"About

"That wasn't
I continued. "It
who'd given Johr

"I'm sure any tattoo artist can touch up the scars he might end up with. Look up tattoo parlors in the phone book."

"It's more than that, Nana. His power as Domn Lup was magically bound into the art. We have to find the artist and make him unbind it." I ran a hand through my hair. "And fast."

"What's the hurry?"

In whispered tones I told her about the wære's head honcho coming on Wednesday. "If I could have just tapped into Johnny's subconscious and gotten an answer, we'd know who did this and could start searching. Instead, I got some cryptic rune reading."

Nana stood at the end of the dinette and twirled my note page to her. "That changes everything, and yet . . . the reading isn't without truth."

"What?"

"This rune, Ansuz, may look like an *F*, but it's alphabetical equivalent is an *A*." Her finger tapped along the row as she mumbled "Uruz is a *U* and Mannuz is an *M*. . . ." Then, more clearly, she announced, "You got your answer, Persephone." Nana handed me the paper. "You got a name. Arcanum."

Turn the page for rave reviews of
Linda Robertson's compelling Circle series

ARCANE CIRCLE is also available as an eBook

Praise for the action-packed fantasy
of
LINDA ROBERTSON

Fatal Circle

"The third in Robertson's Circle series won't disappoint fans who've come to expect lots of romance, mystery, and intrigue from her books."

—*Romantic Times* (4 stars)

"Packed full of action, intrigue, and events that would not let me put this book down. . . . This book was a wild pleasure to read."

—Fangtastic Reviews

"A strong thriller."

—Alternative Worlds

"I love this series and this book did not disappoint. . . . I'm hooked, baby!"

—Book Lovers Inc.

Hallowed Circle

"Robertson brings back the magic and the mayhem. . . . Twists, turns, and narrow escapes keep the pages turning."

—*Romantic Times* (4½ stars)

"An instant classic, featuring a refreshingly wise and likeable heroine."

—*Affaire de Coeur* (5 stars)

"Readers will find themselves swept off their feet, without the use of a broomstick, and into a dangerous world that is teetering on the edge of a war between the nonhumans. Very entertaining!"

—Huntress Book Reviews

ARCANE CIRCLE

LINDA ROBERTSON

Pocket Books

New York   London   Toronto   Sydney

Pocket Books
A Division of Simon & Schuster, Inc.
1230 Avenue of the Americas
New York, NY 10020

First Juno Books/Pocket Books paperback edition January 2011

JUNO BOOKS and colophon are trademarks of Wildside Press LLC used under license by Simon & Schuster, Inc., the publisher of this work.

POCKET and colophon are registered trademarks of Simon & Schuster, Inc.

For information about special discounts for bulk purchases, please contact Simon & Schuster Special Sales at 1-866-506-1949 or business@simonandschuster.com.

The Simon & Schuster Speakers Bureau can bring authors to your live event. For more information or to book an event contact the Simon & Schuster Speakers Bureau at 1-866-248-3049 or visit our website at www.simonspeakers.com.

Cover design by John Vairo Jr.
Cover art by Don Sipley

Manufactured in the United States of America

10 9 8 7 6 5 4 3 2 1

ISBN 978-1-4391-9025-8
ISBN 978-1-4391-9026-5 (ebook)

For Richie.

When you read it, you'll know why.

Maybe.

THANK-YOUS

Red-Caped Hero Thanks:
Shannon & Dave, Beth & Steve, Melissa, Costie
Because making realistic concert T-shirts and buttons
for a *fictitious* rock band just kicks ass.

Java-N-Chocolate Thanks:
Michelle, Melissa, Laura, Faith, Rachel, Emily, and Tracy
As always, I am grateful to my writing group
for reading, critiques, support, and the friendship.

Delicioso Thanks:
Samosky's Homestyle Pizzeria
For making such fabulous pizza,
even my characters love it. *Yum!*

PAMArita Thanks:
Paula Guran
Your keen eyes and wise guidance keep me from
sticking my foot in my mouth,
and to Laura Bickle
for sharing your vast knowledge on
a variety of unusual subjects.

Howlin' Thanks:
Jim Lewis. My own wolfy bad boy.

Reverent Gratitude:
For the many-named Muse. You will always *rock*.

Extra Thanks:
Derek Tatum & Carol Malcolm @ DragonCon;
Larissa @ Larissa's Bookish Life; Rachel Smith @ Bitten
by Books; Abigail @ All Things Urban Fantasy; Roxanne
@ Fang-tastic Books; Susi & Caroline @ Booklovers, Inc.;
Erik & Justin @ nightstalkersradio.com; and Scollard;
and all the reviewers, bloggers, and tweeters
who've helped spread the word.
There are too many of you to list and *that's* fantastic!

ARCANE
CIRCLE

CHAPTER ONE

Nearly dragging the veterinarian behind me, I raced up the tight and twisting stairs, desperate for him to treat my boyfriend. It was just after two P.M. and the vet, Dr. Geoffrey Lincoln, was already well acquainted with his patient, Johnny Newman. What other type of doctor would make an emergency house call to treat a wærewolf?

Johnny, wearing only dark jeans and an Ace bandage wrapped high around his rib cage, lay on his narrow bed in the attic bedroom of my saltbox farmhouse. Despite a grimace of pain, he made no sound.

As soon as Kirk, a wærewolf from Johnny's pack, saw the doc and me enter the room, he rose from the folding chair next to the bed. He hadn't moved since we'd gotten Johnny in the bed hours earlier. Kirk nodded at us and then walked quietly to the foot of the bed.

Dr. Lincoln set his bag on the chair, pulled latex gloves from it, and bent to inspect Johnny's wound. It kept seeping blood and had completely saturated numerous gauze pads and two of the elastic wraps already. In the time I'd been gone, the blood had again soaked through layers of padding and was darkening the bandage like an ever-expanding Rorschach blot.

I hoped that I appeared to be holding myself together and functioning, but my shaking hands threatened to expose my counterfeit calm. *This is all wrong. Johnny was in wolf form when injured. These wounds should have healed when he transformed back, but they didn't.* My fears ricocheted inside me like wild bullets—the crossfire could shatter my cool and collected façade at any moment, exposing my panic.

A veterinarian by trade, Doc Lincoln had experience with the traumatic wounds animals sometimes inflicted on each other, and he had treated Johnny and other wæres before. At five-foot-nine, with receding brown hair, brown eyes, and glasses, the doctor appeared at first glance to be an average man, but the fact that he was willing to provide care to wærewolves—albeit secretly—made him very special indeed.

He took a pair of scissors from his bag and cut carefully through the wrapped bandage. "I need more light."

When Johnny moved his rock 'n' roll self in a few weeks ago, he'd brought a table lamp made from a guitar neck. I jerked the shade off and twisted the little knob. A hundred watts brightened the narrow, slope-sided room.

"Hold it closer."

I stretched the lamp's cord as far as possible. Under the harsh illumination, he peeled the bandage back and exposed Johnny's gruesome chest injury. The three jagged slashes were deep, each at least six inches long. Despite the swelling, each time Johnny inhaled the wounds gaped wider. Fresh blood welled up, flowing across his chest. It was thick enough to hide the winged pentacle tattoo that spanned his pectorals.

Dr. Lincoln examined the gashes, and even though his touch seemed light, Johnny grimaced, compressing his features so tightly the Wedjat tattoos around his eyes almost disappeared. But the "wolf king" does not whimper. He had recently revealed to his pack he was the fated Domn Lup, able to make a full transformation at will, not just when the moon was full.

At least the doctor was here now. He'd know what to do to help Johnny. Doing something, anything, was better than the helplessness I'd felt while waiting for him to show up.

As he completed his examination, the doc's thin lips pressed into a firm line and he announced, "I've sewn up worse on you, John, but this doesn't show any indication of that accelerated healing you wærewolves are notorious for. Was it silver that cut you?"

"Nope." Johnny shot me a grim look that, in effect, passed the task of answering the doctor's question to me.

Johnny's wounds had been inflicted by a phoenix raking him with her claws during a dawn battle with fairies. Another consequence of that battle was the myriad elementals—unicorns, griffons, dragons, phoenixes—now grouped in the wooded grove behind my house. I was planning to ask the doc if he'd serve as their vet—several of them were injured.

But, for now, if I told him the source of the injury was a creature that supposedly didn't exist, he'd go all skittish and spew questions. He wouldn't believe it until he saw it for himself, so I answered cryptically. "It was a creature of magic that cut him."

"Magic?" The doc rubbed at his brow. "Then some residual effect must be preventing the healing."

Magic had a negative effect on wæres. It could force them into a partial shift and leave them forever stuck that way: neither human nor wære. "He's the Domn Lup," I said. "He isn't as susceptible to magic as other wæres." Even as I said it, I realized I'd dismissed the obvious. Mad at myself for missing it, anger squashed most of my worry. The doc's theory was a good one. "This wasn't exactly magical energies being stirred up around Johnny. Magic made *physical contact* with the intent to damage him. Any wære without the powers of the Domn Lup probably would have bled to death from an attack like this."

"Can you cleanse the magic away?" The doc mimed waving a wand.

The answer wasn't going to make Johnny very happy. "Yes. With salt."

"Salt in my wound," the wære grumbled.

My hand gripped Johnny's. "Sounds like a song title," I said. Being the guitarist and front man of a band, he could make lyrics out of just about anything.

The doc peered at me over the tops of his glasses. "Is using salt like that something you specifically, as a witch, have to do?"

"You mean: Does it take magic as well as salt?"

"Medicine *is* magic to me. But," he reached into his bag, "I was thinking more along the lines of washing the wound with this." He lifted an IV bag of saline solution. "It's sterile."

He was a thinker. That made me even happier he was on our side. "Saline should be fine. Give it a shot."

"Are you sure?"

"I use it to magically cleanse a space, but mundane humans often use salt to protect themselves. Ever spilled salt and then tossed a pinch over your left shoulder? You were supposedly protecting yourself from evil."

Dr. Lincoln turned to Kirk. "Would you fetch some towels from the bathroom? Wait, I-I didn't say *fetch* because you're a . . . I mean, I would've said it that way to anyone."

The handsome Asian wære smiled and replied, "That political correctness shit is for pansies who can't stomach the truth." He left the room.

The doc laid the IV bag on the bed and clasped Johnny's shoulder. "I can try just stitching it, but cauterizing it first is my recommendation."

"Just do what you need to do," Johnny said.

"My stitches aren't quite as refined as those of a plastic surgeon working on a starlet, but then my usual clients don't worry much about scarring. Wære healing is good, but I don't know how the magic will play into this. It could leave a scar. Cauterizing it is even more certain to leave a mark."

"I don't care." Johnny's teeth were grinding.

I set the lamp back in its place while the doctor dug in his bag and brought out a small tray and what must have been a cautery tool. It looked something like a soldering iron.

When Kirk handed me the towels, I rolled them up and tucked one on either side of Johnny's rib cage.

The doctor punctured the IV bag. "I just want to make sure you know it's possible the scar will show in all your shirtless rock-star pictures," he said, squirting the fluid into the cuts. I lifted the lamp again—and saw a white flash of rib bone as the solution washed out the slashes. Johnny sucked air through his teeth. The doc blotted around the injury with another of the towels, then dabbed the wounds directly with gauze.

The bleeding continued. I might have thought it was just a reaction to the wound washing if Dr. Lincoln hadn't directed a silent question at me with his eyes.

My icy unease returned, wintry fingers stirring my emotions again, nearly forcing me from hidden fear into obvious panic. *He can't keep on bleeding like this and we can't take him to a hospital. They transfer wæres to state shelters rather than treat them.* State shelters were more like human dog pounds than hospitals.

I wasn't going to give up. "Let's try a higher concentration of salt."

"Easy for you to say," Johnny grumbled as I charged down the stairs to my second-floor bedroom. From the cabinet where I kept magical supplies, I grabbed a pouch of coarse sea salt. This was already empowered for use in my spells, intended to cleanse the ritual area into a sacred space. Surely this would counteract the magic in the injury, but it was going to hurt like hell.

Back in the attic, I apologized to Johnny and dropped an overflowing fistful of the coarse beadlike chunks onto his chest. Immediately, he growled, writhed once and dug his fingers into the mattress. Concentrating, I visualized the salt foaming like baking soda and vinegar being mixed, and imagined it neutralizing the lingering magic.

When a coastal aroma wafted around me, it was a signal that the salt cleansing was complete. I gestured for the doc to take over. He pierced another saline bag and washed away the sea salt.

This time, the bleeding had markedly decreased. My panic receded.

The doc surveyed the wound again, holding the cauterizing tool ready. He motioned Kirk over. "Hold him down."

"Not necessary." Johnny set his jaw; Kirk stayed where he was.

Dr. Lincoln leaned in. "I'll do this as minimally as possible, but your tattoo is going to need a touch up—"

"Wait!" Johnny grabbed for my arm, jerked, and swore loudly. A fresh spill of blood ran across his chest. "The tattoo."

My breath caught.

Someone had found out long ago that Johnny was the Domn Lup. Whoever it was had magically locked his power into the various tattoos on his body. We needed to find out who had done this and have them reverse it to *un*lock that power.

"Will scars on this tattoo keep it from being unlocked?" Johnny asked.

"I don't honestly know." *The real question is: Can magic in a phoenix's talons sever the magic in a tattoo?*

Johnny's cell phone rang from the bedside table—the chorus of Ozzy Osborne's "Bark at the Moon." It was his ringtone for all the pack wæres. Kirk checked the display and announced, "It's Todd. Probably wants a status report."

"Give him one," Johnny said.

Kirk opened the phone. "This is Kirk."

The doc waved his utensil to refocus us all on him. "Am I doing this?"

Johnny released my arm and relaxed back onto the pillow, shaking his head. "I can't risk any more damage. Just stitches. And not where the ink is if you can help it."

"I'll do my best." The doc put the heated tool back on the tray.

"It's not aching as bad now, Doc, after the salt."

"But your moving set it bleeding again. Be still."

"You need to talk to Todd," Kirk said, offering the phone.

The doc motioned Kirk to stay back. "I need his arms down flat to do these stitches." To Johnny he said, "Take your calls later."

Kirk ignored him and said, "It's important."

Due to the recent death of the pack's leader, Todd would have been promoted and given the title *dirija* if Johnny hadn't revealed he was the Domn Lup. Todd retained his place as second-in-command, but he wasn't exactly thrilled about anyone leap-frogging him to gain the position, least of all Johnny.

"Put it on speaker, Kirk," Johnny half-snarled.

Kirk hit the button, kept the phone upraised. Todd's authoritative voice demanded, "Who else is in the room?"

"Red and the doc." Johnny called me Red, as in Red Riding Hood to his Big Bad Wolf.

Dr. Lincoln opened another pack of gauze.

"This is pack business," Todd barked. "I'll wait."

Johnny growled, "There's no one here I don't trust. Just tell me."

Todd's marked sigh signaled his disagreement with the idea.

Johnny growled again in frustration, adding forcefully, "Now."

Todd said, "I've made arrangements for the two wæres we lost, we're contacting and counseling the families." Some members of the pack had volunteered to fight at Johnny's side in the fairy battle. Most survived, but a few were incinerated by a superheated beam that had melted sand into glossy walkways. There weren't any remains left to bury. "You're going to have to meet with them soon. And . . ." Todd didn't finish.

"And?" Johnny prompted.

"I got a call from Romania."

Johnny and Kirk shared a look I couldn't read.

"Word of the Domn Lup has traveled up the ranks. All the way up. The Zvonul didn't send word back down and have some bean-counting *adevar* call. The personal assistant of the Rege called. The Rege is coming to meet you."

Sounded like the bigwigs of the wæreworld were taking a personal interest in their new Domn Lup. This wasn't unexpected, but it was *fast.* Less than forty-eight hours had passed since Johnny had revealed himself to his pack. The wære governing system was unfamiliar to me, so I was listening close, making mental reminders to ask about these new terms and titles.

"When are they coming?" Johnny asked.

"On Wednesday. Unless their travel plans change." It was now Sunday afternoon.

"Make sure we're complying with whatever they need. Call me later if you have anything more."

The phone's screen faded to black. Kirk closed it and replaced it where he'd found it.

"I'd like to numb the area and give you a sedative so you can relax and rest," Dr. Lincoln said.

"No," Johnny said. "No numbing, no sedatives. Just sew me up."

My duties as light source monitor continued as the doc worked. It was a front-row opportunity I'd rather have missed. Watching him stitch the torn muscle, listening to him remark how the sutures would dissolve slowly, and then discuss the area where the bone had been exposed, was not an experience for the pleasant memories scrap-book. I had to verify which line went where a few times while he carefully aligned the tattoo, sewing in stitches to either side of the lines. After he had tended to all the inked areas, he worked outward from them.

Johnny's expression spoke for him; it wasn't a painless process.

When the doctor finished, he rinsed Johnny's chest again. "The damage to the pectoral muscle is going to be the worst of it. Any movement of your arm will pull on the wound. I suggest you use a sling for a few days at least, maybe a week. Maybe more, depending on whether or not your usual healing kicks in. No matter what, no ac-tivities of any kind that could strain those stitches."

He wiped Johnny's skin dry and applied a salve. "Use this. Although you're averse to the numbing additives in it, this stuff will help minimize scarring." He placed the container on the bedside table. "Three to four times a day. I'll bring you more soon."

The doc checked the temperature on the cauterizing device and, satisfied, put it away in his bag. The bleeding was stanched. Johnny had been effectively tended to. I breathed a relieved sigh. Then the doc stood, ready to leave. "Doc, wait." My respite from stress was too short. This wasn't over yet. "I have something to show you before you leave."

"Red," Johnny interrupted, "I want a minute with you first. Kirk, you and the doc step out."

No one questioned him.

I sank down on the bed, grateful for a moment alone with him. My fingers pushed into the jet-black waves of his hair, scrubbing over sand still on his scalp. My mind flashed on the beam cutting a dragon in half, then incinerating a Beholder's legs as the rest of him burst into flame. I could still hear his final scream.

That grit also reminded me of what Johnny had done. In wolf form, he'd attacked the fairy Fax Torris. She'd dragged him beneath the surface of Lake Erie. They'd been under a long time. Too long. In those moments when my fear was most intense, I regretted terribly not yet telling him that I loved him.

My heart compelled me to say those words now, but with him lying there injured, it seemed that telling him here, like this, would cheapen the words. I didn't want to say them out of pity or as a reaction to fear.

I said nothing and kissed him. Not a sexy, passionate kind of kiss, but a so-alive-in-this-moment kind. I put to memory the feel of his soft lips pressed to mine because earlier today I'd thought I might not ever get to kiss him again.

Johnny, however, took it as a "Let's get naked" kind of kiss. His hands rubbed up my arms—and he jerked in pain and said something very improper.

"Doc said no activities that would risk the stitches," I whispered.

Undeterred, he put on a brave face. "I don't care. Any chance you'll do a little voodoo on me tonight?"

CHAPTER TWO

I sat up, rolling my eyes. "Your libido is insatiable. You're not in any shape to be doing—"

"Wait, wait—not voodoo, I mean *probing.* Can we do a little *probing* tonight?" He grinned.

It was such a Johnny thing to say that the words filled me with relief. *He's going to be fine.* "I'll give you two innuendo points, but that's all you're getting." I'd lost track of the score in our little game of who could use the most sexual innuendoes in normal conversation.

He carefully moved his arm and laid his palm across my thigh. "Seriously, Red. We've shared pieces of our souls. I need you to use our connection to find out what you can about who inked me up and stifled my powers."

"I will." I found a clean spot on the towel and blotted the blood that had seeped between the stitches when he moved. "Let's get you past this first."

"Does the process of digging in my memories involve hand-to-hand combat?" he asked sarcastically.

"It might." The point he was making was clear, but so was mine. "I've never done this kind of thing before. It might involve mud wrestling for all I know."

Expecting him to wiggle his brows and make a re-mark about bikini-clad females in shallow pits of mud, I was surprised when his mirth faded and he became very serious. "Red, the top dog is coming. I need this unlocked pronto. I don't want anything holding me back when he arrives."

"Johnny." He'd lost blood and energy. Because his power was locked in his tattoos, transforming at will wasn't ever easy. Right now doing so would have been harder still. "I get it that the Zvonul are the wærewolf equivalent of the Witch Elders Council, and that this won't be as easy as a couple of neighborhood dogs get-ting introduced via mutual butt-sniffing. But what is this Rege going to do?"

"He has to see me change. The rest of the wæres won't accept me until he confirms me as the Domn Lup."

"Other than the Rege, Todd said something about an *adevar*?"

"Titles up the chain of command. Let me start at the bottom so this makes sense. *Dirija* is a local pack lord, like a mayor or a priest. They account for a hundred to two hundred and fifty wæres, depending on area and city size. They answer to an *adevar*—think of them as IRS agents with governorships. Each *adevar* deals with ten to fifteen *dirija*. They aren't well liked."

"Why not?"

"The *dirija* see them as buttinskis and tattletales."

"But 'bean counter' was the term Todd used."

"They're basically accountants who get furry once a month. They kennel with the packs they oversee on a ro-tating basis. Never a fun time. It's like being audited."

"Okay."

"Between them and the Zvonul are the *diviza,* who are more like mafia dons crossed with U.S. senators."

"I think the government official examples help me understand, but the priest and mafia descriptions create a bunch of blanks that I'm not sure I want filled in."

Johnny snorted. "Yeah, but actual government officials are elected or appointed. These guys fight for position. The Zvonul are a pack of the most powerful wæres on the planet, each with a region under his direct influence. They keep control through loyalty they create with spiritual connection, intimidation, and strategy. So the idea of a group of priests, mafia dons, and generals—with a whole lot of Big Brother mixed in—is a more accurate analogy."

"Yikes. Sounds like a cult."

"See why I wanted to stay out of it?"

"Yeah. But you're in it. Big time."

He didn't reply. He just picked at the sheet on the bed.

Though etymology made it pretty obvious, I asked, "And the Rege?"

"The Zvonul's main man. Think of him as . . ." he considered it and said, "Pope-Czarzilla. If he called the packs to unite, it'd take the airlines weeks to handle the exodus of wæres to Romania. No one would dare refuse."

"But the moving industry in America would crumble!" My flippant statement won me the lopsided grin I was hoping for, but it faded too quickly.

Johnny had taken the mantle of his fate in order to help me defeat the fairies: He'd killed Ignatius Tierney, the former *dirija,* who also happened to be his father figure, and in doing so he'd claimed the pack. The responsibilities of his destiny were changing him, siphoning off his lightheartedness, replacing it with new gravity. He'd risked everything for me; to deny him anything would have been selfish.

"Okay. We'll do some probing tonight. But you've lost a lot of blood; you're going to have to drink a gallon of orange juice."

"You should know, Red. This household has the potential to single-handedly keep Florida orange growers in business."

Johnny was referring to my own frequent need to consume OJ. The vampire Menessos was my servant, and part of being his master meant letting him feed from me.

But Johnny had been unconscious on the beach during part of the battle. He'd missed some very important events . . . such as me staking Menessos. If he'd known what I'd done, I don't think he would have made that joke. I'd taken a terrible risk to defeat the fairies. Menessos may be well and truly dead, never to rise again. Just thinking those words caused tears to threaten, so I changed the subject. "Is Todd going to be a problem in all this?"

"No. He must've realized that I'm only in his way until I'm confirmed. Then, the Zvonul will have other plans for the Domn Lup. This pack will be his anyway. I'd bet a guitar or two that, to hurry the process up, Todd personally called them before Ig's body had even cooled."

"What do these 'other plans for the Domn Lup' entail?"

"I'm not sure what they'll expect. There hasn't been a

Domn Lup in centuries. But," his fingers tightened on my thigh, and his warm voice rescued me from the sadness building inside me, "I won't move to Romania."

That deserved another kiss. This time, instead of reaching up for me, his fingers glided around my leg and over my hip. I broke off the kiss when he poked at the contents of my pocket.

"Why do you bother keeping it with you now?"

He meant the protrepticus, an inanimate object—mine was an old cell phone—that housed a spirit. It could never be very far from my person. When I'd created it with Xerxadrea's help, it had bound me with her and the spirit. She'd given her life to save mine at the Cleveland Botanical Gardens late Friday night. We'd had to leave her body behind. It was an awful thing to do.

With her death, the spirit should have been freed, but I hadn't had the nerve to check. "Dunno," I mumbled. "I'm sure it's useless but . . . I feel guilty for leaving her and maybe, somehow, through this thing I can tell her I'm sorry."

"If you figure out how to find the dial directory for specific dead people, I want to talk to Randy Rhoads." He patted me softly. "Hey, you better get the doc on to his next appointment."

I stood. "You want anything?"

"A bowl of Lucky Charms would be nice."

He's definitely on the mend. "I'll send it up with Kirk. And the juice."

"Kirk's going to have to go soon, Red."

"I'll come back as soon as Dr. Lincoln's shock wears off."

• • •

The bar bouncer wære and the veterinarian were standing in the small foyer area on the main floor, obviously uncomfortable with each other. "Kirk, I need you to take some food up to Johnny." He looked grateful for the promise of escape. "And, Doc, do you have plans for this evening?" I asked, even as I headed for the kitchen.

"I was going to order a pizza and watch my latest delivery from Netflix," Dr. Lincoln called.

Without disturbing Nana and Beverley's very serious game of Chutes and Ladders at the dinette, I gathered a small mixing bowl, a spoon, the cereal box, a half-full milk jug, and the half-gallon of orange juice. The items passed to Kirk and he headed up the steps. "What do you like on your pizza, Doc?"

"Why?" He drew the word out suspiciously.

"I was hoping you would evaluate a few animals I've acquired. If you will take a look at them, I'll send Nana and Beverley to pick up some pizzas."

The doctor, bemused, shook his head but conceded. "Banana peppers and sausage."

"That was easier than I expected." The prospect of losing his down time and taking on unexpected work seemed like something he should resist with a bit more force.

"Whatever you've got going on is sure to be more exciting than *Underdog*."

On my way out I grabbed my jacket, an insulated flannel overshirt. The doc followed me through the cornfield, lugging his medical bag. "Is there a corral out here?" he asked.

It was colder than I'd thought. Buttoning the flannel, I answered, "Sort of." We didn't have to fight our way through the cornstalks; the elemental animals' passage had bent the stalks down and created an eight-foot-wide path straight to the grove where the ley line ran.

"What kind of animals did you acquire?"

"You'll see."

He grunted. "How many of them are there?"

"Several. I don't have an exact count."

"Give me a hint or something."

Our approach caused the animals to stir. There was nickering and bird sounds and a noise like a giant burp. It could have been Mountain's belch or one of the dragon's.

"Did you know a ley line crosses my property, Doc?"

"No. I've heard you use the term before, but I'm not sure what it means."

"It's a magic thing, an earth-energy line—but you can't see it. If you're attuned to such things you may gain a sense of it, but the animals are undeniably drawn to it. They're keeping themselves close to the ley line in the grove of trees up ahead."

The crunching of our steps abruptly changed. An over-the-shoulder glance revealed the vet had halted. He stood stiffly and his humorless expression was what I'd expect to see if I'd taken him snipe hunting and he'd just caught on to the game.

I stopped, too. "What?"

"Exactly." He pushed his glasses up his nose. "You're talking magic. What's out there?"

Though he was confident with the farm animals he treated, the idea of magical creatures stripped away his certainty. He had learned some of how wære genetics changed the rules of medicine. I couldn't blame him for being guarded. And, with the exception of a single normal Great Dane puppy, our relationship had involved injured wærewolves, kidnapped and thieving witches, and some very dangerous vampires. But I had hoped to get the elementals into his line of sight before he freaked. The elementals might be even harder to accept, but at least they were closer to regular work for him.

I strode back to him.

He said, "Tell me there aren't any bizarre wære-creatures out there."

"No bizarre wære-creatures. No wære-pigs or wære-platypus. Wære-things probably wouldn't gather at a magic line, anyway. I promise, there's nothing out there that's contagious like that." I used the word *contagious* rather than *dangerous* on purpose. These creatures had done a lot of damage while the fairies had control collars on them.

"And still you won't name what I'm going to see."

"Doc."

He removed his glasses and wiped them clean on the tail of his shirt. "Very well. But I'm billing you. Regardless of the pizza."

"And I'll expect the overtime rate."

He tucked his spectacles determinedly back into place and had just taken his first step forward when a shrill neigh pierced the air. The thump of hooves followed, bringing a pristine unicorn cantering into view.

Dr. Lincoln stopped in his tracks again. This time his jaw dropped.

The young stallion pranced to a halt and shook out his glorious mane as he noticed us. Then the unicorn leveled his horn at us and snorted. He pawed the ground, ready to charge.

"Errol, get your twitchy self back over here!"

Mountain's voice was followed by a whistle. The unicorn hung his lovely head and walked out of view. I'd have sworn he was sulking.

I needed Dr. Lincoln to accept that he was seeing creatures that weren't supposed to exist and to give them medical attention. The world had been forced to recognize vampires and wærewolves for over two decades, but a real unicorn was still inconceivable. "You coming, Doc?"

"Th-that horn . . ."

"Was real." I started walking. "C'mon. You're going to be amazed."

He followed me.

Mountain waved at me when we cleared the stalks. He always wore sumo wrestler–size major league sports shirts and, like his jean-pocket–length black ponytail, the shirts suited him. At least they did when they weren't torn and bloody like the Cleveland Browns jersey he presently wore. His shirt was a victim of this morning's battle.

Mountain was a Beholder, one of Menessos's once-marked servants, and though strong as an ox and visually intimidating, Mountain didn't bother hiding that he was a big softie. He'd struck me as rather shy when I first met him, but shortly after our first encounter he'd told me he grew up on a farm. Now that he was in charge of converting my twenty rural acres into a farm for very non-traditional livestock, he was coming out of his shell.

He scratched under Errol's bearded chin and said, "Don't mind him. He's harmless."

"I doubt that," the doc muttered behind me.

After polite introductions and a quick update on Johnny, I asked, "Errol?"

"Aw, he prances around and swings that horn like he's Errol Flynn swashbuckling with a sword. You don't mind me naming them, do you?"

"Not at all. You'll be tending them. They're yours as far as I'm concerned."

"Elementals? No way. You're the witch. They're yours. I'm just the happy ranch hand."

The doc was gaping, taking in the scene, the animals—even Mountain's obvious vampire bite—when a young dragon slithered forward, sniffing excitedly. The veterinarian backpedaled, but I steadied him with a firm grip on his shoulder. "These animals fought in a battle today. Many of them have minor injuries. Some are worse. Would you check them over?"

The dragon stopped sniffing and a forked tongue shot out. It tasted the air like a serpent's tongue before receding back into the creature's eel-like maw.

"I don't even know what to do with a . . . a . . . a . . ."

I gave the doc's shoulder a little squeeze.

"Dragon."

Mountain laughed. "Neither do we." He offered his hand, palm up, fingers wiggling, and the dragon leaned to get some of that chin-scratching for himself. "But we'll find out, won't we, Zoltan?"

I raised my brows at him and repeated the name.

Mountain chuckled. The dragon raised his head higher

and flicked his gill fins straight out. "I don't really need to explain that one, do I?"

"How many of them are there?" the veterinarian asked.

"Fifteen unicorns, twelve griffons, twenty-six phoenixes, and five dragons," Mountain answered promptly. "I'm going to suggest we need two barns and one aluminum coop. Don't want anything that'll burn around the phoenixes. If you want me here tending them, a studio apartment attached to one of the barns would work for me."

"What are we going to feed them?" I was willing to accept an answer from either of them.

The veterinarian shrugged. Mountain said, "We'll just have to figure that out. I suppose dried corn like chickens eat would work for the phoenixes, and oats and grains for the unicorns. The dragons are water creatures so some kind of fish for them. And griffons . . . would that be bird food or giant-feline food?"

"You're going to need goats," the doc said. "They're part falcon or eagle, not the type of bird to eat carrion. Both lions and birds of prey hunt." He appraised Mountain. "Not sure I'd want the job of feeding them."

"They're all pretty tame, really, Doc." He pointed over his shoulder at a griffon. "All but that one, anyway."

That particular griffon was one of the most beautiful animals I'd ever seen. His feathers were raven-black, as were his front bird-legs, one of which he kept lifted with claws curled in. The rest of him was Bengal tiger, gold and orange and black. The tip of his tail had flaring feathers on it.

He stood with his hooked beak pointed west at the

setting sun, but when Mountain gestured at him, he craned his neck toward us and his golden eye slitted. The other eye was missing, as were the talons from the foreleg he was favoring.

"You're losing daylight, Doc." It was November, and daylight saving time officially changed the clocks last night. In a few more hours, the darkness would be full.

I left Dr. Lincoln and Mountain to their task and walked back to the house, but that little reminder had slapped me in the face. In a few more hours I'd know for certain the consequences of staking Menessos.

CHAPTER THREE

When I returned to the attic bedroom, Johnny was sitting up on the edge of his bed. He'd loosened the adjustment on one of his screaming skull guitar straps and was using it as a makeshift sling. He had just finished the cereal and set the bowl on the floor.

"Nana and Beverley are going to pick up some pizzas. What would you guys like on them?"

"Nothing for me," Kirk said. "I called someone to pick me up." Our ex-military sharpshooter had been in the battle, too. He hadn't napped afterward, as the dark circles under his eyes could attest.

"You wanna eat first?" Johnny pressed.

Kirk shook his head. "I just want to go home."

Johnny conceded and thanked him.

Kirk walked to the door, gave a solemn nod, and left us.

Warmer now, I draped my flannel on the foot of the bed and sat gently on Johnny's not-so-bad side. I had to mind my feet so I wouldn't kick the bowl, the cereal box, or the empty jugs for both the milk and the juice.

"You hungry enough for pizza?"

"Always."

"Your appetite's fine, Frankenstein. I think you'll survive."

"Use my phone. Samosky's is programmed in. Just press seven and send."

Of course he'd have the Homestyle Pizzeria on speed dial. It was the closest one. I lifted his phone from the table and flipped it open. A picture of me sleeping appeared on the screen. "When did you take this?"

"Days ago," he said slyly. "When you were sleeping with your head in my lap on the couch."

That was right after I'd killed a fairy in self-defense. No wonder I wore a mask of worries, even in my sleep.

While I placed the order, Johnny tried to study his stitches, groaned, and gave up. It must have hurt his torn muscles to arch his neck that way. When my call was complete, he took the phone back, snapped a picture of his chest with it, and appraised the damage. "Ick," he said, and put the phone on the table. "I learned something today."

"How to make self-portraiture look easy?"

"Ha. No. It takes a bad chest injury to get you alone in my room." He sniffed, affecting distaste. "Can't say I'm keen on doing it again."

"Do my ears deceive me? You don't want to 'do it'?"

That lopsided grin flashed once more. "Point for you. I meant I don't want to have to get my Frankenstein on every time I want to be alone with you up here." His arm encircled my waist. When he gave me a little squeeze, he grimaced.

I leaned against him. "There you go again. It's *all* connected."

"Ain't connected to my pants," he asserted. "That part feels fine."

"Mmmm-hmmm," I hummed, unconvinced.

"If you don't believe me, I'll submit to a hands-on inspection."

I laughed out loud.

He lay back across the bed. "Go on, feel for yourself. Tell me what *you* think."

Slithering down to lean on my elbow beside him, my palm rested teasingly on his thigh. Peering into those deep blue Wedjat-lined eyes I couldn't help discarding the humor of the moment for solemnity. I'd been so scared of staring into those eyes, once upon a time. Now they had the power to make me melt.

I couldn't imagine life without him. "I think I almost lost you today." Saying those words made my worst fears rise, real again in that instant. My heart lurched in my chest and a big lump swelled in my throat. A long silent moment passed while I reminded myself that those fears had been averted.

"Kirk told me what you did."

Frozen, unable to tear my gaze away, I couldn't maintain it, either. My eyelids slid shut. My lungs pushed a held breath through my tight throat, and a pair of fast and rebellious teardrops rolled down my cheeks.

I hadn't just staked Menessos.

I'd wrapped him in my arms and kissed him.

For good or ill, my actions were mine. *Own it.*

Eyes opening, I nodded because I didn't trust my voice.

Johnny took my hand from his thigh and used it to

draw me closer to him. It wasn't the action of a jealous boyfriend. *Maybe Kirk didn't tell him about the kissing part.*

"Is the vamp dead-dead or undead?"

"We'll know in a few hours." The misery and dread in my voice were as thick as syrup.

He searched my face. "How are you?"

"Good, now. You're going to be fine."

"That's not what I meant. You two were—I mean *are*—bonded."

I tucked hair behind my ear. "I feel fine."

"Now. What about then?"

"It was awful." *In every way.*

"Well," he said cheerfully, "when that vamp does rise, he's going to be hungry. When you go to unlock the kennel . . . be careful."

That he'd said "when" and not "if" meant a lot to me. I snuggled down beside him, head on his shoulder.

It was more than I could expect, to have come so close to losing them both and still have one of them in my arms.

Is it ungrateful of me to wish that I could still have them both?

On that Lake Erie beach, where witches, wæres, a single vampire, and his Beholders had put aside their normal antipathy and united, albeit briefly, against a common enemy, we'd defeated the fairies and I'd sealed the doorway between our two worlds. In minutes, when the sun set, I would know whether I'd slain the world's original vampire and rendered him a normal corpse, or simply ushered him into the realm of being one of the true undead.

Sitting on my cellar steps, I waited, wringing my hands.

Behind me, the door was shut. Before me, the cellar was a dark tomb except for the tangerine candle in the center of the floor. The citrus aroma mingled with the smell of cold cement, old hay, and coppery-sweet blood.

My stomach was in knots and I hadn't been able to eat dinner. The foreboding was more diligent now, gnawing at me with sharper teeth.

I had killed a man once, years ago. It was an accident, but it had haunted me. This . . . this was so much worse. I'd done this on purpose.

Menessos's body lay sprawled in the first cage with the blanket that had wrapped him carelessly flung open. Apparently, Kirk had carried him down here and literally tossed him into the kennel.

The inevitable machismo pissing contest strikes again. It happened whenever vampires and wærewolves crossed paths. The alliances forged for the beach battle had, apparently, expired with our victory.

It made me mad. No one should be treated that way, dead or alive, least of all the *original* vampire. Though Kirk didn't know that tidbit, he and I were going to have a talk about respect in general.

This kind of thing made me wonder if I would ever be able to succeed as the Lustrata. Balancing these preconceived notions of place and rank seemed impossible. I couldn't go around and smack each and every wære and vampire in the back of the head, say, "Grow up," and *poof!* it would be so.

Making them open their own eyes and see the value in each other, that was the trick. And it would be so much harder than planting a head slap on each of them.

But it wasn't just the vampires and wærewolves bickering among themselves. The witches were in it, too. As were the mundane humans. The old dividing lines of skin color, religion, sexual orientation, and class status seemed to have found some common ground in their hate-mongering against the kind of people in and around my farmhouse. Despite human history being full of caveats about intolerance, one particularly hate-filled TV pundit had recently coined the term *"non*sters" to lump witches, wæres, fey, and vampires together—emphasizing that they were not human. Technically, we witches were still human, but sadly, the incorrect term seemed to be catching on.

I checked the time on the satellite phone Menessos had given me.

In about a hundred and twenty seconds, the last edge of the sun would officially cross over the horizon. Menessos would rise. Or he wouldn't. I'd know whether that conspicuously incomplete feeling in my core would ever feel whole again.

On some level I was aware of a metaphysical absence when Menessos was away from me. Though I sat only a few yards away from his body, that sensation was even stronger here. The best comparison I could make equated this to the way those who've lost a limb described their phantom pains.

Though Menessos was a self-righteous bastard most of the time, on that battle-ripped beach he'd gently placed the slender wand into my hands and *told* me to take his life so we might win the day. He'd even placed the tip against his chest to make it easy for me.

The cinema in my mind replayed the moments of his staking repeatedly, seeking some sign that he would come back. I'd placed a second hex on him as he died. That gave me hope. *But did that action come too late?*

Menessos had given up his life. Willingly. He'd given up the light of day forever. If he rose, he would evermore be a child of darkness.

All he'd sacrificed, these hands had taken.

My knuckles whitened around the phone as if it was the embodiment of hope I was silently clinging to. Menessos had to wake and rise and be the good ol' pompous asshole we all knew and . . . *Well, I won't add the L-word there.*

But he had to rise. I didn't want to revisit the web of guilt that had ensnared me after the stalker's accidental death. I didn't want to dream of Menessos screaming blame at me and wake in a cold, shameful sweat for weeks on end. I *needed* not to be a murderer twice over, mostly because of Nana's old saying: Once is a mistake, twice is a habit.

Two witches had lost their lives on the beach, and two wæres. A dozen Beholders died. Those deaths were a weight I couldn't—and shouldn't—be freed from carrying. They died pursuing my cause and fighting for what I needed done. I mourned their passing, but that was a pain I could keep in check.

With Menessos, it was different. My grieving for him had been displaced and tethered to a slim hope. The burden on my shoulders as I sat here waiting for confirmation was so heavy I knew if he didn't rise it would crush me. It would break me.

Eagerly straining to see something in the candlelight, I scrutinized his body for any sign. The vampire's face was angled away. His wavy, walnut-colored hair was strewn across the hay, across his cheek. One arm was thrown free of the blanket and at an awkward angle, not broken, but if it had been me lying there my arm would have been pins-and-needles asleep. But then my heart still beat regularly, maintaining the circulation of blood.

His didn't.

Menessos was dead. Lifeless as a toaster. Like every other vampire when the sun is yet hanging in the sky.

He hadn't been like this before. He'd been alive. It was this, his ultimate sacrifice, that had allowed us to win the day.

Shoving the phone into my pocket, I pulled the sleeves of my flannel past my fingers and let the cuffs dangle. I resituated myself on the step. I re-resituated myself. These were the longest seconds of my life.

His chest rose, minutely.

Or it might have been the flicker of the candle flame.

I stared hard, unwilling to blink.

His chest moved again, this time raising a fraction higher. The hair on his cheek fluttered as he exhaled.

He lives!

I had the urge to stand and shout, "He's alive! He's

alive!" like a parody of Dr. Frankenstein, but I kept my backside planted on that cement stair. I swallowed, hard, and pushed my flannel's cuffs back up, fingers folding together, knuckles pressed to my lips. *Now, will he be the same?*

CHAPTER FOUR

Groaning softly, Menessos stirred. His groan grew louder, rising in pitch. He ripped away the blanket, clawed his shirt and tore it open, screaming in anguish as fingers scrabbled at his chest. He arched his spine until only the top of his head and his heels touched the floor.

Stunned, afraid, I eased onto a higher step. It felt like I was drowning from the inside, filling up. . . .

Menessos's arms snapped out to the side, palms up, shaking. His fingers closed into tight fists. His scream dwindled away. He sank slowly into the hay and lay still except for the rise and fall of his chest.

The sensation of emptiness and the phantom pain were gone.

"Oh, Persephone." His whisper was raspy and dry.

He knows I'm here.

"For a moment it felt like dying all over again," he said slowly, seductively, "and then suddenly it was as if one hundred thousand volts of electricity were delivered straight into my heart—a heart prickling with thorns, pierced by your hand, and broken by your love for another—and then it beats effortlessly, as if it never stopped."

The breath I'd been holding escaped in a rush and I scooted down to the lower stair. My gaze left the kennel for a heartbeat in my repositioning, but when I looked up he stood at the bars and I gasped. This preternatural stealth and speed of vampires still unnerved me.

The wrinkled suit didn't diminish him. His eyes were gray, dark, and sharklike. A pentacle of dried blood—the evidence of my second hex—was on his brow, peeking from under tendrils of messy hair. "Are you yourself?"

"Who else would I be?"

I smirked, but didn't stand or move to let him out. "Hungry?"

"Rapaciously."

The pompous asshole is back. My heart swelled with happiness and a comforted sigh escaped. "We've made arrangements."

"Do tell."

"Mountain is going to come down in a few minutes. I wanted to assess you first, and tell you that I don't think he knows what happened exactly. Only that you were covered and brought here, kept from the sun."

"You didn't tell him you staked me?"

I shook my head no.

He laughed at me. It wasn't kind laughter. "Do you feel guilty? Even though I stand before you?"

"I killed you."

"It was neither an accident nor murder. I offered my life to you, Persephone. You held me to your breast as my life leaked from me." He made it sound sexual. In the candlelight, I caught a glimpse of fang. "And you made claim to me inside of that darkness. You placed another of your marks upon me." He scrubbed irritably at his brow, flakes of blood drifting away. "You own me now, my master. You must own what you did to achieve it."

He was right but I wasn't going to say that aloud. I stood.

"What happened after? Your eyes are bright, your spirit high. Johnny survived, then?"

"He's injured but will heal." I quickly told him what he'd missed, including a little about those who were lost. "I'm sure the painter died as well. He couldn't have survived that. What was his name?"

"Ross." He added, "Good for him."

"Good? His legs were incinerated while he was alive, then the rest of him burned!"

"Your pity is commendable, but unnecessary."

I clamped my jaw shut, wedging my tongue behind my teeth.

"His story is more than sad and I will not burden you with it. Take comfort in his death, Persephone, for it was what he wanted most of all."

"I don't believe that. I watched him flee for his life. He stumbled . . ."

Menessos's grip lowered on the bars of the kennel. "Freudian slips are not always a trip of the tongue. How many Beholders did I lose?"

"Twelve, I'm told."

He nodded, glance flicking to the satellite phone in my hand. "May I make a call? I must have a car sent for me."

"Of course." I took a step forward and stopped, still holding the phone close to me. He did have Regional Vampire Lord stuff to do, but now that my guilt was allayed and it was clear he was as "normal," or, rather, "paranormal," as I could have hoped for, I had an agenda of my own to pursue. "But first, the elementals that survived are in the grove with Mountain. Will you allow him to stay here?"

"If you wish it, my master, it shall be so."

"There's more to it than that. The animals need barns. Mountain suggested that Heldridge's Beholders could build them, as a kind of test of their loyalty to you."

Even in the dim candlelight his aversion to this idea was evident. "They should not be anywhere near you. If any of their allegiance to him remains, they may seek to strike at you in retaliation for the task he could not complete." Heldridge, the local lord, had attempted to kill Menessos using a dagger-throwing performer as his assassin. When that failed, Heldridge had fled. Now his people needed to be dispersed to other havens or taken in by Menessos.

"Regardless, the barns are needed, and quickly. I don't know who else to ask."

"As always, I will give you what you want and more, but you are my Erus Veneficus, and your protection is my utmost concern." Publicly, Menessos and I maintained the ruse that he was the master and I was simply his court witch; very few knew the truth. "Perhaps I could assign some of my most trusted to guard you."

I already had some personal protection: a charm given to me by Beau, a Bindspoken witch and owner of the magic supply shop called Wolfsbane and Absinthe. The charm would only defend me, though. Guards could protect everyone, including Nana and Beverley, and guards could act offensively if required. "All right," I said. "But I don't want Goliath." Menessos's second-in-command, among other things, Goliath was also the brother of the spirit housed in the protrepticus. He'd overheard his dead brother's voice coming from my "cell phone" and questioned me. I'd never supplied an answer.

"It would not be him. He's been set on another task."

"Oh?" When Menessos did not answer the question inherent in that single syllable, I added, "This will be good, Menessos. Your Beholders will work with Heldridge's men, keep tabs on them, and take action if they try anything."

Menessos rolled his shoulders and used the bars to stretch languorously. A wicked little smile spread across his mouth.

"What?"

"I've just decided who to send to protect you."

"Who?"

"Offerlings. They have many skills, dear Persephone. I know a few females whom it might suit you to have as sentinels."

"Women?"

"I have found that often it is better to have the protection of women."

I remembered the one Offerling in particular I'd dealt with at his haven, Risqué. "Tell me you won't send topless women in ruffly orange short-shorts."

"Would your live-in wærewolf like that too much?"

"He didn't seem too fond of Risqué, but that isn't the point."

"Then what is?" He licked his lips.

His fangs seemed longer than usual. Or the candlelight was playing tricks. "One, guards need to be fully clothed if they're here. Nana would have a cow if they're not, and, well, Beverley doesn't need to see that. Two, you need to stop treating women like dress-up dolls. Consider the task, then consider the functionality and practicality of the attire you insist that they wear. If you ask me, thigh-high platform boots should be *outlawed*."

He assessed me with lecherous approval. "But seeing you in them stoked my appetite in ways that have yet to be satisfied."

I held up the satellite phone. "You want to call for a car? Promise me no monkeyshines."

There was no hesitation as he solemnly said, "This I pledge to you, Persephone, my master: I am *dead serious*."

His words carried a heavy weight, but I was more aware that he'd said my name and no power flowed with it. I wondered if he'd lost the ability to "stroke" me by saying my name, or if it was an "at will" power. I offered him the phone.

He noted the distance at which I kept myself. "Trust me so little?"

"Just cautious."

He reached for the phone, but his eyes remained steadily on mine. As a show of trust, I stretched forward an extra inch. His grasp curled around my fingers and the phone—but nothing more. He didn't yank me to him; he didn't do anything except touch me.

But that was enough.

A swift memory flashed to the forefront of my mind, invading my vision. I saw Menessos, walking through hallways unfamiliar to me, but obviously familiar to him. It was as if I were in his mind with him, and he definitely knew where he was going. . . .

The music of hollow drums and flutes, of gently plucked strings drifted after him down long stone hallways, and whispered up a wide stairwell. He glanced out a window; below, donkeys pulled carts and people filled the marketplace.

His hair was longer, well past his shoulders and bound loosely. Shirtless, his skin was bronzed. He wore a pleated skirt secured with a belt, and sandals.

The afternoon was hot, the air dry, and he was thirsty. He'd been at his duties since dawn and now wanted some honeyed wine. As he approached a certain doorway, a sense of relief filled him, a sense of home and family. He entered quietly, eager, and shut the door silently. The echoing music was lost, replaced by a woman's soft laughter. He smiled to himself and parted the curtain only enough to peer into the next chamber. There, a man and a woman lay cuddling upon a bed.

They did not know he was watching.

The young man in the bed had lean but muscular limbs, and he lay on his back. The woman was sitting up, propped by one hand while the other toyed with the man's brown hair. One of her legs lay across his abdomen, and he idly stroked up and down her thigh.

She was thin and elegant, her every motion conveyed the tender grace of love. Her hair cascaded to her waist and was dark like the deepest night. Menessos could tell it had been braided until recently, but now it fanned out over her shoulders with wide waves where it had been plaited.

Their nakedness made obvious what they had been doing. Yet Menessos felt no pang of jealousy or awkward interruption. He watched them adoring each other, and true joy filled him.

His throat rumbled softly as he cleared it. Both looked up at once, and each smiled warmly at him. The woman called his name and gestured him forward.

"Una," was his whispered reply. "Ninurta." He joined them, heart swelling to know that he was loved unconditionally by both. . . .

I blinked, and saw only the vampire before me in the candlelit cellar talking into the satellite phone, completely unaware that his memory had overtaken me.

Johnny, Menessos, and I had traded pieces of our souls, pieces bound in strong memories. We did this in order to protect me from being Bindspoken by the Witch Elders Council for breaking—out of necessity—a few of their rules. As the Lustrata, I couldn't risk having my aura sealed and being rendered magically impotent forever.

What I'd just seen was the memory Menessos gave me in that *sorsanimus* spell. I wanted to see it again, to study these legendary people once more, but the memory's strength had fled.

Menessos shut the phone off. "A car was already on its way. The driver should arrive in fifteen minutes." His tongue ran over those long, sharp teeth. "Is Mountain nearby?"

"Yes. But you fed from him this morning. Will you be able to stop?"

"I have been a vampire for thousands of years, Persephone," he scolded me, irritation seasoning his tone.

"Being undead is new."

"I do not feel different in any way that should alarm you."

It implied that he did feel different in other ways. I would have questioned him further, but his aura of starving-animal impatience warned me not to delay. In the little time we had, however, there was one more thing I *had* to hammer out. "Johnny's asked me to search his mind via the *sorsanimus* link to find what I can about whoever locked up his tattoos. I have an idea of what to do, and how, but I don't want to waste time on the trial and error method. Do you know anything that can help?"

"Are you in a hurry?"

"A bit."

His eyes narrowed with suspicion, but, again, we had little time.

"He shouldn't be able to change at all," I babbled, "because of how his powers are locked up, but he can. It's difficult, but the fact that he can surpass it attests to his power—"

"No. It attests to yours."

"Huh?"

"The spell that forcibly transformed Theo included Johnny and the others. It did more than save her life, did it not?"

I nodded. Though they had all transformed as usual during the last full moon, each of them retained their man-minds while in wolf form.

"Had he been able to transform any part of himself prior to that?"

"Only his hands."

"And afterward, the Domn Lup proved himself and fully transformed. You are supposed to repeat that particular spell for the wærewolves who fought at the beach, are you not?"

"I am."

"Perhaps if you include Johnny again, it will further weaken those locks."

The logic was sound; I'd present the option to Johnny. It might be enough, for now.

Menessos offered the phone to me through the bars. I stepped closer to retrieve it. Both of his hands shot forward and grabbed my wrist. As fast as it happened, my first impulse was to jerk away, but I didn't give in to fear. I stood unmoving, unresisting.

At his lingering touch, the underside of my sternum heated. It was some kind of bonus born of the first hex between us and he could stir this reaction in me by simply saying my name. He called it "kindling my flesh," and he could make it very pleasurable. Now that he bore my second hex, perhaps simply saying my name didn't have the same power, but he showed me how much more thorough a second hex could conduct the kindling: a warm kiss blew onto the nape of my neck, setting my spine afire, burning like a slow fuse.

It wasn't clear if Menessos felt it; he did not react. He did nothing but hold me and stare into my eyes. "You kissed me, before you killed me," he whispered. "The memory of you willingly pressing your lips to mine is one

I will treasure. Forever." He released me and the flame on the fuse died away.

Oh no. This is going to be tougher to resist.

Leaving him, I pushed the cellar door open and a gust of chilled November air instantly curled cold fingers around me. This airstream dragged me up from the underground as if desperate to separate me from the vampire.

Mountain stood a few yards away, the kennel keys in his fist. I touched his arm. "You gave blood once today and have been busy with the elementals ever since. A driver will be here in a few minutes, let him donate instead."

I watched from my living room window as a limousine pulled into my driveway. The driver got out, his steps scrunching on the limestone, and opened a door. Menessos got in without so much as a backward glance toward the house. When the red taillights streaked up the road, a fraction of the completeness I felt in his presence bled away from me.

Retreating from the window, I saw Johnny descending the stairs, barefoot. Every step he took revealed his exhaustion. His hair was damp and he wore a skull-patterned button-down shirt. He balanced a pizza box on one hand, an empty two-liter Dr Pepper bottle wobbling dangerously atop it. His other hand, limp and empty, dangled from the arm supported by the guitar-strap sling.

"Let me take those." I intercepted him before he'd

reached the bottom of the stairs and relieved him of the cardboard and plastic. "Should you be up?"

"I figured if I can't manage a shower and the stairs, we shouldn't try this mind-probing business." He put his feet firmly on the floor. "But I'm good. Saved you some pizza."

"I see that."

"And I see that I was right."

"About?"

"The vamp."

"How do you know?"

"If he'd been toast, you wouldn't have taken so long to get back inside."

Together we walked to the kitchen.

Nana, just finished with the dishes, dried her hands on a kitchen towel. She then ran a hand through her snow-white hair, still adjusting to the new, more modern 'do that had replaced her outdated football helmet of a bouffant.

Dr. Lincoln and Mountain sat at the dinette responding to Beverley's many questions about the unicorns, mostly answering, "I don't know."

When Mountain saw me he asked, "Do you have any camping gear?"

"I have an old tent packed away, but I don't know what condition it's in. Been years since I've used it. Don't you want to stay in the house?"

"Nah, I'll stay with the elementals."

"Temperature's dropping out there."

"I'll be fine. Plenty of insulation." He patted his rotund belly. "Someone should monitor them."

I relented. "I'll get the tent." I went out through the kitchen door and into the garage.

After hauling the hard-shelled tube that contained the tent down from a shelf, I wiped cobwebs and years of dust from its surface. The last time I had used it was back in college, when Michael LaCroix and I had gone camping with another couple. We'd broken up before the next planned camping trip, the one that ended with the other couple hospitalized and lucky to be alive after a rogue wære attacked them.

Back in the kitchen, I handed Mountain the somewhat clean tube. "I'm sorry, but I don't have a sleeping bag." Mine was long gone, not that Mountain would have fit in it anyway.

"That's okay, Doc's loaning me one he had in his truck."

"Sometimes I have to stay with my patients," Dr. Lincoln said. "Always have one with me."

Mountain bid us a good night and headed out, the tent bundled under an arm and a flashlight in his grip.

The doc had gathered his things up as well. I walked him to the front door. "Are we going to lose any of them, Doc?"

"I don't think so. Mostly minor wounds. That griffon, though. If he gets an infection . . ." He shrugged. "Wouldn't let me get close to him. I'll try to come back tomorrow evening."

"Thanks, Dr. Lincoln." I held the door open for him.

"I'm going to be over here a lot, tending your new animals, so you may as well call me Geoff."

"Deal, Geoff."

After I shut the door, Johnny came down the hall toward me. He carried a plate bearing two slices of pizza and held it out to me, features firm with determination. He knew I hadn't eaten.

I accepted the plate and picked up a slice. He'd reheated it for me. Samosky's pizza was awesome. Before I could take a bite, Beverley, escorted by Nana, appeared for a good-night hug and kiss. Unicorns or not, Nana was making sure she kept to her usual nightly routine.

Being home amid all this average family activity felt very . . . satisfying. *It's my destiny to bring balance. As aggravating as it might be at times, this is what it is about. Having this.*

Johnny and I went back to the kitchen. He looked pale so I made him sit down while I poured myself a glass of 7UP. Joining him at the dinette, I said, "I know you're the tough-guy Domn Lup, but you lost a lot of blood and you need to take it easy."

"If you insist."

"I do."

Despite his fatigue, he managed to wiggle his eyebrows suggestively. "I'm not sure I can even climb *all* the way back up those stairs tonight."

"Would you like to sleep on the couch?"

"No," he replied quickly. "I can take the main stairs, they're straight. It's the attic stairs that are troublesome. I have to hunker down *and* twist. It pulls the stitches."

Whining wasn't in his character, so I was suspicious. "Really?"

He shrugged nonchalantly and moved the napkin holder around. "Maybe I should crash in your bedroom." His blue eyes locked on mine with the last word.

That was all it took to make my heart beat a little faster. "Let's see how you feel after we get this 'probing' done."

"Oh." He grinned. "I always crash after intense probing."

CHAPTER FIVE

My bedroom's creamy-yellow walls were bathed in the flickering glow of white candles and the sweet, heavy scent of nag champa incense filled the air. Nana and Beverley were asleep in their beds, and Johnny and I were alone in my room. I'd promised to try this mind-probe thing and, despite feeling more like sleeping than scrutinizing, I would try it. Plus, with the wærewolf head honchos en route, Johnny needed whatever information he could get.

"How do we do this?" he asked.

"First, we take our pants off." I dropped my jeans, leaving me in a long-sleeved tee and cotton boy-short panties.

He growled approval and dropped his jeans atop the discarded guitar-strap-sling without a word. I approved of the black stretch cotton boxer briefs. They were snug where they needed to be snug. Regardless of his injury, it was obvious his libido was doing just fine.

"Since when did you start wearing underwear?" I asked.

"Since the summer's over."

Just below the hem of the shorts, tattoos of blocky

Aztec figures adorned each thigh. Drawn with thick lines and colored in with dark shades of red, these tattoos weren't my favorites. "Sit on the bed and, here, take these pillows."

"Please tell me that this is going to involve some kind of kinky sex magic thing."

"Sorry."

"Damn."

"This isn't even going to stir up a lot of energy like magic does. It's mostly a meditation. The saline and salt should have cleansed the magic completely from your wound, but if you feel even a hint of energy affecting your injuries, let me know, okay?"

"I *am* more tolerant to magic than other wæres."

"I know but . . ."

"But what?"

"When we made love at the haven . . . you know Menessos did something, right?"

He arched a brow. He could have given into anger or laughter. "He didn't have video cameras in our room, did he?"

"Oh, hell. Not that I know of." I had a sinking feeling inside. That bastard just might have. "He did something magically, through his link to me. He said that we'd already imprinted on each other, and he gave it a nudge into a fuller emotional bond. When it happened, we both murmured, '*in signum amoris.*' Do you remember that?"

He squinted. "Now that you mention it . . . sort of."

"Well, if, because of that or the *sorsanimus,* this tweaks you in a way that's wrong, bad, or unpleasant, say so and we'll stop, okay?"

"You imply that I could be tweaked in way that is both wrong *and* bad yet is not unpleasant."

I licked my index finger and gave him a point on the air scoreboard, then began rearranging my closet. Once all of my clothing hangers were pushed from the right side toward the middle, some old poster frames were exposed. Behind those were smaller frames, and behind them, a rectangle of slate, a little more than a foot wide by two feet long and less than a half-inch thick. The slate was cool and smooth under my fingers. I hefted it out and leaned it against the bed. I passed Johnny a fluorite stone and proceeded to cast a circle around us.

Before calling the elements to guard us I corrected my wording to invoke the "spirit of the elements" and not the elementals themselves. Probably not necessary, but it wouldn't do to have any of the elemental animals from the grove trying to break into the house, so better to over-think in this instance.

The personalities of the elements arrived as I had always experienced them before. I knew earth was present when a tingle touched my skin. Air was announced by a warm breath swirling around me, lifting my hair. I called to fire, and felt its nips and small gnawing bites of response. Lastly, I called to water and felt the pressure and the pull of a current, then it subsided and buoyancy took hold until it all faded away.

At this point, I lit an extra white candle. *Goddess, watch over Ross and see that his soul finds its way to the Summerland to heal.*

Sitting cross-legged on my bed in front of Johnny, I used the pillows to elevate my knees so they could touch his and be nearly level. When I positioned the heavy slate on our knees, it took a minute to make adjustments but finally the slate slab rested on our bare skin and seemed reasonably level.

"Is this the genuine version of the Ouija board?" Johnny asked, fingers skimming over the gray-black smoothness. Symbols of all types had been drawn on the surface in faded and occasionally chipped white paint.

"Kinda. 'Ouija' is just a made-up name and we aren't using it to contact spirits or demons or what-have-you. But it is something that can help in . . . well, communication. This piece of slate has supposedly been in my family for generations. The story goes that in the 1860s my great-great-great-grandmother stole this slate from the ruins of an altar to Hecate and painted these symbols on it to ensure she got it out of Greece."

"So your whole family is made up of spunky chicks?"

"Spunky?" *Not the word I would have used.* "I guess you could say that, but we're not even sure her account of things was completely true."

"Spunky and a liar? Say it ain't so."

"More like spunky with Alzheimer's."

"Oh. What are all these fancy scribbles?"

Confident he recognized the numbers and the alphabet, and could read the "yes," "maybe," and "no," for himself, I explained the rest. "Runes, zodiac symbols, planetary symbols, astrological glyphs, the various stars, here . . . you know a pentacle." It was in the middle of the rectangle. I pointed to symbols. "These are just stars with more points. A hexagram—like a Star of David—has six; the heptagram has seven; here's eight, the octogram; and nine, one form of an enneagram. Here's the symbol for infinity, and you know the Wedjat and the ankh." There was no wasted space, yet the symbols weren't crowded. They each had their place.

"Why'd we have to take our pants off to hold this slate?"

"So the physical energies in our bodies have direct access."

"I do like direct access," he said.

I chalked another point into the air for him.

"And this?" He held up the fluorite. The purple and blue hues were frosty, not glossy. It wasn't smooth and round like a marble, but a normal tumbled stone you'd find in the bins of any rock-hound's store. It had edges and flat spots. "It isn't the same as those." He pointed to the purple stones I'd placed with the white candles.

"Those are sugilites and they are receptive. This is fluorite and it's projective."

"Meaning?"

"Meaning those stones around the circle will aid in drawing the answers out of you, while this one will project those answers onto the slate."

"And the purple theme?"

"Spiritual. We're tapping our souls, but we're also tapping your subconscious." I waited a second. "You feel all right?"

"I'm kinda horny."

My nonplussed expression made him defend the statement.

"What?" His attention flitted from my chest to my

face. "I'm in your candlelit room, that little aphrodisiac stick is smoking, and I'm on your bed in my skivvies."

"That little stick is incense, nag champa, and it is for meditational purposes. As in calming."

Johnny sniffed the air, wiggled his brows. "I disagree."

"I meant, does your *arm* feel all right?"

"Yeah, yeah. My arm is fine."

"Put that stone in the middle on the pentacle, then put your hands like this." I held my hands in front of me as if I was going to clap, but instead of bringing them together, I placed them on the outer edges of the slate. The tip of my middle finger rested at the midpoint of the side, and the cool edge of the stone stretched along that finger, into my palm. Johnny mimicked it. "Your fingertip must touch mine," I said.

He adjusted.

Now we held the stone rectangle like a tray we were ready to lift, but we weren't going to be moving. "Will you be able to keep your arm there for a while?"

"Yeah."

"I can get more pillows if you want to prop it."

"Nah. I'm good."

I bit my lip, then said, "I know."

The gleam in his gaze was soft, adoring, a bit sad, and it said much more than flattering words ever could. "I'm ready."

"You're *always* ready, but for now, I want you to close your eyes. Breathe deep. Good. Again." I kept my voice even, soothing, and my words slow. "Ground and center. Feel your heartbeat, feel how steady it is. See the light inside you. Now slowly increase the scope of your vision as if backing up. See yourself, see your light remaining steady in this place, while your view of it moves farther and farther away, until you can see the whole universe, with your light at the center." I gave him a moment. "Now slowly glide back to that light, embrace it and become one with it, calm and steady."

His breathing was deep.

"I am going to ask you questions and make statements. Do not use your voice to answer me. When you hear the stone tumbling around, do not open your eyes. Concentrate on that light, on keeping it in your embrace. Listen to it hum and let it shine through you, down your arms and into the slate."

He nodded.

"Go back, reach into the past. You're waking up in the park. Naked, confused, covered with tattoos. You don't even know your own name." I paused. "Now go back further. Reach into the unknown."

Wrinkles appeared around his eyes as if he was squinting. His breathing had quickened.

"Don't force it. Just feel, feel the weight of time lifting from your shoulders. Imagine a clock, and the arms are spinning backward. I do not expect you to know the answers. They are locked away from your conscious mind. But they may not be locked from the subconscious. Just focus on the clock and let your subconscious answer through the stone between us. Breathe. Breathe." I repeated it a few more times until I could sense serenity around him again.

"Good." Directing my awareness onto the fluorite resting on the pentacle, my first few questions would be easy, to set the tone. "Can you answer?" I whispered as low as possible, almost soundless.

The fluorite remained still.

I asked again, waited again. Nothing.

With closed eyes, I sought that piece of Johnny's soul I now carried. Breathing in the incense, I imagined that ethereal essence searching for that memory and reached out for my alpha state. *Johnny,* I thought. *Johnny.*

What?

I stilled. For an instant, I could have sworn that I'd heard his voice. *Silly me. I'm not searching for Johnny, but for the memory he gave me.*

Targeting that more precise request, the memory awoke and answered my call. It sparked like neurons firing across my brain, and finally it filled my sight.

I saw Johnny, in his late teens. His hair was shorter, and he had no piercings, just the tattoos. As before, with Menessos, I was watching Johnny and yet I was one with him, impossibly seeing this moment from the outside, yet also inside his thoughts, feeling his fear.

His eyes were too wide—the dark blue like lapis lazuli set in ivory and encased in ebony, like on a mummy's sarcophagus. His arms were wrapped tight around him as he paced inside a jail cell, then stopped, staring at the open door. He wanted to rush through it, to flee. The naked bulbs along the walkway beyond the cage were dim, and some burnt out, but he could still see the endless rows of cells, the filthy floor, and dingy block walls. There were no windows here.

Beauregard walked down the hallway, shutting each door, checking that it was locked. Johnny paced away from the door, turning to watch as the door swung shut, clanging like a dull death knell. Beau twisted the key in the lock, gave the door a tug. The pity on the man's face made Johnny feel weak and cowardly. These men around him weren't afraid. But I am, he thought. He could smell the reek of it clinging to him as if he'd pissed his pants. They all knew he was scared. He couldn't hide it.

Beau secured the cell door next to Johnny's. The last one in the row. Ig's cell. After a nod at the dirija, Beau left the cell-block kennel area.

In moments, a wave of heat made Johnny's skin ripple and nausea made him crouch in the corner of the cell. He put his back to the rough block wall. Its coolness chased the rising bile back down his throat. In the cage beside him, Ig had removed his clothes and folded them, stacked them in a neat pile. He moved to the bars near Johnny.

"You okay, son?"

Johnny didn't answer; he didn't want to be naked, didn't want the others to gawk at the strange tattoos now embedded in his skin. After a moment he asked, "What will it be like?"

"I won't lie, it hurts. Hurts more if you fight it."

"What if you're wrong? What if I'm not like you and I don't change?"

Ig gave him a kind but cheerless smile. "I wish that were true, John. But you are one of us."

Johnny knew it was true. He could smell and hear things others couldn't. But he couldn't remember it being any other way. He couldn't even remember his name. They called him John Doe at the hospital. No one knew how old he was, either. They guessed seventeen. Maybe eighteen.

In the twenty-seven days since he woke naked in that park

without any memory, no one had recognized him. No missing person's report had been filed in any state for someone that fit his description, with or without the tattoos.

No one cares enough to search for me.

Ig reached through the bars and put a reassuring hand on Johnny's shoulder.

Johnny put his head down, fighting back tears—a sign of weakness he would never let Ig see.

Then the moon blew her kisses into the cell block and her curse shivered into life. Gooseflesh prickled and erupted thick, dark hair. It felt like sandpaper had been shoved under his skin, scraping and scrubbing under his flesh.

He tore off his clothes just in time.

His face ruptured, and the inner beast was born snarling and fighting, forcing its way out into the world. Molten iron surged through his veins, burning him, dissolving him. He was stretched until his overheated bones felt brittle thin, and then the moonlight hammered him like forged steel, remaking him, pounding him into a new shape, stronger than the former.

For a time he stood on all fours, unmoving, waiting . . . but the pain was gone. He felt like a just-whelped pup, exhausted.

Ig had become a red wolf, growling at him. To the other side, a gray wolf snapped its muzzle through the bars. In cells beyond he saw wolves mounting she-wolves; he saw another wolf throw itself against the bars repeatedly. He watched it fight frantically for a freedom it would not find.

He stared down at his paws.

I'm a wolf. A wolf! I am . . . I am.

None of us, *Johnny thought,* will ever be free of this curse.

No one will want me now.

His muzzle lifted and the saddest wailing howl echoed through the cell block.

Holding on to that despairing sound, keeping it foremost in my mind, I begged, "Who made these tattoos? Who bound his power away from him?"

The fluorite tumbled to the left, rolled toward me, spun on blank slate and rolled toward Johnny. The stone stopped on a rune letter that was shaped like an *F* with the two bars angled down.

"Ansuz," I whispered. The rune represented the spoken word and advice. But when the little fluorite spun halfway around, I knew this was a sign to reverse the rune and change the meaning to trickery and lies. The stone rolled to the right, onto the next rune, Raidho. Upon this angular-looking *R,* the stone again rotated half a turn. Since this symbol normally indicated travel, the reverse meant an upsetting change in plans. The stone rolled to the very next rune like a sideways *V,* called Kenaz, and did its little spin for a third time, meaning poor judgment or ignorance.

The stone seemed to be simply checking out each rune and twisting. I began to wonder if this was a waste of time.

When the fluorite rolled back to Ansuz, then tumbled across the slate as if it were running away and stopped abruptly on Nauthiz, however, my confidence returned; there *was* a purpose in this reading. Nauthiz looked like an *X* that someone had kicked: The line ending its upper right "arm" was shifted vertically rather than at an angle. The stone did not pirouette here, so the symbol indicated a need, but whether that was a spiritual, emotional, or material need had to be assessed by the surrounding runes. The fluorite rolled to Uruz next, then to Mannaz. The former symbol looked like two upright bars, one shorter than the other, a slanted bar connecting the tops. It was the sovereign of strength, determination, and healing: internal transition. The latter symbol resembled an *X* and an *M* combined. The stone spun halfway around— and having just relived Johnny's memory I had to think it was indicative of silence, solitude, and perhaps introspection. It was definitely about personal obstacles and separation.

The stone rolled back to the pentacle and went still.

It had given me a kind of recap of Johnny's story, as if I'd asked for a reading. I hadn't. Though I prompted it a few more times, it did not respond. I counseled myself to keep a heavy sigh from escaping.

Johnny cracked one eye open a fraction. "Is it done?"

"Yeah." I said quick thanks and left him holding the slate while I took up the circle.

I moved the candles to the dresser top, let the stones pile on the bedside table, and took the slate back to the closet, where I shifted the frames forward and bent to replace the slate.

"Well?" He sounded like he was ready for bad news.

From deep in the closet I asked, "Do you know anything about runes?" I twisted to see him as he answered. He was staring at the bed. *He has a prime opportunity to ogle my ass and he's missing it?* "Johnny?"

"Runes? Um, that would be a—" He turned and realized this position and my undies left little to the imagination. He gaped, then shut his mouth and turned away. "No."

Oh hell. This is worse than I thought.

I wanted to come out of this feeling like I was helpful. Instead, I'd disappointed him.

When the chore of putting everything away was done, I reclaimed my seat on the bed. "What's wrong?"

"I can tell you didn't get an answer." There was no blame in his voice, but there was plenty of dismay in his blue eyes.

"Not really. It answered more like a rune reading. I'll have to give it some thought."

He was stepping into his role as Domn Lup and giving up so much . . . his band was on the top of that endangered list. Making it big in the music industry meant everything to the three band members of Lycanthropia, but Johnny's new role as front man for wærewolves everywhere could destroy that rock 'n' roll dream. The band mates weren't sure they should book any more shows and if they weren't playing and packing in the crowds they weren't of any interest to the industry reps.

"I'll cross-reference the symbols tomorrow and see if I can make sense of it then."

He nodded, pensive. His mood had sunk low. It had been a long, wearying day. Still, I decided to give it one more try.

"As the Lustrata," I said, moving onto my hands and knees, "I'm supposed to balance the good and the bad." I crawled closer, until our lips were an inch apart. "It's important to me to make sure I give you something good, for all the bad you're dealing with."

"Well," he replied, his voice taking that one syllable and letting it trail, growing deeper until he was nearly growling. It was such a male sound, like he was wrapping me in thick velvet with his voice, and when paired with the yearning that took over, it caused the ambiance of the room to change drastically. "In lieu of giving me the name of the person who did this to me, I can think of one other thing you could give me that's very, very good. . . ."

With my palms on either side of his hips, I whispered, "Let me guess."

CHAPTER SIX

Later, after Johnny had congratulated me on my "damn good guess," we lay snuggled together, my head on his shoulder and one leg across his thighs. My fingers trailed over his stomach and my thoughts wandered.

I felt sad for him, now that the memory I'd taken from him was so clear to me. I knew what memory I'd taken from Menessos, and that I'd given him my memory of meeting the Goddess in a cornfield when I was a child—though I'd forgotten it until he recounted it to me. I didn't know what memories Johnny and Menessos had shared. And I didn't know what memory Johnny had taken from me. It wasn't the night I lost my virginity; I could still remember that farce.

So I asked, "During the *sorsanimus,* I allowed you to have whatever memory you wanted. What one did you take?"

"Whatever I wanted?" One side of his mouth crooked up. "I don't know if *that* really applies." He considered it for a moment. "I guess I wanted a sense of what it was like to have a mother."

I sat up. "A mother?" *No, not my mother. Anything but*

that. Blood drained from my face. "What did you take?"

He stared at the ceiling, seemingly far away. "I can see you sitting on a cracked vinyl bathroom floor, a dirty bathtub at your back. You're biting your lip . . . just like you still do . . . you're watching your mom as she puts the curling iron to her hair and checks out the window. She's on edge. You're nervous; there's no sense of the security a child should know. I can feel that you can't please her, can't make her smile and you want to so badly. You look at a paper in front of you. You'd made a big red heart and written 'Mommy' inside it. You're so proud of it, the letters are neat, just like the teacher showed you. Your mother checks the window again, catches her breath, and whispers, 'He came!' and she's so happy, so excited and she's smiling. You want to give her your picture now. She comes and scoops you up in her arms and you feel like everything is safe and good. But she hasn't seen your picture. You say, 'Mommy, I drew—' and she sees it. She sees you used her lipstick to draw it, the metal tube is on the floor, its contents worn down by your drawing. She screams at you, screams that you ruin everything. Her embrace isn't warm or happy now, she's squeezing you too tight. You begin to cry. She hurries down the hall with you and throws you into your little bed. Your arm hits hard against the wall and you cry louder. She says . . . terrible things."

Though he didn't tell me what she said, I could hear the echoes of her yelling in my memory. *I'll never have anything and it's all because of you, you stupid little brat. I should have given you away! Instead I've spent eight years suffering, alone.*

"There's a padlock on the outside of your door and she locks you in. From your window, you see down into the apartment building's parking lot. She gets into a truck with a man and leaves. You're there alone, locked in your room, crying yourself to sleep." He took a shaky breath. "You don't know what to do when smoke fills your room. You can't breathe, and then firemen kick in your door and take you away."

His words had brought it all back and my tears wouldn't be denied. "The curling iron," I said. "She forgot to unplug it." I wiped my cheeks. "At least I think she forgot. I'd rather not think that she purposely tried to kill me."

Unable to reach the tissue box, Johnny offered me the corner of the sheet. "That's . . . awful, Red."

"I remember that night in the hospital, my mom snuck in and woke me up. She took me away without getting me discharged. She left me at Nana's. They argued and I heard her say, '*You* didn't want me to give her up, so *you* raise her.' I never saw her again."

I felt stupid for letting it hurt me so many years later—that was a hell of a memory for him to end up with—but I'd learned to let my emotions flow so they could *keep* flowing. When more tears sprang, I blotted them on the sheet. "If you wanted a memory with a sense of a mother's unconditional love, you got cheated."

"We both did." Johnny ran his fingers comfortingly over my leg.

My breath caught; we were positioned exactly as Una and Ninurta were in the memory from Menessos.

Johnny mistook my reaction for something else. "C'mere," Johnny whispered. I scooted down, head on his shoulder again. Moving slowly, he enfolded me in his arms as best he could. My misery drained out as if it had just happened, and I tried not to wonder if our positioning like Menessos's most-beloved meant anything.

Well before dawn, Johnny was awake. He kissed my cheek on his way out of the bedroom. "I'm off to help with preparations for the memorial. I'll see you . . . sometime. Not sure when. Probably after this whole thing is over tonight."

"You must be feeling better." I could have slept half the day.

He moved his arms like a fitness guru showing off biceps. "I'm a little stiff."

"Still? I thought I took care of that last night?"

"Ha!" He used both index fingers to chalk up a whole row of points onto our air scoreboard. His enthusiasm cheered me from my sleepiness. "That you did. I think you have more innuendo points than I do now." He was brimming with adoration—then his phone beeped and he was all business again as he read the text message. "Either Todd's decisophobic, or he enjoys tormenting me with the final say-so of every detail." He drew closer and kissed my cheek again. "I feel like I'm healing up now. That salt did the trick. Good thing, too. The authenticity of my being the Domn Lup would sink if I'm strolling around with my arm in a sling."

Male pride. I stretched, arching my back. "Should I come with you?" I asked around a yawn.

He bit at my nipples through my shirt. "I love it when you do."

Laughter chased the yawn away. "Point for you."

He pulled his arm back at the elbow and said, "Yes! Ow . . . oooo." He rubbed at his chest. "Okay, no celebratory arm movements yet."

"Should I come *to the memorial* with you?"

"It'd probably be better if you didn't."

"Okay. Guess I'll dig into that rune reading today."

That won me a third kiss on the cheek and, too soon, Johnny left.

Determined to unravel the meaning of the rune reading and unable to go back to sleep, I got up. Half an hour later, as I sat in the kitchen writing out my notes, I suddenly felt a shriveling sensation, as if I were a balloon filled with water and all of it was gushing out of me, leaving me empty and depleted. It took my breath away.

But it wasn't my flesh that had been drained . . . it was my soul.

The sun had risen; Menessos had died.

With each gasp of air I gulped, I recovered and the withering and abandoned feeling receded. I resumed writing out my notes.

Soon, the floor above me creaked. The sound signaled that Nana and Beverley had roused and it was time to start breakfast. I started coffee, popped some bread in the toaster, and boiled water for oatmeal. With such uncommon events occurring lately, these ordinary household chores held greater meaning to me. I needed to cling to these moments when I could.

Nana shuffled in, took a cup of coffee, and sat in my spot at the dinette. "Johnny's gone early today. Heard my car coughing down the road." The rusty Chrysler LeBaron did need a tune-up.

"Pack things to attend to."

"Sounds like I've got car things to attend to." She lit a cigarette. "What's this?" She tapped the paper with my notes.

"Runes."

"Shit, Persephone, I can see *that*," Nana croaked. She scanned the drawn runes and the notes I'd made about which were reversed.

Before I could reply, Beverley and Ares bounded down the stairs sounding like a small herd of cattle. I got side-tracked serving the kiddo her oatmeal with brown sugar, and forgot to answer Nana. While Beverley ate, I made her lunch. After affixing a sticky note with a joke written on it to her sandwich bag, I zipped up the lunchbox and tucked it in her book bag.

The party invitations for her classmates were already stashed in the front pocket. I'd promised her a big birth-day party. Though she would officially become ten on Thursday, we were inviting her whole class over on Sat-urday. And I had secret plans for some docile ponies to attend, too.

Ares was sitting by his bowl, tail skimming over the floor in rhythm with his hungry whining, so I fed him.

After finishing my own bowl of oatmeal, I tidied up the kitchen and let the puppy out to do his business. Nana remained uncharacteristically quiet throughout all of this, studying the runes I hadn't explained. When Bev-erley and I headed out the door for the bus stop, Nana was still scowling at the paper.

• • •

As my Toyota Avalon rolled into the driveway, a white delivery van turned in behind me. It had followed me most of the way back from the bus stop. So, curious and concerned, I stopped the car halfway up the drive, put it in park, and got out, ready to go on the offensive if need be. When I saw INCOMPARABLE DELIVERIES, LTD on the van's side, however, I relaxed.

A deliveryman in dark blue coveralls and matching cap stepped out. At Hallowe'en, this same man had delivered a costume from Menessos. "You?" My surprise got ahead of my manners. "Good morning." I saw the name embroidered on his coveralls, and added an awkward "David."

"Good morning to you, too, miss." He offered me a manila envelope then headed back to the van and left.

Inside the envelope was proof of Menessos's ability to swiftly pull political strings. I now had official permits for building two barns and a chicken coop, adding a bedroom-and-bath addition to the house, "site improvement" to and placement of a mobile home, and to dig a second well on my property.

Tossing this onto the seat, I put the Avalon in the garage. Nana opened the door from the kitchen before I'd even cut the engine. The toe of her pink fuzzy slipper was impatiently tapping. Her new, softer hairdo did nothing to diminish the supreme authority she could convey. *Guess it wasn't just the outdated beehive.*

As soon as I opened the car door she demanded, "Are you planning to move into that vampire's haven?"

"No!" Her question stunned me. "I may have to show

up once in a while, though." I slammed the door a little harder than was necessary and clomped up the steps carrying my purse and the manila envelope. "What makes you think that?"

Nana harrumphed as she shuffled into the kitchen and resumed her place at the table. "Your rune reading."

Deciphering that was my whole purpose this morning, so I was eager for her input. "I'm better with Tarot than runes. So explain."

"What pattern were you using for this seven-rune spread?"

"No pattern. That's just how it ended up." I filled my favorite coffee mug; it had Waterhouse's *Lady of Shalott* on it. I joined her at the dinette after dropping my insulated flannel on the chair back.

"Typically, a seven-rune reading divides into four parts. The first two define the problem, the second two reveal the past factors that have brought about this situation, and the third pair give advice. The final rune tells you what to expect if you take that advice."

"Okay." With the powerful irritation Nana was radiating, I didn't dare try to retrieve my notes from her and assess them according to that premise. I'd see what she had to say then tell her the circumstances under which I'd actually gotten this list of runes.

"Well, according to these, the problem stems from someone who wanted what was best for them and *that* caused you to have to change your plans. Sounds like the vampire making you his court witch."

She had a point—if the reading had been about me, which it wasn't. Moreover, Nana didn't know about the *sorsanimus* ritual. I was able to do this reading for Johnny because we now shared souls. No way was I going to explain all that to Nana right now.

"And the next two say that your poor judgment and the chance encounter with that vampire brought this all on you."

I nodded without comment. She was seeing what she wanted to see in the reading. If there truly was a dual reading at work here, then maybe it pointed to my meeting with Beauregard, the Bindspoken witch who owned the witch supply shop Wolfsbane and Absinthe. Because he gave me the spell components to do the *sorsanimus* ritual, I owed him a favor. More likely, though, all this referred to how Johnny was brought into the situation where he was given the tattoos.

"In the next pair, Nauthiz cautions you to think twice before taking action, while Uruz, to me, represents very masculine forces—so you should think twice where any men are concerned."

"Okay." Except that was probably Johnny dealing with other men, like maybe the Rege who would be here in a few days. "And the last one?"

"Tells you to take good advice. Like mine. And I say: Stay home and leave the vampire alone."

My mouth opened, ready to tell her it was Johnny's reading and the "separation" inherent in the last rune was more of a warning against letting any difficulties interfere with or cause a separation between him and the root of his spiritual strength. Before I could make a sound, though, she added, "Let the mundane humans buy all that romantic crap about vampires, but a witch should know better." She thumped the table with her fist for emphasis.

That was when a semitrailer truck bounced past the house, as in, *in my yard,* and headed through the cornfield along the path of the trodden-down stalks.

For a moment, Nana and I just gaped. Then my feet had me hurrying out the door. Nana called my name, stopping me long enough for her to toss the flannel to me. "Can't have you catching cold."

I donned the jacket as I rushed outside—I'd forgotten to shut the overhead garage door because of Nana—and jogged after the semi.

Those hand-delivered building permits had arrived just in time.

Before I reached the pathway, a second truck was crossing my yard, and I got out of its way. A third with a flat-bed trailer stopped on the road to unload a backhoe and a forklift. A small bus rolled to a stop behind it. The bus doors opened and dozens of men streamed out. Or, more accurately, dozens of Beholders.

Mountain came across the cornfield shouting directions for the Beholders to form lines in a certain area for a head count. Menessos's men were dressed in work clothes and heavy-duty boots. They were prepared for a day of hard, dirty work.

Heldridge's men, however, looked more like thugs. Some wore gold chains and rings. Some sported dark sunglasses or bandannas. All of them were wearing clothes that branded them a bunch of badasses while also screaming, "I've got money," because the crisp, clean, new clothes were undeniably designer labels.

Though I was excited that a barnraising was about to

commence, I realized that running out here in the midst of that excitement might have been hasty. We weren't certain whose side these human vampire servants were on. My pace increased as I headed to intercept Mountain.

The forklift barreled over to remove a skid from the first semi. Someone pushed a delivery list into Mountain's hands and he skimmed it, flipping pages and nodding. When he looked up, Mountain saw me and waved. Strands of his überlong ponytail lifted in the chilly morning breeze.

"It's cold," I said, stepping up beside him. "Did the tent keep you warm enough to sleep well?"

His head bobbed. "It did." The bus driver left his vehicle idling and strolled over with a drive-thru bag and a large coffee that he passed to Mountain, who shoved the delivery list under his arm. "Thanks, Derek," he said as the man walked away. "Hold this?" He offered me the coffee and I held it while he dug a sausage biscuit from the bag. "Mind if I eat?"

"Not at all," I answered. I watched the line of Beholders, Menessos's warning at the forefront of my thoughts.

He bit, chewed, *mmm*-ed. "Speaking of eating, the griffons caught a pair of deer last night."

"Oh?" I shot a glance toward the animals; they had all moved into the grove itself. Phoenixes perched in branches, and while the unicorns' alabaster coats were plainly visible amid the tree trunks, the griffons were barely discernable. I couldn't see the dragons, but I heard their distinctive warbling. It seemed they would all stay clear of the Beholders. *Good.*

"So they're fed. The project list shows delivery of

food for the others is pending. Should be here within the hour." He was also watching the Beholders, who had lined up as bidden, though they had taken it upon themselves to separate their line into two groups.

Mountain must have noticed me eyeballing the Beholders. "Heldridge's men are in for a rude awakening today," he said. "There's going to be a lot of sore backs and blistered hands tonight."

"Do you think you'll have a problem with them?"

"When a haven dissolves, everyone wants to go to a master with a reputation for treating his people well, but generally the vampires who step up to take on the extras are the ones who tend to break their toys, if you know what I mean."

"What reputation does Menessos have?"

"That he won't tolerate disrespect and is exceedingly harsh on anyone who opposes his rules, but otherwise safe. They'll behave. Besides, the boss is sending sentinels for you."

"Yeah, we talked about that." I wrinkled my nose. *He promised no monkeyshines.*

"They should've been here first. Before Heldridge's Beholders anyway—wait—there they are." He pointed with his pinky as he pushed the last of the biscuit into his mouth.

A sleek black car rolled past the semis and up my gravel driveway.

"Oooo. Audi A8," Mountain mumbled. He readjusted the coffee, dug in the bag again, and promptly bit into another biscuit.

"They won't know I'm out here," I said to Mountain.

"It's probably best not to have them accosted by my Nana first thing."

He waved me on. "Don't worry about us out here. I've got this under control."

"I believe you do." I patted his enormous upper arm. "Thanks, Mountain."

"No. Thank *you*. The boss let me stay because you asked and . . . I'm glad to have this task."

I jogged away feeling that having him here—in addition to my gratefulness for having someone with farm knowledge in charge of the new livestock—was giving him part of his heritage back. A positive contrast to all those lives that had been lost on my account.

As I rounded the house enough to gain a clear view of the driveway, I saw a pair of women dressed like federal agents. Each had taken a position behind open car doors, holding handguns aimed into my garage.

Sweet Goddess, what's Nana done now?

CHAPTER SEVEN

S top!" I shouted.

The woman nearest me kept her weapon aimed into the garage as she shouted to me, "You are the Erus Veneficus? Persephone Alcmedi?"

"Yes." I couldn't imagine what kind of exchange Nana had instigated to provoke these women, but my Great Dane pup, Ares, was barking his head off inside. "Put your guns away."

"My lady, there's a creature in your garage."

A creature? My jog accelerated into a sprint. The woman who'd shouted at me abandoned her position behind her car door and for a moment it seemed she intended to tackle me to keep me safely back. "Whoa," I commanded, hand up and out to stop my well-meaning defender. She pulled up short but spread her arms to block me. I demanded, "Let me see," even as I thrust past her to where I could view the trunk of my Avalon in the garage.

A feathered tiger's tail swished at the front edge of my car.

At least it's not Nana causing the ruckus.

"Do not shoot," I commanded them. "Put your weapons away and stay back." Walking slowly into my garage, I saw the injured griffon with his beak in the big plastic bin where Ares's dog food was kept. He'd overturned the bin to get it open. His blind side was toward me. "Hey there . . ." I said softly from inside the garage.

His head shot up, neck feathers fluffing menacingly. His wings rose as much as the garage would allow. He opened his beak and made a noise like the rumble of distant thunder. It was the griffon version of a growl. "Whoa, there, Thunderbird," I said softly. "Didn't you get any deer last night?" I eased forward. His wings lowered a little and he moved to keep the Avalon between us. To the women outside I said, "Get into your car. If he leaves, let him."

They unhappily obeyed.

For each of my slow steps toward the hood of the Avalon the griffon countered, hobbling to the trunk. When he was clear, he took to the air. I hurried outside to watch; he went back to the grove.

They were sentient creatures of magic. While they couldn't speak, I was certain they were able to reason and think in ways that typical animals could not. Therefore, I wasn't worried that the griffons would fly off and eat little children, but I was concerned that they might migrate to a ley line in a warmer state.

Sounds of car doors shutting brought my thoughts back to the sentinels in their Audi that Mountain thought was so terrific. The women were approaching me. The one that had been ready to tackle me was a platinum blonde; the other a lovely Asian woman with dark hair.

Being gorgeous was a requirement to be an Offerling, but they had toned that down with the stern effects of their tightly bound hair. The brunette wore her hair in a low ponytail. I was delighted that she was dressed in a suit of battleship gray with a black silk blouse and sensible shoes. She settled her gun into a shoulder holster. The blonde wore a camel-colored double-breasted suit with a black turtleneck. Her pale hair was in a prim bun.

No Menessos monkeyshines. Yay!

As the blonde walked, she lifted the jacket to put her gun into a waist clip holster. "What the hell was that thing?"

"A griffon."

"You're shitting me," the Asian said.

My expression said clearly that I was not. "Right now I have many unusual animals running around here. Don't shoot any of them."

"What else can we expect to see?" the blonde asked.

"In the house is a fast-growing Great Dane." Who, I remembered, wasn't fond of Beholders. Still barking though the griffon had gone, Ares clearly wasn't fond of Offerlings either. "Out in the back there's . . . the unusual livestock." I left it vague.

The blonde nodded, conveying that she was an accept-what-you're-told-and-worry-about-what-it-really-means-later type. That didn't mean she wasn't able to think on her feet. I was willing to bet that, if I had claimed to be Mae West and asked her to set my hair on fire for me, this lady—without losing her unshakable and in-control demeanor—would have simply poured something on my head and told me it was flammable while she texted the higher-ups and ordered a psychiatric evaluation for me.

She extended her hand to me. "My lady, I'm Maxine Simmons. This is Zhan Hong. We'll check the house, then take up our positions for watch."

I introduced the women to Nana while holding Ares's collar as he acquainted himself with them. They must have been carrying some residual scent of things undead, because Ares was unimpressed. I shut the garage door before any more griffons found the dog food, and let the behemoth pup help me clean up the kibble while the women satisfied themselves that no one was hiding under my bed, in my pantry, or under the sink.

I left Ares in the garage and joined Nana in the kitchen, where she was watching out the window. The permits from the manila envelope were on the table; she'd been looking them over.

"About those runes." It was, after all, my intended goal for the day. "That wasn't exactly a reading, and it wasn't for me. It was for Johnny."

"How so?" Her forehead wrinkles deepened.

"I used Great-El's slate." My great-great-great-grandmother had been named Elpis, but Nana had always referred to her as Great-El, so I did, too.

"Lord and Lady, I haven't thought of that eccentric old thing in years."

I hoped she meant the slate, not Great-El.

"What were you trying to do with it?"

"I wanted the name of whoever gave Johnny his tattoos."

"I'm sure any tattoo artist can touch up the scars he might end up with. Look up tattoo parlors in the phone book."

"It's more than that, Nana." I moved closer and lowered my voice, not sure I wanted the Offerling-sentinels to hear. "We've learned that his power as Domn Lup was magically bound into the art. We have to find the artist and make him unbind it so Johnny can change at will without so much effort." I raked my fingers through my hair. "And fast."

"What's the hurry?"

In whispered tones I told her about the Rege coming on Wednesday. "So I tried Great-El's slate thinking if I could tap into his subconscious—some part that remembers—and get an answer, we'd know who did this. We could start searching. Instead, I got some cryptic rune reading."

Nana stood at the end of the dinette and twirled my note page to her. "That changes everything, and yet . . . the reading isn't without truth."

"What?" I asked.

"Because it came out like a reading, indicating reversed meanings and such, you thought of it like a reading. If you think of them like letters, though . . . this rune, Ansuz, may look like an *F*, but its alphabetical equivalent is an *A*." Her finger tapped along the row as she mumbled, "Uruz is a *U* and Mannuz is an *M* . . ." Then, more clearly, she announced, "You got your answer, Persephone." Nana passed me the paper. "You got a name. Arcanum."

CHAPTER EIGHT

Arcanum?" Theodora Hennessey asked, the warmth of her alto voice coming through the phone. She was one of the wærewolves who kenneled in my cellar during full moons. Her day job was owner and sole employee of Revelations, a service providing background checks on anyone from a possible employee to potential spouses.

"Yes." I spelled it to make sure there was no miscommunication.

"Male or female?"

"I don't know."

She asked more questions and got the same answer. Theo sighed. "I'm good, but honestly, finding someone via a pseudonym, without a full, real name and a birthday is seriously iffy. Finding it without an address or even a confirmed city or state is next to impossible. Do you have *anything* else?"

"This person is a tattoo artist and probably a witch." At least I was hoping one person had accomplished this. If we had to track down two . . .

"Well that's something. I'll do my best, but no promises."

"Thanks, Theo. And hey, Beverley's birthday is Thursday, will you come for dinner? We're having a big kid party on Saturday, but I'd like to have all of you who were friends with her mom over on Thursday." I heard pages shuffling.

"I can do that. Just promise me Johnny is making the cake."

I grumbled.

"What?"

"I can't promise that. I doubt he'll have time to bake. The Rege is coming to meet him on Wednesday." Over the next few days the whole pack would know, so I didn't fret about telling her.

"Hell, that was fast. The Rege himself, you say?"

"Yeah." I had a thought. "What do you know about him?"

"Keep your head down and stay the hell out of his way."

"What do you mean?"

"You ever see *The Godfather?*"

"Yeah."

"You see *The Terminator?*"

"Yeah."

"What about the *Nightmare on Elm Street* movies?"

"The scary guy with knives on his fingers? Yeah."

"Combine them. That's the Rege."

The well-drilling team was hard at work in the field when semis and trailers carrying two more backhoes, a crane, and some large sections of concrete were brought in. It seemed someone had quickly decided where the buildings would go and had measured and marked the areas, and the machinery was barreling around the cornfield.

As the first trucks left and the crane began unloading the concrete chunks, another arrived with prefabricated barn sides, trusses for the roof, and more. Some logistic genius was at work here.

All the hubbub was making Nana nervous. She announced that she was going to the store. Though she no longer had a hairdo that required gallons of Aqua Net and regular salon maintenance, she still tied a babushka under her chin before taking my car and fleeing.

Now that the runes had been deciphered, I could get some work done on my column, but I wanted to call Johnny first and tell him about Nana's interpretation. While my computer booted up, I hit speed dial. Expecting to leave him a message, it surprised me when he answered.

" 'Lo?"

"I thought you'd be busy," I said.

"I am. But I wanted to hear your voice."

"Aww . . . Well, thanks to Nana we're making a little progress on those runes." I told him the name and he was ecstatic, until I added what Theo had said. "On top of that, even if this person is found, convincing them to undo the binding may take time."

"We'll go with the vamp's backup plan, then. I'll try to get the forced-change spell scheduled ASAP. It'll reassure the men if I'm participating with them." I'd promised to perform a ritual for pack members who had volunteered to fight the fairies. The spell would force a painful and out-of-cycle full transformation on them, but afterward they would be able to retain their human minds whenever the full moon hauled their wolf form to the surface.

"Good point. I'll get my supplies. And, I was going to ask you to make Beverley's cake for the family party Thursday, but you're going to be busy so I'll order two from the bakery. One for us, and one for the kid party." The idea of the Domn Lup baking was ridiculous, yet the first time he met Nana he'd brought her the most marvelous Macadamia nut cookies. There wasn't anything Johnny couldn't cook.

He was silent. "I wanted to make her something special, but you're right. I can't commit to that. I don't know what to expect from this dog-and-pony show with the Rege."

Maxine, the blond sentinel, entered the dining room where my computer and desk were set up. "Another car has pulled into your driveway," she said, drawing her gun. "A woman is approaching your door."

"I gotta go," I said to Johnny. By the time we spoke brief good-byes, whoever it was had knocked. "I'm sure you can put that away," I told Maxine on my way into the living room.

She followed me.

I stopped.

She stopped.

I spun on my heel. "You don't have to escort me to the toilet, do you?"

"No."

"A little space, please?"

"You're not going to the toilet now. You're answering the door."

"Not usually a dangerous thing."

"It can be. Do you recognize the older blue Corvette?"

I glanced out the picture window. "No, but this isn't the haven."

"You are the Erus Veneficus of the Regional Vampire Lord now. Like it or not, your world is changing."

I was already irritated with her, and those words didn't help. "Back off."

Maxine retreated two steps. At my arched brow, she relinquished one more step and arched her own at me.

This was going to be annoying.

"I answer my own door, okay? I'll call you if I need help."

Maxine took a pose of readiness behind the opening from the dining room to the living room, just out of sight from whoever was on the porch. Stepping into the hall, I opened the door.

And was totally unprepared for who I saw.

In black jeans and a light-blue long-sleeved T-shirt, she stood an inch shorter than me, even in her snake-skin cowboy boots. As she stared at me, her lips moved soundlessly, saying my name. Her hair was the same dark brown as my own, but hers was lightly streaked with gray and fastened into a loose braid. She was me, with twenty-four extra years and twelve extra pounds.

Eris. My mother.

She reached for the screen door and clumsily jerked it open, hands shaking. The smell of menthol cigarettes hit me hard. "I saw you on TV. I traced you through an online people finder." She swallowed hard; her voice was shaking as well. "I thought you might be living at the haven now, but I had to try here before I went traipsing into a place like that." She forced a smile. "And—what luck!—here you are, my girl." Her dark eyes welled up with tears, imploring me to say something.

After sixteen years, she's standing on my doorstep.

I was too stunned to speak.

I opened the floodgates—the reservoir of anger I'd saved for this moment. I let that anger flow free . . . only to find the reservoir had dried up. All the words I'd meant to say were gone.

My heart recognized this was a critical moment, a remarkable chance, but my brain sent a signal down my arm and, without breaking my stare, I slammed the door shut in her face.

"I was such a fool," she pleaded from the other side.

I flipped the lock. *This is how things are supposed to be. The barrier of a door between us, me locked in.*

The knocks become angry pounding.

I'd felt those fists on my body, once. I turned and walked away.

How dare she show up here.

Why now?

The news coverage. Was she *worried* about me now? *That would be ironic.* It was more likely she thought I'd acquired some status that might benefit her somehow.

She didn't say she was sorry.

I don't know how long I stood there in the kitchen or how many times Maxine prompted me by calling my name. When the car's motor revved, it snapped me out of my astonishment. I found I could breathe again when the sound of the tires throwing gravel was followed by an engine's roar as it rocketed up the road.

"Get out," I said. The women sent here to protect me couldn't shield me from this pain.

No one moved.

I grabbed the *Lady of Shalott* coffee mug from the counter and pitched it at the wall. It shattered. "Get out!"

My favorite mug was in pieces all over the floor. With my vision blurry from tears, the cleanup process was more troublesome than productive, and it wasn't until my fingertips were bloody from multiple little nicks that my emotional fog dissipated enough for me to remember a broom and dustpan were ideal for this kind of chore.

I wiped my face on my sleeve and turned toward the pantry to see Zhan silently shutting it. She held the broom and dustpan. "Allow me, my lady," she said. Her voice was so soft.

"I can get it," I snapped, grabbing the broom from her. I wasn't mad at her, I was just *mad* and I'd told her to get out and she hadn't. But it wasn't like me to be so rude. Even as I rejected the basic human kindness she was offering and got back to the mess I'd created, the tears welled up again. It wasn't like me to be angry with an innocent bystander over something I did myself.

But it *was* like my mother.

Suddenly I felt so ashamed. "I'm sorry."

Zhan took the broom back with a gentle smile and I

fled to my bedroom. With the door locked, my shaking fingers sprinkled an imperfect circle of salt around me on the floor. I sat.

> *"Mother, seal my circle and give me a sacred space,*
> *In which to think clearly and solve the troubles I face."*

My meditation switch flipped "on" and I hit the alpha state. In my visualization, the lakeshore stretched before me, and the familiar willow tree was at my back. The sun was blazing, the breeze anxious. "Amenemhab!"

The jackal, my totem animal, did not answer.

I stomped around the shore looking for him, but normally he appeared after I'd dipped my toes in the water and let my chakras cleanse. Realizing I was wasting my time searching, I jerked my shoes and socks off and sat where the lapping water would ebb and cover my feet. It took an effort to relax my chakras into opening and releasing my negativity—no surprise—but several minutes later, I had achieved it.

Letting go of all the negative energy made me calmer and more in control of myself . . . but my pain wasn't resolved when the rumble of the garage door opening invaded my meditation and I knew Nana was home. I left the tranquil vision before I could get my totem's counsel and awoke in my room.

I was grateful for something to do, even if it was hauling in the groceries. I met Nana in the driveway, Maxine on my heels. Nana climbed from the car humming to herself. As she loaded my arms and Maxine's with bags, she was *grinning.*

In the kitchen, I saw Zhan had cleaned up the mess. I was unpacking box after box of Twinkies when Nana entered. "Leave them in the bags," she said. "It'll make carrying them out to the men easier."

Out to the men?

I couldn't imagine the big, burly Beholders eating Twinkies, but Nana could. She wasn't naïve about what these men were, but she'd seen the building permit for her new bedroom: Nana was grateful they were going to build it. She was walking on clouds right now. I didn't want to ruin her mood by telling her that my mother— her estranged daughter—had finally shown her face.

Eventually, though, I *would* have to tell her.

Nana had gone upstairs to quilt and I'd herded Ares into the room with her. Neither of them seemed to care for the women in suits. For the next several hours I worked on my column. Maxine interrupted me when the gravel trucks showed up, when the electric company arrived to put in poles, and again when men came to measure the back of the house. Since a noisy backhoe was about to commence digging up the area destined to be Nana's room addition, I decided my work for the day was done, saved the document, and went to watch out the window.

The prefab walls of the first barn were going up, and gravel was being dumped into the footer spaces around the second. I noticed some of the odd concrete chunks had been deposited near the house. "Any idea what those are?" I asked Maxine.

"Mountain said they were precast panels for the footers. You can build on them right away, don't have to wait for the concrete to cure. He said it was a miracle the right sizes were in stock, but we lucked out." She handed me a paper with a rough drawing of the layout for the addition. "Mountain brought that earlier, while you were upstairs."

"Wow. This is bigger and much sooner than we'd anticipated," I said.

"Might as well get it done while the equipment is already here," she replied.

I had to agree. Nana's knees had failed her before, so I wanted to spare her from my staircase as soon as possible.

Minutes later, a truck rolled by with a giant cake pan on the trailer. "Any guesses what that's for?" I asked.

"Not a clue," Maxine replied.

Donning my flannel, I headed for the door. The sentinel blocked my path.

"You can come with me, or you can piss me off trying to stop me. Which is it going to be?"

"Give me two minutes to re-secure the doors and windows so we're certain your home and grandmother are safe in our absence."

"Or Zhan could stay here while you escort me."

"One against that many Beholders?"

"Heldridge's men may not even be a threat. And if they are, they've been up and working eight hours already."

"We are both going with you."

I shrugged and conceded. With a dog treat for Ares in hand, I told Nana what we were doing. Maxine locked the front door, then we headed out to the garage, intending to exit via the man-door. On a whim, I halted our little parade to fill a gallon-sized bucket with dog food.

Maxine and Zhan waited for me, both with guns drawn. I appreciated that they took their duty here very seriously, but their bared weapons didn't make me comfortable. "Is that absolutely necessary?"

"Better safe than sorry," Maxine said and opened the man-door. She locked it behind us and we walked toward the construction.

After we located Mountain and waved to get his attention, he walked over to us.

Behind me, Zhan gasped as she took in the flock of birds, strolling like peacocks from the far end of the grove. Their flame-colored feather configurations were brilliant in the afternoon light. "Phoenix?" she asked, incredulous.

I nodded. The unicorns and griffons remained hidden within the grove. The dragons were near the edge, curled in big piles.

"They're eager to get into their coop," Mountain said. The metal roof on the aluminum shed was being attached as he spoke. "They must know it's theirs. They keep meandering out to have a look at it."

He gave me a brief update about pipes being laid in trenches below the frost line. Goddess help me, but Johnny's dirty mind was rubbing off on me; nearly all of the report sounded like innuendos.

"What is *that*?" I pointed at the newest arriving truck, backing into position according to the commands of onlooking Beholders. Before Mountain could reply, the answer hit me. "A swimming pool?"

"For the dragons."

"Dragons?" Zhan echoed.

"There. They're sleeping." Mountain pointed to where the dragons lay. They looked like coils of giant drainage tubing. "Once we get the pool installed and filled, they'll be much happier."

"Did they eat?"

"Ten *cases* of those little cans of tuna! I think I killed the hand-crank can opener. I've got someone trying to contact the Cleveland Metroparks Zoo, to ask about their suppliers. Bulk frozen fish would be far less hassle."

The animals were being taken care of, their shelters were coming along fast, and Mountain had it all under control. *Speaking of eating . . .* "You'll have dinner with us, right?"

"There's no need to go to any trouble on my account."

"You don't want *me* to go to any trouble? Look at all this." My hand flapped at the scene around us, and I nearly dropped the bucket of dog food. "I won't take no for an answer."

Apparently, griffon hearing is good enough to detect the rattle of kibble amid a cacophony of construction. Thunderbird emerged from the edge of the grove. The griffon arched his neck in my direction.

Immediately I started toward him. The sentinels followed.

As we neared, I held out the bucket. "You want this?"

Thunderbird lurched forward eagerly and his lame paw caused him to stumble. It looked as if he was about to attack.

We all halted, but movement to my right caught my attention and I realized that Maxine had raised her gun.

The griffon recovered his balance and stopped.

"Lower it," I whispered. "Get back." On my left, Zhan backed up several paces. The griffon considered Maxine with a steadiness that had an undeniable cognizance behind it.

She lowered her gun and stepped back.

"C'mon, Thunderbird." I shook the dog food again. "This is all yours."

His one golden eye assessed me in an altogether human manner, not at all like a bird. He came to me, dipped his head into the bucket, came up crunching.

I couldn't resist stroking those black feathers gently.

He jerked away, but did not retreat.

"Sorry," I whispered.

In one swift movement, his beak darted in, wrested the bucket's handle from me, and swung it away from me. He limped deeper into the grove, tail twitching irritably.

Mountain returned to the worksite. Maxine and Zhan followed me across the field.

I'd hiked only a dozen yards when my back pocket erupted with the guitar riff and chorus of AC/DC's "Back in Black." I took another step before I realized: *The protrepticus is ringing!*

CHAPTER NINE

Stopping in my tracks, I jerked the phone out of my pocket and flipped it open so hurriedly I nearly dropped it. Samson D. Kline's voice hailed me. "Heads up, little girl; Xerxadrea's body has been identified."

The phone issued a burp of static and the screen went black. I shook it, closed it, and opened it again. No light at all and no chance to ask him how the protrepticus could still work.

"My lady?" Maxine prompted.

"Nothing." I pushed the phone back into my pocket and hurried on.

As we crossed the yard, a dozen witches swooped down from the sky. My sentinels raised their guns once more and, again, I insisted they put them away. This time my most authoritative facial expression accompanied the words, "Holster them, now." The sentinels obeyed.

The witches hovered above my grass. That they did not dismount their brooms meant they weren't staying. That they wore their formal black robes and charm-bedecked pointy hats meant they were on their way to or from official business. Thanks to my phone call, I could guess what.

Foremost was Vilna-Daluca. Ruya, the raven that once sat on the shoulder of the Eldrenne Xerxadrea, now sat on Vilna's shoulder. The rest of them were high priestesses, members of the *lucusi* that I'd had the honor of being a member of . . . for about twelve hours. They had given me my own flying broom, amped up my house wards, and promptly severed their ties to me as Xerxadrea had instructed them when they learned I'd become Menessos's Erus Veneficus. Ranking witches didn't allow status, titles, or respect to witches who used their power in service to vampires.

Only Menessos and I knew that my becoming EV had been Xerxadrea's idea and she had intended that severing to be temporary. She knew my role as EV had many purposes, and that Menessos's "benefit" was the least of them. She'd assured me of this as she lay dying, having taken a bolt of fairy fire to save me.

"To what do I owe the pleasure, ladies?"

Vilna-Daluca dismounted her broom and advanced, steps soft and certain. She stopped before me, expression blank. Her long hair was loose, straight, smooth, and so white against her black robes. I was searching for a clue, scrutinizing the set of her mouth, the hazel of her—

She slapped me. Ruya screeched.

Before the bird could resettle its feathers, Maxine had her gun to Vilna's temple. She cocked it for emphasis.

I recovered. "Max, put it away."

"But—"

Without shifting my focus from Vilna, I said, "Either you do as your Erus Veneficus commands, or you suffer the consequences."

I hadn't pulled rank to threaten Maxine before. She obeyed.

Citing my rank, however, didn't please the Elder before me. Blame hardened Vilna's features. She whispered hotly, "We protected you!"

She was referring to the witches having aided me during the battle. "And I am grateful for that."

"Grateful?" Her lips barely moved as she snarled the word at me.

Jeanine glided close. In a voice meant to lure jumpers away from high ledges, she said, "Our actions were still in the best interests of the council."

Vilna-Daluca shrugged her off brusquely. Silent teardrops slid down her cheeks. She cleared her throat. "What came before is what Xerxadrea wanted. Out of respect for her, I leave it." Her words cut like a keen-edged blade. "I leave your wards and even the elementals, as you are evidently accomplishing their house and, I assume, their care. But I am telling you now, before these witnesses: henceforth, we are enemies. Do not call on us. Do not expect our favor. What we had is gone."

Xerxadrea was right. Vilna hadn't asked me what happened, so it was clear she had her mind made up—without the facts. I considered defending my actions, but she needed someone to vent her grief upon more than I needed to be vindicated. *Maybe in time . . .*

I bowed my head slightly. "Blessed Be, Vilna."

She mounted her broom and took to the air. The rest of the *lucusi* followed.

• • •

Knowing Beverley wouldn't recognize the Audi if I let one of the sentinels drive me to the bus stop, I hurried inside to get the keys to the Avalon. Nana was leaning against the counter in the kitchen, arms crossed, slippered foot tapping again. With a jerk of her head she indicated the yard beyond the kitchen windows and demanded, "What was all that about?" Her tone was clipped, as if trying to decide whether to sound angry or sad.

So much for her good mood I tried to preserve.

I shook my head, searching for words. Upon coming home after the beach battle I'd promised to tell her and Beverley everything that had happened. In the telling I'd admitted we buried Aquula at the Botanical Gardens, but I had left out the fairy attack that followed. If I'd revealed Xerxadrea's sacrifice, I would have broken down. It wasn't that I didn't want Nana to know, just that I wanted to wait until the sting of that loss wasn't as sharp before I spoke of it.

Nana continued. "The news just announced the body found in the Botanical Gardens Friday night was the Eldrenne Xerxadrea. I knew they'd said the gardens had been broken into and that a body had been found, but I guess it was in my mind that they had found the body of the fairy or something."

My chin dropped almost to my chest.

"Did their visit have something to do with that?"

I nodded.

"She struck you. . . ." Nana's crossed arms fell limp at her sides. "There's more to the story than you told me."

I bit my lip and nodded again.

She snorted. "Makes an old woman wonder what else you're keeping secret." She shuffled out.

The hurt in her voice was like *another* slap in the face. Not only had I not told her about Xerxadrea, now I'd not bothered to mention Eris had showed up after ignoring us both for damn near twenty years. I'd just won myself an all-expenses-paid guilt trip.

There wasn't time to fix it right now, so I grabbed the keys and left. *The day had started with such promise, and then gone steadily downhill. Now it's officially an all-out disaster.*

Zhan elected to ride with me to fetch Beverley from the bus stop. My having wrongly snapped at her earlier left me feeling too guilty to refuse.

"How did you come to have those creatures?"

I had expected Zhan to make some inquiries, and was glad her curiosity was focused on the animals and not my mother. "Their forefathers were stolen from this world millennia ago by the fairies. We kind of inadvertently stole them back." The explanation was radically over-simplified, but true.

"We?"

"Many people played a part."

"Menessos?"

"Yes. He was a part of it."

"He knew?" The blame in her tone wasn't ambiguous. "He knew these creatures were real?"

Oh hell. I couldn't be honest with her. No one was sup-posed to know he was the original vampire, and that he was there when the fairies entered our world. Though he was unaware the fey were taking these elementals from our world at the time, he did know of it later.

Will today's disasters never end? "We only found out yesterday morning when the fey showed up with the elementals," I lied.

Nana had put something into the oven while Zhan and I were gone, and now it smelled wonderful. I sat at the computer working on my column and, to counteract all the terrible things that had happened today, I was imagining this was just a normal evening for a normal family at home.

My make-believe was more convincing because Nana had gone upstairs to quilt while dinner baked, and the kiddo was doing homework at the dinette. The phone had rung a few times—Nana answered the cordless upstairs—but other than that, everything was quiet. Peaceful. *Normal.*

Then Nana trudged down the stairs and began fixing something to go with the scrumptious-smelling dish in the oven. She must have decided we should have a side of Raucous with Earsplitting Sauce—because she was being anything but quiet.

At the dinette, Beverley twisted around to watch Nana clanging pans. That caught my attention; it didn't surprise me that Nana would be this angry with me, but to show her anger to Beverley was unexpected.

Two could play the not-talking-but-not-silent game.

Pushing away from my desk, I stretched, rose, and left

the computer. Johnny's stage pants were done in the wash and I decided to be helpful.

Once the dryer was jingling and thudding with the studded and chain-adorned clothing, I joined the kiddo. Even with a cantankerous old woman battering my cookware and some knight's battle armor apparently rattling in my dryer, I kept telling myself we were just an ordinary family . . . until the Beholders began filing out of the field and boarding the bus parked out front.

Ordinary families don't have the Regional Vampire Lord's servants building barns in their backyard.

The thuglike men from Heldridge were as dirty as Menessos's men, but they were moving much more stiffly. Some were inspecting their hands and I recalled Mountain saying they'd have blisters.

There was no evidence of animosity among them; it seemed from their behavior that some had made friends with Menessos's men. That was encouraging. I needed something to go right today.

Mountain brought up the rear, talking with a wiry older man. Mountain pointed at the house and the two of them approached the new foundation with a tape measure out.

"What are they doing?" Beverley asked.

The phone rang. Nana moved to answer the long-corded kitchen phone.

"Making plans for Nana's room," I whispered.

Beverley nodded. "What's got her so grouchy?"

"Dunno." I wasn't going to tell Beverley that Nana was mad at me because I'd kept secrets from her. I didn't want to be the do-as-I-say-not-as-I-do brand of foster mother. "How's the math?"

"Easy." She wrapped her arms around me in a hug. "I'm so glad I'm here, where the unicorns are."

"Me, too." I rubbed her back. "How's the history?"

"Same."

Seeing how small, innocent, and eager to please she was, my heart ached. How could anyone ever treat a child wrongly? Beverley wasn't even my child but I couldn't imagine hitting her or locking her in a room. Sometimes I doubted myself as a parent, but unlike my own mother, I'd never resented the existence of the child in my home, or wished that she weren't here.

I can't fess up about Xerxadrea or my mother now. With the snit Nana's in, that additional information might turn the kitchen into a war zone. Maybe tomorrow.

Behind me, Nana hung up the phone with more force than necessary, and shuffled back to the stove, grumbling. Beverley peered up at me questioningly.

"Must've been a sales call," I whispered.

The buses were leaving. I moved into the bench seat across from Beverley, where I could evaluate Nana.

That was when the sun sank away; I knew it because I felt Menessos awaken screaming in torment, felt him suck down his first breath of this night, felt him whisper my name as he regained control of himself. That sensation of filling up, of being whole, returned. A few deep breaths later, my body felt equalized.

Mountain left his muddy boots at the front door and entered the kitchen in sock feet. He washed up at the sink—he was so tall and thick that he didn't fit in the little bathroom under the stairs. "Where's Johnny?" he asked.

"I don't think he's going to join us," I said. "He's still at the memorial for those lost on the beach."

"Mountain, you're in charge of security for now," Maxine said, coming in from the living room where she'd supervised the Beholders' departure via the window.

"The head count on the bus was the same for the number that arrived," he said.

"Noted. We're going to check the perimeter and then get supplies."

Nana set the casserole dish she'd just taken from the oven onto the stovetop. "Will you eat?"

That's my Nana. If she didn't like someone she could give them the cold shoulder all day, but when dinner was served she'd still expect them to eat. She'd be mightily offended if they snubbed her dinner in retaliation.

"No, thank you. We're going to make our rounds, and get some supplies. We'll eat while we're out. See you in two hours."

Nana wordlessly transferred the meal onto the plates, but clanking dishes and spoons voiced her irritation for her.

I meant no insult to the sentinels, but some time away from them suited me just fine. Having lived alone for a few years before Nana moved in, sharing meals had developed into a special activity.

Mountain sat in the chair adjacent to Beverley's. I was in the back corner on the bench. Nana served everyone a plate of salad, crusty bread, and a chunk of her casserole, then slid in beside me. Beverley appraised the food on her plate, dissecting it with her fork to inspect the layers. "It smells good, but I don't know what it is."

"My mother called it mousakas kolokythakia. It's moussaka with zucchini."

"I like zucchini," Beverley said. "My mom used to slice it and fry it."

Nana pointed at her. "She gave you more than a beautiful face and a sweet disposition then, young lady. She gave you variety in taste. Good for her, and good for you." Nana dug into her food.

I enjoyed taking a meal with a small cozy group, and with these three people in particular, it felt like a satisfyingly domestic exercise. A chance to sit calmly together and have some peaceful conversation . . . it was a common thing that my hectic life promised to allow less and less. For me, struggling through the balance-driven destiny of the Lustrata was paid back like this, in these quiet moments breaking bread with family. It was right and warm—Nana's irritation notwithstanding.

Or maybe Nana's fabulous bechamel sauce with cheese was making me sentimental.

"Are the barns done?" I asked Mountain.

"Almost. The animals are in them, but the roofs and the insides need some final touches."

"So, Mountain," Nana began conversationally, but the edge of annoyance in her tone couldn't stay hidden, "what kind of mess-making can we expect tomorrow?"

He wiped his mouth on a napkin. "Here at the house, they're going to cut through the new house-side foundation panel and into the cellar, to route the electric, plumbing, and heating for your addition. When that's done they'll put up the floor joists and subflooring, erect the prefab walls. This is where the Beholders really shine. Once the foundations are set to build on, we're fast." He paused. "Out in the field, the water truck is coming tomorrow to fill the dragon's pool. The well pump will be put in, the electric wired."

"Did the electric company get the poles in?"

He nodded. "The foundation for my mobile home is in, too. It'll be delivered and set up. Since the semis have already torn up the yard, I requested that a gravel driveway be put in, running to the barns, but I'm not sure if they'll do that tomorrow or the next day. And I asked for a truck for myself."

"You're so lucky," Beverley said.

"Because I might get a truck?"

"Because you get to live out there with the unicorns."

"I'll technically be closer to the dragons." He covered his mouth like he was sharing a secret with her. "And let me tell you, they snore like buzz saws."

She giggled.

"Did Heldridge's men give you any cause for concern?" I asked.

"They didn't have any construction sense." He readied another bite of moussaka. "And they weren't accustomed to physical labor, either."

"Didn't slow you down any," I put in.

The phone rang *again*. Nana slammed her fork down and rose to answer it. The rest of us were politely quiet. She glanced fleetingly in my direction before stepping into the living room to talk privately. I tried to listen in, but even with my hearing being amped up by my connection to the vampire, Mountain and Beverley's discussion of unicorns combined with the clattering dryer kept me from hearing. When Nana reappeared, she was more disgruntled than before.

And I was more curious than ever.

Which is probably the point. She wants me curious so she can deny me some knowledge as payback. So I resolved not to be curious. Outwardly, anyway.

CHAPTER TEN

When the meal had been eaten, Mountain headed into the living room. He was on guard duty until the sentinels returned. Beverley and I cleared the table and did the dishes. While we were drying the silverware, Nana took a third call, whispering in the dining room. Again I couldn't hear. The clanging silverware and the television program that Mountain was watching interfered. The call ended right after Beverley fed Ares and hurried upstairs to run her bathwater.

Nana was usually right behind her, but not tonight. Instead, she joined me in the kitchen. "We need to talk."

Good for her, being direct. "I know." I hung the drying towel on the little bar inside the lower cabinet door to dry. It was my turn to be direct. "I didn't tell you about Xerxadrea because it hurt. I didn't want to—" I stopped there. Saying her name had caused a lump to clog my throat. The culpability and grief were still so close.

"Didn't want to what?"

"Cry." Hot drops rolled down my cheeks. "Once Aquula was buried, the fairies attacked. Xerxadrea gave her life to save mine." My statement was as blunt as I could make it, and still it ended with my voice cracking.

Nana's brows flew up.

"I was going to tell you. I just wanted a little distance from it first. I didn't mean to hurt your feelings."

She came and put her arms around me and I let the tears fall. "What happened?"

"The fire fairy sent a ball of flame at me. Xerxadrea flew in and took the hit before it could reach me."

"That's why she crashed?" Nana patted my back and released me.

I nodded, wiped my cheeks again. "It was . . . awful. She knew it would happen. Said she'd foreseen it."

Nana gave me a moment then remarked, "Does this mean you'll get off my ass about scrying?"

Her crass statement drew a choked laugh from me. "No. I don't want you to do anything noble with that high of a price."

She dug a cigarette from her pocket case and lit it. "Since we're being all open now, you need to know . . . we have another problem." She used the ash end to point at the long-corded phone on the wall. "Those phone calls." She said it like she was ratting on someone.

"Oh?"

"They're RSVPs for the party." Nana sounded discouraged.

"Are they saying no?"

"Not exactly. They're from concerned parents."

"Concerned about what?"

"That *you* might try to be here."

That stunned me so much I almost gave myself whiplash.

"They all saw the news. They think you're still at the haven, but one said she thought you'd gotten Beverley from the bus stop this evening. They want to make sure you won't be here because they don't want 'that kind of person' around their children."

I sank into the dinette chair. "Oh."

"At first," Nana said, sitting on the bench across from me, "I thought I'd tell them to kiss my wrinkled-up, lily-white ass, but . . . this party is for Beverley, not me, not you. So I said that the bus-stop inspectors were wrong, that I hoped I never saw you again, and that I had no reason to think you'd be here."

Head dropping forward miserably, my fingers raked through my hair. *Yup. This is the rotten, train-wreck kind of day I'm having.*

I'd stood up for a greater justice to lure out killers and to set up our fight against the fairies. It had worked in favor of my friends. And it had worked against my family. Doing the right thing for the right reason was biting me in the ass.

"You *have* to be at this party," Nana continued, "but we need to figure out a way to make this community open its arms to you."

As if on cue, the phone rang. Dismal, Nana rose to answer it. Again, she took it to the dining room. However, now that she'd told me, she didn't restrain her voice on this caller. I heard her say, "No. To my knowledge she will not be here." Silence. "Yes, yes, I understand, but I don't care who you *think* you saw. I do have *other* relatives, you know." Silence again. "I don't want Persephone here for the party either."

During Nana's next wordless moment, Beverley stuck her head around the wall of the hallway. "What's going on?"

There was no gurgle of bathwater running upstairs. "Why aren't you in the tub?"

"I wanted a drink of milk. May I?"

"Of course."

When she'd poured herself a full glass, she came to the dinette, sipping. I patted my thigh. "Come on."

She slid the glass onto the table then climbed up in my lap. "Why is Demeter telling someone she doesn't want you here for my party?"

My arms encircled her. "Remember when I had to go to the haven for a few days with Menessos?"

She nodded.

"I told you Nana would have to say some mean things about me, things she didn't really believe but had to say to keep you both safe. That's what she's doing now."

"Telling people she doesn't want you here keeps us safe?"

"It's getting complicated. You see . . . some of your classmates' parents are objecting to me being here."

"Why?" she asked. "They're not the bad guys, are they?"

"No, no. Nothing like that." I could sell myself the illusion that we were a normal family but I couldn't sell that fantasy to the community around me. We *weren't* normal and I'd broadcast it all across the news. I swallowed my dejection and stuttered out the answer. "In order to let the bad guys think Nana and I were mad at each other, we had to tell *everyone*. She was on TV and so was I. The bad guys saw what we wanted them to see and all of that worked out. Unfortunately, your classmates' parents saw it, too. Now, they're not sure they should let their children come to a party being held by us."

"I don't understand."

"They don't approve of what I was doing on TV. But Nana's telling them I won't be here, to make sure they do come."

Her arms gripped me tight. "But I want you here."

"I know. And I want to be here."

Nana shuffled in and hung up the phone. She was ready to shoo Beverley off to her bath, but even as her mouth opened the phone rang again. Her mouth twisted in exasperation and she answered crossly.

"We'll work something out," I said to Beverley.

"Why are they being so mean?"

I rubbed her head. "They are doing what they think is right, protecting their children. I don't blame them for that."

"That's stupid. You wouldn't hurt their kids." She crossed her arms and frowned deeply.

"Of course not. But they aren't sure of that. Parents want to make sure the places their children go are safe." *Except for the parents who leave their children locked up in apartments about to catch fire.*

Nana hung up the phone again. "That was the vet," she said. "He's been called to an emergency, and won't be able to make it out tonight." She gestured at Beverley. "Come along."

"Can we have just a few more minutes?" I asked.

"Of course. I'll draw the bath and pour in the bubble juice." She shuffled away.

"They are being good parents," I reiterated to Beverley. "Even if it's not what you or I want them to do, they're doing their job. Be glad your friends are loved that much."

Her brow puckered. "They're being dumb."

I'd never seen her like this. "No, they are not."

"What did you do that was *sooo* bad?"

Her sarcasm clued me in that she didn't think I'd do anything *bad*. It made telling the truth harder. "I let Menessos drink from me."

Her eyes widened as much as possible and then some. Her crossed arms fell limp. "On TV?"

"Yes. Everyone knows what I did *and* they know I'm a witch *and* they were told that I'm in a position to take orders from a vampire. Any one of those things is reason enough for parents to question whether letting their children around *me* is safe."

It sounded awful even to me. *I'm a fool to think I can provide a normal home life for Beverley.*

She pushed my hair back and examined my neck. The wounds had nearly healed; all that remained were two pink marks. "So because of you no one's going to come to my party?"

The blame in her words struck me harder than Vilna's hand.

We remained silent for heartbeats. With my fingers making a V, I touched her forehead and pushed gently upward as I said, "Hold on there, wrinkly-mad eyebrows."

That made her brows knit tighter. "My mom used to let Goliath drink from her. Then everything got messed up!" She jumped off my lap, flinging her arms out and knocking the glass to the floor where it shattered. "Now she's dead!" Beverley ran from the kitchen.

I was left alone with the spilled milk and shards of broken glass. I dropped to my knees and started piling the larger pieces in my palm.

My breath caught.

My mother had showed up and it ended with me smashing my favorite mug. Her words from so long ago echoed through my mind: *I'll never have anything and it's all because of you, you stupid little brat.*

Eris was selfish. She did what *she* needed—locking me in my room so she could go on dates and ultimately she abandoned me with Nana.

As I stared at the sharp fragments in my hand, I wondered if I was any different. I'd done what I needed to do as the Lustrata. Though I'd acted to safeguard Beverley since her mother died, I wasn't exactly Mary Poppins. Because of me, Beverley had been kidnapped and nearly killed by the fairies. Now, because of me, she may not even have any friends.

Maybe she'd be better off—and safer—with someone else.

CHAPTER ELEVEN

A half hour later, with the milk and glass cleaned up, I sat in front of my computer trying to work on my column when the phone rang *again.* Nana had the cordless with her so I didn't move to answer. Not that I was getting much work done while sitting there feeling like a complete failure and social pariah.

I took the protrepticus from my jeans' pocket and opened it. No light. I shut it and laid it on the desk. Earlier that day, it had rung. Sam had spoken to me. And Xerxadrea was dead. Her death should have broken the bond between her and Sam and me. His spirit should have been freed and gone from the device.

Questions piled up in my mind like a traffic jam. It was after sunset; maybe Menessos could provide some answers. I reached for the satellite phone.

"Seph," Nana croaked from the top of the stairs. "It's for you."

I left the satellite phone where it was and replaced the protrepticus in my pocket as I walked to the kitchen and picked up the corded phone. *Phones everywhere.* "Got it," I called back. "Hello?"

"It's me," Theo said. I heard the click telling me Nana had shut off the cordless.

"How's the memorial going?" I asked.

"Depressing. I just left." I heard her car door shut. "The wife and family of the one guy are shocked and sad and grieving like you'd expect. The other guy's girlfriend is totally losing it. Last I saw, the crying women had Johnny looking overwhelmed. He said to tell you he'd be late getting in, and that the wæres who survived are scheduled for tomorrow around ten or ten-thirty."

"In the morning?"

"Yeah. Seems weird to be doing a moonlight spell during the daytime, huh?"

"The moon is in the sky during the day as often as it is at night," I muttered. The time they'd set meant I couldn't have Menessos with me. While the wæres would probably have objected to the vampire being present anyway, having him as a backup would have made me feel better.

I heard papers rustle and Theo said, "The moon rises tonight about five minutes to midnight, and sets tomorrow afternoon at one-thirty-ish. They want to do this at the den and someone calculated it all for him and said the westward windows will have the moon in view by ten in the morning."

A heavy sigh seeped out as I stretched the cord and sank into my desk seat again.

"Are you all right?"

"Yeah, I'm fine. I knew he was going to schedule it for tomorrow but it's been one train wreck after another here today and I haven't gathered the supplies or reviewed the ritual. I'll need to do that tonight."

"You'll be able to do it, though, right?"

"Oh yeah," I assured her. "It's not that." I didn't want her to think any of the wæres might be endangered due to a lack of preparation on my part. "There's just a lot on my metaphorical plate right now."

"I hear ya." She gave her own little sigh. "And speaking of other things we have to do . . . my source at WEC got back to me. She can't find any leads on witches named Arcanum who are tattoo artists. Is there anything else you can tell me, anything at all, that might refine the parameters even a little?"

"No," I whispered. *If this is two separate people, why did I get just one name?*

Most witches took an alternate name for spell work. Typically, they used an animal, flower, or gemstone, or a combination of names. Sometimes it was simply an ancient name or archaic word. "Arcanum" sounded to me like it fell into the latter category. Either way, since these magical names were attached to spells, witches didn't share them on the WEC rosters. Theo's source wasn't going to find anything helpful. "Can you flip the search? Try the name itself or the tattoo artist aspect."

"I'm on that, but the witch angle was a smaller net to cast and sort through so I concentrated my efforts there," Theo said. "You're a solitary. You're listed."

She'd looked. *Hmmm.* "That's because my family's lineage is traceable back centuries on their rosters. I'm the black sheep doing my own thing without a coven, but Nana wouldn't let me *not* register."

"So it's optional?"

"Yes. Some people prefer to keep their religious beliefs a secret."

"Ahhh. Speaking of secrets, do you care to share what all this is about, or do you have to keep it on the down low?"

"Do you remember, after I did that spell that forced you to transform, when you asked Johnny about his tattoos and he got all tight-lipped?"

"Yeah. Found out they're his sore spot."

"They're more than that. They're the crux of his past." This information was Johnny's to tell, but she needed to know it to do her job. She kenneled at my house and I'd saved her life, so I trusted her. "Johnny's power is bound in his tattoos. We need to find the person who gave them to him and get that power unlocked so he can transform easily. Hopefully, he'll get his memories back, too."

"You didn't say this was for him."

"Can I claim the multiple train wrecks again?"

"Sure. But if this is for Johnny, I'm going to call in favors across the network."

"Hey, don't broadcast that he has a weakness."

"I know better than that. No offense, Seph, you're one of my very best friends and your requests rank high, but my pack takes priority. Knowing my *dirija* is involved makes finding this Arcanum my prime objective."

"No offense taken, Theo. None meant to you, either. Protecting the people I care about comes first. Sometimes, it seems like saying less is safer for everyone."

"It's okay, Seph. If I've learned anything in the investigative business, it's that knowing when to share and when *not* to share is just as important and dicey as knowing whom to share with."

• • •

With the spell scheduled for early tomorrow, and Nana busy with Beverley, it was time for me to get some answers to my lingering questions about what I intended to do.

Using the satellite phone, I called Menessos from my bedroom. He answered on the third ring. Laughter in the background preceded his delayed greeting. "Hello, Persephone." The sound of his voice caused warmth to flow over me like a slow, heated tremor. "What might I do for you?"

"I wanted to ask you about the forced change ritual we did for Theo."

"The moonlight amplifying spell. Yes?"

Another trill of female laughter trickled through the phone. My ears detected other sounds—rustling fabric?—and I heard a woman call, "Come back!"

"Yes, that one," I said quickly. "I need to repeat it for the wæres tomorrow morning and I have questions."

"By all means ask them, but give me one moment?"

"Of course."

As I waited, the silence sounded like the inside of a seashell, and I guessed he had covered the receiver. Though muffled, I heard, "Get out." Momentarily the sound of a shutting door followed and Menessos said, "Now you have my undivided attention. You will be casting the spell after the sun rises?"

"Yes. You intervened before. You took over and all I did was sing. How can I be sure it will go the same way this time?"

"You cannot be sure," Menessos replied. "Since you have slain me and I cannot be with you in the daylight, it is impossible for the ritual to be executed in the same manner. In my opinion, it should *not* be the same."

"What do you mean?"

"We used the energies of others to help supply the magic because you had limited experience with using ley lines. Perhaps now you can fully fuel the ritual from the line."

"I was thinking I'd have to do that, but I'm not certain I want to." Using the line could be dangerously addictive, more so in larger quantities, and this would definitely involve a larger quantity.

"We forced four wæres to fully transform the first time—that was no simple task. How many are you attempting now, my dear, ambitious Persephone?"

"There will be twenty or more. And it's not because I'm ambitious. It's because I agreed to reward them for coming to your aid."

"You have so many admirable qualities, not the least of which is your witchcraft. And speaking of witchcraft, I must say Heldridge's witch is quite satisfactory."

"Was that her you just put out?"

"Oh, yes, she's put out."

I wasn't certain how to take that, but I was convinced that he'd intended for me to be unsure.

"She's a very talented witch, you know. Not like you, my Lustrata master, but she has certain skills." He cleared his throat. "She's headstrong. She was not satisfied to be merely pampered in Heldridge's court. She owns a confectionary shop. It is called DeMonique's Boutique of Unique Chocolat, and is in Terminal Tower."

"I take it she's French."

"Eva de Monique is many things, but first and foremost, she is French. French couture. French chef. French witch."

I wondered if he was trying to make me jealous. And then I wondered if he was succeeding. "That's great," I said quickly. "Perhaps you can publicly renounce me—send me home as unwilling to take orders or something—and make her your Erus Veneficus." Maybe that would appease the local parents and Beverley wouldn't be left in the middle, friendless.

"You would leave me?" He sounded hurt.

"If you have another witch you don't need me."

"Forever will I need you, my master." He put special emphasis on the word "need." "She could be your apprentice."

"That's backwards. She's an experienced court witch. I'm not."

"That hardly matters since I dictate what her place is."

"But taking her would be a benevolent gesture to the others in Heldridge's court."

"I have taken her."

Ignoring the remark, I went on. "What I meant was if you make her your EV then it shows the rest of them that you are willing to take them on. It might be the very thing to cement their loyalty to you."

"There are many ways to cement one's loyalty. I could use her to show them the depths of my cruelty. Fear accomplishes much."

"Menessos." I hoped he was teasing me.

"It is expected that I should take Heldridge's trophies. To give up my own for them is illogical."

"So dismissing me in favor of her *would* have meaning for them?"

"You have been the single bright spot in all this darkness, Persephone."

When he said my name, I could smell cinnamon. He clearly hadn't *lost* the ability to affect me by saying my name, but it *had* changed. The second hex evidently provided him a broader range in which to influence me, and a refined amount of control.

I thought of the vampire PR campaign broadcasting the idea that vampire lords were merely executives who keep their employees, the vampire underlings, in line. I gave it one last shot. "This would be a good business decision for you, wouldn't it?"

"I find myself unwilling to part with you in that way."

But you'll join with her in my stead. My jaw was clamped shut and I did not voice the thought. It was as if our bond, and the predilection for him it gave me, stoked up false jealousy. My inner smart-ass had always been easily riled.

"And," he continued, "since the witches have denounced you for becoming my EV, if I denied you as well, you'd have only the wærewolves left. They have little tolerance for witches. What you suggest is folly."

"Maybe this spell is folly," I grumbled. "They will retain their man-minds without you being a part of the ritual, right?"

"Yes. Magic is so fluid that spells are rarely performed the same exact way twice, what with planetary alignments always in motion changing the mixture of energies. Do not fret over this detail. The desired result is often reaccomplished. That is because of the spellcaster, and you, dear, delicious Persephone, are quite capable."

I'd just saved the final version of my column on the computer in the dining room when I caught a glimpse of headlights turning into the driveway. "Maxine and Zhan are back," Mountain called out. He held the door for them as they came in, each with a sleeping bag and a pillow tucked under her arm. They allowed him to return to the grove and informed me it was their plan to alternate for night watch; whoever wasn't on duty would unroll their bag and sleep on the couch.

I handed Maxine the TV remote and headed upstairs. Pausing atop the steps, I eavesdropped on Beverley and Nana playing Old Maid. On any other day, I would have tried to get in on a game, but not today. Not after Beverley's outburst. Not with all I still had to do.

I considered telling Nana about Eris showing up when she was done with Beverley. But it wouldn't be that simple. I couldn't just drop the bombshell and walk away. She'd want to talk. Nana had her own guilt trip about the way she'd raised me.

I was already emotionally drained and still had to review the spell for tomorrow. Plus, Johnny had had a hell of a day himself. He'd be home soon. He'd need me, too.

Eris hadn't been part of Nana's life or mine for a long time. Announcing her sudden reentry . . . and exit . . . could wait.

I got my Book of Shadows out, took the copy of the Trivium Codex from Nana's room, and sat down to study.

• • •

When Johnny finally arrived home, he snuggled in beside me, naked, spooning his warm, warm self right
against me. His arm snaked around my waist. I ran
my nails lightly up and down his forearm and asked,
"How'd it go?"

"The families of Robert Connor and Brian Kimball are
grieving and in disbelief," he said.

It seemed important to him to say their names, just as
it had been important for me to know Ross's name. "Did
you know either of them?"

"No." His whisper was full of regret. "But now I know
about them. Robert was laid off when his factory job was
outsourced and his wife, Donna, is waitressing at a Bob
Evans out in Beachwood. He'd been jobless for months and
she said he thought if he got in good with me, he might be
able to work as part of my security. She didn't want him to.
She thought it was too dangerous." He squeezed me. "She
was right." He sighed into my hair. "They had two sons
before he contracted the virus. They're twelve and fourteen
now. Bright kids. He volunteered in order to provide for
them, and now they don't have him anymore."

Recognizing the guilt in his voice all too well, I rolled
to face him.

"It's hard for them with no body." The superheated
beam had left nothing of those it claimed. "Seeing him,
his corpse, that would make it more real."

"Not just for the families."

"Yeah. I'm having a hard time, too, Red."

He was silent while I stroked his cheek.

"You know what it's like," he whispered. "The Eldrenne gave her life for yours." His fingers fidgeted with the bottom of the tank top I'd worn to bed. "In my mind, I can understand that Robert and Brian did the same, they gave their lives for a greater good, but . . ."

He didn't finish, so I did. "But your heart has a hard time accepting that you're the instrument of that greater good."

"Exactly," he whispered. He grasped a lock of my hair and tickled under my chin with the tips.

I pushed myself against him under the covers, slid my knee up to his hip.

He shifted gears but not in the way I expected. He asked, "Are you all set for the ritual?"

"I made a list of the supplies I need to gather up tomorrow morning, but I have everything so it'll be quick." My hands wandered. My lips found his. My tongue tasted an oaky sweet flavor. "Todd get the Laphroaig out again?"

"When it was all over, Todd, Kirk, and I toasted our fallen comrades privately. Said some words to the crescent moon."

He took my roving hands in his and said, "Tell me about your day."

Is he seriously not in the mood? "Are you drunk?"

"No."

"You realize you just asked me how my day was *and* stopped my hands from fondling you?"

"I'm a regular dreamboat, ain't I? Being the sensitive guy interested in your monotonous day and all that."

"Yeah, because 'monotonous' is *certainly* the one word I'd use to describe my days lately."

The sarcasm made us both feel better. So I tried another dose of it. "What'd that Laphroaig do to you?"

"I didn't think it could get any worse than you making me hold that vamp's hand and sharing a piece of my soul with him. But a battle, a chest wound, the probing you and I did, all followed by the long-ass day I had . . . it left me with some tight muscles in my neck and shoulders. The single-malt Scotch loosened 'em up. I get a rain check, though, right?"

I smoothed his black curls away from his forehead and fingered the white-gold loops piercing his brow. He'd removed the little studs from his nose and hadn't worn them in a while. "You can have whatever you want."

"Oooo." He kissed my forehead. "So tell me. What'd I miss here?"

He had no desire to make love at all. I'd seen him like this once before: after seeing his father figure, Ig, bedridden and terribly ill. Right now he needed intimacy, but not sex. "The good news is, the barns and the coop are up and need minor finishing touches tomorrow. The poles are in and ready for electric to be installed. The well is dug. You met Maxine and Zhan?"

"Zhan must be the one asleep on the couch. Maxine introduced herself, told me she was security sent by the vamp. She recognized me from the ceremony at the haven, but I couldn't say I remembered her. Though I did compliment her on the Audi."

Nana's old LeBaron with the AARP sticker in the back window really wasn't the kind of car Johnny could be comfortable in. And the Domn Lup should have at least eight cylinders in his engine. If things ever settled down, maybe we could do something about that. "Tomorrow the well pump will be installed, Mountain's mobile home is coming, and they'll get more of Nana's addition done."

He was silent, then said, "Was there bad news?"

"Plenty. Xerxadrea's body was identified. Vilna-Daluca stopped by with the *lucusi* to be sure I knew they were pissed at me."

"Oh goody."

I snuggled under his chin and let my arm drape over his side. "And guess what else?"

"There's more?"

"Always." I started to tell him about my mother's visit, but I could feel tears burning my eyes at the thought of mentioning it. Considering what Theo had said about Johnny being overwhelmed by weeping women today, I decided not be another crying female he had to deal with. I could tell him later, too.

I did, however, tell him about Nana and me having our little disagreement and fixing it, and about the calls from worried parents coming in this evening. "And to top it all off Beverley's mad at me." I felt awful again just thinking about it. I told him what had happened with her. "I'm not sure what to do about her party. I guess I'll have to leave for the day, but the bigger issue remains."

"What bigger issue?"

"Me." I sat up and wrapped my arms around my knees. "I want her to have a normal childhood, Johnny. She deserves that. But with me being the Lustrata and you being the Domn Lup, how is that ever going to happen?"

Johnny's fingers trailed over my back for a few heartbeats, then he sat up and mimicked my pose. "Her mother became a wærewolf when Beverley was just a baby. From the very start, Red, her path was never going to be the Norman Rockwell version of a normal life—whatever that is. Her mother had a vampire lover and she was murdered by a rogue witch. Don't beat yourself up because you can't provide *normal*. You provide love."

I bit my lip. "What if that's not enough for her?"

"How could it not be?"

Laying my head on my knees, I let the sadness rise up. "She said that everything got screwed up after her mom started letting Goliath drink from her. She depends on me, she's lost everything, and now her party may be ruined because I'm letting Menessos drink from me." The tears fell. "She's never going to trust me."

Johnny's arm wrapped my shoulders and he pulled me to him. "Yes, she will."

"I'm bound to him, Johnny. I can't undo it."

"Would you, if you could, for her?"

"I might."

"You did the right thing for the right reason," he said.

It was my former mantra, but now I hated each syllable. "I chose to act for justice. But I didn't see how any of it could trickle down and encroach on her life." Miserably, I added, "I should have."

"You acted. Of course the situation changed afterward. Most people would have been immobilized by their fear. Not you. In the moment, you did what was right. You always do—because of that you saved her life at the Covenstead. Because you're willing to take action. You can't reevaluate your past based on current events. What's done is done. You can only make changes to the present and hope for the best future to come."

Johnny laid back and pulled me close so my head lay on his shoulder. I felt safe in his arms and I let his words reassure me as he idly stroked my hair.

Sleep had almost claimed me when he whispered, "Maybe you could wear a disguise to the party."

CHAPTER TWELVE

Johnny cuddled close and whispered into my ear, "You know, technically, a shower is a lot like rain."

"What?" I asked over my shoulder, wiping away sleep. The clock read six-fifty. The sun wasn't up yet.

He ran his fingers from my thigh to my hip and let his warm palm rest on my waist under the tank top I'd slept in. "Thought I might cash in that rain check in the shower."

"You mean the shower that's so close to Nana and Beverley's rooms?"

"We can be quiet."

"The day I orgasm quietly will be a bad day."

He beamed at that remark. "Yeah, you are noisy. I dig it." He brushed hair from the nape of my neck and bit me gently. My reaction to that was arching my back and wishing ardently for thicker walls. When I moaned in quiet frustration, he twisted to sit on the side of the bed. "But that would be a little brazen, wouldn't it?"

I rolled over to watch the red foo dog and black dragon tattoos dance on his back as his muscles bunched in a stretch. "Nana hasn't breathed a word about us sharing a bed, *yet*. It's a good idea to refrain from tempting her beyond her ability not to butt in."

"Good for whom?"

He had a point.

Johnny grabbed his pants from the floor and held them modestly in front of him as he stood and faced me. "Probably a wise call, but," moving the jeans aside, he added, "I can't say my 'morning wood' agrees."

Every nerve ending sizzled when I saw him. I threw the covers off and knee-walked across the bed. His deep blue eyes, framed in messy dark curls, capture me as I reached out and fondled him. "It'd be a shame to waste it."

"It would."

Though he slept naked, I didn't. I released him to roll my tank top up slowly, teasingly. He followed its revealing progress, breathing faster. When I pulled it over my head, he responded by pushing my boy shorts down and letting his hands wander until he discovered how wet I was. I wiggled out of the shorts and dropped them to the floor. "Ta-da."

"If you skipped the pj's you wouldn't have to go through all that." He moved closer. Holding me, he nibbled on my ear and nuzzled into my hair. "You smell so good," he said.

"Yeah?"

"Yeah. Sweet like lilacs." He caressed my breasts, my nipples. I trembled, ensnared by Johnny's touch, his scent, and his voice. A decadent heat engulfed me. This wasn't like the enflamed yearning Menessos could incite with his voice. This was a more deliberate reaction, triggered by certainty. The pleasure Johnny could give me—had given me repeatedly—was flawless.

"Get behind me," I said, twisting onto all fours. Growling in approval, he joined me on the bed and stroked me with his fingers, pressing them slowly inside me. I moaned softly and rolled my hips. "Please."

His cock pressed at my opening, but didn't thrust inside.

He knew me, he knew I was greedy for him and wanted all of him deep within me. He grasped my hips and held me firmly while he rubbed just the tip in and out. In and out. Over and over, until I was desperate for all of him, yearning for gratifying release, and shaking with the need of it.

I pushed against his grip; he was strong and maintained the distance. Only the tip. "All of it, Johnny," I whispered, my voice hoarse.

"All?"

"Now. Please."

"As you wish."

I was so wet, when he shoved his length into me, there was no resistance. A whimper of pleasure passed from my lips and I tossed my head, throwing my hair across my naked back.

Johnny took a handful of my hair and twisted it around his hand until his grip was at the nape of my neck. He held me there with my head raised. It was aggressive and controlling. It was dominant. I liked it.

I liked the power play. The idea that he claimed a position of control excited me. But I was not without power.

My back arched, knees flexed, almost drawing me off him. Then, with his other hand's fingers pressed on my hip bone, he urged me back. I thrust myself onto him again.

We had a rhythm, a balance of control and consent. Still, I swiveled my hips every so often just to remind him his control wasn't absolute; I could veer from the rhythm.

An incredible orgasm was ready to overtake me—

Then I felt Menessos clinging to life despite the rising sun. I could feel him kindling my flesh, burning under my sternum, heating deep in my core. It was so good, so powerful I lost myself in it, moving faster and more forcefully. I was almost there.

—Menessos died.

The kindling warmth disappeared. I was alone with Johnny again.

But none of the urgency faded. None of the desire dwindled. Somehow, knowing this was mine, all mine and mine alone, made it better.

Johnny was building up to his own orgasm. All he needed was a squeeze from me. *That* squeeze. He was waiting for me, in full control of himself, and now that Menessos had succumbed to his curse, I gave Johnny full control. I let go. I obeyed his rhythm precisely.

The orgasm hit me like free-falling, a glorious sensation rippling across my body, my heart pounding, my breath racing.

My elbows gave and I thrust my face into a pillow as I cried out. Johnny maintained his grip in my hair, but stretched his arm to allow me distance.

When the angle changed, my sensitivity to his movements redoubled and the climax was revived. My fingers clawed into the sheets until my body was overloaded, until the low growls from Johnny's chest had stopped, until we collapsed onto the bed, twisting to lie side-by-side until we caught our breath.

While Johnny showered, I lounged in the bed. His return was quick, and he wore only his jeans. His wet hair was in a towel-dried but adorable mess. I left my warm bed and inspected his chest because I couldn't *not* touch him. "You took the stitches out."

"Yeah. Oh, look, it's a tit bit nippy in here," he said, performing his own inspection on me.

"I'll crank the heat up if you like."

"I do like it when you crank up the heat . . . but don't touch the thermostat. More fun for me."

I felt very grateful that his mood and his libido were elevated again. He'd laid out another button-down shirt and as I passed it to him, he volunteered to make breakfast and Beverley's lunch while I showered. I accepted the offer.

The aroma of coffee and bacon lured me down the stairs. Though I had been a vegetarian for several years, as Menessos had warned me, my connections to Johnny were making the savory scents of meat more scrumptious to me with each passing day. I joined the rest of them in the kitchen where I discovered Johnny's cooking had won over the sentinels. Outside, the night was fading. It was light enough that Johnny could see the dark shadows of the barns. "It's like in the cartoons: ACME barns. Just add a drop of water and *poof.*"

Beverley thought that was hilarious.

Maxine and Zhan were in suits of navy blue and pale gray this morning. They donned their suit jackets to make a round outside before the Beholders showed up.

Johnny passed a plate into my hands. Though two greasy slices of bacon lay beside the eggs and toast, I accepted it eagerly.

Soon Beverley put her empty plate in the sink and left to brush her teeth. She hadn't spoken a syllable to me.

"Enjoy your coffee," Nana said. "Since we have spies in minivans, I'll take her to the bus stop from now on."

"Spies in minivans?" Johnny echoed.

"One of the objecting parents recognized me picking up Beverley yesterday." For a few minutes, the three of us brainstormed about how we could get this party on track. Johnny pitched his disguise idea to Nana. She gave it her approval.

Beverley strolled slowly into the room. "If I get an A on the math test today, can I see the unicorns again?" she asked, studying the floor where the broken glass had been. With the very last word, her eyes lifted to meet mine.

She was blank; I hadn't a clue about what she was feeling. But I conceded, "That would be a fitting reward."

Nana drove her to the bus stop—after Johnny assured me he'd remembered to stick a joke in her lunchbox—and I began gathering my supplies for the ritual.

I packed white taper candles. Green, yellow, red, and blue votive candles. My incense holder and incense. Two bowls. A bottle of crystal water and a pouch of sea salt. I had hematites, aventurines, bloodstones, and coral. I tucked all of these into my overnight bag, added my wand, and had my broom ready. It was not the ritual broom that had been used in the previous version of this spell, but I felt that having my flying broom from the *lucusi* couldn't hurt.

Hearing the LeBaron sputtering outside, I zipped up the bag and headed downstairs with the Codex copy in hand.

In the kitchen, Maxine and Zhan had completed their rounds and were having a discussion. Curious, I stepped down the hallway. From the muffled growling sounds, I guessed Johnny was rough-housing with Ares in the garage.

Nana shuffled through the front door and immediately joined us. She had brought down her notebook with translations of the Trivium Codex this morning, and she dumped her coat on the back of her chair then sat. "You take the Codex copy?"

"Yes." I handed it to her.

On cue, Johnny strode in. After planting a quick kiss on my cheek, he claimed the last pieces of bacon.

"We should go with them," Maxine said to Zhan.

"I believe one of us should stay," Zhan countered, "to make certain that no one enters the house."

Maxine said, "We were told to protect *her,* not her house or her grandmother."

"Is it not implied?" the Asian woman asked. Maxine did not respond. "It would be negligent not to have considered all the implications," Zhan added.

"But she will be *surrounded* by wærewolves."

"Hey, Red won't be in any danger there," Johnny said.

"You don't know that," Maxine pressed.

His shoulders squared at her challenge. "Yes, I do." His tone was more authoritative than I'd ever heard. The voice of the Domn Lup made Maxine swallow whatever retort she might have considered. From the garage, Ares barked. *Guess he heard it, too.*

"However," Johnny added in a more conversational tone as he let the puppy into the house, "if you'd like to let me take the Audi, I won't object to that."

Maxine crossed her arms. She wisely did not say a word, but let her body language speak for her—although she lost some of the affect with Ares sniffing her ankles. I scolded him and he trotted off through the dining room. I was just glad he was past his growling dislike of these particular Offerlings.

"C'mon," I chimed in. "The Domn Lup can't keep showing up in a rusty Chrysler LeBaron."

"I heard that," Nana grouched, lifting her head from the notebook.

Maxine said to Zhan, "You stay." She pulled the keys from her pocket, studied them for a moment, then tossed them to Johnny. "You drive."

His adorable little-boy grin spread.

After I claimed the necessary pages from the Codex copy and tucked them into the overnight bag, I asked Johnny, "When do you want to leave?"

He checked the clock. "We have some time, but I can't wait to do the test drive."

While shaking my head at his glee, I hugged Nana good-bye then rehefted the bag onto my shoulder and headed for the hallway. "Then let's go. You can take the long way."

We passed the doorway to the living room. Ares was on the couch, paws on the back, tail wagging vigorously. I was about to scold him again, when the low growl in his throat made me stop. Beyond him, I saw a dark Chevy Impala in the driveway. A shadow appeared on the glass of the door, and someone knocked.

"Let me," Maxine said.

"I can still answer my own door." Without waiting for her I jerked the door open.

Two men stood on my porch.

One was broad-shouldered with a near-ebony complexion. His head was shaved but he had a trim goatee surrounding unsmiling lips. I was willing to bet even this guy's baby pictures were stern. Combine his facial expression, and the methodical assessment in his dark eyes, with the serious black suit, and I knew he wasn't here on a whim.

The other man was pallid, and was decidedly not broad-shouldered. He had pale weasel-like eyes that remained fixed on me. Ivory's no-nonsense suit screamed "government official" just as much as Ebony's.

I didn't open the screen door. Instead, I pointed to the front window. "The building permits are posted."

Ebony reached into his pocket and produced a badge and an ID. "I'm Special Agent Damian Brent, this is Special Agent Clive Napier. I have some questions for you, Ms. Alcmedi, if you have a moment."

CHAPTER THIRTEEN

Special Agent Damian Brent pointed at my overnight bag. "Going somewhere?"

"I was going across town for a few hours."

His gaze shifted to focus past me. "Do you have a permit for that gun?"

"I do," Maxine said.

I'd jerked the door open and, as usual, she had her gun out. I could have at least checked before opening the door, or waited until she'd retreated out of sight.

"Concealed carry?" Agent Brent asked.

"Yes. May I see your identification?"

I stepped out of the way so she could move forward. Her gun was lowered but still available as she drew closer to the screen door to make her inspection of his credentials. A moment later she said, "I've never heard of the S-S-T-I-X." She spelled it out, letter by letter. "What's it stand for?"

"I'm not surprised you haven't heard. SSTIX"—he pronounced it like the famed river Styx of Greek myth—"is a newer and little-known task force."

We all waited; he didn't go on. "And the acronym stands for what?" Maxine pressed.

"Specialized Squadron for Tactical Investigation of Xenocrime."

"Xenocrime?"

"As in crimes committed by those members of society deemed . . . strange."

"Nonsters," Clive added with a twisted smile.

It had been only a matter of time until nonhumans had a task force devoted to their crimes. This *should* have been a good thing, as law enforcement officers increasingly had refused to investigate crimes involving vampires and wærewolves for years. Insurance companies and governmental agencies had lost numerous lawsuits brought by families of slain or disabled police officers whose attorneys had cited circumstances "far superior to normal risk." Based on Agent Brent's vibe, I was betting the federal government had found a solution . . . and that it might not be all good.

Maxine removed the cell phone from her pocket. She still hadn't holstered her weapon. "With so many freaks able to make realistic documents, you'll of course understand if we verify your credentials before talking to you?"

"Of course, but it'll take you longer to make that verification than it will for Ms. Alcmedi to answer a few simple questions."

"The number?" Maxine insisted. She dialed as Agent Brent rattled off a series of numbers.

I stepped forward. "What do you want?"

"I have questions about the death of Xerxadrea Veilleux and the break-in at the Botanical Gardens."

A pang of loss resonated in my chest at the mention of her name. Keeping my expression blank, I said, "Xerxadrea was a friend. I mourn her loss. Someone told me the authorities thought she lost control of her broom and crashed."

"May we come in?"

"Not until she verifies you."

He took a small notepad from his pocket and flipped it open. "The alarms went off at the Botanical Gardens at eleven-twenty-six P.M." He tapped the notebook. "Local television stations broadcast live coverage of you from eight-twelve P.M. until eight-thirty-eight P.M. A ceremony of some kind, and you wore a red hooded cape."

He took a breath, so I said, "I'm not sure of the exact times, but I have to assume you've done your homework and that you are correct." Nothing about my installation as Menessos's court witch was criminal. *Although I would arrest Menessos for making me wear those boots if I could.*

"I also have sources that say at approximately nine P.M. you were seen leaving the area of the vampires' haven with a man on a motorcycle. The motorcyclist drove on the sidewalk for a short distance."

That *was* illegal. At least for the "motorcyclist," Johnny. My mouth stayed shut.

"So where did you go when you left in such haste, Ms. Alcmedi?"

"To see me," Maxine said, shutting the phone and tucking it away.

"And you are?"

"Maxine Simmons."

He asked for her address and wrote in the little book as she answered. "May we come in now?"

"No," Maxine said firmly.

"How long did you two ladies stay together?"

Maxine shrugged as if unsure. "I don't remember. Do you?"

In truth, I'd gone with Johnny to The Dirty Dog, then flew on the broom to the gardens. After the encounter with the fairies that left Xerxadrea dead, I left with Menessos. We revisited The Dirty Dog, then continued on to the haven. Security cameras might have picked up the cab arriving at the haven downtown, so I didn't dare lie about that. "Until Menessos came for me. We arrived back at the haven at . . ." Menessos had given me the satellite phone then. I was afraid to call Nana because it was after one in the morning. "It was just after one A.M., I believe."

"Nine until one." As he wrote that down, Agent Brent asked, "So what were you doing during those four hours, Ms. Alcmedi?"

"Playing cards with me," Maxine said. "Uno. And staying clear of vampires. If you've seen the TV footage then you'll recall there was an attempted murder at the ceremony."

Agent Brent pursed his lips, a sign that he wasn't convinced.

"We weren't certain who the target was, but the Regional Lord thought it best she be elsewhere," Maxine replied. "What's any of this got to do with the Eldrenne's death?"

I made a mental note to remember that Maxine was a convincing liar.

Agent Brent continued. "Eyewitness police reports say that at approximately eleven-forty P.M., someone wearing a red hooded cape was observed flying away from the Botanical Gardens on a broom." His bland tone supported the disgust he was conveying to me. "You were there, Ms. Alcmedi. I want to know *why* the deceased lost control of her broom."

It was Menessos's second-in-command, Goliath, the police had seen. I had given Goliath my cape to wear in hopes it would draw off the fairies that were after us. Menessos told him to wait until the last moment to leave, to buy us time to make our escape on foot.

"Enough of this," Johnny stepped up. "Do you have a warrant?"

"I do not. Do you have a motorcycle?" He quickly assessed Johnny.

"If you don't have a warrant, then you're done here."

Johnny's voice exuded an unmistakable threat. The agents, after glaring briefly through the screen door, left. Johnny shut the door when they had exited the porch.

"They're likely calling to get access to all the city's traffic cameras right now," Maxine said. "Where did you two go?"

"We took Superior into Cleveland Heights to The Dirty Dog." I watched the two men stride to their very plain, government-tagged Impala.

"East." She paced a few steps, took out her phone again, and made a call. She told someone to get a couple tech geeks to the Blood Culture, pull video surveillance, and doctor in an arrival and departure of two women who could pass for the two of us, with me in the ceremonial outfit. She gave them times and the proper date. When she shut the phone, she grinned. "Now we'll have corroborating evidence if he needs it."

"It can't be that easy."

"For the tech geeks it is."

"Women who could pass for you and me?"

"The Boss knows a lot of women, my lady. A lot of size sixes. Me in shades, you with the hood up. Easy."

Nana and Zhan had been listening, and joined us in the living room. Though apprehension radiated from her, Nana didn't speak.

"You said we were together and gave him your address," I said to Maxine.

"I said you came to see me. I didn't say where. He *asked* for my address because he assumed that's where we were."

Good point. "Still, I didn't kill Xerxadrea. Fairies did."

"With magic," Nana said. "Hard to prove you did it, hard to prove you didn't."

"I have no motive!"

"She kicked you out of the *lucusi* before witnesses, Persephone."

I swallowed hard. My stomach iced over.

"Don't worry about it," Maxine said reassuringly. "Now you weren't even there." She nodded toward the door to indicate we needed to get moving. "Boss won't allow them to make a media martyr of you."

There were many who bore me ill will for various reasons. Some of them were in the Witch Elders Council. Using the angle that someone was setting me up was viable, but having to lie to protect my innocence was a kick in the gut to my notions of justice.

Johnny and Maxine were waiting for me in the car.

As I stepped off the porch I noticed an empty bucket in front of the garage, the one I used for dog food. Thunderbird had brought it up for a refill. I grabbed it and hurried to the car.

Though Johnny had his phone to his ear, at my approach he revved the engine happily and grinned at me through the windshield. My blond sentinel had taken the passenger front, leaving me to get in the back. I tapped the driver's window and Johnny lowered it. After only a few words I realized he was telling Theo about our visitor, and requesting that she see what she could find out about SSTIX.

"Pop the trunk," I asked. Maxine had to tell him where the lever was. After my bags were in the trunk, he'd put the window up again so I mimed filling the bucket followed by flapping wings. I doubt either understood it to mean, "I'm going to feed the griffon."

I hurried to the grove with the dog food, stopping at the edge and holding out the bucket. Thunderbird stretched, rose to his feet, shakily, then settled his feathers and ambled weakly toward me. I set the bucket between my feet. Thunderbird stopped and cocked his head. He made his trademark sound, but it lacked force.

I reached down and scooped dog food into my palm and held it out.

He puffed his neck feathers up and kicked one of his hind legs, tail swishing. He'd seemed weak and was acting tough now. I was sure it cost him. "C'mon."

Slowly, he continued forward and snuffled at my hands.

"They're clean," I said softly.

A long moment later, with his sharp beak hovering over my offering—and me hoping his aim wasn't impaired by his lacking vision—his beak opened and the odd bird tongue licked up a few pieces of kibble.

"At least they *were* clean," I added.

As he continued to eat from my hands, I studied his wound. Runny pus and goop. He needed Dr. Lincoln.

Gently, I closed my grip around his beak, not blocking his nostrils.

He stilled, except for rolling his remaining eye up at me.

"You have to let the doc treat you, Thunderbird."

My fingers loosened, and he reared his head up regally. It reminded me of a man, standing tall and declaring he was fine and didn't need a doctor.

I bent to pick up the bucket and quickly examined his injured talons. Standing straight, I offered him the handle. "Let the doc do his job and help you heal."

His craned neck twisted away and he snuffled again. Now he seemed like a child who'd stuffed fingers in his ears and declared he wasn't listening.

With those glossy feathers and that sleek tiger body, he was a gorgeous creature. Griffons were symbolic of nobility for centuries, though not exactly shown in tiger form. Tigers were enigmatic and powerful. He was mysterious nobility. I didn't want him to die.

I placed the bucket on the ground before him. "I don't want to lose you, Thunderbird."

He thundered again and spread his wings as if to prove his might.

Reaching up, I stroked him gently from the neck to shoulder. He was so soft. He hadn't resisted, so I did it again, ending in a reassuring pat. Then I jogged back to the driveway.

As soon as my car door shut, Johnny backed up the driveway. I momentarily got over the smooth leather seats and asked Maxine, "Who answered at the number Agent Brent gave you?"

"Department of Homeland Security."

CHAPTER FOURTEEN

The idea of this government task force ruled my thoughts as Johnny drove us to town. One of their agents using the derogatory word "nonsters" signaled a lack of good intentions. They'd even coined a *new* word for offenses: xenocrime.

"As in crimes committed by those members of society deemed . . . strange," Agent Brent had said. They were drawing the lines. Since SSTIX fell under DHS jurisdiction—*under Homeland Security; Goddess, it sounds so possessive*—this could turn into a firestorm.

Fire.

I didn't pack a lighter for the candles. The thought hit me as we arrived at the edge of town. "Will anyone have a lighter at this meeting?"

"I don't know," Johnny answered.

"Make a stop at the drugstore up here, will you? I didn't pack one." Doing rituals away from home was new for me.

Maxine led me into the drugstore, and we walked briskly to the far side of the building where the candle section was located. After I selected a butane candle lighter, we headed to the register. On the way, I caught sight of the endcap display of Hallowe'en items, marked seventy-five percent off. I stared at a frog costume and a pair of fake cow's horns.

Johnny suggested I wear a disguise to Beverley's party . . .

While these wouldn't work, maybe there was something here that would. I crept down the aisle where the Hallowe'en items and candy had been gathered.

A man stepped into the aisle next to me, and the urge to hide overwhelmed me. The guy's aura exuded hostility. I kept my focus on the items before me while mentally reinforcing my own aural shielding. Then, from the corner of my eye, I checked him out. He was staring down the aisle—right at me.

Maxine pushed past him. "There you are."

Her arrival caused the man's attention to shift onto the sale items and that gave me an opportunity to make a quick assessment of him. I decided that this guy had no real business here. Though he scrutinized the cheesy plastic vampire teeth and ladies' fake fingernails with spiders on the tips, his fancy suit, gold watch, and alligator shoes made me certain he wasn't buying either item.

"What are you looking for?" Maxine asked.

"Just checking out the sale," I murmured. Rotating on my heels, I checked the items on the opposite side of the aisle. The brief spin allowed me a second hasty appraisal of him. As tall as Johnny, with a military high-and-tight haircut, this man's shoulders made Agent Brent's broad frame seem comparatively narrow. The slight bump under his jacket—similar to the one Zhan had from her shoulder holster—told me the most.

Another special agent. Following me. And not very sly about it.

Maxine caught my evaluation of the man and made one of her own. She must've noted the gun under his jacket as well; she moved herself directly between us.

Hoping he would leave, I studied the discounted Hallowe'en items. Just as I picked up a blond wig, Maxine said in a clipped voice, "We're going to be late." She pointed down the aisle, away from the man. Maxine kept herself expertly between us as I carried the wig and lighter to the register. Remembering my thought about calling myself Mae West and Maxine lighting my hair on fire, I smiled to myself.

While Maxine and I were in line, Mr. Alligator Shoes left the store.

After paying, I exited and hurried to the Audi. Maxine practically pushed me into the backseat, but remained outside scanning the other parked cars.

Johnny twisted in his seat. "This thing has a built-in massage-and-ventilation mechanism!" His glee faded. "What's wrong?"

"Did you see the guy in the fancy suit leave?" I asked.

Johnny said, "No. Why?"

"I think a special agent may be following us."

Johnny's bright mood darkened. "Are you certain?"

"Yeah. He was fairly obvious."

"What makes you think he was a G-man?"

"Gun bulge under his coat."

Maxine opened the door and got into the passenger seat. "Nothing," she said, "but let's get out of here."

Johnny had us on the road in seconds. I kept watch out

the back. He took an alternate route, cutting down side streets before returning to the main roads. "See anything?"

"No, but he may be more adept at road surveillance."

"Or," Maxine added, "he may have done everything he wanted to do."

"What do you mean?" I asked. "He didn't touch me or anything."

"Yeah, but he smelled wolfy to me, and he got close enough to scent you."

I met Johnny's eyes in the rearview mirror. The last thing either of us wanted was to think that SSTIX had *nonsters* on the payroll.

Fifteen minutes later, we headed east on Abbey Avenue and turned onto West Fourteenth. When Johnny turned again, I had to admit, I was surprised by where this forced-change spell was going to take place. "The Cleveland Cold Storage building?"

"Yup."

Long abandoned, or so I thought, and subject to disputes—the Ohio Department of Transportation wanted it demolished to make way for their new I-90 projects—it was legally still in limbo.

The twelve-story building had windows on the second and third levels only. In its heyday the upper floors were basically a series of big refrigerators and freezers. Now, the windowless upper levels served as a canvas for huge billboards seen from I-90's current route. Theo had said they wanted to do this at the den, but it hadn't hit me until now that this was *the* den. No wonder the disputes had been going on for years. The wæres were trying to work out a deal.

I checked the sky. The moon was still visible, and I was sure I would be able to see it from the west-side windows. "You'll herd the wolves to the kennels after they change?" I asked as Johnny drove up a newer ramp and into the open lower level. We passed through the loading dock access and into what looked like another parking garage.

"I will."

He parked. We all got out. As I retrieved my things from the trunk he told Maxine, "This is as far as you go. We have our own security." His decision didn't surprise me; she worked for Menessos, after all.

"Where she goes," Maxine pointed at me, "I go. By order of the Regional Vampire Lord."

"His orders mean nothing here."

"You don't want to cross him," she said.

"And you don't want to be a lone Offerling in my den."

Her eyebrows lowered and her lips tensed: conflict turning to anger.

"Maxine, as your Erus Veneficus, I'll take responsibility if Menessos is displeased."

"I'm just supposed to wait here in the car?"

"Actually," Johnny said, "I suggest you drive over there." He gestured. "Just on the other side of I-90 is a place called University Inn. The best eastern European food anywhere. I recommend the Salisbury steak and pierogies. Eat slow. Have some dessert and strike up a conversation with someone. I guarantee you'll learn something interesting." He opened the Audi's door. "Whenever you're ready."

Seconds later, she drove down the ramp.

Johnny said, "This way." We entered the building.

There were twenty or so cars in this lower level. A stairwell sat next to a wide, open elevator. The lift was big enough for a car and had rickety wooden gates. The elevator in the vampire haven had struck me as unsafe and I'd been concerned about riding on it, but it wasn't nearly as ramshackle as this one.

As Johnny led me onto the elevator, I said, "Now would be a good time to offer me a few words of reassurance."

He laughed and replied, "It's safe." When he shut the time- and termite-damaged gate, pieces of wood splintered to the floor.

"How . . . romantic," I muttered.

He entered some code on the keypad and jabbed his thumb on a red button that made the gears shudder. The elevator rose with a rhythmic jerkiness that was not at all comforting. His charming lopsided smile beamed at me until we stopped at the second floor.

An open expanse sprawled before us, and the men were grouped to the far western side. Todd was approaching, having heard the elevator's gears kick in. Blond and built like a pro wrestler, he was two full inches shorter than me. The meanness in his features was constant. He didn't bother with a greeting. He said simply, "They're ready."

The men stood silently watching. It would have made me feel more at ease if they had been chattering among themselves. Instead, they shifted their weight and locked keen eyes on me. They were likely as uncertain about their safety in this spell as I had been about mine on that elevator. I'd make sure to reassure them with more than "It's safe," and a smile as I'd gotten from Johnny.

All eighteen of them were here, Kirk included. They bowed their heads and murmured respectfully, "Domn Lup."

This spell was going to be their reward for volunteering to stand with Johnny against the fairies. It would give these wæres the ability to retain their man-minds whenever they transformed naturally with the moon cycles. They had done as he asked and they deserved this gift. But I was also doing this for Johnny.

Theo was doing her best searching for answers, but we had little to go on, and the wærewolf head honcho would be here tomorrow. Not much time to find this Arcanum, let alone undo the magic, but Menessos had indicated the spell should somewhat weaken the bonds restraining Johnny and enable him to transform more easily. The Rege would see only the fully ascended Domn Lup.

Johnny introduced me, and said, "While she checks the windows and decides what spot will suit the needs of the spell, let me just say once more how grateful I am that you volunteered . . ."

While he continued addressing the men, I walked to the western wall, set down my bag and broom, and gauged the view from the various windows. The glass was clouded with years of weather and grime, so I resorted to checking those that were broken out, trying to find a spot where the moon was in the best position. Once located, I could mark my spot on the floor and arrange the wæres accordingly.

My ears detected a regular *tap-tapping* sound and I searched for the source. The men heard it, too, and Johnny's words trailed off. It seemed to be echoing from a stairwell beside the elevator. The shadows darkened with movement beyond. The men were all actively sniffing the air.

Cammi Harding stepped into the light.

The spoiled bank heiress had, apparently, gone shopping and found a pair of shiny gold, thigh-high platform boots not unlike the red ones Menessos had provided me for the Erus Veneficus ceremony. When I'd gone to The Dirty Dog to talk to Johnny, Cammi had ogled my boots. That particular run-in had ended badly for her, as had our last run-in, which occurred at a church. Clearly, she was back for more.

Her glossy black miniskirt was as tight and short as possible, and meant for someone at least fifteen years her junior. She did seem to relish flaunting what wære genetics had graced her with. The gold top was low-cut and sleeveless. Despite the chill in the November air, she wore no coat. Even from this distance I was certain her nails, makeup, and fluffy platinum hair were flawless. The only thing that surprised me was the absence of her more subdued twin, Sammi.

As soon as I saw her, I found myself wondering what Eva de Monique looked like. *I am secure that my relationships with both Johnny and Menessos are all I want them to be.* I hoped that affirmation would squelch these seeds of jealousy.

"Hello, boys," Cammi purred, strutting forward.

"What are you doing here?" Todd demanded.

"I'm here to be the voice of reason."

"Get out," Johnny commanded.

"Someone needs to remind them what a risk they're taking, letting magic be stirred around them." She angled her path to avoid Johnny and stopped in front of the gathered men three good paces out of anyone's reach. "You haven't forgotten how that witch threatened me, have you? Or that she threatened to call the energy up and leave me half-formed? You heard her, Pete. I know you did. And so did you, Josh. And yet you line up like puppies in a pound, wagging your tails, eager to be petted." She tossed her head and struck a pose of defiance as she looked them up and down, taking the measure of every man present. "There's not an alpha among you."

That won her angry growls all around. *She can't think insulting them—and their Domn Lup—will sway them to see her side of things.*

"Oooo. I love that sound," she taunted. "Do it again."

The men gave her their best growls.

"There it is . . . there's the evidence of the backbone of real wæres. I know you've seen him change, you've found your Domn Lup. But he's not doing this, is he? She is." She pointed at me accusingly. "The *sange stricata*." She sauntered toward me, and the group of men parted to let her through. She stopped just past them, as if to give the visual effect that she was leading the wæres who flanked her. "They say she's the Lustrata. What-fucking-ever. What does the witches' messiah matter to us? Have you all forgotten your training? The witches are—" Her features manifested arrogance and seemed to scream, *I know something you don't know.* "Well, we'll not discuss that in front of her. Let's discuss what we all know: she's a witch tied to witches, she's also tied to vampires—you've seen her on the Regional Lord's lap, feeding him—and she's tied to our Domn Lup."

"You're walking a thin line, Cammi," Todd barked.

"Oh shut up. I'm not anti–Domn Lup. I'm merely connecting the dots and making sure you see how she could be a danger to us all." With a flick of her wrist she cut Todd off before he could get another syllable out. "I want you all to do what the Lup asks of you. But not *blindly.* Ask yourself: Do you trust *her?* Are you willing to become another half-formed monster?"

"Get out," Johnny said. "Now."

"Make me," she cooed. "Show me what a big strong alpha you can be."

"Heel, bitch." This new, deep voice echoed from the stairwell.

As its source stepped into view, I recognized Mr. Alligator Shoes from the drugstore.

Men filed in, forming a line behind him. Yet, as Johnny, Todd, and the other pack wæres squared their shoulders and emitted low growls, I wondered what, exactly, was going on. How had these guys gotten through the security Johnny had boasted about, and whether I should let Johnny know this was the guy from the drugstore.

Mr. Alligator Shoes marched into the room, and his men maintained their line behind him, though one not-so-brawny man lagged back, carrying a briefcase.

Cammi sucked in a breath and sashayed toward him. "Finally, a true alpha!" She gave a coquettish little shimmy at the last.

Maxine was right; he was a wærewolf.

As she neared, Mr. Alligator Shoes swiftly slapped her—hard enough to knock her to the ground. "Never speak to your *dirija* again." He spat on her.

My mouth opened to protest—standing silently by while someone hit a woman wasn't in my nature—but Johnny caught my attention as he threw off his leather jacket and his shirt. His hands, arms, and shoulders darkened, sprouted fur, and bulged. It wasn't pretty, but it bulked his size closer to that of Mr. Alligator Shoes, who had pointed his finger at Cammi as she had pointed at me earlier. "You will *never* trouble him with the sound of your voice *ever* again, do you understand me, bitch?" He spoke with a thick accent.

That was when Johnny leaped forward, launching himself at Mr. Alligator Shoes. Both fell, rolled, and rose up swinging.

The two groups of men growled at each other, but none interfered with the fight. Cammi, reflexively touching her smacked cheek, struggled to get her feet under her. I could attest to the difficulty of this when there's two extra inches of platform attached to the bottom of a high-heeled shoe.

The men fighting seemed well matched; for what I could tell, each was blocking the other's punches. Then Mr. Alligator Shoes took a hit to the kidneys, but it gave him an opening to hit Johnny in the jaw. Johnny's growl rumbled in his chest and I felt a wave of energy.

He punched Mr. Alligator Shoes in the stomach so hard it lifted him into the air and sent him back six feet. Johnny was fully transformed before Mr. Alligator Shoes had landed.

He hadn't taken off his jeans, though. Wriggling and kicking out of the fabric and the undies gave the beast some trouble. By the time Mr. Alligator Shoes had been helped up by his men, the pony-size black wolf stood snarling before them.

"It's true," Mr. Alligator Shoes whispered.

CHAPTER FIFTEEN

Having reverted to man form and put on his pants, Johnny glowered at the invaders. "*I* give the orders here."

"You told her to get out. I was just enforcing your word." Mr. Alligator Shoes' lip was busted and bleeding.

"I don't need your help."

"I think you do. She still hasn't left."

Johnny flashed dark, scathing eyes at Cammi. In seconds, she was trying to run to the stairwell in the stupidest shoes on the planet. I couldn't help smiling at how ridiculous she looked. Everyone watched her go, including Mr. Alligator Shoes. Before she could disappear up the stairwell, he remarked, "She's a bit old for my tastes. Not sure I'd keep her around. Is it sentimental? Did she teach you things when you were a pup?"

"Unless *you* want to be banished from speaking to your Domn Lup, you will speak only when spoken to."

Mr. Alligator Shoes bowed his head.

"Who the hell are you?"

"You may call me Gregor."

"What are you doing here?"

"I am the head of the Omori, elite protectors of the Zvonul." He pulled a leather bifold from his breast pocket and flashed an ID. "These are my men; we have come to secure the area. I was so charged by the Rege."

"Does he think there is cause for concern here?"

"This is standard procedure. May I ask a question?"

Johnny let him wait for the answer. "One."

"Why would you take such verbal abuse from a pack bitch, and in front of your men?"

"I would have dealt with her my own way."

"You Americans are weak, letting your women wag their tongues as much as their tails. Discipline is the fastest, surest way to achieve obedience. Especially with women."

I'm liking him less with every word.

Johnny stalked forward. Gregor's men retreated from him, lowering their heads. Gregor did neither.

"If a woman's tongue wagging is a threat to you, Greg, I'd say you're the one who's weak."

Gregor lowered his head. Glancing around, he observed my broom and supply bag. "May I ask what is going on here?"

Johnny gestured toward me. "She was about to reward these men, who volunteered to stand with me in battle. I believe that freely given allegiance should be rewarded."

"Allegiance is *expected*. Anything less is punished."

Johnny didn't miss a beat. "Then I'm relieved that you're not the Domn Lup."

Gregor assessed me lecherously. It was clear my layers of shirt, hoodie, and blazer, paired with jeans and hiking boots, didn't fit the mental picture he was forming. He gestured toward the stairwell. "The other one was dressed to give rewards." He glanced again at the broom leaning against the wall, eyes narrowing suspiciously. "What will this one do?"

"She's a witch."

"Fuck!" Gregor shouted. "This is your *den,* man! What is a witch doing here?"

With a roar, Johnny all-out slugged him. Gregor's head snapped to the side, his knees buckled. He barely caught himself on the heels of his hands.

"*Your* tongue-wagging is pissing me off, Greg. This ain't Romania. However you do things there, you can count on our ways being different."

Transferring onto his haunches, Gregor wiped blood from his lips. His expression was utterly hostile, but he stayed down.

Johnny pointed at the floor. "My house. My rules. Got it?"

Gregor delayed his nod for as long as possible, but when Johnny had that acquiescence, he turned to the men this Omori brought with him. "Got it?"

They each went down on one knee and bowed their heads.

The pack led the Omori upstairs, moving into a meeting room. Johnny, Todd, and I took the long way around. I thought we might be going to the *dirija*'s office and I wasn't disappointed. I leaned my broom on the wall beside the door and dropped my bag beside it. Kirk immediately opened the little refrigerator and passed an energy drink—Rockstar—to Johnny, who gulped it down. That transformation had taken a lot out of him.

"Did you know the Omori were coming?" he asked Todd.

"No."

"He said it was standard procedure."

Todd's cheeks reddened at the unspoken accusation in Johnny's words. "I've never been a *dirija* and I'm not privy to what secrets of protocol they might keep. Did you get a handbook?"

Johnny didn't answer.

"I didn't either. Ig never told me anything about the Zvonul, the Rege, or Omori. Why would he? He didn't intend for me to lead."

"Todd . . ."

"Don't expect me to have the answers you need on this, John." Though he'd spoken forcefully, he continued in a less aggressive tone. "The grooming Ig gave me for the position was incomplete at best."

Realizing that prolonging a conversation that reopened Todd's deepest wounds was not a good idea, I asked, "What are the Omori?"

"Apparently they're the wærewolf version of the Secret Service with a whole lot of special ops included." He shot a look at Kirk. "I want to know how they got in."

Kirk left. Johnny tossed the empty can into the trash. "Let's go."

I followed him and Todd to a gymnasium with hardwood flooring. A carpeted platform about three feet higher than the rest of the area was situated to one side about ten feet from the doors we entered. Furnished with a long table and executive chairs, it looked like it belonged in a boardroom rather than a basketball court. The high ceiling was dotted with arena lights, but only one was powered up, illuminating the table and its occupants.

The wæres ahead of me ascended the steps to the dais. The "home team" sat in the comfortable chairs with their backs to the wall; the "away team" faced them, the dark openness and drop-off behind them. I stopped just atop the stairs, close enough to see and hear them, but well out of reach and out of the illumination.

Johnny and Gregor were midtable across from each other. Johnny's men pushed their seats to the wall and stood, eyeballing Gregor's men who remained seated. Gregor, with his black eye, bruised jaw, and bloody lips, was a mess. He hadn't been offered ice or even paper towels. I wondered if the wæres lacked ice packs and a first aid kit, or if the big, bad Omori leader was expected to lick his wounds.

"As head of security for the Zvonul, I must know why you found it reasonable to have a witch in your den." Gregor sounded almost submissive as he spoke. He was moving his mouth very little. Maybe pain had something to do with the diplomatic tone.

"I don't answer to you."

"Respectfully, I remind you that you have not been confirmed by the Rege. Even when that occurs, the authority you wield is not without limits."

"I revealed myself to you. You're obligated to acknowledge me as Domn Lup."

"True. But my first obligation is to the Zvonul. Until the Rege offers you his acknowledgment, his orders remain supreme. While your confirmation is yet pending, I am under his orders to secure this den and this area. And he expects you to comply."

"If I don't?"

"He will not come. Your confirmation will become . . . unlikely."

Johnny considered for a moment, then answered, "As I told you, she was about to bestow these men with a reward."

"What manner of reward?"

"She can perform a spell that amplifies moonlight. Amplifies it enough to force them to fully transform."

"That's impossible!" A fresh spill of blood ran from his cut lip as he spoke, but he ignored it and continued: "The moon is waning. Less than half her face shows."

"Three of my friends have already experienced this spell and have been enhanced for it. They now retain their man-minds during their transformation with the full moon. It is a gift I intend to give these men for their service."

I heard the briefest hesitation before the word "friends." Erik hadn't exactly been happy with Johnny since he learned that Johnny could transform at will. I didn't think it was jealousy, but it was clear that the Domn Lup would have lofty responsibilities to attend to, and that it would cut into band time. I hadn't known their very friendship might be at stake.

Gregor's gaze rapidly bounced back and forth as if he was thinking fast. When his jaw flexed, I knew it was a bad sign. "No," he said.

"No?" Johnny echoed.

"I cannot allow this to proceed." He spoke not to Johnny but to the men. "This spell must be canceled." He spat the word "spell."

Johnny leaned across the table. "Your job doesn't give you authority here."

Kirk joined us then, and made knuckle-popping fists as he took his place. The rest of the local pack shifted into ready stances, preparing should this become a fight.

Gregor relaxed into his seat. "The Rege arrives tomorrow. I cannot allow anything to transpire here that may be the first stage of a strike at my lord."

"You can't seriously think—"

"The witches have long threatened preemptive attacks on wærewolves. As impossible as your claim is, for security purposes, I refuse to allow her to even attempt it."

"It's not up to you, *Greg.*" Johnny stood and glowered down at Gregor. "These men decide for themselves!"

Immediately, Gregor bowed his head and said, "I yield to your suggestion. Let us ask your men to decide for themselves. Surely you would not have them go through with this spell if they wish to wait until the Rege has returned to Romania? We would, of course, consider such a decision to defer your own plans as a high act of respect in favor of the wishes of the Zvonul."

Gregor's smooth. He'd just gotten his way while acquiescing to Johnny's demands, reminding everyone here that the Zvonul had all the clout, *and* hinting that the men should vote to wait so that their leader could avoid any discredit.

Gregor called out, "If you vote to delay this spell until the Rege has gone, let it be known by raising your right arm."

Slowly, every arm rose.

"And you, witch, do you agree to wait, or do you protest this notion?"

I dropped my crossed arms and stepped into the edge of the illuminated area. "I will reward these men whenever it pleases their Domn Lup and them."

"Persephone?"

It was one of the men with Gregor who called my name, the not-brawny one with a briefcase. He was at the far end of the table, and he stood so the wære-bulk between him and Gregor no longer blocked his view of me.

"Chris? Christopher LaCroix?"

"Yeah." He smiled, then, with everyone staring at us, the moment soured into awkwardness. "Yeah," he repeated, quieter, as if he wished he'd kept his mouth shut.

Chris was the younger brother of the one serious boyfriend I'd ever had, my college sweetheart, Michael LaCroix. Chris had been inadvertently turned wærewolf by a girlfriend he was trying to kennel. Word got around and Chris was threatened on campus by some wære-hating jocks. It led to a wære coalition forming and even some non-wære's like me joined. Michael, who waffled between being a private investigator, a personal trainer, and a kung-fu master (his nickname then was Pi-fu), instructed a training series for self-defense. They had access to one of the campus's smaller gymnasiums at a certain time every week. He taught wære's methods that took their superior strength into consideration and kept them from hurting mere humans, even if those mere humans were instigating an attack.

The demand for this training had been more than any

of them had expected. When Michael opened a pay-for-training center in a nearby town—a business venture he'd not even hinted about to me—I'd told him it bothered me that he would do this behind my back. I just wanted to be kept in the loop. He'd said he didn't have to "clear" anything with me and he dumped me. I hadn't seen either of them since. Until now.

Breaking the awkward silence, Chris offered a polite "How've you been?"

"Good. You?"

Gregor cut in. "There's obviously no further need for you to be here, witch," he said pointedly to me. "Don't let us keep you any longer."

Not really passive-aggressive, just aggressive.

Johnny gestured to Kirk. "See the witch to the University Inn."

At that, I knew three things for certain. One, he wasn't going to let on about our relationship more than necessary to these Omori; two, he wasn't coming home with me; and three, it was highly unlikely that I'd have another chance to perform this spell before the Rege arrived. Could Johnny repeat another man-to-wolf transformation without what he would have gained from the spell?

Maxine said, begrudgingly, that the pierogies were fabulous. When she asked how I was done so quickly, I told her some unforeseen other pack business sprang up and we'd rescheduled. If she was suspicious that there was more to it than that, she didn't show it outwardly. I didn't want to talk about it and she was keen enough not to need it spelled out for her.

In the car, I switched the radio to WMMS. I was hoping to crank up some rock 'n' roll, but the morning show's aftermath crew was blathering on. So I found WKDD out of Akron and gave the sound system a workout.

My thoughts ran to Johnny. And worry.

His second-in-command, Todd, resented him. Todd wanted to be *dirija* in the worst way, and while that would happen once Johnny was confirmed as the Domn Lup, in the meantime, Todd had to wait *and* he had to take orders from Johnny.

And then there was Cammi, who was a power-hungry bitch. She'd used her looks to work those men over, and fast. I hoped that the Omori's threat held, that Johnny wouldn't ever have to hear her speak to him again, but she was cunning. She'd use her feminine wiles to influence others. The threat she represented wasn't gone.

He struggled at every step, and while I had no doubt he could handle it, the fact that he literally had to fight for his position saddened me. It was barbaric. Bottom line, I didn't want Johnny to lose the man he was now in the process.

It occurred to me his problems weren't unlike mine. The responsibilities of my role were changing me. Months ago I couldn't have imagined going into a vampire haven, let alone having my own apartment inside one. I couldn't have imagined feeding a vampire, much less being *doubly* bound to one.

And despite being the Lustrata, I still wanted to give Beverley a normal childhood. I could have given her that easily before all this Lustrata business began. *I'm losing who I once was.*

Through Beverley, I realized, I was anchored to that struggle, to the desire to keep a tight grasp on my sense of self, of the here and now, so I didn't completely lose myself.

Maybe if I can give Johnny back his memories, there will be something in them that will anchor him.

I was more determined than ever to get his tattoos unlocked.

When we pulled in the driveway, the first thing I noticed was the power lines were strung along the poles, providing electric to the finished barns and Mountain's mobile home, which had arrived. Nana's prefab walls were going up.

Mountain gave me the update, remarking that the wiring and plumbing had been accomplished, and that the floor joists and subfloor were in.

"Any chance of getting that heated flooring for her?"

"I'll certainly make every effort to get that for you." With a nod, he beckoned me aside and I followed so we were out of Maxine's earshot. "The men cut through your basement block wall and installed a small door that will lead to the crawl space under the addition. Far as they know its standard access for the plumbing; better from inside the house than in the block foundation. More weather tight and all. But," he added with quiet grimness, "it will be a good hiding place for a vampire. If it ever becomes necessary. Only you and I will know."

"Gotcha."

He gave me a wink and headed back to supervise.

Doc Lincoln arrived just after dinner. The house was still full of the delicious smell of Nana's lahanodolmathes she'd fixed for dinner. Greeks think the best cabbage is found after the first frost, and I guess the frosty mornings had inspired her to make the recipe: ground beef and rice with eggs, dill, and onion rolled up in cabbage leaves. Nana must have noticed that I was eating some meat. Topping it all was the avgolemono sauce—egg yolks, water, lemon juice, and corn starch—poured on right before they're served. I asked Geoff if he'd like to have some.

He admitted it smelled wonderful, but said he'd already eaten and offered me another pill bottle full of that salve for Johnny's stitches. "Sorry. Don't need it. They've healed up and he took the stitches out already."

"Good. That wære healing kicked in." He dropped the bottle back into his bag. "The barns have lights now, yes?"

"Yes." I told him about Thunderbird. "Maybe with some dog food you can coax him into trusting you. He needs some help, his eye is . . . icky."

"Icky how?"

I described the yellow oozing pus, about the same shade as the avgolemono, but I didn't mention that or, for the sake of my digestion, let myself dwell on it long.

"Yeah. That's not good."

"You'll need the dog food, though. He let me touch him today because I've been feeding it to him."

"You should go with him," Nana said. "I'll wash the dishes tonight."

"But you cooked," I protested. Johnny hadn't come home yet. He didn't have a car with him, but someone would give the Domn Lup a ride. Eventually. *Hope he and Gregor aren't still duking it out.*

Beverley pointed to the refrigerator where a magnet prominently held her math test with a big red A+ on it. "I aced the math test. Can I come out and see the unicorns?"

"Absolutely," Nana said quickly. "Maxine will help me with the dishes. Take Zhan with you, too." She shot a glance at the sentinel. If Nana knew Zhan was curious, that meant they had talked some today. Good for Nana, not being completely antisocial toward the Offerling. *But I hope Zhan didn't mention the visitor who upset me so much.*

CHAPTER SIXTEEN

After bundling up, I checked by the garage for the bucket. Thunderbird had not brought it back, so I filled a mixing bowl instead. The four of us walked to Mountain's mobile home first. Beverley knocked. "You're my first guest, Beverley," he said happily. "Come in! I don't have much in the way of seating to offer, but it's out of the cold air."

I could smell pizza, then saw half of one on the stovetop on a round cooking stone. "The oven works. Anyone like a slice?"

Beverley took a small one. I didn't blame her. Nana's lahanodolmathes wasn't going to be her favorite. I had a suspicion Nana's traditional Greek food phase was actually an unspoken effort to get someone else to volunteer for cooking duty in Johnny's absence.

Something bumped the back door lightly and emitted a gargly whining sound. It commanded our attention but Mountain simply shrugged it off. "I think Zoltan wants some pizza."

"I wouldn't advise giving in to that," Dr. Lincoln said.

"Don't worry, Doc. The way that little dragon belches

his tuna there's no way I'm letting him have a garlic-tomato sauce."

"Can I see him?" Zhan asked.

"Certainly." Mountain grabbed a Lysol spray. "Hopefully this will kill the pizza smell for him." He doused the area of the door then led the doctor and an eager Zhan outside and over to the barn.

Beverley and I remained behind so she could finish her pizza.

An awkward moment later, she said, "I'm sorry about breaking your glass."

My glass. "This is your home now, kiddo. It was your glass, too." I hoped she understood what I was trying to say. "I'm sorry that I have to do something that your mother did, something that bothered you."

Beverley set the pizza on a napkin. "She always acted like Goliath biting her was no big deal. It's got to hurt. It's . . ."

When she didn't go on, I took a deep breath and steeled myself. "I'm the Lustrata, Beverley. I am bound to Menessos and to Johnny, and to you and Nana." I searched her face and added, "There's nothing I can do to change any of that."

The corners of her little mouth angled down. "I don't want you to die."

"I don't, either." I took her into my arms. *But my path is a dangerous one.*

"I don't want to lose you," she said. "I don't want to go anywhere else. I like it here."

I pulled away and got on my knees to be eye level with her. "This is how things are here. Vampires and witches and wærewolves are always going to be in the mix. I can't promise it will be easy for you. It won't. But I can tell you that I truly want you to be a part of my life. I want you to have a regular childhood, but a lot of my life isn't regular."

She wiped her cheeks with her shirtsleeve. "I don't want a 'regular childhood.' Regular kids don't get to ride unicorns and play with dragons."

My heart swelled. She couldn't have said anything that encouraged me more. Grasping her arms reassuringly, I said, "Then you have to accept the good and the bad. You have to accept that living here means riding unicorns and playing with dragons and it means knowing that one vampire gets to drink from me and a certain wærewolf gets to kiss me." I squeezed her gently. "Can you accept that?"

She bit her lip, then nodded. I pulled her to me and said, "I love you, Beverley."

They were words I couldn't bring myself to say to Johnny, but they slipped out for her easily.

She threw her arms around me. "I love you, too."

It was like those words sealed all the cracks of concern between us. They gave her security. They gave me hope.

When we joined the others, Zhan was still awestruck and trying to make friends with Zoltan, who slithered away every time she tried to touch him. His constant aversion wore her down until she looked hurt.

"He's playing with you," Mountain told her. "Turn your back like you're sulking, and he'll sneak up on you.

When you spin around, see if you can avoid him until he pretends to sulk."

She did as he instructed and for the next several minutes the two of them played this variation of Keep-away. It was amazing. Zhan was nimble as a ninja, flipping and somersaulting through the barn. Watching the two of them was like watching an acrobatic stage show. When finally Zhan stopped, breathless but delighted, Zoltan coiled around her and let her pet him.

The rest of us applauded.

"He's incredible," she said.

"Indeed," Mountain said. There was a sparkle in his eyes I hadn't seen before. *He's sweet on Zhan!*

When Geoff finished with the dragons we proceeded to the phoenix coop. Their staccato chirps made it clear that they did not like being disturbed after sundown, but Mountain pulled a box of Hot Tamales from his pocket and gave each of the fire birds a piece of the zesty candy.

"Is that what I think it is?" Geoff asked.

"I dropped some earlier accidentally," Mountain said, his cheeks flushing. "They went into a feeding frenzy."

It didn't take long for the vet to finish up and we moved on to the unicorn and griffon barn. I peered across the night-shrouded field toward the grove. I couldn't detect Thunderbird if he was there, but he would have been well camouflaged.

A sense of urgency filled me, an eagerness to get to him, but we needed to let Beverley see the unicorns first. She'd earned her grade and had been very patient. I could be, too.

When the barn doors rolled open, every pristine white

unicorn head rose up. Some quiet nickering greeted Mountain. A young colt backed out of his stall in the middle and trotted the short distance toward us. "Hey, Errol." Mountain scratched under the colt's chin.

"Can I pet him?" Beverley asked.

"Ask him," Mountain said.

Beverley moved one cautious step closer. "May I pet you, Errol?"

Errol backed up two steps. I thought he was declining, but then he ceremoniously bent one foreleg under and bowed down until the tip of his horn touched the ground at Beverley's feet.

Wide-eyed, she whispered to Mountain, "That's a yes, right?"

He was as surprised by this gesture as the rest of us. To me, he said, "I think that's an invitation."

With the unicorn making his dramatic display, I couldn't possibly have said no. I nodded. Errol raised up. Mountain slid his hands under Beverley's arms and lifted her, placing her gently on the unicorn's back. Errol moved away, slowly. With high parading steps he walked toward the rear of the barn where the griffons had made nests out of hay. The colt brought her back, and took her toward the griffons again.

She was, of course, delighted. "He's so beautiful, Seph! Can I tie purple ribbons in his mane and tail?"

With lifted brows, I redirected her question to Mountain, who said, "If Errol doesn't protest, sure."

Assured that Mountain and Geoff had everything under control, I announced, "I'm going to try to bring Thunderbird here, so you'll have the light."

"I'll come with you," Zhan said. I opened my mouth to object, but she cut me off by adding, "Menessos assigned me to make sure you're safe, so you won't be going out in the dark alone. I promise to stay back once we get near him."

It was proof that the sentinels were getting to know me. Zhan hadn't even pulled her gun when we left the house. "C'mon."

We tromped across the field toward the grove, pushing aside cornstalks to take a direct path. The moon was a crescent hidden behind clouds full of cold rain waiting to burst open. Half the distance in, my vision had adjusted.

"Now will you tell me how you happened to steal these phenomenal creatures?" Zhan asked.

"The fey had control collars on them. The only way to stop them was to remove the collars. They're quite dangerous when forced to be, so it wasn't easy. It was like the reverse of mice trying to bell a cat. Once freed from the collars, though, they stopped fighting against us and actively helped us as if they were eager to be away from the fairies."

"Eager to be home." Zhan's steps slowed, then stopped, and she emitted a light sigh. It wasn't the long, breathy, "wow" kind of sigh. It was the brisk, irritated-with-myself kind.

Though I had pressed on a few more steps, I waited for her and spoke through the stalks. "What is it, Zhan?"

She shook her head as if clearing her thoughts and moved forward. "It's just so extraordinary."

That, I could tell, wasn't the whole truth, but she didn't have to share more.

A dozen yards later, we left the cornfield and emerged onto the grassy edge of the grove. I shook the bucket. "Thunderbird," I called. "Hungry, boy?"

Nothing. Not even nest-bound birds or squirrels awakened by my voice deigned to answer. After trying a few more times, my patience was ended. Minding my footing, I entered the grove and watched for movement amid the trees. I called his name again.

Maybe he'd gone flying. There weren't any injuries to his wings.

I walked around the more open part of the inner grove, searching for the other bucket, thinking to fill it from this one.

When I found it, it was still full.

"Zhan! Help me find him!"

I dropped the metal mixing bowl and launched into a frantic search. As I pushed through the branches, my arms got scraped and I stopped.

He didn't come this way. Where would he fit?

I scrutinized the dark . . . and found his path. Following a trail of broken branches, straining to see, I neared the far side of the grove and tripped over Thunderbird's leg.

I plopped down, twisting to keep from landing on him. Jumping up, I called out, "Here!"

Thunderbird hadn't made a sound. On my knees, my hands groped all over him. He felt cold and he didn't respond. *Don't be dead.* Pressing on his rib cage, I held my breath trying to detect his breathing or a pulse.

There! Weak, but beating.

Zhan appeared from the grove a few yards away. "Get Mountain and the doc," I called.

It seemed like forever, but the two men arrived. Mountain tried to lift Thunderbird but couldn't. "Please, Mountain, I've seen you carry a couch!"

"Sorry, Seph. Couches aren't limp. They don't have wings and paws and claws flopping this way and that putting me off balance."

"We can't leave him here!"

"I could drag him," Mountain suggested.

In the end, we lifted his front half, pushed a half-rolled tarp under him, then lifted the back half and spread out the length of the tarp. We threaded rope through the tarp grommets and tied it to the backhoe and pulled him to the barn. Mountain dragged the tarp inside.

The griffons left their nests and watched as Dr. Lincoln tended Thunderbird's damaged eye socket, then inspected the claw. The three front talons had been seared off at the same point. Fax Torris's beam must have burned them away. Geoff bandaged those, readied a syringe. "This will fight infection," he said, "but I have no idea what dosage is appropriate for a griffon. I'm calculating it according to weight, and I'm guessing at his weight, so . . ." He drew a long breath. "Don't be mad at me if Thunderbird doesn't make it."

"I trust your best guess, Geoff."

He administered the shot, then stood. "Keeping him warm now will help. Can we get him into one of those nests?"

"We can try."

Mountain hauled the tarp into the sawdust that padded the rear of the barn, and got him near an empty nest, then he put his arms around Thunderbird's rib cage behind his wings. "When I lift, you yank the tarp away, okay?" When that was done, the griffons crowded around. Mountain tried to shoo them away. "I'm trying to get him into a nest," he told them. A griffon pushed in between him and Thunderbird and continued to push Mountain until he was off the sawdust.

Two eagle-and-lion griffons moved in on either side of Thunderbird, lying with their bodies against his, and they covered him with their wings. Another hawk-and-cheetah griffon moved in behind them, and the smallest one wriggled under Thunderbird's neck until his head was cradled upon the other's shoulders. The rest of them resumed their nests.

"I've never seen the like," Geoff murmured.

My satellite phone rang. It was Menessos. "Hello."

"Ah, the sound of your voice warms my heart." He paused. "Or maybe that's just my dinner going to my head."

I walked away from the others to a more private spot. "How's Eva?"

"Drained."

His blasé answer evoked my sarcasm. "Well, at least your hunger's satisfied."

"Ah, my sustenance is the nightly charity of my good people. But finding satisfaction, Persephone, is not so simple as the insertion of my fangs into flesh. That requires the insertion of another part of me into warm and eager flesh."

"Doesn't Eva have warm and eager flesh?"

"Of course. But the sweet thrill wanes somewhat when eagerness is so easily elicited. The succulent bliss of the moment is lost."

Johnny could've written a whole song around that one sentence, so I committed it to memory. However, I was in no mood tonight to cater to Menessos's need for bliss. I selected my next words carefully. "So what's the purpose of your call?"

"Goliath had some news."

"Oh?"

"He's uncovered clues concerning Heldridge."

Heldridge was the vampire who'd coerced a performer at the Erus Veneficus ceremony to kill Menessos as part of his act. I'd been on Menessos's lap at the time, so initially we weren't certain which of us had been the target. "And?"

"It seems the traitor was seen in Pittsburgh but has moved on to Harrisburg."

"Goliath's closing in on him?"

"Yes. The word is out that Heldridge has acted traitorously against his Regional Lord, so he has no access to funds, the Vampire Executive International Network has placed a bounty on him, and he will have trouble finding anyone who will speak to him and not betray him. But Heldridge, too, seems to be closing in on his goal. The only question is whether he'll be able to find appropriate lodging for his days as he makes his way to Washington, D.C."

"Why would a vampire try to reach D.C.?"

"Our North American headquarters are there."

So instead of hiding in shadows and disappearing

completely, Heldridge was racing to get to the topmost blood drinkers? "Is he seeking some kind of political sanctuary?"

"I believe it more likely that he has information."

"Valuable enough to save himself?"

"Perhaps. It depends on how he pitches it. And whether or not it can be proven."

"What does he know?"

"What the fairies wanted him to know."

That Menessos was alive. Or had been. Thanks to me, he was now truly one of the undead. "Is that relevant now?"

"As I said, the usefulness of it depends on whether or not he can prove it."

"Can he prove it?"

"Persephone, your own words could be used against you."

"*My* words?"

"You are very strong, but if you became his hostage—"

"Hostage? You just said he was in Harrisburg and heading for D.C."

"I will not underestimate him. He is clever. And, should he capture you . . . I know his methods. I believe he could make you talk."

CHAPTER SEVENTEEN

Wednesday morning arrived with a cold, cold rain. With Menessos's message I hadn't slept much and was still awake when Johnny came in late. Now, he was sleeping in. The recent injury, the fighting and transforming left him drained, and the energy drinks had only delayed the inevitable crash. When Nana took Beverley to the bus stop, I checked on Thunderbird with Maxine at my heels, gun in her hand. Menessos had told her of his concerns and now she was on alert. The griffon remained asleep and surrounded by warm friends.

Then I focused on my column, which was due today. Maxine paced.

Despite the noise of Beholders working on Nana's room addition, I polished up the column and emailed it to my editor, Jimmy Martin. Not long after I hit the send button, though, Mountain informed me that they were ready to break through the exterior wall and install Nana's bedroom door. I opted to completely relocate my computer instead of merely covering it against the dust they were about to stir up.

By eleven o'clock, everything that could be moved was

out of the dining room. Dust barriers were put up to minimize the effect throughout the house. Then the *real* noise
began. Nana retreated to her room upstairs with Ares and
cranked up a country music station on her clock radio.

Having someone tearing a giant hole in your house in
November, I found, was cause for pacing. Which had me
and Maxine at cross purposes.

Maxine suggested, "Aren't there any errands you can
run?"

By "you," she obviously meant "we." "Groceries."

"Great idea. You'll need help with bags?"

"Of course."

We left Zhan in charge and fled, grateful to be away
from the cacophony. The Audi was a smooth ride, even on
the rolling country hills. Max drove as if the road was her
personal course to test the vehicle's maneuverability. On
the upside, it took only twenty minutes to get to town.
I'd been quiet during the ride, clenching the handle on
the door, but she was now obeying the speed limit and I
loosed my grip and found my voice. "So, Maxine, how did
you come to be an Offerling to Menessos?"

"I've always been a risk taker, craving excitement,
y'know?"

After that drive, yeah, I believe her.

"I never had the typical girl goals," she said, a tinge of
sadness in her voice.

"Do you feel differently now?"

"No . . . it's just . . . my mom got a tomboy when
she wanted a princess. Growing up in Connecticut, she
wanted me to be in beauty pageants. She couldn't understand why I wanted to rock climb, why I wanted to

know how to pilot a helicopter or shoot guns." Maxine drove into the grocery parking lot. "She didn't understand how I could *like* getting dirty. She thought I was being defiant."

"Were you?"

"Not of her. Of her illness. My mother had multiple sclerosis."

"Oh," I said.

"My teen years were spent watching her get weaker, get older, frailer. As the illness gripped her more and more, she wanted to think I'd have the happily-ever-after kind of life, even though she wouldn't be around." Maxine parked in a space at the back of the lot where there were few other cars. "In the end, she was bedridden. She couldn't even move." She plucked the keys from the ignition and got out.

I grabbed my purse.

Over the car's roof Maxine continued. "I wanted to *live.* To feel my heart pound every day and never fear the risk so much that I missed out on a thrill. Before she died, she told me, 'Run, Max. Climb and get dirty. Just don't stop moving.' I did. After she died, I did *more.* I pushed the limits. I pushed for her as much as I pushed for me."

We started across the parking lot. I asked, "So she did understand."

"Yeah." Maxine nodded. "If I have to die, it'll be quick. No long years of fading."

The "if" in there made me understand why she was with a vampire. "So how'd you end up with Menessos?"

"There are services, not unlike eHarmony, that try to

match people up with vampires. It's a complicated process, secretive and labyrinthine to the point that many times I thought I was being fleeced. Four months later, I met Goliath. Six weeks after that, I met Menessos."

"Were you scared?"

"Hell yes. But I loved it. Better than any roller coaster."

"Oh."

"Being an Offerling provides the excitement I crave, and the pair of marks Menessos placed on me means I won't be fading anytime soon."

"So you want to be a vampire?"

"To be ageless and never die? Absolutely. Where do I sign?"

We stopped at the end of the parking row as a white delivery van rushed by, apparently in a hurry. When it stopped nearly in front of us the driver opened his door and we angled our steps to go around the back of it toward the grocery entrance.

As we cleared the back, the rear doors swung wildly open, nearly hitting us. Maxine lurched around the door and snapped, "Hey, assho—"

I heard a *thunk* and Maxine dropped to the ground.

Even as I thought to bend over her and help her up I realized there was a hole in her forehead. A circle of blood was spreading on the pavement like a wine-red nimbus around her head. *She's never getting up.*

I heard another sound, like the *whack* of a baseball bat meeting a fastball. My world went black.

• • •

Consciousness returned in brief snippets, each a little longer than the last. I wanted to hold on to it—*where am I?*—but it kept escaping and that made me angry. Or maybe it was the dull ache that made me angry. Or the fact that I was nauseated and there was a soppy gag in my mouth and I wasn't sure how to throw up around it.

I was also blindfolded. That part I was almost grateful for. It felt like the backs of my eyes had been stung by bees and I was certain that any light would have intensified my headache. The downside was having no idea where I was, except that there was cold cement under me. I'd been hog-tied—my hands and feet bound behind me—and now lay on my side. Every movement shot splinters of pain through my head so I didn't try very hard to inspect further. I did try very hard to just breathe and listen. Then the shivering set in. Too bad the cold didn't help the nausea.

Voices echoed to me as if from a tunnel, muffled enough that even with my amplified hearing I made out only a word here and there. *Maybe I'm at the bottom of the well. Where's Lassie when I need a big collie rescuer?*

As the voices continued, I realized they were arguing. Something about that anger got through the punch-drunk fuzz inside my head. It swept away the confusion and reality hit home: *I've been kidnapped and Maxine's dead. They shot her in the head!*

Menessos's warning about Heldridge replayed in my memory.

The shouting continued and I strained to hear, needing yet fearing to have confirmation that Heldridge had me.

The prospect of being tortured didn't help my stomach settle. Was I so weak and scared that I would tell everything immediately to avoid Heldridge's methods?

Then I caught the word "Bindspoken."

That left me wondering if maybe it wasn't Heldridge but the witches who had me. Xerxadrea had played up to the high priestesses of her *lucusi* the notion that Menessos was a serious threat when she officially ousted me from the group. Because I'd become his Erus Veneficus, WEC certainly wasn't happy with me. Killing one of Menessos's Offerings wouldn't have been their style, however, with "Harm none" being their motto and all.

Besides, Xerxadrea's claims were all for show.

Not that Vilna-Daluca was aware of it. And now that Xerxadrea was dead, Vilna blamed me. Problem was, Vilna wasn't exactly wrong. But who else would have cause to throw the word "Bindspoken" into an argument?

The shouting voices seemed to be male. Men could be witches, but there weren't that many of them.

Maybe Heldridge was trying to use me to barter the witches into protecting him.

"She is a threat!" another voice said clearly.

Oh hell. Maybe it was some rogue parents who'd seen me on the news, though I didn't think any of them were the type to commit or commission a murder.

My brain felt muddy inside.

Think! It didn't matter who had me, I had to get away. *I can't fail. Beverley will be devastated.*

Despite the pain of moving, I stretched my head so I could scrape the blindfold up, little by little. Once it was off, it was obvious how futile the effort had been.

Wherever I was, it was completely dark except for a sliver of dim light about ten feet away from me.

After long minutes of straining at the bindings, I had to admit my struggles were only giving me friction burns. Not very Lustrata-ish. Of course the protrepticus, my satellite phone, and my purse had all been taken from me. They'd even removed my necklace with Beau's charm. So I pondered what magic could get me out of this. If I called to a ley line, anyone but mundane humans would sense it. Whoever had me could probably get in here quick and dole out another whack to the head before any sorcery could be completed.

Footsteps approached beyond the door. Panic seized me. *I don't have a plan yet!*

The door opened and I learned who had kidnapped me.

By the shape of the shadow, I recognized Gregor. He had a long blade in his grip. He advanced and crouched over me. I held my breath. *Poor Beverley. Will she ever understand how much—*

He sliced through a rope behind me and the length uncoiled from my ankles. My wrists were apparently a separate binding and remained taut. He yanked me up to stand, not at all good for my aching head, and strong-armed me to the door. There, he jerked the gag from my mouth and let the drool-saturated fabric slap against my neck.

"Stir the slightest energy, witch, and I'll twist that pretty head of yours until it pops off." He pushed me through the doorway into another nearly dark room.

I stumbled and, because each step equaled a thudding kick in the cranium, it was only by dumb luck that I managed to keep my feet under me. When steady enough to stand upright without fearing my balance was compromised, my smart-ass mouth opened. "Hey, asshole, I had nothing against you guys until someone killed Maxine and kidnapped me."

Gregor crossed his Mr. Olympia–size arms and gave me a smugly satisfied expression. I was like a toothpick next to him, and with me being bound and having that goose egg trying to hatch on the back of my head, he did have the advantage . . . unless I wanted to call to a ley line and half-form every wære in the area, which I didn't. *But I am debating how far I'd have to be pushed to willingly cross that line.*

"This is the witch?"

The voice came from behind me. Slowly, I turned. We were surrounded by tarnished steel walls. At the corners where the metal panels had been secured in place were circles of rust with trails of the corrosion leaking downward. Pipes snaked across the ceiling.

Then I saw the man wearing a crown and sitting on a throne of ebony.

The Rege.

The throne seemed to be made from cylinders of wood, tall ones forming the two rear posts, shorter ones supporting the arms of the seat. The dark wood was decorated with various skulls, horns, and tusks. It was like four phallic symbols with hunting trophies nailed together to create a royal, manly-man chair. If it had a voice, it would have bellowed, "Behold! Virility incarnate!"

The phallic symbolism was continued in the black waist-high pilasters of marble on either side of him, topped with green pillar candles. They were the only source of light in the tomblike room, creating an intimate dimness while casting an eerie glow upon the skulls.

All in all, this was where I'd have expected the leader of the wærewolves to lounge. Though I'd have thought he'd look different.

Thick silver-gray hair hung from under his emerald-studded crown and brushed his shoulders. It was utterly Ricardo Montalban from *Star Trek II: The Wrath of Khan* and I almost laughed—but choked on it when I realized he was wearing a long black robe that resembled a cassock. And the crown on his head was more of a mitre than something a king would wear. This dude was *not* playing "Warrior King," he was into "Insane Holy Man Ruler."

Johnny had pegged it. *Pope-Czarzilla.*

Underneath the unbuttoned robe was a collarless black silk shirt with a slitted neck embellished with bright green embroidery. I couldn't tell anything about his pants but he was wearing riding boots—one ankle was propped upon the other knee. The pose conveyed contentedness.

His eyes were chalkboard green and he stroked his square, shaven chin slowly as he assessed me. When his hand lowered to the armrest, he lovingly fondled the skull at its end. He wore wide rings on nearly every finger.

All the iconic imagery in his carefully chosen costume was unnecessary. One look in those callous eyes, pitiless enough to match the cruel, bent line of his mouth, and I knew this was a man who had seen extreme horrors, enjoyed the show, and bought the entire season on DVD.

It made me want to be invisible.

"Do you know who I am?" His accented tone was thick

with inflections of authority and his deep voice scratched in a way that conveyed age as much as his silver hair did.

"The Rege," I answered.

"The Omori think you are a threat, little witch." He shifted his weight on the chair, leaning slightly forward. "Are you?"

The words I'd just spouted at Gregor in my aching and anger echoed through my mind. "You're certainly giving me reasons to think I ought to be." It wasn't backing down; it wasn't admitting anything directly, either.

He stood and advanced on me, each step both graceful and threatening. Not quite six feet tall, he had probably been handsome until something ugly inside reached maximum levels and seeped out, eroding him until only an expression of scorn remained. His powerful build matched the Omori leader's, as if Gregor was the latest version, new and improved, now ten percent bigger. *Romania must have gotten rid of all the grocery stores and replaced them with GNCs.*

Glowering down at me coldly, the Rege let the moment linger, as if waiting for me to lose the stare down and collapse at his feet in fear and submission. But his furrows and lines were not daunting. Johnny's Wedjat tattoos had once scared me more than this guy's best glare. Of course, I'd never been tied up back then.

His arm swung up, ready to backhand me.

Resolved not to reward him with evidence of how frightened I truly was, I didn't react—not to hold my breath, not to tense against the strike, and certainly not to cower before this man. If he hit me, though, I was going to try my best to throw up on him.

"You are brave," he whispered. His breath smelled like burnt earth. His arm lowered slowly. "Brave enough to try defiance." He didn't strike me, but instead put his thumb under my chin and applied pressure to the soft triangle of flesh where there was no bone.

I jerked away; it forced me to take a step back.

With a sardonic smile and a down-his-nose glare, he turned back to his macho throne, satisfied I had given ground.

He'd received the indication of submission he wanted from me, but my mouth didn't always know when to stay shut. "I'd prefer to be known as brave enough not to back down when I've been wronged."

He spun back. "It was the Omori that wronged you, killed your friend." He flicked his fingers dismissively at me as if that would wipe the blame from my eyes. "They are within their rights to act preemptively, though I gave no such order."

Leaders shouldn't pass the buck. "You fear me."

He laughed. "You flatter yourself."

"Then why are my hands still bound?"

In a flash he gripped my arm so hard it seemed he meant to break it. With a jerk he compromised my balance and put me on my knees. Aftershocks of pain rippled through my head. My vision blurred for a moment.

That's worrisome.

The Rege bent and gripped the lower half of my face, lifting my head roughly. "You are bound, little witch, because," his tone dropped to a gravelly lower register as he finished, "I like it that way."

I tried unsuccessfully to jerk away again but I had no leverage. He continued laughing at me. On my third attempt, he got fed up and shoved me hard enough to throw me onto my side.

Keeping my head from cracking on the floor was a small victory. It cost me a strain in a neck muscle and a new wave of nausea. "I get it now," I snapped, struggling to tell up from down. "You bind what you fear in order to control it. And your true weakness is your inability to admit it."

With the toe of his boot, he rolled me onto my back and straddled me, glowering down at me for a long moment. I considered shoving my foot in his groin, but wasn't certain my blurry aim would be true. He lowered himself to his knees and sat on my stomach. Aside from recognizing this as similar to the dominance tactics I read about in Ares's puppy book, I could barely breathe and my arms felt as if they were being smashed. One of my wrists would break if he didn't get up soon. *C'mon stomach. Help me go all Linda Blair on him.*

"I have heard you possess the skill to perform a spell that can render a wære the keeper of his man-mind, even when in wolf form. And that, if true, could make you valuable. But tempt me, and you will discover what happens when I decide someone is worthless." His fingers slithered forward to seize my neck and give a little squeeze as if to hint at how easy it would be to kill me. Then his nails scratched over my collarbone and jerked the neck of my shirt, snapping threads in the seams at the back. He licked his lips lecherously.

I sneered.

He stood, shrugged out of his long coat, and took a step away. He placed it, his mitre, and shirt on the seat of his throne. The Rege may have been old enough to have lost all the color from his hair, but he had maintained his muscle tone. He was actually ripped.

With a wicked smile, he said to Gregor, "Leave us."

CHAPTER EIGHTEEN

I rolled, kicked, twisted, and had my feet under me in a flash, backing away.

The Rege chuckled; it was punctuated by the dull sound of Gregor shutting the door.

"I will teach you to be docile, witch."

I put my back to the steel of the insulated wall. Earlier I hadn't wanted him to know how truly frightened I was, but now I needed him to think I was helpless, so my brave mask fell away and panic crept into my features.

He bought it gleefully.

When he advanced, I kicked up—stopping him with one heel planted firmly on his chest. The steel behind me bowed as he leaned into it. I thrust my foot against his breastbone even as my other foot kicked up. The steel made a warping sound as it gave under the pressure and rust rained down. The toe of my hiking boot caught him on his square chin and knocked his head back.

It was a struggle to get my feet back under me—my back scrubbed down the tarnished and corroded steel wall as I plummeted a few inches. I barely kept my ass off the floor.

My actions had surprised the Rege enough to force him back a few steps. He recovered instantly.

Fighting for balance, I spun away. The wall flapped open, broken through on one side, revealing studs and a block wall. I ran from him. It wasn't as easy to do as it should have been; my vision blurred and refocused just in time for me to stop short in front of the throne and turn to keep him in sight.

He stayed on the far wall, watching me. Maybe his age had slowed him some, but he was physically in such good shape that it was doubtful. I had the feeling that the Rege would gladly allow me to tire myself out.

Reaching out mentally, sweeping metaphysical arms back and forth as if signaling to a landing airplane, I searched for nearby energies to stir. Not big energies like a ley line—though I was getting ever closer to crossing that destructive line. For now, I still wasn't willing to risk every wære in the vicinity. I could target ley energy just on the Rege, but others nearby would sense it and come to his aid. I'd be forced to defend myself even more aggressively, and I didn't want to do that. Calling just enough energy to make a point to him, and calling it from nearby to avoid alerting the others, was my best option.

But the steel and cement left me wanting.

The Rege pushed from the wall, slowly, cautiously closing in just as I found latent energy in the stones of his mitre: they weren't emeralds at all, but green tourmalines. Knowing I could use this man's status symbol to help me keep him at bay, I hid my smile and sank down on his throne, projecting defeat while my fingers stretched toward the mitre.

Green tourmalines are supposed to increase the wearer's self-confidence and aid communication by creating openness and patience, as well as sincerity toward others. But not these tourmalines. These had been tainted by him. They had become overconfident and boastful. Oppressive. *Even better.* Drawing that energy around me, that ostentatious disdain prickled over my aura like a porcupine's quills.

The Rege halted six feet from me, gauging me and surely deciding how to proceed.

"Touch me, and what happens to you is your own fault."

His hostile frown remained as he said, "And the black widow witch spun her delicate web." He laughed. "The risk is minimal; I secured my Regency by proving resistant to magic." He inched forward, hand stroking downward on my aura.

I knew he would now stroke upward and feel the quills. I put every ounce of my will and belief into meeting his merciless eyes. "What you want to achieve will not be accomplished this way."

A single barb, primed to convince him I was more dangerous than he had assumed, pricked his finger. His features slackened momentarily, then he blinked, shook his head, shifted his weight back.

I stood and willed every barb to rise defensively.

His scornful smile resumed its place on his face. "I assure you, I have accomplished many things this way."

"You don't even know who *I* am." The edge of conviction in my voice was sharp. It stalled his steps again.

He held his position on the verge of my aura's circumference. "It matters not."

Though he was aiming for snide, I heard a note of doubt in his tone. It was the signal for me to laugh at him and try to reinforce the idea that the advantage here was mine, and he just hadn't seen it yet.

"If you're so proud of who you are, then, tell me."

Borrowing lines from Johnny and others, I said, "I am a pure-blood witch, a caster of spells, an element master, and ringer of bells." Feeling an empowering swell of energy swirling inside me like raging rapids—and hoping it wasn't just some bad side-effect of brain trauma beyond a concussion—I advanced on the Rege. "I am the witch of old," I said as my aural quills sank into him, "delivering justice and voicing truths untold. I've been called the moonchild of ruin . . . don't make me ruin you."

As I spoke, his eyes glazed over. His jaw slackened.

It was the same reaction I'd witnessed in the policeman at the Botanical Gardens when Menessos had mesmerized him. I wasn't certain it was even possible that I had impressed my will upon him, but if it was . . . "You're finished here. Leave. Now."

The Rege walked away.

I held my breath, waiting for him to return and attack, to announce that he'd played me for a fool. When the door shut behind him, the reality of what I'd done hit home and left me stunned.

But I couldn't be too impressed with myself. After he had gone I realized I should have said: "Untie me and *then* leave."

So. Getting free of the ropes was my new goal, but I took a moment to collect the icky-feeling energy of those tourmalines from my aura and release it from the stones on his mitre.

The candles could have burned through the rope, but before I gave myself third-degree freedom burns, I considered other options. I discovered that the teeth on one of the skulls adorning the throne were serrated and sharp enough that I was able to saw through the rope at my wrists and get free in about ten minutes. Though I've seen TV protagonists free themselves similarly, none of them ever acted like their triceps ached with effort afterward. Just then, lifting a glass of water—and I badly wanted something to drink—would have proved painful.

Now that I was free, I had to choose my next move. Redoing what I'd just done to the Rege was questionable, and unlikely en masse, so staying here waiting until *more* wæres showed up wasn't an option. That meant it was up to me to quickly get my ass out of here.

There were two doors to the room. One led to where I had been when I woke; the other was used by Gregor and the Rege as an exit. A quick inspection with one of the candles established that the former led to an empty chamber without any other doors. The floors of both rooms were cement and had drains in the floor.

I glanced up at the old pipes winding their way across the ceiling, studied the walls. The place had me wondering if I was up to date on my tetanus shots. The lack of windows made me think this place was underground.

Not good.

I knew which way to go, but I couldn't guess what to expect once I passed through the door.

Making an assessment of what was available, my options were few. I considered the candles, rope, marble pillars, and throne. Since pointy things usually made good weapons, I tested the horns on the throne to see if any could be detached.

Just as I mentally whined about the ache in my arms, one of the horns broke off. And I do mean *broke*. The base of it stuck jaggedly up from the back of the throne quite obviously.

Great. Now the Rege has another reason to be pissed at me.

What I now held was dark and grooved, more of an antler or a prong than a horn. It was as long as my forearm and thicker than was comfortable to grip, but this was no time to be choosy. It was unquestionably pointy enough to be dangerous and that was sufficient. With the rope coiled around my shoulder—because if they discovered I had escaped, they would think I was still bound and that might give me an advantage if needed—I hurried toward the door.

Rushing made my footfalls harder and faster, which brought a resurgence of nausea. I slowed down and moved carefully. The door's strange push handle gave freely. *Hooray, he didn't lock me in.* I opened it with such patience I impressed myself. But the sneakiness wasn't necessary. Beyond was a block hallway, industrial wide, dirty and lit by bare, dim bulbs. To my right was a dead-end; I had to go left.

Cautiously, and with a white-knuckled grip on the antler, I walked down the hall. My ears burned, straining for a sound.

This place felt like it was underground, so I wanted

to go up. Up meant out and away. My brain whispered about the underworld and how the goddess Persephone was escorted back to the world by Hecate and Hermes. But that same brain seemed to be throbbing as relentlessly as a metronome keeping time.

As the hallway ended on a wide space, I saw no one, heard nothing. After sniffing and smelling nothing but the dusty cement, it was easy to decide to hit the stairs. *Up and out.* Chanting that to myself kept the underworld whispers at bay.

I climbed one level, peeked into a similar open space, and stepped out to head up the next level. Here, the silence finally ended.

That didn't surprise me. Of course there would be people guarding the exit. As I neared, however, the sounds weren't what I expected. They weren't the noises of guards playing cards or watching sports. They weren't human sounds at all.

I inched around the final turn and slinked along the wall at a snail's pace. What I could see was a re-creation of the previous floors. With my cheek against the cold concrete blocks, I peeked out into the open area. Empty.

It seemed every floor had the same layout, and the noise was coming from down a hallway not unlike where I'd been kept. Wary, I eased into the open area and edged onward, only to find there was no stairwell cutting back in. If there was a way out from here, it was down that hall. Past the noise.

I wiped my sweaty palms on my thighs, then resettled my grip on the antler and moved into the hall. From my new position I could tell the doors were different. The sound was coming from within the rooms ahead; the doors might be open or altogether absent.

Nearer, the smell of barn straw filled my nostrils. The dried grass rustled as something inside moved. It was followed by the sound of brusque sniffing. *Definitely animal. If there are animals of some kind in there, they would be out roaming if not confined.*

That reasoning steeled my nerves enough to proceed. I could see the doors were recessed just a little, and the first one was barred. A relieved sigh deflated my lungs; glad to know whatever they had in there wasn't coming out.

I passed without seeing anything inside but cement and straw in the first caged room. If there had been steel on the walls here, it had been removed. The second cage was on the opposite side. There was more of the same movement and sniffing sounds, followed by a whine. I could see the tip of a furred tail, but that didn't tell me much.

The third room seemed empty. No shifting straw to reveal movement, no sniffing.

Just as I passed, something launched itself against the door, paw swiping out. I threw myself to the hallway floor, but even so, I felt one of the claws catch on my jeans pocket and tear it.

Landing on my forearms with a thud, heels kicked up, I saw stars again. The antler skittered away.

Lying there until the dizziness faded would have been my preference, but something was snarling a few feet away and my instincts didn't allow me that luxury. I rolled to my side and the rope slithered away from my shoulder. Keeping my knees bent so my feet were clear of the still-grabbing paw was the priority.

The claw that had reached for me was scrabbling over the floor between us. But it wasn't like any claw I'd ever seen before. There was only one actual claw . . . the rest of it was—

—a human hand.

My mind couldn't make sense of what I was seeing at first. I chalked it up to the concussion, but even in hindsight, I don't think I could have comprehended it any faster if I'd been clear-headed and fully caffeinated.

It was a human arm, stretching through the bars, an arm lightly covered in fine gray hair like the downy feathers on a chick. The fingers were shortened, the palm lengthened, and the index had a single dark claw on it instead of a fingernail. At the shoulder, the arm attached to a deformed body, one with a doglike rib cage, deep rather than wide. The fur here was darker, thicker. The creature had human buttocks, human thighs, but at the knee the limb became the lower leg of a wolf.

Again my eyes scoured the grotesque, misshapen body. My brain screamed at me, *Don't look!* But I couldn't help it. My rebellious gaze locked on its face. The all too-human head had fangs—more teeth than any person should have in their mouth. There was no snout, just a human jawline and human nose turned dark at the tip. The ears were elongated. The eyes, one wolf-gold, and one human-blue, slammed home the realization of what I was seeing.

This was a wærewolf. One exposed to the energies a witch can stir, the insufficient energy that leaves them half-formed.

This man, this thing, snarled at me and saliva dripped

from its horrible maw. There was nothing even remotely human in the eyes that were locked onto me. They were feral. They were hungry. And they saw meat.

He lifted his head at an angle no human neck would be able to match, and howled. But that howl wasn't wolfish. It was the scream of a man being tortured.

"Admiring the handiwork of your peers, witch?"

Snapping my head around toward the voice was a mistake. My head complained mightily about it even as my limbs prepared to get my feet under me and flee. But Gregor didn't come after me. He simply crossed his bodybuilder arms and fixed me with his usual scowl.

This time, the nausea wouldn't be denied. I threw up. When the nasty-tasting nothingness on my stomach was gone, I dry heaved for several minutes.

CHAPTER NINETEEN

About an hour later, after an elevator ride down to a familiar parking area beneath, I realized that I'd been brought to the den. Maybe without a concussion I might have realized sooner, but the upper floors, which had no windows, were nothing like the lower area, and the elevator had steel secondary doors, not just a wooden gate.

They had bound my hands again, this time in front of me, but there was so much of the prickly rope wrapped around them that it was, truly, overkill—like eight pounds of anchor line. If my arms didn't ache, I could have started building up my biceps. Enough reps with this load and I could give Gregor some competition.

A black limo was waiting. Gregor, three Omori, the Rege, and I all climbed in. Omori thugs sat on either side of and across from me. Gregor opened a brown paper grocery bag and set it on the floor space before my feet. "In case you vomit again," he said mockingly. "Do not miss."

Other than that, no one spoke. We were subjected to some classical music that was much too upbeat for the state of my head. Watching out the windows made my stomach very unhappy, so I focused on the floor and the beat of the throbbing inside my head. But I wanted to know where they were taking me, too. I recognized Carnegie Avenue and East Seventy-ninth Street. We took a right on Superior, then a left on Martin Luther King Jr. Drive.

Are we going to the Cultural Gardens? I lowered my eyes again as my stomach shuddered.

Nana and I had picnicked here a few times in my childhood. She liked, predictably, the Greek Garden with its Doric columns framing the entrance to a reflecting pool. *Nana and I ought to bring Beverley here next summer and picnic. If I make it out of this, that is.*

My stomach squeezed; I fought against it. Back at the den I had asked for a drink of water and Gregor had declined, saying I would only "make a mess" if he did. He was right. I leaned over the paper bag just in case.

The Omori thugs beside me inched away.

The limo zipped past the Greek Garden area, pulling over to the left just before the stone bridge that supported St. Clair Avenue. The arched stonework in the bridge was gorgeous, reminding me of the entrance to the Arcade that Mountain had shown me. There was no time for daydreaming, however. The men unloaded and I was expected to stay with them. *Damn it. I want a bottle of water and a nap.*

I thought the wealth of rope around my wrists would be a red flag to drivers passing by, but one of the Omori thugs was wearing an overcoat. Gregor ordered him to remove it, then draped it over my arms as if I was merely holding my jacket as I strolled along.

I made sure to breathe my puke breath on him.

So, in the dying light of the day, we walked up to the life-size statue of a man in a long coat, seated comfortably, yet clearly deep in thought. The Rege seemed particularly glad to see it.

The bronze had taken on the green patina of age and local pigeons had added their artwork as well. The plaque told me it was George Enescu, the years of his birth and death, and that he was a composer. *A Romanian composer.*

Maybe the long cassocklike coats are a Romanian thing.

If this was just a little sightseeing trip around Cleveland to take in spots that offered some cultural homage to these foreign visitors, hooray. But there was no reason to take native-Ohioan me along for the ride. I was no tour guide.

So what is going on? "Are you guys all fans of Mr. Enescu's?"

"I am," the Rege said. "That was his *Romanian Rhapsodies* we were listening to."

Gregor's cell phone beeped. He gave it to the Rege.

"We're waiting," he said tersely. Pause. "Not coming? What do you mean not coming?" The displeasure in his voice was succinct. That someone could irk him that much made me smile. Then, whoever was on the other end said something in response that caused the Rege's attention to shoot to me. He stormed away, snarling whispers into the phone that I couldn't understand.

Smiling at Gregor like I'd just won the lottery, I asked, "Things not going according to plan?"

He said nothing, but simply gave me a fine example of what utter contempt looks like. If he'd been on our team, it would have been a plus in our column. We started

another stare down. The wounds Johnny gave him had
healed nicely.

"*We* have her, so get your ass down here and claim
her!" The Rege shut the phone so hard the sides clacked
together and he tossed it at Gregor with such aggrava-
tion he didn't realize his best pal wasn't paying attention.
Gregor took it in the face.

Shoved into the back of the limo, I climbed onto one of
the side seats. These guys were definitely not gentlemen.

The Rege sat inside with me. Gregor remained just beyond the car door.

"Who's coming to claim me?"

"Ah." He gave a snort of laughter. "A witch with so
many enemies she cannot tell whom to fear first. How
many lives have you befouled and besmirched?"

I scowled at him. Surely he understood that I could tap
the ley line and change all of them into the things I'd seen
in the upper floors of the den—

Even as I thought it I knew I could never do that to
a person on purpose. I felt the hardness fade from my
features.

"Who do you think would pay the most?"

Chin lifted proudly, I asked, "The Rege is an
extortionist?"

The Rege backhanded me with enough force to propel
me against the side seat. "Never. But I cannot refuse the
opportunity to add to the coffers."

My already-concussed head did not take that blow
well. I blacked out for I don't know how long. When I

woke, I lay there dazed and reeling for several minutes be-fore feeling recovered enough to sit up.

I wondered what time it was. The road through the Cultural Gardens wound through like a meandering stream at the bottom of a valley, and here the day's last light was blocked by the sloping heights of the garden. The tinted limo windows made it even darker. I hadn't detected Menessos waking, so this had to be dusk.

"I always get my way, witch. As you should recall. Or do you need another lesson?"

In answer, I scooted as far from him as I could and tried to rub at my now puffy jaw. The way they had me tied up, all I could do was scrape the rope over it. *I've been abused enough for one day.*

Considering his words, however, I had to infer that he believed he did rape me when I had invoked that power and influenced him. I'd said, "You're finished here." Maybe in his mesmerized mind, that implied the deed had been done.

Another car pulled in behind the limo. Because it was now the time period of civil twilight, this car had the headlamps on and they were the new Xenon kind. They made me squint even through the tinted rear windshield.

Then another car arrived behind that one, and another. I detected nearly a dozen dark figures coming toward the limo. The driver of the first car exited and joined those moving in.

I was ready to throw up again. *Where'd that bag go . . .*

Menessos awoke. After a moment of adjustment, the sense of completeness filled me, and took the edge off my pain. I abandoned the interior bag search. Peering out the rear window I saw the driver of the car with the offensive lights.

Johnny.

The local wæres formed a line to the side of the Audi Johnny had driven. The car gave them some cover from any prying eyes of passersby. Drivers wouldn't think much of cars stopped here, and the presence of a limo would likely offset the oddness of suited tough guys standing around in the garden.

Gregor opened the door and the Rege slid out with a grace not unlike Menessos's. He stepped forward and the door slammed before I could exit. Another guard came to stand at the door to the other side. I was reduced to watching out the window like a kid.

"Where is she?" Johnny demanded.

The Rege used his thumb to point at the limo. "Inside." He tilted his head, assessing Johnny. "Gregor documented his wounds. They were quite nasty."

Johnny held up his fists. "If you're after a matching set of your own, I've got 'em right here."

The Omori all growled and moved half-steps forward. "Never insult your Rege!" Gregor snarled.

The Rege stopped Gregor with a gesture.

"You're the Domn Lup?"

"I am."

"Prove it."

"Give me the witch first." There was an edge to Johnny's voice. I heard it even through the glass.

The Rege hadn't missed it, either. "Why?"

"Why not?"

He shrugged nonchalantly like a man who knew he

had the advantage. "Are you sure you want damaged goods?"

I hadn't expected he would play his hand so soon.

Johnny shifted his weight, tensing. "What did you do?"

The Rege spread his arms. "I *entertained* her."

I thought for certain Johnny would go into an all-out transformation. But he didn't. His chin lowered. "Show her to me, or I'll tear you apart."

"I'd like to see you try."

"What I did to him," he indicated Gregor, "was restrained."

"I'd say she's faired marginally better. But not by much."

Either he was trying to instigate Johnny to change, or male pissing contests had just been taken to a new level.

The good thing was that everyone was focused on the two of them. Inside the limo, I was sitting right next to the door. Twisting, I put my feet against the door, levered the handle, and kicked out with all my might.

The rearmost edge of the door caught the Rege in the small of his back, scraping him and sending him forward.

Gregor reacted. He reached for the door, but the window hit his knuckles hard; it forced his arm back and left him to be broadsided by the door—right in the balls. He doubled over.

As I shot between them, Gregor grabbed my leg. I fell flat, elbows hitting hard and my bound hands flapped out before me. In a heartbeat Johnny was there, helping me up.

"Leave her," the Rege snapped.

Johnny stilled. I craned my neck to see why.

While Johnny had bent to help me, the Rege recovered and drew a knife from somewhere. He held it against Johnny's throat.

"Sharing power with you isn't in my plan, boy."

"My whole pack knows about me."

The Rege shrugged; it made Johnny suck air through his teeth. A thin line of blood appeared where his skin and the blade edge met. "The Omori are very good at what they do."

Johnny wouldn't give in. "So is my pack."

"Ha! Welders. Construction workers. Movers. What do they know of being hunted?"

No one was paying much attention to me. I was on the ground and therefore helpless. But if I could draw attention to me, Johnny might get a shot at getting out of his predicament. "He underestimates everyone, Johnny. It's his personal flaw."

The instant my voice distracted the Rege, Johnny threw himself backward, kicking up his feet. Johnny's foot strike drove the Rege's arm upward, and the knife sailed into the air. The Rege lost his balance, pitching forward onto his knees.

Johnny's flip left him neatly crouched.

The dagger *thunked* into the ground between them.

Johnny snatched it and stood, glowering down at the Rege.

Gregor put his foot on the back of my head and applied pressure to my lump. I screamed. Grass and leaves got in my mouth. All I wanted to do was keep him from grinding his heel on my head.

Reaching behind my head, I groped up his shoe and

under his pant leg, I clawed down Gregor's sock and dug my nails into his skin as I screamed again.

Once, I had pulled power from Menessos. Being bound to me, he fed on my energy and I had been able to call that power back to me. But through him, I'd also pulled from Goliath. While Gregor didn't have any power of mine to call, his power was pooling on the surface of his aura.

I drew on that power; I *yanked* on it. The earth roiled under me and it seemed I became a geyser of fiery acid ready to erupt.

Suddenly, Gregor wasn't accosting me anymore.

Wiping grass from my mouth, I rolled over. He was scurrying, crablike, away from me. "She tried to make me change!" he shouted.

I was mad enough—and hurt enough—to spit nails now. I got my feet under me and shouted back, "I did not! If I'd meant to do that you wouldn't be in man form right now," I said, stalking toward him. "What I did was remind you of what I can do." I kept advancing. He twisted to get his feet under him, trying to run even though he wasn't up and balanced yet.

The big, brawny Omori retreated before me, drawing their guns.

I heard Johnny laugh. "Those pussies are your brave Omori?"

I stopped and turned to face him.

"Greg there said we Americans were weak . . . right before I kicked his ass." He shook his head at the Rege. "Fuck. You guys are clueless."

CHAPTER TWENTY

I strode toward Johnny as he told the Rege, who was still on his knees, "Tell your pups to put their guns in a pile on the ground. *Now.*"

The Rege made a gesture of conciliation. Metal clacked on metal as the guns were dropped. Johnny motioned to Todd and Kirk, who patted the Omori down and collected the weaponry.

Johnny untied me and took my face in his hands to give me an inspection. Johnny's touch was so light, so warm, I didn't want it to stop, even when his thumb stroked my cheek. I flinched; being walloped twice today by the Rege had left me bruised.

His rigid posture yielded to embrace me. Emotion radiated off him. His face filled with relief and protectiveness. He understood how I'd felt when he disappeared under the Lake Erie surface.

"You were skipping your intro with the Rege?"

"Max was murdered, you were missing. Kind of took priority."

"She's not just a witch to you," the Rege said disgustedly.

"Deal with it," Johnny growled.

The Rege rose up onto his knees. "I left my mark on her insides."

Johnny jerked away. I grabbed his arm—his skin darkened under my grip and fur pushed up between my fingers. Claws sprouted from his fingertips as I watched. His breath rasped harshly and he leaned threateningly over the Rege. "No," I said. "He didn't."

"Yes, I did!"

"Do you remember it? In detail?"

Uncertainty clouded his features.

"He thinks he did," I said to Johnny, "but he didn't."

The Rege's confusion was replaced with vehemence. He spat at our feet. "You used magic on me?"

I didn't answer. I didn't even deign to acknowledge that he'd spoken to me.

Todd and Kirk returned to our side with the weapons, and passed them out to their own people. Kirk ordered, "Keep them handy, but out of sight. We don't want the police crashing our little shindig." Chris LaCroix was on our side. That was interesting. Kirk didn't offer him a gun.

Johnny said, "Explain how murder and kidnapping became a good idea."

The Rege put one foot on the ground, preparing to stand.

"Down!" Johnny commanded.

"I am the Rege! If you are to be crowned, you'll need *my* endorsement."

"But you don't share, remember?"

The Rege shook with rage. "You *need* me!"

Johnny shrugged. "And if you're dead? Do you think your replacement might understandably be more accommodating to my needs?"

The Rege put his knee back on the ground.

Bully the bullies; it's all they understand.

"Now explain," Johnny commanded.

"Ask Gregor," the Rege replied.

"Kirk," Johnny said, as he stepped away. Kirk positioned himself so passing motorists could not see he held a gun on the Rege. Johnny stopped before Gregor. "Answer."

"I intended to question her. I wanted to kill her, too, but first I wanted to know if there were others who could do what she could do. When the Rege arrived I told him what I had done and what my intentions were and why—"

"Tell me why."

"The humans, if not the witches, will eventually seek to destroy us."

Johnny shook his head in irritation.

Gregor continued. "He wanted to question her personally. I didn't think that was safe. I suggested we set her up so that WEC would have no choice but to have her Bindspoken. Then we could recapture her and question her when she'd been magically spayed."

Now I understood why I'd heard these wærewolves use the word "Bindspoken" in their conversation. Gregor was taking high rank on my Least Favorite People list.

"But I, as always, obeyed the will of my superior." Gregor bowed his head submissively in the direction of Rege.

I suspected that was a hint, a suggestion, or a call to action of some kind and kept my attention on the Omori behind them.

"And what was your purpose for questioning her personally?" Johnny asked the Rege.

"I agree with the Omori's assessment of our enemies. I add only a reminder that as the Rege my vantage point of the situation is better, the scope of my sight broader. When the day of our challenge comes—and it will—it is my intention that we are prepared."

"Are the grimasa-azils not enough?" Johnny asked.

"It is the best we have, but I would be a fool to ignore the opportunity to surmount our one weakness when it stands before me. If she can truly bestow us all with permanence in our man-minds, then we eliminate our only moment of weakness: when the animal takes over and we cannot work as a united front. What she can give us better equips us for the inevitable."

It was basically the same argument Johnny used to convince the pack wæres that the spell was worthwhile, but when the Rege said the words, the idea lost its charm.

"And what if I don't agree that the Fate you see is 'inevitable'?"

"Then you are naïve."

I'd thought Johnny must know what answer he'd get to that question and had been mistaken in asking it, but when he bristled in response, I understood he knew exactly what he was doing.

"You need to stop insulting the Domn Lup," Kirk said.

Subordinates telling the Rege what to do evidently pissed him off. His reaction was unsympathetic. "*I* rule the court. That won't change even *if* he proves himself the Wolf King."

Kirk had jumped in, so I took my shot. "You don't believe he's the Domn Lup?" I asked. "Gregor witnessed a full change for himself. Did he not tell you?"

The Rege's compassionless gaze shifted to me. "If he is to be crowned, he'll need my endorsement. Or, as he has already suggested, he can kill me and hope my successor is more pliable. But he'll want something, too."

Of course. Being the Domn Lup wasn't enough; the bigwigs expect their political favor to be bought.

"What do *you* want?" Johnny asked coolly.

The Rege stood. This time Johnny didn't argue.

"I want *her*," the Rege said, pointing at me. "The witch becomes mine, my tool. You"—he arched a brow and frowned distastefully at Johnny—"tone down your image, learn the talking points, and make the rounds of your American media." He smoothed his suit jacket, tugged on his cuffs to straighten the sleeves. "Draw their attention while the witch gifts us all."

"All?" Todd questioned.

The Rege glared at him. Todd shifted back a half-step.

"How many wæres are there now?" Johnny asked.

"I don't have an exact count," the Rege said casually.

I was sure he was lying.

"Over a quarter of a million worldwide," Chris LaCroix offered helpfully.

The Rege's rigid glare found Chris. To his credit, Chris held his ground.

"If she transformed fifty a day," Kirk said, "every day, aside from the scheduling nightmare that would be, it would take over fourteen years."

I was not signing on for that. Though stunned at being the bargaining chip on the proverbial table, I found my voice. "No way."

"You see?" Gregor's voice cracked like a whip. "She is not on the side of the wæres!"

"I'll *give* you the spell," I countered. "You can find another witch who can perform it for you." It wasn't like the Lustrata was the *only* witch who could do this spell. It was in the Trivium Codex after all, the book of sorcery spells from the fairies. Not that finding another witch to do it would be easy. Sorcery required a lot of energy and the moonlight enhancing spell was no different. Most witches simply wouldn't have the power within themselves to perform it. That meant it had to be powered by the ley lines, and not many witches were willing to tap a ley because of the initial pain and the addictive ramifications. Of those who did perform sorcery, few would hazard such repeated exposures, and fewer still would be willing to take such a risk to aid the wæres. "All you need is a witch willing to perform sorcery. She can use a ley line to power the spell."

Gregor flung his arm out, pointing at me, but addressed his superior. He marched closer to the Rege. "Agreeable, logical aid being placed at our feet, and all spoken softly from a pretty mouth. We are being soothed into a sense of security, so that we may be struck down!"

I wondered if all the Romanian wæres hated women.

Walking forward and making a conciliating gesture,

I said, "Look, I'm not against wæres keeping their man-minds. I'm all for it, actually. The need for kenneling would be nearly eliminated. Rogue attacks would be a thing of the past. That's good for everyone."

Gregor spun on me. "I'll never trust *any* witch that much."

"Why?" I pointed at the pack members here with Johnny. "They trusted me, and rightly so. If you hadn't intervened, it would have been to their benefit. It was to the benefit of the three who've already experienced it."

"They did not trust *you*." The Rege inched forward. "They trusted the Domn Lup. What exists between you and that pack exists because of him. Your worth is based only on the value he places upon you. That is not something that will carry over to your allies in WEC, because witches and wæres weren't meant to mingle."

Oh, Goddess. Not the tenet of the good ol' days.

The Rege caught my eye-rolling. "You mock me?"

My arms crossed. "I mock the irrationality of that old idea."

"Irrational?" His shout resonated inside my head, reminding me of my goose egg. "Witches have the power to misshape us, destroy us!"

Despite the flecks of spittle on my arms from his raging, I remained calm. "I saw what I could do to you. And yet I haven't."

He squinted suspiciously. It made him look all the more evil, which until then I hadn't thought was possible.

"Yes, witches have the power to misshape you, but the truth you don't want to acknowledge is the counterpoint that balances that. Witches also have the power to eliminate your weakness, Rege. All you've been willing to see is the danger they represent. Your fear has created a wedge where there should have always been a bridge. The time for that dogma is past and now it's your attitude that has to change. Let it trickle down to all wæres. Guide them to desire man-minds as a means of safety. Use the benefits—like the fact that kenneling won't be necessary—to convince them." If I was to be involved in this, I didn't want them to misunderstand. "I know it will take time to find the *right* witches who can do this, but I can help you find solitaries or those disaffected by the organization. If you develop a businesslike relationship with them, WEC will eventually have to see that doing their part to build that bridge of trust will take us *all* into the future with firmer footing." I uncrossed my arms. "This world will keep spinning no matter what, but all of your people—and all of mine—must take personal responsibility for their own progress."

Gregor growled. "Personal responsibility? Your words sound unsettlingly close to those that would incite a rebellion."

"Good! You all need to rebel against that notion that has kept you afraid of witches."

The Rege turned to his men. The expectancy on their faces was plain; they were waiting for him to guide them. Would it be "as usual," or would he lead in a new direction? Some, like Gregor, clearly wanted to stay on the path they knew well.

The Rege spun back. "Who are you?"

I'd taunted him earlier that he didn't know who I was. He hadn't gotten my name then. I supposed now would do. "I'm Persephone Alcmedi."

"You speak pretty words, Persephone. A spell in each charismatic syllable, but I cannot—"

"She's the Lustrata," Johnny said, interrupting before the Rege could bestow judgmental words he might have to eat later. The Zvonul's main man did not move, but seemed frozen in place. Only his eyes moved, flicking over to Johnny as he added, "And you've tempted her wrath quite far enough." The Rege again drew a breath, ready to protest, and Johnny cut him off. "She deserves respect, Rege."

His face pinched up so tight I thought it was caving in on itself. Giving respect to a woman was blasphemy for a man afflicted with the kind of misogyny that allowed him to qualify rape as a means of punishment. *And because I'm a witch—a woman with power—it flavored his bitterness with acid.*

Now I understood how the rift had become so wide. Witches were predominantly female.

"You really don't get it, do you, Rege?" Johnny spoke up. "You see her gift will make the wæres *always* powerful and eliminate that one full moon night of weakness. You see that it will raise us above the vamps, who lose half of every day and rely on Beholders and Offerlings for their safety. What you can't seem to recognize is that she's offering to let *you* guide the wæres, to have the credit of wise guidance, because she's not in it for the power or glory." Johnny moved toe-to-toe with the Rege. "You haven't shown her any respect yet. Kidnapping her, killing a friend, trying to rape her. Think about it. The only reason you're *not* half-formed right now is because she intends to fulfill her destiny."

"She needs me," he spat. "I won't be a puppet to a . . . a witch!"

I had the distinct feeling he'd almost said *woman*.

Johnny shook his head. "You're wrong. She doesn't need you. She has me, the Domn Lup. But the influence of your long years as Rege would make this easier for everyone."

Silently, Gregor positioned himself just to the side. It was clear he was showing the Rege he backed him up. So I took up the opposite side. Kirk moved in a step behind me.

Johnny went on. "Only with her willing aid can we be lifted above our animal minds. Placed equal to witches in that we have no time of weakness."

"Why would she lift us equal to her own kind?" the Rege demanded.

"To bring balance," I said.

All three of them looked at me. The Rege's attention bounced from me to Johnny and he studied Johnny for a long moment. Without another word, he turned and walked to the limo and got in. His men followed him.

I hope he recognized that he had a hell of a lot to think about.

When the limo drove away, the pack sighed collectively in relief.

Chris strolled up to me. "Lustrata, huh?"

It still felt awkward to just openly claim it, but after a deep breath I nodded. "Yeah."

"I've heard the rumors . . . now I understand why you never backed down. Ever."

It was almost eight o'clock when I got home. We'd been delayed when Johnny used his cell phone to let Nana know they had me back safe. As he spoke to her, I remembered the Omori had taken the necklace with Beau's charm, the protrepticus, my satellite phone, and my purse in the kidnapping. We had to make a stop at the den to collect them. Kirk and Todd dealt with the awkward situation while we waited in the parking area.

"How'd you make the Rege think he'd . . . hurt . . . you, when he hadn't?"

The word he couldn't bring himself to say was "rape." "That's a question for Menessos. It was almost like I mesmerized him. I told him he was finished, to leave. In his mind, I guess, 'finished' meant 'mission accomplished.' " I paused, rubbing at my goose egg.

"I should take you to the ER."

"I'm fine. Ever figure out how they got past your security to the second floor?" I asked.

"They flashed their official IDs at the guards. While the doc was stitching me up the other day, I gave the order to make sure we were complying with whatever the Rege's people needed. The guards thought they were adhering to my order. Now they know better: no one is allowed entrance without checking with me first, not even the Zvonul. The Rege and the Omori may think compliance means they run the den, but not *this* den."

Todd and Kirk returned. My stuff was no worse for wear.

The bad news was that Johnny, Todd, and Kirk had decided they needed a private meeting, at Todd's house, to discuss among themselves their bylaws, options, and what could be done about the Rege. Todd made it clear he didn't want their conversation to occur at *my* home.

I suggested they give Beau a call and ask him about pack lore. Beau may be a Bindspoken witch, but he had the trust of the former *dirija* and he knew an awful lot about everything. He'd told me he'd had cause to do "an enormous amount" of research. That was how he had been able to recognize me as the Lustrata, and how he'd been able to manipulate me into helping him. He'd made me promise to come and see him before the next full moon, which was still three weeks away.

Johnny drove me home, but before we got out of the Audi, I asked him to tell Beau that I'd stop by and see him soon.

"Have I got competition?" he asked, affecting innocence and shock.

"Of course not." I leaned to kiss him.

His lips were gentle against mine. "Sure you don't want to go to the ER and get checked out?"

"It's nothing ibuprofen and an ice pack won't fix."

He touched my cheek again, tenderly. "You're going to have a shiner."

"I think our combat training needs to start again."

"Deal."

I moved to get out, but he stopped me with a touch.

"I could have lost you today."

The fear in his tone made me instinctively want to lighten his load. Sarcasm was in order. "Sucks, huh?"

"Yeah." One side of his mouth crooked up, adorably. I rubbed his cleft chin and pulled him to me for another kiss, this one lasting long enough to run my fingers through his hair, forceful enough to notice the evening stubble on his chin, and sensual enough to set my heart pounding.

When we broke, we lingered with our foreheads together. As he sat back, so solemn, so serious, his mouth opened, closed, opened again. "Red, I . . ." His grip on my hand tightened, but he didn't finish.

I had a distinct feeling that the "L" word was about to follow. *No. No. No. No. No.* I gulped, audibly, and tried to be cheerful as I asked, "What?"

The weightiness lifted from him and he shook his head. "Another time."

Todd and Kirk turned into the driveway behind us in a Chevy Tahoe. Johnny flashed me an enigmatic smile and passed me the keys before he climbed out to go and ride with them.

CHAPTER TWENTY-ONE

Just inside my front door I was trapped in a bear hug from Nana that I didn't think was ever going to end. Zhan was in the living room, and came to her feet. "Welcome home, my lady."

I saw Beverley sneak to the top of the stairs in her pajamas, and I called out to her. Nana released me and Beverley rushed down the steps, throwing herself at me before she'd reached the bottom. With her arms and legs wrapped around me, she buried her face in my neck. "I was so scared," she whispered.

"Me, too." I wondered what she'd been told and what she'd overheard while in stealth mode.

Nana gave me a nod that indicated I should take Beverley back to bed. *Easy for her to say; she hadn't gone two rounds with the Rege.*

Atop the stairs, winded, I said, "You sure are growing, kiddo. In a month or two I won't be able to carry you up here."

She didn't answer. Instead she sniffled into my hair.

I carried her into her room and lay her in her bed. After rearranging the covers and tucking beside her the teddy bear that wore one of her mother's sweatshirts, I sat and smoothed her dark hair back.

"I'm trying, Seph. Trying to do what you said, to accept the good and the bad. But this was *really* bad. Everyone was so scared."

Several statements crossed my mind. I settled on, "When I said it wouldn't be easy, I didn't anticipate days like this." I gripped her hands. "They knocked me unconscious, but when I woke up, the first thing I thought of was you and I fought with everything I had. I fought to get back home to you."

She noticed my cheek. "Looks like it hurt."

"It did. But Johnny took care of it." I shifted to something more reassuring. "Did you get to see the unicorns this evening?"

A sneaky grin appeared. "Errol let me put ribbons in his mane and tail."

"Did he?"

She told me about Mountain letting her ride outside the barn, and that the young colt had been very careful with her and didn't go too fast. On that happy note, though I was exhausted, I asked if it would help her sleep if I read her a story.

"No. I'll sleep now that you're home." She sat up and hugged me, pausing to study my bruised cheek. "You need an ice pack," she declared as she lay back down, arm encircling her bear.

I leaned down and kissed her forehead. "Love you, kiddo."

"I love you, too."

• • •

Nana told me Mountain had said only some odds and ends remained to do at the barns. Her room's roof was finished and the interior was nearly ready for paint. She also informed me he'd called Geoff because Thunderbird was still asleep. They decided that since the griffon was breathing deep and his pulse was strong, that was okay. Geoff promised he'd come out tomorrow after work. I knew Nana was running on nervous adrenaline because only after telling me all that did she offer to feed me.

She dropped some bread in the toaster and started making scrambled eggs. While she cooked with shaky hands, she updated me on some of the decor choices she'd made for the room addition. Evidently Mountain had presented her with paint swatches and her choice of bath and lighting fixtures.

Presenting me the egg sandwich, she said, "That cheek of yours. Everybody's taking a whack at it this week."

I snorted. Vilna had slapped it, too.

"You want some ice?"

"Just ibuprofen."

She got up and retrieved the medicine for me. Nana then listened to the abridged version of my story, after which I headed to my room where I peeled off my jeans, pulled my arms through my T-shirt's sleeves, and performed a feat of female dexterity that allowed my bra to drop to the floor as my arms were jammed back into my sleeves.

I crawled into bed and tugged the covers up around my ears. Sleep had almost claimed me when the satellite phone rang.

I groaned and answered.

"And how did the world fare under the sun today, dear Persephone?"

Menessos was calling to chitchat? *Not likely.* "Dandy," I lied. I didn't want to tell the tale of the day again. "And yours?"

"I'm feeling rather low." His pouting tone transformed accusingly. "As if I'm missing the life essence of one of my twice-marked Offerlings."

Maxine. Anguished, I repeated all their names to myself. *Aquula, Xerxadrea, Ig, Ross, Robert, Brian.* Countless fairies and elementals. All dead. Now Maxine. In an instant, I recalled everything she'd told me about her life and her mother. *No fading.*

The growing list of those who'd died as I climbed toward the Lustrata's destiny hurt my heart. *I must not fail.*

"Maxine is dead," I whispered. "I'm sorry."

"Did you kill her?"

I sat up quickly. "No!"

"Then what are you sorry for?"

"For your loss. But it doesn't sound as if you're worried about her, just the decline in your life essence."

"It *is* something to worry about."

"How? What does the damn life essence do for you anyway?"

"I meant to concede that the loss of *her* is something to worry about."

"Oh."

"How did she die?"

"Protecting me."

"Are you all right? What happened?"

"I'm fine." I didn't want to demean her death. I also didn't want to implicate any wærewolves. I did want to flop back on the pillows, but even the softest pillow would put pressure on the goose egg I was still sporting. Instead, I reclined slowly, twisting to the side and letting my weary eyes shut again. "I really don't want to go through it all again. Can it suffice for now to say she died doing her duty?"

"Yes. If that is your wish, Persephone . . ."

As if the Sandman had cast his dream dust over me while I was yet awake, the vampire's voice stirred imagery into the darkness. A warm summer sun shone in a cloudless sky. The bed under me became a blanket upon the ground in a field of wildflowers. He whispered my name again and I could feel his fingertips gliding up my arm like champagne bubbles up the side of a glass.

"I need to see you. Tonight."

The image fluttered, losing vibrancy as I almost sassed, "Can't Eva satisfy you?" but I held my tongue. After a moment the scene was restored. Still, I didn't answer him. I wanted nothing else to happen today. Except dreamless, restful sleep, that is.

Menessos pressed, "To compensate, my master."

Damn it. "Then you have to come to me," I grumped.

"As you wish."

He wasn't deterred by my demand, but the way he worded it made me feel like I should explain this wasn't a command from his master. "I've had a full day. You just got up."

"Indeed," he whispered low and breathy. "I just did."

• • •

Hours later, I awoke to the ward alarming in my head. The clock read eleven-eleven.

The house was silent around me. I left the mental alarm alone, though it aggravated my still-achy head, and rose from my bed. I was expecting Menessos to show up, but he didn't trip my wards. He carried my hex, and it granted him an all-access pass.

Tiptoeing across the room and jerking my robe on, I opened the door slowly and silently. The house was dark and—if things were normal—Nana and Beverley were in their rooms asleep. From Beverley's room I heard Ares emit a low growl.

I tiptoed to her door. "Easy, boy," I whispered.

He growled again.

I opened the door a crack. "Ares! Shhh."

The dog lay down in his crate, wagged his tail twice.

I shut her door and proceeded down my stairs, weaving the odd path I knew would keep squeaking boards from announcing me. Midway down, I could see into the living room. Nana had left candles burning. *Or Zhan is setting a mood.*

I remembered how Mountain had reacted when he looked at her. I considered returning to my room, but Mountain wouldn't set off the wards either.

A few more steps, and Menessos came into view. Well, his unmistakable backside did, anyway. He was admiring the Waterhouse painting he'd given me. He wore his usual flattering trousers and a businesslike white-on-white striped shirt. His jacket was draped over the arm of the couch.

I lingered there on the staircase. He stood in the room that, once upon a time when I lived here alone, had been my sanctuary. It held my Pre-Raphaelite posters and my bookshelves full of everything on the king of Camelot. Lit by wick flames, the room held an ambiance redolent of ages past. And, moreover, he simply *fit*. Admittedly, I was projecting what I knew of him into the mix, but one thing I wasn't embellishing: despite his modern clothes, there was a majestic quality to his posture and aura. He was innately regal and no one in his presence could deny it.

Especially me.

My mind flashed on the moment before I staked him, before I kissed him, on the moment when I knew the sacrifice he was about to make and saw not the meddling vampire, but the Arthur I dreamed of so often.

I remembered how in the memory we now shared, Menessos was alive, his skin sun-kissed, shoulders thick from hard labor. His hair curled to his shoulders now, but then, in the memory, it was much longer—the kind of hair a woman could run her fingers through just before she passionately raked her nails across his back. . . .

Surely this adoration is a side effect created by the bonds. All masters must struggle with this.

No need for surprising an intruder now; I released the ward alarm. Menessos strode toward me.

"You tripped the wards on purpose?" I asked quietly.

"Would you prefer I enter your bedroom and wake you personally?"

"No. Where's Zhan?"

"I sent her to get a report from Mountain. I told her to take her time."

He gave me his hand over the rail as I took the last few stairs. It was ceremonious and unnecessary, but as soon as he touched me, the power of the hex awakened and again lit my spine like a fuse. My mouth opened to protest, but when my feet hit the floor I found myself eye-to-eye with him, witnessing the mixed need and danger in the blackness of his pupils, swirling like a thing alive. And I didn't really want to scold him. *He gave his life for victory.*

"I waited until your grandmother and the child would be at rest."

"I thank you for that."

His arm snaked around my waist, drawing me to him, inspecting my bruise.

"I'm fine," I said before he could ask anything.

He backed across the hall, guiding me as if we were dancing, and the fuse continued to smolder, its flame caressing me as he guided us to the couch. What I felt wasn't heat like the other times he'd employed his supernal seduction on me. This was different; my second hex was on him now, making him not unlike an Offerling to me. And this blazing fuse felt like . . . a promise . . . a promise that the warm slow burn could detonate with earth-shattering force.

When he sat on the couch there was no resisting the strong arms clinging to me. I sank onto his lap, straddling him. His shirt, I realized, was mostly unbuttoned and when we were seated he tugged it free from his pants and finished unbuttoning it. Deftly maneuvering his knuckles, he stroked my aura and sent sensations rippling over me.

Goddess, he knows what he's doing.

After removing the shirt, he flung it atop the jacket then reached for the belt of my robe.

My hands stopped him. "I'm not comfortable with the sexuality of this."

"The nature of my feeding imitates intimacy."

"But you don't *need* to remove your shirt to feed from your master. It's not like bloodstains are uncommon in your laundry." Besides, this was where, and very much *how,* Johnny and I had first made love.

"You do not like this, my master?"

Apprehension buoyed me above the blissful euphoria to speak my objection more firmly. "Menessos."

His touch on my legs sent sparks through me. Fingers splayed, he guided his caress toward my hips, thumbs on my inner thighs and just millimeters from touching my—

"Let me warm you, Persephone . . . it is cold in here."

He went on, making it all sound so reasonable. For a moment, I was lost, submerged in desire as he kindled my flesh, engulfed in ecstasy as he draped me with adoration the color of candlelight. I sighed over the stimulating tone of his voice and marveled at the melodic quality of his words and how I could feel them seize me tighter in the seconds after he invoked my name. When he finished speaking, I realized the belt was untied and my robe was on the floor. But I wasn't cold. His fingers rounded my arms, and brought me nearer.

Tilting his head, Menessos put his mouth to my throat. He knew better than to kiss my lips, but he eagerly kissed from my jaw to my collarbone. If his touch wrapped me in the blanket of his seduction, if his voice was an irresistible siren song calling to my soul, then his kisses were a web of mystery and flaming exultation. Every time his lips touched my flesh, it was a tender and reverent exploration. And each time my pulse answered, growing stronger, faster.

His lips pressed over the vein. He lingered there, just breathing. His touch trailed down my arms until he could thread his fingers between mine.

Motionless, caught in the glow of the burning marks I'd placed on him, I waited, testing, feeling, trying to break through the surface of this hex haze. This was new, a glorious arousal of body and soul—I wanted to know more, but I was also afraid.

Since it seemed he was giving me a chance to dictate how this would go, I dared not move to respond; it would only encourage him. Giving in to this feverish desire would end with my love and my world in ashes. So I remained stock-still.

When the moment peaked, threatening to become the most arduous exercise of my self-restraint, Menessos ended his immobility. He stroked the backs of my arms. When he reached my shoulders, his touch rounded forward, fondling downward, gliding, caressing my breasts, slowly, reverently—

"No," I whispered, denying him.

"But you kissed me," he whispered back. He tantalized every part of me he touched, and his breathing so warmly on my neck all the while only enhanced the torture.

It was all so sensual, so careful, so delicate. I was being charmed. I nuzzled into his walnut-colored waves.

His hands strayed low to rest on my hip bones. Again, I said, "No."

And the seduction ended. With quick ferocity, he struck—jerking my body against his as his fangs stabbed into my flesh.

My instinct was to fight, to throw this attacker off and to struggle against giving him blood, so I had to convince my instinctual self this was not an attack. Not like that.

He was rock hard beneath me, and as he drew my blood, he used his grip on my hips to rock me as if we were engaged in much more. But I knew what he was doing—baby-stepping me into an affair that robbed me of my loyalty to Johnny.

"Stop," I whispered.

He didn't.

"Stop," I said more firmly. I weighed my options about which to try removing first: his viselike grip or his razor-sharp teeth. Though he'd drank from me before, this was the first time he'd done so as a truly undead vampire. "Menessos."

His body stilled under me, his teeth slid out of me, and his suckling decreased, fading to gentle licking in seconds. The fuse, once full of potency, tapered off. A sense of self-control resumed. My thoughts were clearer.

Finally, with his head thrown back against the couch, the vampire sighed up at me with deep satisfaction. "That was better than sex . . . almost." He licked his lips and gave a little thrust with his hips. "I really need more from you to make that comparison."

I leaned back. "You're wasting your time."

He rubbed my thighs again. "I think you enjoy being a cock tease to me."

At that, I stood, though it wasn't exactly a graceful dismount. "I'm not a cock tease. You're the one who insists on making our situation sexual. You do it to yourself." I headed for the stairs.

He called after me conversationally, "I've heard that the Rege is in town."

I turned and rolled my eyes for emphasis. "What's that? Some new band?" He was fishing but I wasn't taking the bait.

"No." His tone, and the silence afterward, were patient.

"Okay then, don't tell me. Lock up before you leave."

He let me get three steps away. "Persephone."

I stared straight ahead. He'd said my name and I felt weaker. The warmth of his presence faded more as I moved farther away.

I care deeply for him, but I can't love him. I love Johnny.

And I can't even seem to tell Johnny that.

Over my shoulder, I said, "Go back to the haven, Menessos."

"I will. But I'm going to sit here for a while," he mumbled.

At that, I faced him again. "Why?"

With a gracious gesture like a maître d' presenting a succulent dish, he drew my gaze down to the bulge in his pants. "Until I can walk normally."

I pursed my lips. "Well, if you're just going to be sitting for a moment, I have more questions about the moon amplification spell."

"How did that go?"

"It didn't. Something else came up and we rescheduled." I shrugged as if it was no big deal. "What if I had to do this spell for more than twenty wæres?"

"How many?"

Throwing caution to the wind, I firmly said, "All of them."

"And you said you weren't ambitious." He rubbed at his temple. "What are you asking?"

"Is it possible to do this all at once? Say, if I did it during a full moon as they changed anyway?"

"I doubt it. Why would you want to give them all their man-minds?"

"It could eliminate rogue attacks, keep their numbers stable. Kenneling wouldn't be necessary."

"Very practical." He stood, adjusted his pants, and muttered, "Your eager willingness to perform for the wæres certainly dwindles an erection." In normal tones, he said, "You wouldn't be going to such extremes to impress the Domn Lup, for he's already enamored with you. So how long is the Rege staying?"

My mouth stayed shut. I hadn't meant to confirm his earlier suspicion. Aggravated with myself, I ran a hand through my hair and discovered my goose egg was gone. *So I got a perk out of feeding him. Yay.*

"I'm not only the Quarter Lord here," he said, donning the shirt though he didn't bother to button it. "I'm now the lord of this area with Heldridge gone. Matters under his jurisdiction are things of which I must stay apprised." He donned his jacket and sauntered closer, radiating every ounce of masculinity he possessed. "And my court witch must not be plotting to aid the wære-wolves globally."

"But the Lustrata must." I wasn't letting him name-drop his titles and roles as if they were exclusively mean-ingful. "I guess you have reason to renounce me after all."

"We've already discussed that without the vampires or WEC all you have are the wæres. I understand why you would seek to sway them to your side, pacifying them with your excellence, but this is supercilious, especially for you." He caressed my cheek, then let his touch drop away. "Why would you even want to do this?"

"I told you, to—"

"You told me the practical side, yes. But . . ." He sighed. "Have you even met the Rege?"

"You could say that, yes." I wasn't telling him more than that.

"Would you truly remove *his* weakness if you could? He is not like Johnny. The Zvonul are bigots who cling to antiquated dogma—no pun intended. The Rege is the worst of them. To give them what you suggest would not dull their arrogance."

He was probably right. "I'm supposed to bring balance."

Softly, he asked, "And would you give my kind back their days?"

"If I could, of course. Why wouldn't I?"

"Then would you give us the means to enter places where there are wards? Would you give the undead the freedom to roam unchecked as wærewolves do?"

Those were tougher questions. Ones with a myriad of

other questions waiting in the wings, no matter which way I answered.

He reached up again, this time grasping my shoulders. "Your motive is noble and your reasoning is close, but it is not perfect. You're striving for equality, to level the playing field, as they say. But equality is not balance."

"Why not?"

"Because no matter what you do, you cannot make us human again."

CHAPTER TWENTY-TWO

When the alarm clock buzzed, I realized Johnny hadn't come home last night. With all the threats aired between the two wære factions, I wasn't surprised.

Nana had taken Beverley to the bus stop. Mountain was using an expensive paint that included primer—a timesaver—on Nana's new room, a pretty lavender color. The subflooring was in place. Stacks of prefinished tongue-and-groove flooring were just outside the door, topped with bundles of the gray radiant heat padding. I asked him about Thunderbird.

"I checked on him at dawn and he had moved into a nest, but was still sleeping. The other griffons were nearby but not covering him as before."

That put me in a very happy mood, for a few minutes, at least. As I flipped through the phone book to find the number for the grocery to make the cake order for Beverley's party, I noticed Zhan staring down into a cup of tea. There were tears on her cheeks and she seemed resigned to let them air dry. I could understand that. Wiping them only draws attention to the fact that you are crying.

She and Maxine must have been closer than I knew.

"You know what?" I asked her, still searching the phone book.

"What?"

"I'm thinking that instead of buying the kiddo's cake, I could actually make one."

"Do you have the ingredients? The pans?"

I checked the pantry; it gave her a chance to wipe her cheeks unseen. "That would be a no. Not much cake-baking goes on here."

"You'll have to order it, then."

It would be good for her to get out of the house. "Let's just go pick one from the bakery case. They'll write what we want on it."

Outside, Zhan got in the driver's side, but as she reached to put the keys into the ignition, I could see her hand was shaking. "Are you okay?"

"No." She squeezed the steering wheel until her knuckles paled to white. "This was Maxine's car. She loved this car." She grabbed a tissue from her pocket. "Maybe you should drive."

I kicked myself for not insisting on driving in the first place. "Sure." We switched. It was a silent ride into town.

I didn't go south to the Lodi Grocery, where Maxine had been shot. Instead, I headed southwest into Ashland. It was slightly farther, but Hawkins had better cakes anyway. By the time we arrived, Zhan had recovered.

Inside, we chose a chocolate cake from the bakery section with pink and purple in the frosting edges. The attendant took it to write "Happy 10th Birthday Beverley" on it.

We roamed around tables displaying cookies shaped

like turkeys and cornucopias. I picked up one of the stiff plastic containers and considered buying them.

"I want to go home," Zhan said.

I set the cookies down. "I wasn't planning on any other stops."

"To San Francisco," she clarified. "Actually north of there in Contra Costa county."

I hadn't expected this. A dozen questions flooded into my mind. *When did you leave? How long has it been? Does your family know you're an Offerling to a vampire?* Lamely, I said, "Oh?" *Nothing like a death to throw around some perspective.* If she was homesick, I could make Menessos let her take a vacation. "I'll talk to Menessos. I'm sure he'll let you—"

"It isn't him keeping me from it. I did this to myself."

I wanted to help, but there was nothing to do without more information. "Mind if I ask what you did?"

She paced away and I was sure she had decided to go and wait for me in the car, but her steps slowed and she came back. "Unlike many Chinese-American families, mine still practices ancestor worship. They follow the oldest of the old ways. My father is an artist. All my life I was aware that he wanted a son to teach his trade, but my mother had no children other than me. By the time he accepted that he would have no sons and deigned to break tradition and teach his art to a daughter, I had decided his pride was false, that he painted lies, and in doing so he furthered the lie to the next generation. I vowed not to be a part of that and I ran."

I didn't understand. "What did he paint that was false?"

"Dragons. Phoenix. Creatures I believed never had existed. But now," her eyes welled up and she brought out the already damp tissue again, "now I know they do exist, and that they always did. My ancestors weren't fabricating lies. My father's honor is intact. Mine is not."

Geoff arrived at five-thirty. In the back of his dually pickup truck stood six full-grown goats. They were on leashes that were tied to the roll bar. I put my shoes on and walked out to greet him. Beverley stepped up behind me at the door.

"Goats?" she asked.

He said, "I don't think the dog food is doing much for Thunderbird."

"Oh." Beverley's sunny demeanor dimmed.

I was somewhat disturbed myself. "Geoff, you're not going to walk them into the barn on leashes, are you?"

"No. I'll let them loose in the field. I'm sure the griffons will do what griffons do."

"What if Thunderbird doesn't come out?"

"After what I saw the others do to keep him warm, I have to believe that they understand things in a way that normal animals do not."

"Meaning?"

"Either he'll understand and come out, or the others will take him what he needs."

"Let me tell Mountain before you set them loose, okay?"

"Sure."

I put my jacket on and headed out. Beverley was right on my heels. "You probably shouldn't be out here, Bev."

"I'm okay," she said. She didn't convince me.

Mountain had finished the painting and returned to his mobile home. We went there and told him what was going on.

"Good idea," he said. "They'll like that." I gave him a signal indicating Beverley; he understood. "Would you come and help me feed the unicorns and make sure they have water in their buckets?"

"Absolutely!"

While the two of them walked over to the unicorn barn, I called Geoff on his phone and told him to let the goats go free. Then I caught up to the others. The unicorns had spent the day grazing on the grass around the grove and soaking up sunshine, so their stalls were empty. Mountain was instructing Beverley in how many scoops of grain to put into each unicorn's feed bin. He rolled out a hose to fill the water buckets.

I walked into the rear where the griffons gathered. A lion-and-eagle male rose and took a position at the edge of their space.

"Who's this?" I asked Mountain, confident he'd named them all by now.

"That's Eagle Eye. He watches everything."

Mountain followed me as I crouched near the nest where Thunderbird had curled up. Gingerly, I petted his neck. "Hey, you," I said softly. "Wake up. It's time to go hunt."

It took a few more strokes, but finally he stirred. A moment later he stretched. He lifted his head, weakly, and craned his neck to see me. He cocked his head and gave a soft version of his thundering cry.

"There's meat outside," I said.

The other griffons had already smelled prey and wandered out of the barn. I stepped away from Thunderbird to watch. As they cleared the barn doors their mighty wings spread and they took gracefully to the sky. I couldn't help following the last one out and taking in the sight of the majestic creatures circling the cornfield.

One swooped down in a lithe, plummeting attack so swift the goat never knew what hit it. I was grateful the kill was quick. Another and another made their kills.

Thunderbird limped up beside me, butting his shoulder into my hip the way a cat rubs itself on someone's leg as it passes. I stroked down his neck again. "Go on."

He hobbled out, occasionally putting weight on his injured foreleg, as if testing it. Geoff had apparently walked the goats to the field, removed their collars, and walked away. He was approaching on the newly graveled driveway and together we watched the griffons. Just as Thunderbird neared the edge of the cornfield, Eagle Eye landed before him and dropped the carcass of a goat, then backed away, bowing his head.

The doc and I shared a glance.

Thunderbird reached out with his injured foreleg, gripping at the goat. He had no talons left to make the grip a sure one. So, carefully, he switched, putting his weight on that one, and gripped the carcass firmly with the talons on the other. Voicing a thunderous call to the air, he tore into the kill and began to eat.

That evening, Kirk dropped Johnny off just before seven. He looked like he hadn't slept all night, but he kissed me and launched himself up the stairs to take a quick shower and shave. The usual suspects showed up just after him. The diverse crowd was certainly atypical of a kid's birthday party. Not only was the birthday girl the only child, she was the only mundane human among us.

When Johnny joined us, dinner was served and the party officially began, but Beverley and Ares were both already wearing birthday hats and, remarkably, the huge puppy tolerated it.

Nana had made chicken nuggets and cheesy potatoes as our guest of honor had requested. I ate two of the nuggets and more of the potatoes than I should have. After dinner, I presented the cake with ten pink candles. It set the room aglow. Johnny sang her a rocked-out version of "Happy Birthday." Theo took pictures for me.

Beverley blew out the candles and the celebratory dessert was consumed while we passed Beverley's joke book around and read random jokes aloud. Then it was on to the gift opening.

Theo's BlackBerry beeped. She snapped another photograph, handed me the camera, and checked her phone. A moment later, she tapped me on the shoulder. "My source got a hit," she whispered. "Can I use your computer?"

"Sure." It had been returned to its usual spot after Nana's room was finished.

Beverley was delighted with the iPod, digital camera, and clothes she received, but it was the electronic photo frame we'd all chipped in to get her that stole the show. Celia had preloaded it with pictures of Beverley's mom,

Lorrie. The images faded in and out, continually cycling through the files. We shared a tearful moment, Beverley hugging Celia tight.

When the party was over and Beverley was happily carrying her presents upstairs, Theo motioned Johnny and me over. "This is the Web site of a tattoo shop called the Arcane Ink Emporium."

"Okay." Not unlike the frame Beverley had just received, the site had a slideshow cycling through images of happy customers sporting their tattoos.

Theo clicked on the link to the staff page, scrolled down. The artists were listed with their photo and name to the left, and a paragraph about them to the right. At the bottom, an emoticon wearing dark sunglasses rested above the name *Arcanum.* The biography stated:

> The elusive Arcanum has been tattooing professionally for nearly a decade and the edgy, innovative ideas of this artist won AIE the coveted Badass Needle Award and that national recognition made AIE one of the topten tat shops in the Continental USA. Five years running, our name has been in the top five.
>
> If you want to wear the stimulating colors of this artist's imagination in your flesh, you'll have to be patient. Arcanum personally evaluates each potential client and the art they desire; applications available during regular business hours.

No guarantees are made about Arca-
num's availability or willingness to undertake
your project.

Theo tapped her fingers irritably on the desktop.
"It doesn't even indicate whether Arcanum is male or
female."

"Where is this shop?" I asked.

Theo clicked the *contact/directions* link. "Pittsburgh."

"Print that page. It's got the address and the hours,"
Johnny said. "Pittsburgh is only a few hours away. We
can go tomorrow, arrive by eleven, and if all goes well
we could be back in time for dinner." He acknowledged
Nana and added, "That is, if you can get Beverley from
school and cook again."

Nana frowned. "You're supposed to move me into my
new room!"

"I'll do the bulk of that tonight, and the rest I'll do
when we get back. Lickety-split." He grinned at Erik.
"Remind me of that word later. I've got a new song forming even now."

"I'm sure it's not dirty, either," Theo said.

"I need to talk to you, John," Erik said. Without waiting he headed through the living room and continued on
to the front porch. Johnny wiggled his tongue at us before
joining Erik outside.

I focused on Theo. "Tell me you've found something
on this SSTIX task force."

"You're not an easy customer, you know?" Her com-
plaint was given in a light tone. "Government agents . . .
their stuff is sealed and buried. I'm still working on it."

Zhan was helping Mountain with cleanup. Celia joined Theo and me at the big dining table where they discussed the housing market—Theo was tired of her apartment and interested in buying a small home while the market was in the buyer's favor. Nana was putting leftovers away so I went and started the dishes. Beverley must have heard the water and hurried down to help.

"You may have the night off from chores, birthday girl."

She drew closer and whispered, "What are Johnny and Erik arguing about?"

"They're arguing?"

"Outside. I heard 'em on my way down."

Pulling away from her I said, "I'll find out." Without making any kind of announcement to the others, I crossed the dining room to the living room and neared the window overlooking the porch. The two wæres had stepped farther out into the yard, making their voices hard to hear, but they were definitely using unhappy tones. Thinking about the *extras* I'd picked up in being master to a twice-marked vampire, I listened harder.

"Yes I can!" Johnny stressed.

"How can you be a Domn Lup and a touring rock star, man?"

"Why do you presume there's a line dividing those two roles?"

Erik muttered, "Common sense, maybe."

"The Rege wants me to make the rounds with pretty pro-wære speeches. The two agendas can work together! I'll just give those speeches in whatever town our show is in."

"Our *show*? We don't even have a contract, let alone a professional studio disc. I'm wasting my time, John, pissing away my shot by pinning it on someone who can't do the job."

"I *can* do the job."

"Not both."

"Stop it, all right? Don't you get it? You're telling me how the lines you're drawing around *me* mean *your* failure. You just have to stop drawing those lines and let me prove it."

"Prove what? We still don't have a contract."

"We had one from the vampire."

Erik paused. "You're not fucking serious?"

"If you're not *comfortable* with that either, you big pussy, then maybe you'd feel better knowing that the Zvonul have to provide the Domn Lup with personal funds. Who says we can't produce our own disc, shoot a video or two, and buy distribution from a midlevel label? Then we tour and make a name for ourselves."

"And what name are we making? Lycanthropia: The pet project of the Domn Lup. That'd be as embarrassing as Paris Hilton making another album." He paused. "And what would your justice-minded girlfriend think of you extorting funds from your higher-ups?"

"It wouldn't be extortion. They want me to go out there and be the face of wærewolves today. What better way than through music?"

"Sure. Hard, rockin' goth-industrial music that the majority of the population considers junk noise. The Zvonul will definitely want to promote *that* as the new wærewolf image." Erik's sarcasm held low, angry tones.

"I've said everything I can to convince you, Erik. Nothing's good enough."

"Go be the poster boy for the Packs and Allied Wæres, John. I won't be the timekeeper of a politico-façade band."

"Won't? *Won't?*"

"I'm done, man. I'm out. Feral's with me." Feral was the nickname of Phil Jones, their bassist.

"You two discussed this already?"

"Yeah. We did."

A long silent moment passed before Johnny said, "Well then, good luck in your next project." The shushing of grass told me he was walking away.

"Tell Celia I'm ready to go," Erik called.

I moved away from the window and headed back to the kitchen. Beverley was doing dishes. "Hey, you're supposed to be having a free night." I playfully pushed her away from the sink and took the sudsy plate and rag from her.

"I know." She dried her hands. "What did you hear?"

"Hear about what?" Nana asked.

I gave Beverley a now-you've-done-it look. "Not much."

That was when Johnny entered the front door. "Celia, Erik's waiting for you in the car," he called.

Celia asked for and got hugs from Beverley. Theo got one also and in the minutes that followed, both departed. Mountain left for his apartment and Zhan unrolled her sleeping bag on the couch. Johnny hefted every piece of furniture—except the bed—from Nana's old room. I helped him maneuver the chest of drawers through the door, then he carried it down the stairs. He didn't act as if anything was upsetting him, but his silence said enough.

By the time Beverley and Nana were ready to retire for the night, all that remained in Nana's room was her bed and the clothes in her closet. Johnny and I each took an armload—his encompassed everything I couldn't carry—and made the last trip down the stairs, around and into the new room. We dropped the clothes onto the new area rug and I set about resituating the items on their hangers and organizing them into some semblance of order. Not that it would matter to Nana.

"I've got this. Why don't you go watch TV?" I asked.

Johnny passed me the hanger with Nana's cabbage rose shirt on it. "Don't want to disturb Zhan."

"I thought disturbing people was a personal goal for you."

"Just on stage." After the words were spoken, he sighed.

Hands on hips, I asked, "What's wrong?"

"Erik's mad. Real mad. We have a rehearsal scheduled for tomorrow, and I assured him despite the Zvonul being around I'd make it to the practice studio. I clean forgot about it when I realized we might be able to go to Pittsburgh and find this Arcanum." He spent the next thirty minutes or so letting me drag out of him what I already knew about Erik. "I know I screwed up. But he won't let me make amends. It's not like him. It makes me think this is about something other than the band." We had moved on to Nana's laundry, most of which I'd hung up. We were nearly done.

"What else could it be about?"

"If I knew, I'd be doing something about it."

As I peered down into the laundry basket, all that remained were underwear and bras. "You going to help me fold her bloomers?" I held up a pair.

Johnny blinked. I'd seen him fight the Rege and the Omori, but wave an old woman's underpants at him and it left him aghast with fear.

"How'd it go with Todd and Kirk?"

"I called Beau like you said; he drove over." Johnny shook his head. "He brought a bottle of bourbon with him."

"Ah ha. No wonder you didn't come back all night."

"You miss me?"

"Of course. But . . ."

"But what?"

I lifted my hair to let him see my neck. I wasn't keeping secrets. "Maxine's death taxed the vampire."

He took a moment to hedge his reaction. "Did he behave himself?"

"He tried not to, but I insisted. He didn't stay long."

His jaw flexed, relaxed. "Good. Is he going to send another sentinel?"

I shrugged. "What'd you guys come up with, besides hangovers?"

"The Zvonul have to fund the Domn Lup. They won't want me to have a day job. The guitar store will be able to replace me, but Strictly 7 will soon be out a painter and tech and that's not a position that's easy to fill."

"Are you okay with that?"

He shrugged. "I'm not quitting until I've got someone trained. I won't do that to them."

My satellite phone rang. It was Theo. "Hello?"

"I did some digging on the Arcane Ink Emporium. Just a general query, how long they've had their licenses, whether they're current, that sort of thing."

"And?"

"This is too weird. It must be coincidence, but . . ."

"But what?"

"The licenses are in the name of AIE, but there's no lease on file for the building. It's privately owned, but the tat shop isn't listed as the owner."

"Who is?"

"Someone whose last name is Alcmedi. An Eris Alcmedi."

CHAPTER TWENTY-THREE

I thanked Theo and hung up. Dumping the last of Nana's undergarments into the chest of drawers, I announced that the bathtub was calling out for me to come and soak.

"Can I join you?" Johnny quipped.

Just then, Nana passed by the door carrying a glass of milk. She called out, "It isn't big enough for two." Then she added, "Besides, you two should save your naked leisure activities for when the rest of us are sound asleep."

My heart leaped to my throat, but Johnny laughed out loud and took me in his arms. "Demeter's awesome."

"Yeah. That's *definitely* the word I was going to use."

Johnny followed me up the stairs pinching my bottom, and while I gathered my pajamas, he crawled into bed with a notebook open to a fresh page with the words "Lickety Split" scrawled across the top.

I shut the bathroom door, started the water, and sat on the edge of my tub. My head dropped forward and my fingers kneaded the tight muscles in my neck and shoulders.

My mother owns the building Arcanum works in.

Damn it.

Can't I just be done with her?

I slid into the warm water, eager to soak as I'd claimed, but the bath was actually a cover for what I truly meant to do: meditate and talk to Amenemhab.

Relaxing, I entered the meditative state I call alpha and visualized the familiar scenery. Beside the willow tree, I waded out into the water, ankle deep, and cleansed my chakras. When that was complete, I sloshed to the shore and saw the gray and tan jackal trotting up. "What's troubling you?"

There's never a prelude here. "My mother."

"We knew you weren't done hating her." He sat on his haunches. "And that we would be doing a lot of work on the 'challenge to your heart' before we were through."

After telling Amenemhab of her showing up at my house and my reaction, I concluded that part of the story with, "I'm just done with her."

"So you said nothing. You shut the door in her face. That's not a resolution, Persephone."

"What's to resolve? I'm *done.*"

He afforded me his most sage, "that's what you think" expression. "Then why, pray tell, are you here?"

I explained about Johnny's tattoos. "The best lead we have takes us to a tattoo artist in a building owned by my mother. I'm going to have to confront her to find out about this Arcanum person and see if she thinks he'd be willing to undo what he did to Johnny, or if we're going to have to force him." I sighed. "After what I did, she may be disinclined to help."

"Hard to be *done* with someone if you need their help."

"Exactly. So, here I am."

"You don't want *her* to shut the door in *your* face, hmmm?"

"Look, she nearly got me killed, dumped me, left me for Nana to raise. My reaction is justified. Hers never was."

"Perhaps." He lay down, crossed his front paws. "This situation with your mother will never be over until you either truly let it go, or you accept it and go forward."

"Then I accept that she hates me and I hate her and we will leave it at that and go forward."

"If she hates you, why did she seek you out?"

"I don't know," I said, throwing my arms up in the air. "All I know is she didn't look for me until it was made public that I've become court witch in a vampire's haven. If that's her motive, it speaks for itself. I just want it to be over, done, and behind me."

"And it was . . . until she made her move. But now, to help Johnny, you have to make a move."

"I hate chess analogies." I couldn't play chess. Checkers was as ambitious as I got with a checkerboard. "I guess you're going to tell me that chess players gauge all their options and their opponent's possible reactions to each before they decide on their move?"

"I apparently don't have to."

"I wanted my move to be a nullifying nonmove so I could remain in the 'nothing is changing' frame of mind," I muttered.

"But that's not an option if you have to confront her

about the people in her building in order to accomplish Johnny's goals." He sat up. "You're going to have to make a move toward acceptance."

"Acceptance isn't a light switch I can just flip on and off."

"But it *is* time to shine some light on this. It's been in the dark too long."

I snorted. *Just like a totem to twist my metaphors against me.* "Okay, for argument's sake, say I *do* move toward acceptance. That will alter that core fundamental issue that honed me into who I am. And going a step further, if I reexamine this and it's 'resolved,' it may change things."

"May? Something this big *will* change things. It will change you." He lifted a paw and gestured at me. "Whether that change is for better or worse, depends on you."

I was being asked to surrender the sorrow and pain that molded me, that had forged me to be a survivor, a fighter. "I can't forgive her."

"Can't or won't?" The jackal's voice was as firm and demanding as I'd ever heard it.

"The choice she made hurt me so much, so very much. She didn't care about anyone but herself."

"What if she cares now? What if she has learned?"

I snorted.

"Then that means you 'won't' forgive her. And that is less noble than 'can't' forgive her." He stood. "You have a few hours of drive time to figure what you will do." He padded away.

I wasn't done. "Oh, hell, Amenemhab! I expected her to do what she was supposed to do as my mother. She failed. And now you're acting like I'm supposed to let her get away with how she treated me. I'm the Lustrata! I'm supposed to be an instrument of justice." My voice broke. "What she did was not just."

Over his shoulder Amenemhab met my eyes, my anger and grief, briefly. When he spoke, his words were soft and aimed at the ground. "Sometimes justice cannot be served. Sometimes only forgiveness will do."

I left the visualization and woke to pruny fingers and lukewarm bathwater.

Quickly washing up and shampooing, I worked up a little preamble to tell Johnny about my mother's visit, and about her owning the building where Arcane Ink Emporium was housed.

When I entered the bedroom, however, I found him sound asleep. The notepad teetered on the edge of the bed. I placed it on the nightstand; half a page was scrawled with lyrics. I stepped on the pen that had fallen from his grip.

I sighed, turned out the light, and crawled in beside him.

When my satellite phone rang at six-thirty, I grabbed it and shot out of bed. It was Menessos.

"Did I wake you?"

"Of course," I whispered back. I grabbed my robe and headed across the hall and into the bathroom so I wouldn't disturb Johnny.

"I apologize."

"Don't. My alarm would go off shortly anyway."

"I was calling to invite you to the haven tonight."

"I can't."

"A date?"

"We might be out of town."

"Oh?"

"Yeah." I started to tell him that we were going to Pittsburgh, but I remembered that he had said Heldridge was seen in Pittsburgh. "Any news on Heldridge?"

"Baltimore. We have some surprises waiting for him."

So long as he keeps putting distance between us, I'm glad. "That's good."

"Any chance you'll reconsider your getaway? I'm having a party tonight, officially accepting his people into my fold."

"All of them?"

"Those who preferred to be somewhere else have relocated." He sighed. "I am very selective about who I want around me. We have interviewed them all now. I admit, some were forcibly relocated, but in truth, few required such action. I'm keeping almost half of them." He covered the phone partially and spoke to someone else about a caterer for the Beholders and Offerlings. I heard, "Eva, dear, I am certain your chocolates must be divine, but keep them out of my haven." His tone was firm. "I feed upon these people. I find the caffeine in it . . . distasteful." He stopped there, but this time when he continued his voice was deep and angry. "I don't care what Heldridge thought. Get out." To me he said, "Pardon my rudeness."

"Don't worry about it."

"I will fret if you're not here. Taking them on was your idea; the building of your barns was a large part of their test."

It was unlikely we would get back from Pittsburgh in time to make his soiree in Cleveland, but then again we might not even find Eris and be turning around and coming right back. "Maybe."

"Maybe? What if I promise to provide you with a sensible outfit for the evening?"

Every event he hosted had a dress code. "There's a lot going on today. I'll let you know, okay? That's the best I can do."

Johnny came out of the bedroom, stretching and yawning.

"An Erus Veneficus cannot deny her master," Menessos said.

Johnny looked askance at me. With his wære hearing he'd probably caught that last bit.

"But the Regional Lord can say she has been set on an important task." I both rebutted Menessos's point and answered Johnny's look with that statement. "Especially if his *real* master tells him he should." Seeing Johnny had grabbed a towel from the linen closet, I twirled the shower handle and the water rained out.

"We will begin at eight o'clock. If your important task is completed in time."

"Thank you."

"No, thank *you*. I can hear the shower running and now I am imagining you all wet and lathering yourself." His laugh was the last thing I heard before he ended the call. I didn't get to tell him it was actually Johnny's shower running.

• • •

By dawn, a little after seven, I had packed an overnight bag for our trip to Pittsburgh. I could hope we didn't have to stay more than the day, but realistically, Johnny had a lot of tattoos. If we did find this Arcanum and he cooperated, I had no idea whether one spell would suffice to unlock them all at once or not. Regardless, we had to be back by noon tomorrow. That was when Beverley's second party would start.

After silently counting out ten thousand dollars from the duffel bag I kept under my bed, I stuffed the hundred Benjamins into an envelope. The urge to write on it "Money to Bribe Arcanum" tempted me for a moment, but I resisted and shoved it into the overnight bag.

A door slammed downstairs. *Nana's up.*

I'm telling her. Right now.

Amenemhab had told me a truth I didn't want to accept. Forgiveness just wasn't the emotion my heart was anxious to grant my mother, and I was certain Nana would agree with me. So I took my bag downstairs prepared to fess up about what I'd been keeping from her. It would mean taking some of her wrath, but I'd end up with her support. I hoped.

She'd made coffee. *Bless her.*

"Is Beverley up?" she asked.

"Her alarm won't go off for another ten minutes or so. Ready to move into the new room?"

"Smells like paint."

"Open the windows today."

"I opened them when I came downstairs. That's why the door's shut."

That explains the grouchy slam she'd given it. "You want some air freshener?"

She clamped her jaw and glared out the window, fingers tapping impatiently on the tabletop. I poured two cups of coffee and joined her at the dinette. "I have a confession to make," I said.

"I'm no priest."

She was in a serious snit. Maybe telling her was a bad idea. "What's wrong?"

"Last night, Beverley brought me my money back." Nana had given the girl four ten-dollar bills as her present.

"Did she say why?"

"She said she'd rather have a different present."

That sounded rude, and not at all like Beverley. "What did she say she wanted?"

"She wanted me to buy myself those Nicorette patches they advertise on TV. She asked me to quit smoking."

Now the reason for her snit and for her asking whether Beverley was up yet became clear. She hadn't yet had a cigarette. "Good for you."

Her attention snapped to me. "What?"

"You're obviously trying."

She snorted and glared at something in the field.

"Though it's a double-edged sword, I suppose."

"What's that supposed to mean?"

"You're the toughest lady I know. If you set your mind to something you'll do it or die."

"I passed on that quality, you know."

I smiled. "Wouldn't have it any other way."

She lifted her coffee cup and drank.

"But I also know that someone telling you that you *can't* do something is as good as daring you to do it. And you never back down from a dare."

She put the cup down. "What are you saying?"

"I'm saying that if you want to quit smoking, you'll only have to defeat the tough lady who raised me. Are you tough enough to defeat yourself?"

She snorted again. "We'll see. Where's your favorite mug?" She pointed at the plain black mug I was using. "I was going to set it out for you."

"Broke it."

She tsk-tsked. "Well, what's your confession, my child?"

Her sarcasm is not something I'll ever get accustomed to. "This past Tuesday, while you were at the store. I had a visitor."

"Who?"

I hesitated so I could take a deep breath and steel my nerves for this.

"Wasn't that old boyfriend of yours, was it?"

"No."

"Not the boy you went to the prom with?"

"No."

As Nana stared down into the dark fluid, she wrapped both hands around the base of her mug, clinging to it like a life raft. I was willing to bet she'd initially try to pacify her nicotine addiction with additional caffeine.

"Why are you bringing them up?"

"Because there's a sense of hurt about you this morning. Old hurt."

I pushed my coffee cup away and sat back, crossed my arms. "My mother stopped by."

Nana didn't move—even blink—for a long moment.

"Apparently, I made the news in Pittsburgh."

"That's where she is?"

I nodded. It was my turn to stare angrily out the window. I saw Mountain in the distance, shutting the door to his mobile home and heading over to the phoenix coop. A moment later, the door opened again and Zhan stepped out, hurrying this way.

The possibilities of what that meant derailed my train of thought.

But Nana promptly set the locomotive back on the tracks. "What did she think of you being on the news?"

"Dunno," I said flatly. "I shut the door in her face."

Nana considered it, then shook her head. "That's mean."

"Mean? After what she—"

"Not *that*. I know you don't want to have anything to do with her." She paused. "I don't know that I'd have opened the door in the first place."

"Then what's mean about it?"

"You telling me about it *this* morning. Now I want a cigarette more than ever."

After breakfast when Beverley went upstairs to brush her teeth, I told Johnny about my mother's visit, and announced to him, Nana, and Zhan that Theo had discovered Eris owned the building the tattoo parlor was in. Zhan finally understood who the upsetting mystery guest had been. Johnny and Nana now saw that this little road trip was going to be harder for me than originally thought.

While Johnny took Beverley to the bus stop in Nana's car, Zhan, who was going to Pittsburgh with us, packed an overnight bag. I'd packed a second bag with magical supplies and Zhan helped load the Audi's trunk. Once the bags were in place, I laid my broom atop them and shut the trunk.

I hadn't had the nerve to ask Zhan about seeing her come out of Mountain's mobile home earlier. I hadn't even let on that I was aware that she'd snuck into the house. She could just claim she'd stopped in while making her rounds—and it might have been true, for all I knew. The sleeping bag on the couch was rumpled. All my suspicions were based on seeing how the Beholder had reacted to this particular Offerling.

We waited in the house. Johnny was late.

When he arrived, his face was flushed and his jaw set. "I think I fucked up."

"Why?"

"One of the moms came over to the car and set into a cop-worthy interrogation of me. She wanted to know who I was, how I was related to Demeter, and whether I was going to be at the party tomorrow."

"What did you tell her?" I asked.

"I gave her the short answers, and added that there were circumstances to the whole thing the news hadn't covered and if she had any common sense she'd understand they only report stuff that will entice people like her to tune in—truth notwithstanding." He shook his head. "She didn't like that. She said, 'I don't want my daughter around *your* kind,' and headed back to her car. So I got out and followed her."

"You didn't."

"I did. I told her the party wasn't for me or you or even her, but for Beverley—a sweet kid we all care deeply about, a kid who deserves to have a fun birthday party. I said, 'Beverley hasn't done anything wrong, lady. She's respectful, does her chores, and gets outstanding grades. If you prefer your daughter not be friends with a kid like that, then you're clearly one of those people with a cranial-rectal inversion and we don't want *your* kind at our party.'"

Stunned, somewhat horrified, and yet wanting to laugh, I covered my mouth until I figured out which reaction to give full rein.

"Did I just totally screw up her party?"

Before anyone could answer, the sound of firm knocking on my front door interrupted.

On my way to the door, I recognized the plain, government-tagged Impala in my driveway. Special Agent Brent and his pal Napier stood on my porch again. This time they were smiling.

"Now what?" I asked through the screen door.

"I wasn't certain we'd find you here," Damian Brent said.

"Did you think I'd skip town?" I detected Zhan moving into the living room. Johnny stood behind me.

Damian Brent shrugged. "Your friends keep ending up in the city morgue."

My jaw clamped shut. *Maxine.*

"Five patrons of the Lodi Grocery witnessed the murder of Maxine Simmons in the parking lot. According to their statements, someone matching your description was hit in the head with a baseball bat and stuffed into the back of a white van, which then sped away. Seems you were kidnapped, Ms. Alcmedi, but here you are safe and sound at home." He gave the impression he was quite concerned.

With witnesses and Maxine being dead, it wasn't as if I could deny it.

"How is your head?" he asked.

"My head is fine. Now."

"It *was* you the murderers stuffed into the van?"

"Yes. I escaped." It would only cause trouble for Johnny and the pack if I admitted I knew who kidnapped me; it would mean I knew who had murdered Maxine and that was a can of worms I didn't want to open. "Maxine's death is tragic."

"Ah, yes, but the death of the *one person* who could provide you an alibi for the time when Xerxadrea Veilleux was murdered must have you quite worried."

"I actually hadn't considered that." *It was worrisome* now *because he mentioned it.*

"When I was informed the deceased was Maxine Simmons, I remembered her name from my notes. We're here as a courtesy. Since you're here and safe, however, I have to ask, did you get a good look at the men who took you and murdered your friend?"

"No. As we walked around the van, they shot her and I

thought she'd tripped. I bent to help her up. Just as I saw the bullet wound, I was hit. I blacked out."

"But you escaped. Did you see anyone then?"

"No."

"Where were you being held?"

Johnny put his arm around me protectively. "Back off, man. This has been traumatic."

"Since Ms. Simmons was an Offerling to the Regional Vampire Lord, this murder investigation has fallen to me. I'd like Ms. Alcmedi to come down to the station and give a formal statement. If you'd like to initiate the paperwork for kidnapping charges, we can tend to that as well."

"I can do that on Monday," I said bleakly. "This weekend is pretty tight."

"She's been through so much we are going to visit some family," Johnny added. "She can give you a statement Monday." I was impressed he'd twisted the current events so fluidly.

"It doesn't work that way, Mr. Newman," Clive Napier said. "And we have some questions for you as well."

"Me? About what?"

"Let's talk at the station, okay?"

Johnny and I exchanged glances. In the living room, Zhan waved to get our attention. She nodded; she was already on her cell phone. Nana shuffled down the hall bringing my jacket. "I'll make some calls," she whispered.

They were calling in the cavalry.

CHAPTER TWENTY-FOUR

The agents put us in the back of their gray Chevy Impala. The black upholstered seats were clean and the new car smell was pronounced. Into the formal silence that descended as Napier typed an address into the GPS device, Johnny asked, "You guys don't get anything better than an Impala?"

"No," Special Agent Brent answered flatly.

Johnny seemed to have touched a sore spot.

The men up front didn't engage us or each other in conversation so it became a tedious ride. Thank goodness it wasn't long. Shortly after he turned onto US 303, I knew where we were going. Evidently SSTIX, although a federal agency, didn't rate space in the Homeland Security offices in Cleveland or with the FBI in either Cleveland or Akron.

When we arrived at the little station, however, Brent glared at Napier. "This is the local law enforcement facility?" he asked quietly.

"It's the closest one. I called and confirmed we'd be using it as a field station."

Brent got out and slammed his door.

"He keeps that up," Johnny said to Napier, "and he's gonna slam this little bucket of bolts apart."

Napier ignored him and got out.

In sync, the two agents opened the rear doors for Johnny and me.

Brent wasn't happy with the rural cop shop. The brick façade was approximately two feet wide on either side of a white, single-car garage door that took up the bulk of the building's front. The rest was a white door with two full sidelights. The roof peaked in the middle and had a niche. Someone had filled the niche with cement and finished by shoving a black clock into the mortar.

At our approach, the door opened and the part-time sheriff of these parts waved in greeting. He wasn't much older than me, and he was lean in a bookish way. A scientist's lab coat would have suited him better than a badge. "Howdy," he said. "Are you the fellow that called about using the room?"

"We are," Special Agent Brent said. Polite introductions followed and I learned that our part-time law enforcement was the township mayor's nephew, Robbie Carter. *The only action he was likely to see out here was a paper cut.*

"This way."

We followed him inside, passing through a small waiting area with four dusty folding chairs in it—no butt prints, even. In the hall, we walked past a room with a door where Officer Carter's desk sat to our right. At the end of the hall were two more doors. The left one, I assumed, led to the garage area where his patrol car must have been parked. The one straight ahead opened into a nine-by-nine room with a table and four more folding chairs. A file and a tape recorder rested on the table. Beyond it was a countertop with a microwave, a small sink, and a tiny refrigerator.

"It doubles as the break room," Officer Carter said proudly. "I laid out our local forms for you, and the tape recorder you requested. There's some bottled water in the fridge. Help yourselves." Robbie let himself out and disappeared down the hall.

"Agent Napier, Mr. Newman, wait out front, will you?" Agent Brent said.

I sat down and dropped my purse onto the floor, feeling grateful I hadn't ended up in one of those narrow rooms with a one-way mirror. Still, it was an interrogation room: a windowless box with one stretch of overhead fluorescent lighting. On the ride over, I'd pondered several angles to explain how my kidnapping occurred without implicating the Omori or the Zvonul, but I hadn't come up with an answer. Where had I been held? I was going to have to lie and say I didn't know, claim traumatic memory loss. *I hope they don't want to examine the knock on my head since it's gone now.*

Special Agent Damian Brent shut the door then removed his jacket, exposing his shoulder holster. From his jacket pocket, he removed a few of those drive-thru packages of salt. He snapped the end and shook the granules around the room.

Have to give him credit for trying to protect his ass from magic. But his information was somewhat flawed. Salt could be used to cleanse sacred spaces, counteract magic in motion, clear old magic away. It wouldn't have stopped me from starting a new spell and it certainly wouldn't hinder me from calling on the ley line.

He pushed the record button on the device, checked to see that it was running. After speaking a perfunctory intro—our names, location, the date and time, he said, "There's a few things you need to know."

"Like?"

"If you so much as make a move or give a hint that you are using magic, I am authorized to use my weapon."

"Understood."

"Secondly . . . I believe you went to a different grocery on Thursday and bought a cake."

They had me followed? "Yeah. Didn't much feel like going back to the Lodi Grocery. What's that got to do with me giving a statement about what happened to Maxine?"

"We'll get to that homicide in a moment. You picked up a package of decorated cookies in the bakery."

"So?"

"My agent bought the cookies you'd handled and we lifted your prints from the packaging."

"Okay."

"We also printed the Glass House of the Cleveland Botanical Gardens after Xerxadrea Veilleux's body was discovered there. A bit daunting that, being a public place and all, but our team has been cataloguing all of those prints this week, and when we got yours yesterday . . ."

He let that dangle for a several seconds. I resolved not to say anything. Then I did anyway. "So you brought me down here to question me about the incident at the Botanical Gardens, not about the death of Maxine Simmons, as you led me to believe." I wanted that on the tape.

His little victory made him smile. "We have your prints on both doors exiting the Glass House. No matter what Maxine Simmons claimed, you *were* there. And we can prove it."

I thought back. Menessos and I had left through the doors in the mirrored section, where people are supposed to make certain no butterflies have landed on them and are about to leave their protected area. I *had* touched both doors. *Shit.*

"Did you kill Xerxadrea Veilleux?"

"No!"

The door opened.

"My client will answer no more questions."

I couldn't believe who I saw.

It was Vilna-Daluca.

Damian Brent rose from his seat, hand politely extended, and introduced himself. "You are?"

"Vilna-Daluca Veilleux." She did not accept his hand, though she did give his extended appendage a look that said she found the notion repulsive. "I've been appointed by WEC to represent Ms. Alcmedi."

My shock had to have been apparent. Not only was I stunned that this self-professed "enemy" of mine was here acting as my defender, but her last name was the same as Xerxadrea's. *Were they sisters?*

Brent hadn't missed it either. "Veilleux? Are you a relation of the deceased?"

"A distant cousin." She waved off any inference he might have been reaching for. "Come, Persephone." She opened the door.

"You can't leave," he protested.

"Do you intend to arrest her?" Vilna asked pointedly.

"I can. Her prints were found among those at the scene."

"*That's* your probable cause? A public place where anyone can visit? I'm sure you found plenty of prints."

"And an eyewitness saw her fly away on a broom, through the hole torn in the Glass House roof."

Vilna opened the file under her arm, flipped through some of the pages. "The report says the officer observed a red cape flapping as someone flew away on a broom. He could not identify this person."

"She was on TV in a red cape."

"Circumstantial, Agent Brent. Little Red Riding Hood has been seen on television."

"Her prints were found on two doors exiting the Glass House. It puts her at the scene of the crime."

Vilna shook her head sadly. "Young man, she lives here. She could have been a visitor to the gardens anytime. And if your witness saw her leave through the ceiling, why would her prints be on the exit doors?"

Brent sneered at her. "The prints and the witness are enough to place her at the scene of the crime."

"And the murder of the one person providing her with an alibi will lend credibility to the notion that she was set up. I have many character witnesses who can and will testify to the profound love my client had for the deceased. There is no motive for her to have perpetrated such a crime."

"Motive? Ms. Veilleux, your client had just become the Erus Veneficus of the Regional Vampire Lord." His syllables were clipped and curt, voice deepening just enough to make sure we all knew he was getting pissed off. "That's a position that puts her at odds with WEC, reason enough for an Eldrenne to confront her."

Vilna-Daluca wasn't fazed by the anger brewing around him. "Not if Ms. Alcmedi was planted there for purposes of espionage."

Damian Brent's face blanked in surprise.

"You're not the only special agent in the room, young man. And I can assure you that my client did not murder the Eldrenne. If we doubted that, I wouldn't be here. And," she added ominously, "neither would she." She tossed a business card into the air and it flipped and floated down onto the table where it skittered directly in front of him—guided by sorcery. "Please have your people send me the full disclosure paperwork as soon as possible. I have found it is always illuminating." She may have been old, but she showed him an evil-granny smile that nearly made me shiver. The wicked-witch expression trumped human anger every time. "Good-bye, Agent Brent."

I followed her down the hallway. Agent Brent called out, "Do you represent Mr. Newman as well?"

Vilna spun, incensed by the idea. "A wærewolf?" She gave him a single-noted derisive laugh. "Did you catch the part about me being from WEC, Agent Brent? We don't represent wærewolves." She stomped out.

I waited long enough for Johnny to give me a nod, then followed her.

"What really happened?" she demanded as we proceeded along the sidewalk.

"The fairies poisoned one of their own, a mermaid fairy named Aquula, and killed her," I said. "Xerxadrea and Menessos were burying her at the Botanical Gardens. After she was laid to rest, the fairies attacked."

Vilna-Daluca stopped dead. "That's a very neat explanation, now that you've sealed the doorway and the fairies cannot be questioned."

"Menessos and Goliath can corroborate my story!"

"Vampire words are worthless in a witches' court."

"Vilna, I swear to you. The fire fairy was the one throwing the fireballs. Xerxadrea dove in and . . ." I swallowed hard. "She took a fireball to save me. Then she crashed. She died inside. Menessos had been accompanied by Goliath and we gave him my red cape and my broom, thinking he'd draw off the fairies while we made an escape. Goliath waited until the last moment to buy us time to get out. We took a cab to The Dirty Dog, then returned to the haven." I left out the part about Menessos mesmerizing a police officer. That was definitely illegal.

Vilna-Daluca shook her head. "A vampire piloting a witch broom alone?" She thrust her finger at me threateningly. "I know better than that."

"I awakened it to life and commanded it to carry him as he bid that night. It did."

"Impossible."

"It *did*! Goliath was taught the ways of magic before he was turned."

She walked away from me, grumbling. I hurried after her. "Vilna! Wait!" I caught up to her just as she was joined by Celeste and Ludovica, who had stepped out of an antique shop. In street clothes the *lucusi* members could have been average older citizens out for a stroll, but their malign mugs made me keep my distance as I added, "I can't believe you showed up here. Thank you."

"Don't thank me," she snapped. "I came to ensure I get the disclosure files, not to hear your lies."

"But—"

"WEC takes care of our own, Ms. Alcmedi, and in this case, that's the Eldrenne. WEC's punishment won't be doled out by human courts. I will see you Bindspoken yet."

No you won't. "Vilna," I said softly, almost pitifully. She said nothing; the gleam in her eyes was pure hate. "Will there be a Crossing Ceremony for Xerxadrea?"

For a split second, her gaze softened. In one blink, though, all the severity resurfaced. "We've had it already. You weren't invited."

As the three of them marched away, leaving me standing on the sidewalk alone, my heart sank. Tears spilled.

To make matters worse, Johnny was still inside the police station.

Adjacent to the station was the Town Hall, a quaint and tiny brick building with a more formal flavor to its façade. I settled on the steps there and dried my cheeks with my sleeve. *I'll perform my own remembrance ceremony.*

Head in hands, I waited for Johnny to come out.

Though Vilna had gotten me out of the station, this wasn't over. *She made me out to be an undercover witch in*

Menesso's's court. That didn't seem like the kind of information that would make someone like Agent Brent back off, now that I thought about it. It seemed more like the kind of challenge that would add fuel to his fire.

The chorus of Judas Priest's "Breaking the Law" erupted from the flannel's left breast pocket.

I didn't recall bringing the protrepticus, but I grabbed it with such haste I nearly ripped the pocket. Even as I opened it I blurted, "Sam? How are you doing this?"

"Ha ha ha, little girl. Wouldn't you like to know? Zhan's bringing a car. Almost there."

The light on the protrepticus faded out again.

I pushed buttons. I opened and shut it. I removed the battery pack, shook it, and put it back. The lights didn't even flicker on the dead little scrap of technology.

A familiar Audi sidled up to the curb. Zhan waved. All I could do was nod and get in.

And wait for Johnny.

CHAPTER TWENTY-FIVE

We didn't have long to wait. Johnny emerged from the police station less than ten minutes later.

"In addition to the Eldrenne's death, they're investigating the long strips of melted glass found on the Lake Erie shore," Johnny said as he buckled his seat belt. Zhan was letting him drive; she sat in the back.

"How'd they link that to you?" I asked as he accelerated onto US 303.

"A man's wedding ring was found embedded in the glass. Though partially melted it had some unique markings, which led to the item being ID'd as one that was sold to Robert and Donna Conner."

"Oh no."

"Yeah. They paid a visit to the Conners' house, trying to locate Robert to ask *him* about the glass. Donna told them they should ask me where he is."

"What did you say?"

"I asked him if I was under arrest. He said they were just looking for information. I said I didn't have any and couldn't help him." Johnny shook his head. "It won't be the last of it, but he had no reason to hold me. I mean, Donna didn't even file a missing person's report."

We were coming up on a road that would connect us to the interstate. "Are we heading home or to Pittsburgh?"

"It's two and half hours one way," Zhan said.

Johnny shook his head again. "We're going home. This day's fucked."

"But I thought you wanted to get this taken care of ASAP."

"I do . . . but we never moved Demeter's bed to her new room and there should be a sense of hope in the onset of what we're undertaking. Not this. Nearly being arrested is like a bad omen, you know?"

"I didn't think you were superstitious like that."

"Me either."

I wondered if this "bad omen" should keep us from the haven tonight.

After lunch, I ordered the cake for the kids' party the next day and we set about taking Nana's bed apart and relocating it in her new room. When we were done, Johnny decided to track down Feral, Lycanthropia's bass-ist, and talk to him about the band situation.

Before he left, I asked, "Has the Rege set a date to confirm you?"

"No. I think he's got his people working on ways to alter the interpretation of their laws so he can deny me even after I prove that I can change at will."

I broached the subject of the party at the haven. "Should we go?"

"Yeah. You have your duties. I should be back in time for it."

"Should be?"

Zhan let him take the Audi. I think it was a means to coerce him to return on time.

Nana worked on her quilting. I settled in at the dinette in the kitchen and wrote up a reminder list for the party. It was the first kids' party I'd ever thrown, and even though I'd be disguised as someone else, I wanted Nana to have a reference to make sure everything was proceeding according to plan.

Zhan stepped into the room. "I've been thinking," she said, "about Maxine, about life, and about what you said the other day."

I gestured for her to join me. "Which part of what I said?"

"That you'd talk to Menessos for me." She sat across from me. "To ask him if I could go home."

"You'll let me ask now?"

She nodded. "But wait until after Pittsburgh. You've got enough going on right now."

"Okay. I'm sure he won't have a problem with it." I'd pull rank if I had to.

"Can I take pictures of them, the animals, to show my father?"

"Absolutely." I stopped. "Oh, and talk to Mountain. If he thinks it would be all right—and if your family can house them—maybe you could take a few of the phoenixes. If your family would like to be charged with their keeping, it might be like a peace offering from you."

She was stunned. "You would do that for me?"

"Of course." When I answered, her chin dropped, her mind surely racing with the logistics of getting phoenixes to the West Coast, as well as the family reunion playing out in her imagination. Movement outside caught my attention. Mountain had emerged from the field.

He was hammering in some metal posts to erect a temporary fence across the new driveway to the barns: no need to provide a tempting pathway for our young guests.

Sneakily, I added. "But if you go . . ."

"What?" She sounded concerned.

"Mountain would miss you." I pointed through the glass.

She saw him. Her concern converted into guilt. "Don't tell the Boss."

"I won't tell. Why would I?"

"Offerlings and Beholders aren't supposed to . . . to . . ."

"Like I said, I won't tell."

"Mountain is good to me," she said softly, wringing her hands. "He sees me. Other men see . . . something else."

"You don't have to explain, Zhan."

She had resumed staring at the tabletop.

"Why don't you go ask Mountain now? Work the plan out."

She rose from the table, but lingered long enough to say, "Thank you."

• • •

The sun set at five-thirteen and my now-expected connection to Menessos clicked in. It was full dark when Johnny arrived at six o'clock as promised. It felt much later than it truly was. We sat together in the back as Zhan drove us to the haven.

Johnny told me how his afternoon had gone. "Feral didn't believe I kicked an Omori's ass, or put the Rege on his knees. I had to conference call Kirk and Todd to corroborate."

"What did he say then?"

"He grunted, but that was because he was under someone's sink."

"Huh?"

"He was on a service call." Feral's day job was plumbing. "So I drove out and joined him."

"Did you help?"

"I fetched him tools. Helped him carry things in and out."

"Did your labor have a payoff?"

He nodded. "He called Erik, had him meet us at Triv's restaurant. Over a beer, Feral told Erik what the other guys had told him. And then he says to Erik, 'I'm telling him.'" Johnny set his jaw momentarily, demonstrating his irritation before he continued. "The Rege had sent Omori to their houses and they were told the band would be breaking up eventually, but if they quit and made the process go smoother, they would be given 'severance pay.' They each got an envelope with twenty-five grand."

"No way."

"Way."

"They took it?"

"When the Omori shows up on your doorstep, you comply."

"You didn't."

He smirked. "I'm the Domn Lup."

It occurred to me that we were talking rather freely about pack stuff in front of Zhan. Johnny had wanted to avoid Maxine's knowing too much. I took his hand and, concentrating, tried to figure out how to word what I wanted to say.

He squinted at me. "It's all right," he said.

"Huh?"

"I could . . . hear you."

He gripped my hand tight. *Menessos called me. We talked.*

His lips hadn't moved. Yet I'd heard him.

In signum amoris. Menessos had admitted he'd used magic on Johnny and me when we had sex at the haven. He'd claimed it was a link, a shared mental connection by which we'd be able to sense each other's moods. If the emotions were strong enough, like fear, it might call to the other—a benefit that we might find "as worthwhile as the more physical one." The vampire had also said Johnny and I had already imprinted on each other, inflaming that physical bond. The *in signum amoris* made it an emotional bond as well.

And then we shared pieces of our souls, making it spiritual, Johnny added.

"Lord and Lady!" I said aloud.

"Everything all right back there?" Zhan asked.

"We're fine," Johnny said and winked at me, adding, *Wanna see how she reacts if we make out?*

CHAPTER TWENTY-SIX

Menessos's haven was in the lowest levels of the old May Company building on Euclid Avenue, facing Public Square. The eight-story building was beautiful, with white glazed terra cotta tiles framing the nine bays of Chicago-style windows and all of it topped with a scrolled pediment and a Renaissance Revival clock.

Well, it's beautiful above street level, anyway.

The ground level had a flat industrial-type awning that jutted out. While it provided cover from the elements, it seemed to me that the plainness below that awning detracted from the rest of the building. The restaurant next door to the haven had a strange portico embellished with an old car, neon lights, and tall arborvitae in containers. It didn't fit with the majesty of the rest of the building.

But then Menessos's frontage didn't add any class either, being comprised of plywood walls and a primer gray door. Or it had been on my *last* trip to the haven. As Zhan rolled to a stop to let us out, I saw a newly refurbished exterior, dazzlingly lit.

The vampire haven's entry now matched the white glazed tiles and architectural trimmings. There were also sections that encroached just slightly on the sidewalk, like half an octagon, with four six-inch-wide panels of glass separated by narrow strips of white tile.

Two sets of doors were lit from the front and behind; the white of the frosted glass seemed to glow, and was interrupted only with the universal vampire symbol—six gleaming white teeth on a field of black inside a red circle. Of course, the outermost teeth were razory fangs. The word HAVEN was written below in bold lettering.

A foot-wide plastic banner was stretched across the left set of doors. It read OPENING SOON.

Johnny held the door for me. Inside, the cherrywood ticket booth gleamed under soft lighting, and I saw that the entire lobby was finished. A metal security fence separated this from the open space beyond, which was now blocked by plastic sheeting.

"Guess he's refinishing in there, too."

"Didn't he tell you?" Johnny asked. "He's putting in a nightclub. That's what those two angled things out front are for."

So Menessos and Johnny were getting chummy? Not necessarily a bad thing. "Those bay windows indicate this is a nightclub?"

He gave a throaty laugh. "They will when there are scantily clad young women dancing in them."

I groaned and headed for the stairs, but I saw the elevators were now unbarred. I punched the button. The doors opened and Johnny and I stepped in. He waved up at the corner. Seeing the question on my face, he said, "Always cameras in elevators."

It must have been true. When the doors opened on the

lower level, Risqué was waiting for us in all of her red-eyed, blonde-ringleted glory. She bowed her head toward me and murmured, "Erus Veneficus." She followed it with a nod at Johnny. "Gorgeous." She twisted on her clear plastic heel and barked, "This way," as she strutted off.

We followed without a word. Tonight Risqué wore aqua blue ruffled satin short-shorts. I hoped there was a top of some sort under those mounds of curls, but considering Risqué's proclivity for a topless tease look, it was not likely.

She escorted us to the same rooms where she had fixed my hair for the Erus Veneficus induction ceremony. "Damn it," she murmured. "They didn't bring the beauty case over yet. I'll be right back."

In the back room I found zippered bags holding clothes for us. A piece of cardstock with a hole punched in the corner had been fastened to the zipper of each. My name was written in calligraphy on one. Johnny's was on the other.

Though Menessos had promised me a sensible selection, I wasn't convinced we'd have the same definition of how that word related to apparel. "I'm afraid to open this."

Johnny stepped up beside me. "On three, we unzip and see what he expects us to wear."

"Deal. But first, about that . . . telepathy . . . in the car." I was still astounded by that. "It must be linked to the *in signum amoris* thing, but why didn't it happen before?"

"It did happen before. For me, anyway. A day or so after you were inducted as the EV, when you asked me if I wanted the burden of knowing another big secret, Menessos's secret, I could hear your voice in my head. You admitted you hadn't told me everything yet. And you asked me if I wanted the responsibility of keeping it."

I remembered that, now that he reminded me. I had been thinking those words to him, but I had no clue he actually heard me. Then, "Yeah. I kind of heard you weighing the pros and cons of it." *And I'd heard him at the beginning of our probing session with Great El's slate.*

"We were touching then, and touching in the car. Maybe physical contact makes it happen."

He, of course, made physical contact sound dirty. "But we've touched a lot since the *in signum amoris* thing."

"Okay, maybe we have to be touching *and* be in the right frame of serious-mindedness. Focused. Something. We should experiment. Maybe even when we're naked and—"

"I agree. But not here and now."

The moment wore on silently for a heartbeat, then Johnny said, "On three."

He counted. We unzipped as one.

I was judging the contents of Johnny's garment bag, not my own. He had been given a suit. Not a department store one, either. It was absolutely not anything Johnny would wear, but it was black, with a black silk shirt and tie. Even as I studied it I knew it was something that would clothe the Domn Lup. "Wow."

"Touché." He gestured toward my own garment bag.

A black silk evening gown with a sequined top cascaded from the hanger like glittering spilled ink. I held it up. It was floor length, with a high slit up the side.

The straps crossed behind the neck, and the bodice had a plunging neckline, but all in all, it had good coverage. Then I turned it around and realized the back was virtually nonexistent.

Johnny gave a howl of approval.

"Keep it up," I said.

"Not a problem if you're wearing that."

I shot back, "I hope you know how to tape a girl into her evening gown, because I'm going to need tape if I'm going to stay in this modestly."

He laughed at me. "I've never taped a girl in a dress before, but it sounds like it includes man-handling. Let's get started." He grinned wider and added, "And since we have to get undressed, we could experiment . . ."

Before I could answer, however, Risqué returned.

"My second-in-command is off on a task tonight, so it pleases me to have the newly revealed Domn Lup honor me by sitting at my right."

With a spotlight on him, Johnny descended the steps, crossed the theater's house, and strolled up the ramp to make a show of clasping forearms with Menessos before taking a position in front of Goliath's usual seat. When the polite applause died, Menessos said, "And now my Erus Veneficus."

As I made my crossing, I mentally repeated how grateful I was for the practical two-inch heels on the sequined pumps Menessos had provided.

Risqué had not only done my hair and applied my makeup, she'd presented me with a scarlet garter. Though the hosiery that had also been provided wasn't the thigh-high kind that needed a garter, I wore the red satin-covered elastic as the symbol of my rank in the vampire's court. The bright color and the high slit skirt of this dress meant the garter was apparent to everyone.

Bestowed with a gorgeous gown and sensible shoes, my hair and makeup done, it was one of those moments when a woman should feel confident and beautiful, and I did. As I neared Menessos and Johnny, however, and took in the spot-lit view of them, both in stunning suits, standing side-by-side as if there had never existed any animosity between them, their attractive faces attuned to me, their eyes seeing only me, it hit me that I truly was the luckiest woman in the world. Not only because they were such handsome devils. Not only because I knew how desirable each was without the suits. But because I had nearly lost them, and I still had both.

My hand slipped into Menessos's hand, and he guided me to my place, presenting me to the applauding crowd.

The house area was filled to capacity, with all of Menessos's people and those he was taking on. I saw familiar faces in the crowd, specifically, Zhan, Seven, and Mark. There were others I recognized but didn't have names for. Only Mountain was missing, and he had an excuse—tending the animals and especially Thunderbird.

Menessos kissed the back of my hand and bid Johnny and me to take our seats.

"Now. Eva de Monique. Join us on the stage, and sit on the dais steps to my left, that all may know you have rank here, second to my own Erus Veneficus."

A tall slender woman in a dove gray one-shouldered

sheathe dress stood up from a table in the house. She moved with a liquid grace uncommon for a mortal. Her ebony tresses were arranged in short angled lines that I guessed must be all the rage in Paris. Her skin was like smooth-chiseled white marble. Her gray-blue eyes seemed to capture not only the color but the threat of stormy seas. It was a face that would have been beautiful no matter what, with or without makeup, no matter the hairstyle. Not everyone could wear glossy black lipstick and make it look good, but Eva could.

Yeah. She was someone I could legitimately envy.

Menessos gestured to the steps before me. She sat, posture remaining as rigid as if iron bars lined her spine.

"Allow me to welcome all of you who are new to our haven. Let this celebration symbolize the first embrace of the family you are joining. Once your hungers are sated, you will be called up, table by table, and I will bestow your new marks individually, according to your previous rank. Henceforth, you will be mine, and this will be your haven. But first . . . feast!"

Menessos clapped his hands and caterers entered, taking lidded plates and placing them before those, like Zhan, seated at tables draped in black cloths. Those seated at the tables swathed in scarlet received tall stemmed glasses of dark fluid.

Ornate tray tables were placed before Johnny, Eva, and me. We were then each served by Risqué. Menessos was given a tall flute like the other vampires.

The meal was delicious, but being on stage made eating awkward. The fact that no one engaged in conversation made it more so. My appetite simply didn't exist.

Our tray tables were carried off and as the servers moved into the house to clear the tables, Risqué crossed the stage with a silver-lidded dish. She lifted the shiny top and offered me chocolate-dipped strawberries. Eva twisted around and whispered, "I made those myself."

Her French accent was thick. Menessos had told me she had a chocolate shop in Terminal Tower. The huge strawberries had to be luscious and juicy, and the dark chocolate was striped with white. I reached to take one.

Menessos laid his hand on my arm. "No," he said gently. However, he graced Eva with an angry sneer. "I said no chocolates here."

She smiled broadly. Eating her meal had not smudged her lipstick. I wondered what brand would stay that glossy even through a meal. "I mean only to share the best of me with my superiors, my lord."

"We discussed this already. I said no. I will not have the chocolate tainting my sweet."

"I've never even heard of such a thing affecting the taste of blood."

"My refined palate is no doubt more sensitive than your former host's."

I'd stayed out of their conversation, but it was clear Menessos meant to enforce his rule. *Fine by me.* My hand dropped back into my lap.

Eva pouted up at Menessos. "I am trying to make a good impression with her."

"Your defiance of me has ruined that possibility."

At his tone, Risqué eased a step back, then another. Moving the way a person backing away from a wild bear would, she put distance between her and Menessos.

"Let me reclaim it," Eva pleaded. "Let her see how delightful my chocolates are."

Menessos sighed, relenting. He nodded. I reached and Risqué moved in again so I could take one. As I opened my mouth, however, the vampire said, "Wait."

"What?" I asked.

"Give it to Eva."

This was getting weird and all eyes in the silent house were trained on us as if we were the after-dinner show. Maybe we were, but I didn't have a script, so I did as told and held out the confection.

Eva stood and accepted it. "Shall I feed her, my lord? Shall I tease her with it for your pleasure?" The twisted corner of her mouth said she would enjoy it, too.

"Eat it," Menessos said.

Her crooked smile broke. "I am allergic to strawberries."

"Eat it," he said again.

"B-but . . ."

"An allergic reaction is a small price to pay for your disobedience." He leaned forward. "Eat. It."

Eva threw the strawberry to the ground and stomped it with her foot. "I will not!"

Menessos flew from his throne amid gasps from the audience. In a flash he had her by the nape of the neck. He held her head back, throat exposed. She clawed at him, trying to maintain her balance on needle-thin stilettos. Her hands found purchase in the layers of his suit.

"You defy me a second time," he snarled, "before all these people!"

She swallowed, her throat working hard at that angle.

"You are not allergic."

"I—I am."

He threw her to the floor and her cheek smacked the flooring with a thud. Most of the audience flinched. As did I.

My thoughts ran to the Rege, and how he treated women. I'd been ready to come to Cammi's aid when Gregor hit her, and I had reason to hate Cammi. While Eva wasn't on my list of favorite people either, I couldn't sit here and watch Menessos beat a woman. And yet my feet did not move. My outraged tongue did not cry out.

Menessos was not a male chauvinist like the leadership of the Romanian wæres so blatantly was. He was a master and he was within his rights to punish someone who, as he had made clear, defied him twice. And I knew in my heart that he would have reacted similarly, had the offender been male or female. The Rege could not say the same.

Menessos motioned Risqué nearer. By the time she had moved close, Eva had recovered enough to rise to her knees.

His fist closed in her hair and he jerked her head back again, forcing her to look up at him. From my position, slightly higher atop the dais, I saw that whatever brand of lipstick she wore *would,* after brute contact with a floor, smudge. Ugly darkness smeared onto her cheek, marring her exquisite beauty like dirt on an angel's face.

"Open your mouth," he said.

She clamped her mouth shut and no longer looked dazed.

Menessos gripped her jaw so tightly that his fingers

pressed her cheeks in. She tried to keep her mouth closed, but couldn't. A single sob wracked her lean frame.

Releasing his grip on her hair, Menessos reached across his chest to select a beautiful strawberry from the tray and held it over Eva's mouth.

Her arms flailed. Her nails clawed at his wrist. She wrenched herself away, crying out, "It's poison!"

My stomach flipped and flopped.

I'd almost eaten it!

The master vampire's demeanor had remained calm throughout the gruesome display, but just then as he set the strawberry back on the tray, he was positively icy. "Are you allergic?" he asked, as he reclaimed his grip on her hair.

"No. No, master."

"You *lied* to me," he spat the words on her. "You tried to murder my Erus Veneficus!"

"It is the way of my former master's court."

"Defiance was the way of Heldridge?"

"No. Survival of the fittest, of the most cunning."

"You were told it is not the way of this court!"

"Mercy, master!"

She had nowhere to go. No one to protect her. And she knew it.

With his one fist still wrapped in her hair, Menessos's other hand shot down with enough force that as he grabbed her by the lowest part of her rib cage, his fingers stabbed through her dress and into her flesh. She screamed as he jerked her up, lifting her as if she weighed no more than a rag doll, and brought her bared throat to his mouth.

Her voice filled the renovated theater . . . until his fangs pierced her. Until his jaws clamped onto her throat and he shoved her away from him even as he tore a wide gash in her flesh. Blood squirted and gushed.

His bloody fingers slid free from her rib cage as Eva's fingers clutched at her neck. Menessos snatched a strawberry from the tray and shoved it deftly between Eva's fingers and into her opened throat, then took his hand from her hair. She fell back onto the stage floor, thrashing and kicking for long seconds.

Above us all, the scream echoed, and finally, like its maker, died.

"Destroy those," Menessos commanded, gesturing at the tray Risqué held.

She hurried in her ruffled short-shorts to obey.

I just witnessed a murder. My heart thudded in my chest, my ears buzzed, and I felt cold to my core. My spine was wrapped in a thick weaving of anxiety, fear, and repulsion. But underneath my sternum was heat. Not lust heat. This was like the sharpest edge of a blade heated in forge-fire. It sliced through me and its blazing edge severed me from the naïveté that once would have denied that such things happened even in a vampire's haven. But I could not deny it now. In the wake of that severing was a residue of cinnamon.

"This is *my* house," Menessos bellowed to the stunned audience. "My rewards for loyalty are grand, but I tolerate no threats. I permit no defiance! I allow no harm to be doled out among you, one to the other. I will give you death if you defy me! My punishment is swift. Do you hear me, members of this haven?"

"Aye," answered those who were already claimed as his.

"Do you hear me, initiates?"

"Aye."

"Then come forth and receive your master's embrace, accept my mark, and become *mine*."

CHAPTER TWENTY-SEVEN

Once upon a time, I'd killed a man. It was an accident. He was a low-life druggie who was stalking Beverley's mom and when I'd intercepted him he threatened me with a knife. In the struggle, we fell. He landed on the blade.

Those seconds as he died were seared into my memory.

It was my dark secret, a shame I would always carry.

In seeing Eva's body and the pool of her blood, in peering out at the crowd, in having heard the words Menessos just uttered, and in knowing that Eva had meant to kill me, I knew for certain this was a murder no one would ever know about except those who'd witnessed it. And all those in attendance, save Johnny and me, belonged to the vampire who'd perpetrated the killing.

It was haven justice. An eye for an eye. Heldridge may have ruled his haven by keeping his people fearful of him and each other, but those were his rules. No master could allow insubordination.

The initiates would have to walk past Eva's body and blood to reach Menessos. The corpse was left to remind them what was expected of them, and the consequences of disobedience.

The Beholders were first. He bit them as a show of laying claim to them. Then, as when he had marked me, he opened his wrist. What was different, however, was he comingled his blood with their own and asked each one, "Do you accept me as your lord, your defender, to whom you will provide all your loyalty?"

When they affirmed they would, he drew an ankh on their bared chests. As the mark claimed them, their knees gave out. They writhed. Heldridge's claim was being ripped from their souls and replaced by that of Menessos.

When he'd marked me, it felt like his bloody mark called up pieces of my soul to be bound by his blood. Those pieces then took the essence of him and sank inside me to hide in intangible places.

To reclaim all the seventy-two male Beholders took over an hour.

Next were the Offerlings, six women and one man, who received two marks each. They were a gorgeous group and though they lacked the brutishness of the Beholders, they still gave every appearance of being dangerous.

Or maybe that's just my reaction to them as Heldridge's people after nearly being poisoned by one of them.

The Offerlings were rendered unconscious by the pain of being given a pair of marks to cancel out the previous binding to their master. They were removed by Menessos's established Beholders, and Menessos called for the initiate vampires to come forward.

Fifteen vampires walked single file up the ramp and

formed a line before the dais. I recognized one of them by the golden brown curls that hung past his shoulders. His name was Sever. He'd been with Heldridge at the Eximium. Apparently, he always gave the impression of being a delighted frat boy who'd just strolled unseen into the ladies' locker room.

"I charge you all with the tasks of managing your fellow initiates and monitoring your Offerings and Beholders; report to me that I may anticipate their needs and meet them in order to maintain the peace and balance of my haven. From this day forward, one of you will speak for all of them." He glanced down the line of them. "Sever. I appoint this task to you."

Sever bowed his head. "As you wish, my master." He bared his neck and made the vow, "I offer you my allegiance, my loyalty, and my undeath. Henceforth, I am yours. Your vampire. Your soldier. Your servant."

Menessos drank of him. "Henceforth, I am your lord, your commander, your master. For your allegiance and loyalty, I will protect you." He offered Sever his wrist, and Sever drank. Menessos moved to the next in line.

When all of this was complete, the tables were cleared, and the music blared. Jaded Jason had been hired once more to DJ the party, or perhaps he was a nonhaven servant like the Incomparable Deliveries guy.

As the dancing commenced, Eva's corpse remained as Menessos had left it.

"Come with me," Menessos said as he rose. Johnny and I followed him off the stage and accompanied him to his private rooms.

His chambers were as I remembered them, from the

round stone altar table that sat opposite the entry door, neatly arranged with candles, a bell, his athame, and various other ritual items; to the stacked stone walls and leather seating in-the-round with two plush, armed seats across from each other and two armless semicircular couches. On the back wall, between two white marble pillars, the wooden door with iron studs was shut.

"Please make yourselves comfortable." He gestured with his bloody hand. "Allow me a moment to wash." He passed through his iron-studded door without waiting to see if we complied.

Johnny removed his suit coat and loosened his tie before sinking beside me on the couch. "You okay?" he asked.

I nodded. "I may never eat strawberries again, but I'm fine."

His arm snaked across my shoulders and he pulled me close. I laid my head against him until, minutes later, Menessos returned. He'd not only washed up, he'd changed into fresh trousers and a clean shirt.

"First, allow me to thank the two of you for coming tonight." He carried two goblets, a bottle of wine, and a corkscrew. The last two he passed to Johnny, who set about opening the bottle. "Because I am well aware of how Heldridge ran his haven, I knew Eva would make an attempt on your life—"

"You knew?" I demanded.

"I wanted to get it out of the way, as this would make the best example for the others." Still holding the goblets, Menessos lowered himself onto one of the plush, armed seats. "When you were not sure if you could join me, I worried that she might find some way to make her strike beyond my haven's walls."

"You knew," I repeated.

"Of course I knew. Why else would I object to chocolate?"

"You said—"

"I lied." He reached for my hand and I gave it to him. He squeezed. "She tried to endear herself to me over these last few nights. She took the chance that I would allow it and not punish her." He shrugged. "She lost."

I felt better knowing my safety was never truly at risk, and worse knowing the murder had therefore been pre-meditated. *The whole time he was with her, he knew it would end this way.*

I detected a fine trembling in his fingers, squeezed reassuringly.

In that instant, I felt his thoughts swirling, so fast and not all of them in English. *In signum amoris.* He'd played a part in it, and now I knew he owned a piece of that bind-ing. What I did catch was the notion that he wanted me there when he made claim to Heldridge's people because he had never marked anyone as a fully undead vampire. He wasn't certain if he'd be deeply drained by so much activity. He'd wanted me nearby to empower him if necessary.

He pulled his hand from my grasp.

Johnny had the bottle open and Menessos provided him with a goblet. Johnny poured and gave the half-full glass of wine to me. I hesitated.

"Drink it," Menessos said, offering the other goblet to Johnny. "You're pale."

I drank. It was tart and warmed my tongue.

Menessos stood and paced before us. "On to the other business. It has come to my attention that we have been misled."

"How so?" Johnny asked. He filled his goblet and set the bottle on the floor.

"Heldridge is very clever. The performer he hired refused to admit any guilt. He claimed to have no idea what he had done. On the surface it all appeared very tidy: a crazed man claims memory loss. We suspected he'd been hypnotized and commanded to attack."

"And?" I prompted.

"I had assumed the blade, a steel throwing dagger, had been ensorcelled in some manner to strike me down. I had the man at Wolfsbane and Absinthe examine it."

"Beau," I clarified.

"Yes."

"But he's been Bindspoken—"

"And he had no reaction to it. There was no sorcery or witchcraft placed upon that blade."

Beau had felt pain at shaking my hand. Being Bindspoken meant forever avoiding contact with magical things. Him keeping Wolfsbane and Absinthe, a witch supply shop, was more of a statement to WEC than I had realized at first. I now understood why he'd put together the items for the *sorsanimus* spell so hurriedly, and why he had a mundane human working for him. Someone had to touch the goods he sold.

Johnny set his goblet by the bottle. "You're saying you weren't the target at the ceremony."

My thoughts on Beau, I hadn't caught that.

Menessos said, "Correct."

"Me?" I asked. Heldridge had been after *me*? "To hurt you?"

Menessos stopped pacing. It was clear he was weighing his words, and I knew this was going to be bad. I took a quick gulp of the wine.

"I told you he knew what the fairies wanted him to know. I assumed they had told him that I was alive."

My mind was racing. "For him to strike at me would weaken you, then the fairies could take action?"

"That was my first thought as well. And one in our favor as now that I am undead, he would look a fool." He again took to pacing.

I'd never seen him this edgy. I had seen him angry and prepared to kill, but then I'd never actually seen him take a life before.

I stood and went to him. Gripping his arm, I turned him to face me and searched his eyes. My hands slipped down to take his.

"The fairies knew something else."

"What?" Johnny asked.

Menessos did not answer.

"That I'm the master." My voice was hollow. My stomach churned with ice.

Menessos gauged my reaction for a long moment. "I kept thinking he was a fool to flee to VEIN. I felt it must be a ploy of some kind. But if he knows *that,* he has good reason as it may be enough to save his existence. If he reveals to the Lord Executives of VEIN that their northeastern Quarter Lord has been hexed by a witch and is under her sway . . . I will be the next vampire with a VEIN bounty on his head. And you, my lovely Lustrata, won't be left out."

Johnny came to his feet. "What do we do?"

"Goliath is unequaled at what he does. When he finds Heldridge, he will kill him."

Johnny stood. "What if Heldridge makes it to these Lord Executives?"

"All manner of unpleasantness shall ensue."

CHAPTER TWENTY-EIGHT

At eleven-twenty A.M. on Saturday, Zhan was pinning my hair tightly against my head. "Sorry I didn't ask Menessos about letting you go home."

"My request wasn't the dominant thing on my mind last night either."

Zhan slipped the last bobby pin into place and declared me ready for step two of my disguise. I tugged the blond wig on.

One look in the mirror proved that everyone would recognize the cheap flesh-colored cap that formed the base of the wig. No one would ever be deceived by this disguise. "This is going to be a problem."

"Give me one minute," Zhan said. She left the bathroom, hurried down the stairs. She came back with a black knit hat that had a skull with wings silkscreened on it in white. I recognized it as matching a shirt Johnny had recently bought; he'd left the hat on one of the coat hooks at the back door. Zhan put it on me. "No fake roots."

I had on a nice blouse under one of Nana's sweater cardigans, dress pants, and loafers. When Johnny had seen my attire—before rushing off to a band rehearsal and strategizing session—he'd proclaimed me frumpy and said he'd be worried about me if he didn't know I was trying not to be recognized by the witch-hating-parent-patrol.

The knit hat was totally wrong for the look I was trying to achieve. "I'm trying to be the socially acceptable niece today."

Zhan thought about it. "Unless you have a flowered chapeau, you'll have to change your role. Come with me." I followed her across the hall. She sorted through my closet. "Wear this and your flannel." She held up a thick pullover hooded sweatshirt with a pocket in front. "Add jeans and your hikers and you'll be more comfortable. Instead of being the snooty blond niece—which is conspicuous and more likely to get you busted anyway—you can be the farm-girl unicorn trainer. Mountain won't mind."

"What if Errol minds?" All the animals knew Mountain better than me.

"Mountain will still be there, as backup."

Her idea was good enough that I probably wouldn't have argued, but I didn't get a chance anyway. Nana shouted up the stairs to announce that the ponies had arrived.

Beverley burst from her room. "Ponies?"

The six rented half-size equines were unloaded from their trailer, saddled, and ready to go.

The owner, Mr. Purdy, could have easily won the casting call for an aging carnie in his Carhartt jacket, dirty jeans, and a ball cap with "Ford" scripted on it. He was all angles and his Adam's apple jutted. He spat tobacco juice on the ground as I approached him.

"You Ms. Alcmedi?" he asked.

"No, I'm Red. Red Newman. Family friend. Ms. Alcmedi isn't here."

"Oh." He scratched at the three days' worth of stubble on his cheek. "Who's payin' me, then?"

I took an envelope from the hoodie's pocket. "They told me to give you this."

He opened it and counted it—twice—then folded it and shoved the envelope into his back pocket. "Thank you. I need to walk the route in the yard now, to make sure we're all good."

"Fine. I'll walk with you?"

"No need."

"Actually, there is."

He stopped, spat again, and his wrinkles deepened. "We're not staying longer than an hour. That's what I agreed to. That's my rate."

"Nothing like that is changing. As I said, I'm a family friend and, well, the birthday girl wanted a unicorn ride so . . . a friend of mine and I devised an attachment—"

"You ain't putting nothing on my ponies. And I ain't got no all-white one, neither."

"I own a young white stallion. We fitted it for him. I just wanted to let you know that we'd like Beverley to lead the pony parade, and I'll handle the horse."

He squinted at me, wrinkling his sun-dried face even more. "Does your young stallion have a fiery temper?"

"Not that I'm aware of."

"What breed is he?"

"A mix," I said. I didn't know enough about horses to answer.

"I hope he doesn't have any Lipizzaner in him. I hear they're mighty feisty. Don't want no horse getting aggressive toward my ponies." He pointed at a little black one tied to a bar on the side of the horse trailer. It was the same size Johnny was when in wolf form. But this animal lacked the pointy teeth and the snarl. "My Smokey Bear there, he's a stud. Might set your stallion off if he's picky like that."

"I don't see that being a problem, sir."

"Better not. Any other interruptions you plan to insert on my regular routine?"

"Nope."

"Then let me walk the yard and make sure there's no holes that could injure my livestock—or yours."

I got out of his way just as the first of the guests arrived.

We'd invited twenty-six kids and parents, everyone in the class. Six showed up—four girls, two boys. Celia was here as well; Johnny was still at band rehearsal. Mr. Purdy's sourness aside, the guests seemed to be in a happy, festive mood and we had just enough ponies for every child.

Beverley, Nana, and Zhan came outside and the kids gathered to pet the ponies. Celia stayed with Nana and Zhan and helped to greet everyone while I hung back at the horse trailer.

Mr. Purdy noticed. "Why aren't you with the others?"

Thinking too long about what to say, I decided to try for embarrassment as I admitted, "Large groups of people make me nervous."

When it was time, Mr. Purdy called the kids together. "Now, either you can all pick a pony to ride, or you can draw numbers out of my hat. If there's gonna be an argument about who rides what pony, we'll definitely draw numbers. Can you pick for yourselves and be satisfied?"

He was so awkward and rough that the kids simply nodded. Lily ended up with Smokey Bear. I only knew Lily's name because Beverley called it a few times. I was glad she had come; she was the girl who'd first befriended Beverley.

Mr. Purdy had each parent set their child onto a saddle, then hold the reins until he got the ponies lined up like he wanted them. "And I hear the birthday girl has a special ride for the day." He gave me a nod, and I jogged to the back where Mountain was waiting with Errol.

The unicorn had deigned to wear a purple halter, and a matching lead rope was attached. It matched the ribbons Beverley had put in his mane and tail perfectly. Mountain had tied some twine around the base of the spiraled horn, covered it with the curly forelock, and then wound the twine under the unicorn's jowls to give the impression of it being fake.

Together, we led Errol around front.

It was like he knew he was on stage. He strutted around the house, neck arched, lifting his legs high and showing off. Beverley couldn't contain herself. She ran toward us. Errol did his elegant bow again and Mountain helped her onto the unicorn's back. Parents applauded.

The ponies raised their heads high, too. Errol's beauty and charisma captivated everyone. Smokey Bear and the other ponies pranced around the yard following him—no encouragement needed.

When the time was up, Nana took over and called for everyone to come inside and wash up for "cold cuts and chips to be followed by cake and ice cream." Mountain lifted Beverley down; she hugged Errol and ran inside with her friends. We petted and praised the unicorn for being such a show stealer.

Mr. Purdy drew near us, intent on the unicorn. He jerked his bill cap off and scratched his head. "In ten years, I've never seen my ponies prance like that."

"They just need a little inspiration, I guess."

"Would you sell me that horse?"

"Sorry, Mr. Purdy."

"How'd you make that horn?" He reached up as if to analyze how we'd attached it.

Mountain cleared his throat. "Check eBay for antlers or movie props."

Mr. Purdy spat, resettled his ball cap, and said, "If you had a half-dozen white horses, all with those horns, you'd make a killin' doin' the county fair circuit. If you weren't bothered by large groups of people, that is." He walked away.

"No doubt." Mountain scratched under Errol's chin. "But I'm not sure your back is meant for anyone but Beverley."

Errol nickered and bobbed his head. I was sure he was agreeing.

"How's Thunderbird?"

Mountain glanced toward the barns. "My truck arrived last evening; had a side of beef in it. The griffons let him have first dibs. He ate lightly, then one of the others brought in a deer leg after dusk, offered it to him, and he ate that, too." He absently plucked at Errol's mane. "I'm trying to figure out why the others treat him differently. Sometimes I think it's his injury, sometimes I'm not sure that's it." He paused. "Zhan tells me you want her to take a few of the phoenixes to her family in California."

"If it will make things better for her, absolutely."

"She said her folks lived on a small farm north of San Francisco. Her mother grows Chinese medicinal herbs."

"Sounds like they could easily house and care for some unusual poultry."

Mountain smiled at my description. "But how do we get them there?"

"Would they prefer a private jet or to go in some type of wheeled vehicle?"

"Not sure."

"Well, when you figure that part out, I'm sure Menessos can handle the rest."

When the party was over and everyone was gone except Celia, it was safe for me to go inside. Ares trotted out to greet me and thumped my leg with his tail all the way down the hall. As I walked toward the kitchen I jerked the hot wig and hat combo from my head, loosed the bobby pins, and finger-combed my hair.

Only Beverley was missing from those gathered at the table. "Where's the guest of honor? The party was a success, yes?"

"Yes. She's upstairs packing an overnight bag," Nana said.

"She's going to stay with me until Monday morning," Celia added quickly. "I'll see her to the bus."

Noting my confusion, Nana clarified. "I've decided that I'm going to Pittsburgh with you. I have some words of my own for Eris."

A road trip with Nana? Thank the Goddess Pittsburgh is only two and a half hours away.

CHAPTER TWENTY-NINE

Everyone slept in late the next morning, but by ten-thirty we'd all showered, eaten breakfast, and were ready. Atop the stairs I paused to check my overnight bag.

"C'mon! Let's hit the road," Nana called out. She held a grocery bag in one hand and had the other on the doorknob.

"What's in the bag?" Johnny asked, stepping over to her.

"It's not a bag, it's a poke."

"A poke?"

"It's like a bag, but it's not."

"Okay. What's in it?"

He didn't know how lucky he was he hadn't asked her what the difference was.

Nana said, "A nightgown and a change of clothes."

"Then it's not a bag or a poke," he quipped. "It's a suitcase."

I descended the steps, imagining how exhausting this little trip was going to be.

Johnny was wearing black jeans, Harley boots, and the long-sleeved tee that matched the knit hat I'd worn yesterday. The silkscreened skulls with wings had a distressed quality, but the brightness of these embellishments made the black of the shirt deeper, darker. Like his eyes. Though still blue, his irises were shadowed today, and were indicative of this day's magnitude.

"Take this," he said and tossed me his leather jacket.

The first time I'd worn his leather, we rode the motorcycle to the hospital because Theo had been in a car accident. We'd both come a long way since then. "Why?"

"If you're undercover as someone in the market for a tat, you should look the part."

"Don't I?" I had on my jeans and boots, too. A black tank top with spaghetti straps paired with a velveteen black hoodie served as my top.

"Yeah, but if you ditch the hoodie and just wear the tank and my leather you'll really sell the idea that you're a newbie biker chick in search of her first tattoo."

"I thought *everyone* had tattoos these days." I shrugged out of the hoodie, aware that Johnny's eyes were roaming over me appreciatively. "They're not just for mechanics, military, and the rock 'n' roll types anymore. Doctors, teachers, and even corporate suits have 'em now."

"Still. It'll help."

I put the leather on, enveloped in the cedar and sage scent of him. "It'll help you to be a distracted driver."

"Mmmm-hmmm." He ran his fingers through my hair, mmm-ed again, then encircled me with his arms.

"Can we go now?" Nana tapped her foot impatiently.

Zhan emerged from the little bathroom under the stairs. "Load up."

Nana was out the door before the rest of us took a step.

Johnny held the door open for Zhan and me. As I passed he mumbled, "Promise me Demeter won't ask, 'are we there yet' every five minutes."

"So, before we arrive," Zhan said from the backseat, "do I need to know the history behind the bad blood?"

Beside her, Nana answered, "Eris is my daughter. She was an unwed mother and abandoned Persephone with me and ran off to be with some man."

"What are you hoping to accomplish, Demeter?" Zhan asked.

"I don't know, but if a confrontation is going to take place, I deserve to be a part of it. I'm the one who picked up where she left off."

"And what's your goal?" Zhan aimed the question at me this time.

"I'm not after a confrontation. I just want answers for Johnny."

" 'Just'?"

Though she meant, "Only that?" I heard the other meaning of the word: "What's right and fair."

"Have you nothing you want to gain for yourself, Persephone?" Nana prompted.

"Part of me wants to shout at her. To let her know about all the hurt she caused. To tell her to her face that she's selfish and clueless and . . ." I stopped because the passionate anger that filled me clamped my teeth together, hardened my voice, and surprised me.

This was the rage and hate I thought I had abandoned. It wasn't gone at all.

All that business I'd told Amenemhab about being done with her—no wonder the jackal was skeptical.

Quietly, Nana asked, "Are you tough enough to defeat yourself?"

I twisted in my seat to meet her eyes.

Gaining Johnny's answers and having my vengeful little encounter was unlikely. Achieving one would rebuff the other.

Which side of me would I let win?

Nana's expression remained intent. I sighed and let my shoulders slump. *I'm the one who picked up where she left off,* she'd said. *Unwed mother.* My gaze fell to Nana's lap, to her fisted, wrinkled, old hands.

Nana had picked me up and set me on my feet. Angered by the responsibility thrust upon her by my mother's flawed character—worried I might grow up the same—she'd been hard on me. It was an imperfect situation, like mine and Beverley's. But Nana was always there. She never gave up.

As I watched, her fists unclenched . . . opened. Searching her face, I saw her sigh, too, as if she'd just let something go. Something heavy. She nodded at me.

Am I that strong?

I faced forward in my seat and stared at the road before us.

The silence lasted for several minutes. Johnny was the one to break it.

"I know the two of you have plenty of reasons to be really ticked at Eris. But to put my two unrequested cents in: I just lost Ig. I hadn't gone to see him in years, but I knew he was there. Now I know he isn't." He adjusted his seat belt. "He was all I had. I'm hopeful this Arcanum may be able to unlock my past and let me know if I have parents out there. I want to know. I *want* that. You have that and it seems you don't want it but . . . just think about the other side of it."

I touched his arm and made my voice soft. "But, Johnny, what if your family is . . ." It was harder to say than I'd thought. I had to push the words out. "What if they are biased against wæres?"

"Then I'll know it's their loss for having their heads stuck up their asses."

"It's not as tidy as you make it out to be. The pain of not knowing how your parents feel can't be as bad as knowing that they feel only animosity." I wanted Eris to feel the pain of *my* animosity. As I stared down at the Allegheny River we were crossing, I wondered, *Am I an awful person for feeling that?*

"What have you got to lose, Red? Can she possibly hurt you more than she already has?"

"If I let her back into my life, yeah. She could."

Johnny snorted just as the GPS commanded that we take the upcoming exit. He switched lanes. "You're scared."

"I am not." My palms were sweaty but that wasn't the same thing.

"Yes, you are. You're scared because you want to be good enough in her eyes, you want to be loved by her so things will be like they're supposed to be."

"No, I don't. Nana loves me. Nana raised me. That's *good enough*."

Johnny guided the car around the ramp to Bigelow. "If

a stranger flips you off because they don't like the way you drive, would you even remember it at the end of the day?"

"Probably not."

"Because their opinion means nothing to you. But what if it was your overbearing boss and he recognized you? You'd remember that."

"This isn't about road rage."

"Oooo. That's a great analogy. Road rage is angry people being unconditionally judgmental of other's actions and behaving aggressively and putting the lives of innocent others in danger."

I twisted around, seeking Nana's support in fending off this absurdity. She shrugged. "I'd give him that one."

I wasn't giving up so easily. "Bullies with cars might work as a metaphor for child endangerment, but not so much as a metaphor for the emotional abuse of a child."

He was zigzagging through the impressive downtown area of Pittsburgh with its myriad tall buildings. In their shadows, I felt small—as small as the defenseless child I once was. With all that we were talking about, I didn't *like* feeling small just now.

"Okay, how about this," Johnny tried again. "Road rage can occur at high speeds or in traffic jams. One is the moment when you must act or lose your chance to get ahead, the other is the moment when the feeling of being stuck overwhelms you to the point of lashing out."

I rubbed at my temple. "So are you making the child represent the car or the road conditions?"

"The child is a passenger, swept along with the bully driving."

He was beginning to sound a lot like Amenemhab. "Okay. What's your end point, Mr. Freud?"

He drove onto South Tenth Street and ahead was another bridge. We'd be over the Monongahela River in seconds. "My point is, it's *your* car now." Under his breath he added, "And what a lovely ride it is." Continuing in normal tones, he said, "So who did you learn more about driving from, Red? From Eris or from Demeter?"

On the south shore, we made a left onto East Carson as the GPS instructed. "Arriving at destination," the voice crooned.

Johnny cruised through the intersection of South Fourteenth and there it was, beside Pittsburgh Guitars. "Huh," he said continuing past.

"What?"

"The guitar shop. I'm still not saying I'm superstitious, but I'll take that as a *good* omen."

We stopped in a parking lot up the street and a dark blue Chevrolet Tahoe pulled in beside us on the driver's side. It was Kirk and Todd. They had intended to ride in the back with Zhan between them, but when they heard Nana was coming they happily agreed to drive separately.

I twisted my hair up, poked bobby pins in to secure it, then donned my blond bob wig. The knit cap again hid the most obvious fakeness of the wig. After checking in the mirror and smoothing the ends, I asked Johnny, "What do you think?"

He wiggled his brows at me and drove back up Carson,

parking in front of the guitar shop. Kirk and Todd drove around the corner to wait.

"Five minutes," Johnny said.

"Give me ten."

"Eight," he countered.

"Deal."

"Here." Nana punched me in the arm with something. "Wear these, too."

She handed me her oversize sunglasses. They were one step removed from those post—glaucoma treatment glasses. With much eye-rolling and a deep sigh, I slid them on. As I opened the door to get out Nana said, "What? No smooch for Johnny-boy?"

I slammed the car door and stomped away.

Still unsure what I was going to say, I was glad Nana set me off before I headed in. The edge of anger felt right.

I passed the guitar shop, walking slowly, taking in what was beyond the glass. As the edge of their storefront ended, I could see into the Arcane Ink Emporium. Their glass had an inner covering of UV protection, darkening it. The front was set up like a waiting room, but no one was behind the counter.

I went inside, jingling the bell on the door.

Scream-o metal music was playing just one increment louder than any background music should be, and the smell of menthol cigarettes filled my nostrils. The weak track lighting from above was subdued. I let the glasses slide down my nose a bit and looked around over the top of them.

To my left and right were red leather couches, each paired with a rustic-style coffee table laden with binders bearing printout sheets with a photograph and a name in large lettering placed into the front display pocket. A counter sat ahead to my right, and a narrow hallway stretched down the center of the building beyond it.

Around me, the black walls were cluttered with metal band posters and movie posters in dark red frames hung at odd angles. Smaller frames held things like concert tickets, or photos of famous people with tattoos. Motorcycle paraphernalia—wheels, handlebars, fenders—were also displayed like art. There were large pots with ficus trees and smaller ones with spider plants or cacti set here and there.

The floors were old, the wood worn, and, as I stepped farther in, I discovered they were also creaky. The floor was covered only by oriental area rugs under the coffee tables. There were more binders and bar seats at the counter. Behind it, on a slightly lower table, I could see a monitor screen divided into eight squares. In one, a male artist was working on another man's arm. Each of the others revealed an empty room set up like a doctor's office, except the last one—in which I saw myself standing in the main front area.

"Hello." From the rearmost area of the building, my mother stepped into the hallway.

She's here.

Though I had rarely seen it, I remembered that smile.

She walked toward me, smiling like a good shopkeeper. "Welcome to the Arcane Ink Emporium. What can I help you with today?"

She wore a black concert T-shirt for some band called Shatter Messiah. The sleeves were rolled up and the length of the shirt had been cut, revealing both her excessive tan and the spike-studded belt threaded through the loops of her black jeans. Snakeskin boots completed the whole badass fashion show.

"I'm considering a tattoo," I said. "I've heard good things about . . ." I frowned, as if searching for the name. "Arcanum."

She sidestepped to take her place behind the counter. "Everyone says good things about Arcanum. My other artists are work-on-demand, but Arcanum decides on a case-by-case basis. Here." She put a clipboard with a single sheet of paper on it before me, added a pen. "Take a seat and fill that out. I'll make sure Arcanum gets it."

"Don't I get to meet Arcanum first? I mean, what if I don't like him? I don't want to yank his chain."

"Doesn't matter if you like Arcanum or not. All that matters is if you like the art." Eris took a binder from under the counter. "Here. Scan through this." After offering the binder to me, she relaxed into the seat behind the counter and did something on the computer.

I flipped quickly through the photographs in page protectors. The art was certainly not contained in one style. There were brightly colored tattoos and grayscale ones. There was tribal art, modern skulls, standard Chinese dragons. The last dragon in the binder reminded me of Johnny's tattoo.

"You like the dragons?" Eris asked as I lingered over that image.

"I do."

"Why?"

"Does that matter?"

She shrugged. "To some people. It can relate to the

dragon's pose, color, where it goes on the body, whether it is oriental or more fantasy. A tattoo should say something about you, it should have meaning beyond the art and color. It should be a badge you give yourself, like a rite of passage."

"You make it sound magical."

"It can be."

I caught the suggestion in her tone. "Are you saying Arcanum makes magical tattoos?" I sounded skeptical.

"All tattoos are magical, if their owner wants them to be."

"And what if the owner doesn't want them to be? Can a tattoo be magic against someone's will?"

She squinted then, but before she could answer, the door opened behind me. I knew it was Johnny. Eris patted the countertop. "Lance has some fabulous dragons in his binder. Why don't you explore his portfolio, too? It's on the table there."

I watched her round the counter, smoothing her hair and not truly looking at her new patron until she'd stepped into the main area. "Welcome to the Arcane Ink Emp—" She stopped in her tracks, swallowed hard, and didn't finish.

"Hello," he said.

Johnny had fixed her with a look, and I knew how powerful his dark blue eyes ringed in the ebony Wedjat lines could be, peering out from under those black waves, the only sparkle coming from the white-gold hoops in one brow.

Eris was staring, openmouthed. "You . . ." She said it so softly, I almost didn't hear it. *But she recognized him.*

My breath caught. My heart sputtered in my chest.

Sweet Goddess . . . my mother is Arcanum?

Before I could recover, she said, "Just a minute," and headed down the hall at a quick pace.

I looked at Johnny; he nodded. We moved into the head of the hallway.

In seconds, Eris, who had disappeared, was backing into view again. Todd and Kirk had come in the back door when she tried to go out that way.

To her credit, she didn't scream or call for help from the other artist. I could hear the men talking quietly and the tools of the trade buzzing now that I was in the hall. The rooms were separated only by curtains.

Eris faced Johnny squarely. "What do you want?"

"To talk," he said.

She took a well-balanced, square-shouldered pose. "Then talk."

Johnny walked forward three paces. "You recognized me. That means *you're* Arcanum."

A man burst through the curtain, slamming into Johnny. They crashed through the open doorway of the workstation opposite. The curtain was torn down and the curtain rod clattered on the wood floor. I glanced into the room to see the client—brows high and mouth hanging open—holding the still-buzzing tattoo gun that had been thrust in his grip.

The men grappled on the floor. The artist was straddling Johnny, and limbs were flailing every which way. Then Johnny got tired of trying to stop him without hurting him and cold-cocked him.

"Lance!" Eris shouted.

The guy slumped to the side, unconscious.

Johnny wrestled his way out from under the dead weight still partially atop him.

Then I felt a distinctive tingle.

It was energy, buzzing not unlike the instrument in the room beside me. Eris was calling on a ley line. *Todd and Kirk are too close.*

My feet moved, I raced and launched myself in a move not unlike the tackle that had just taken down Johnny. "Mom! No!"

CHAPTER THIRTY

Eris dropped whatever magic she'd been calling when I knocked her to the floor. She lay stunned and groaning under me.

Crouched over my mother, I craned my neck to check on the wæres. Todd, stricken, rubbed at his arms. Kirk shivered and resettled his overcoat. Behind me, Johnny was standing in the hall, where he could monitor the knocked-out artist and his customer. "You two okay back there?"

They nodded. *Thank the Goddess it hadn't been enough to cause either Todd or Kirk to go into a partial shift.*

A hand jerked my hat and wig off. "Persephone!"

I must have been a frightful sight as I glowered down at her. "If you try a spell or call any energies, before *I'm* through with *you,* you'll wish your curling iron had set a faster fire."

After I let Eris up, she checked on her artist, then his client. She relieved the man of the buzzing thing in his grasp and set it aside. "Ray, you better just go on home."

"But . . . are you okay? Is Lance?"

"They'll be fine," Johnny said.

Ray's dirty fingernails made me peg him as a mechanic, and he sized Johnny up like he was considering whether or not he could take him.

I tore the bobby pins from my hair and shook it out, but maneuvered the metal hair fasteners around my fingers with the pointy sides out, just in case.

"Let me bandage your arm then you can flip the closed sign and lock the door on your way out," Eris said as she pulled bandaging items from a drawer. When she put the last piece of tape on him she patted his shoulder. "You know the drill, keep it covered, blah, blah, blah. And don't forget to turn the sign and lock the door."

"B-but," Ray stammered. He clearly hadn't made up his mind yet that he couldn't lick Johnny.

"No buts, Ray," she said. "And no fighting. Just go. Lance will finish you up soon and I'll pay for your next tattoo."

"Walk me out?" he asked.

"I'll be your escort," Johnny said. Ray stood, and the defiant glimmer in his eyes made his intentions clear. "Try it, Ray, and you'll leave with some part of you broken."

"Ray," Eris snapped. "We're fine. They just want an explanation and I owe them that. Don't do anything stupid, just go home and fuck Julie. Come back tomorrow."

Johnny walked Ray out. Eris crouched over her artist and smacked Lance's cheek with increasing force. Lance looked like he'd barely graduated high school. "Shake it off, bitch boy." His eyelids fluttered. "There you go, show me those baby blues." He moaned, then blinked and focused on her. "How many fingers am I holding up?" she asked as she flipped him off.

"One," he groaned.

She stepped back, offered him a hand up. On his feet, Lance moaned again, fingers inspecting the back of his head. "Holy shit." He nearly toppled over. Eris grabbed him and kept him on his feet by slipping her arm around his waist.

"Whoa. I'm glad I never tried out for the football team. What hit me?"

"I did," Johnny replied, rejoining us.

Lance faced him, then his gaze fell past Johnny.

Nana and Zhan stepped into view. Nana summed up the situation—and Eris's clinging to the young man—in a glance. "Robbing the cradle now, Eris? I thought you didn't like kids."

Eris plopped Lance down in the nearest seat when she entered the break room. Lance propped his elbows on the table in front of him, face in hands. We were right behind her.

To one side sat a trio of tall stainless steel storage cabinets that would be the pride and joy of any car enthusiast's garage. A refrigerator, a section of countertop with a sink, and a narrow dishwasher were lined up across the opposite wall.

"I've known this reckoning would find me sooner or later," she said as she gave Lance an ice pack. Todd, Johnny, and I claimed the seats on one side of the table; Nana and Zhan sat opposite us. Kirk remained on his feet where he could take quick action if need be. Eris strode around to the table's other end, her boot heels clacking authoritatively. She sat, then stood again immediately and retrieved a pack of cigarettes and an ashtray from the drawer.

She shook the pack until one stuck up from the others. After putting it to her lips, she offered the pack to Nana, who refused, muttering, "Menthol shit."

Eris lit up, took a long drag on it, blew smoke slowly at the ceiling, then rejoined us, her seat slightly angled from the table, her legs crossed.

"When I left you with Nana, I stayed with Larry. He was an armorer and blacksmith who trained horses and jousted at Renaissance Faires. We traveled constantly. I read palms and picked up tattooing from a woman I befriended on the circuit.

"About nine years ago, Larry was cited for felonious assault outside a bar in San Diego, again at a bar in Oakland, and, a few months later, he did the same shit a third time in Sacramento. You cause someone serious bodily harm with a weapon three times back-to-back in Cali, and they send you up for twenty-five years. That's what they did to him, anyway."

She shrugged like it was no big deal, but her crossed leg had begun bobbing to a nervous rhythm.

"His sister took the horses and the equipment. She sold them all at auction, and the bitch left me with nothing." She seemed to be talking to her employee now more than me; he was the only person in the room who wasn't giving her a pissed-off stare. "My last bit of cash was spent on a hotel room and that night I ran up a tab in the bar even though I hadn't any hope of paying it. Lucky me, the bartender hadn't checked to see that my room wasn't secured with a card. Just before last call, a stranger approached me and asked if he could cover my tab. I figured he wanted sex." She clicked her tongue. "Instead, he wanted magic."

She swallowed hard enough to be heard and appeared to be mustering some inner resolve. I thought she was just being melodramatic.

She looked up at Johnny. "This guy paid me—in cash—to perform the magic on you." She breathed false calm from the cigarette again. "I knew it was unethical, but I had nothing. I was desperate. I bought this with it." Her index finger made a circle meant to indicate the building around us. "Opened AIE. I'd never known independence before . . . I couldn't resist."

Johnny asked, "Who was the stranger?"

"I don't know. He never gave me a name."

"What did he look like?"

"I don't remember."

"Convenient." His tone was mocking.

Eris leaned over the table. "I. Don't. Remember. What I did to you was awful and I washed it out of my mind. I never wanted to remember, damn it."

"But I do. I want to remember."

The palpable glares they exchanged made it clear that neither intended to back down. So I interjected my question. "How did you do it?"

Again, she took a hit of nicotine before answering. "It was done over seven days. Arms first, eyes second, navel, then thighs. Each was bound to an element, set to a purpose. The chest was next, binding the previous four together through it."

"Thought you washed it from your mind," Johnny accused.

"Some of it won't come clean." She flicked the cigarette in the ashtray. "Your memories were bound down with that one, like an offering to seal the first five together and locking your past away. I'd worked a little on the foo dog and dragon each of the previous days, because the detail was too great to achieve in a single day. On the sixth day, I completed the foo dog. On the seventh day, I completed the dragon. The last three were more spiritual in the purposes I assigned them. And after the last tattoo was empowered and sealed, I locked each tattoo to a chakra point as an extra precaution."

"How is that even possible?" I demanded.

She pushed the ashes around with the burning end of her cigarette. "Perhaps I misspoke when I said the stranger wanted magic. He wanted sorcery."

"Who taught you sorcery?" Nana asked.

"The woman I knew on the Faire circuit."

Silence filled the room for half a minute, then Johnny asked, "Did I talk while you did this to me?"

"You were unconscious."

"For a whole week?"

"He was drugging you."

Johnny took another long pause. "Why the variation of cultural symbolism in the tattoos?"

"For the strength in the diversity. Bringing so many pantheons to the task . . . I'd never even considered doing anything like this. So in my planning, I was thorough. I wanted to be certain. It's still holding, isn't it?"

"I can transform in spite of it."

"The moon's curse claimed you first, nothing I could do would stop that."

"Perhaps I misspoke," he mocked her. "I can still transform *at will* in spite of it."

Eris's leg stopped bobbing. She didn't even seem to breathe. "At will?"

He nodded.

"Bullshit."

Johnny stood and approached her end of the table. He put the heel of his hand on the corner and leaned over her so the room's lights cast his shadow across her. "I'm the Domn Lup, Eris." As he spoke, his hand darkened and fur sprouted, his nails thickened, black and sharp. "And now you're going to unbind it all."

"I can't."

"You fucking better figure out how," he growled, nails piercing into the wooden table top.

"I'm not prepared. I need supplies, and . . . and . . . even if I was, I couldn't guarantee that I could undo it. Spells can be broken, but this was sorcery."

That wasn't exactly true, but I wanted to know how long she'd lie.

Johnny shifted to rest his hip on the table edge and held his hand up between them, letting the transformation reverse. "Make a list of what you need." He snapped his fingers. "Todd. I saw paper and pens at the front desk." Todd retrieved the items.

Eris studied my boyfriend, who had switched on his

intimidating persona like a true master, comfortable in his own power. Her features were stiff with fear. "It's sorcery," she repeated.

"I hear tell that witchcraft is like sand that touches the sea and the air and stretches along the coast and inland to the soil. Like waves of power that represent the gods and goddesses of the various pantheons, the tide touches the energy of nature, influencing and shaping it to a witches' will through rituals and spells. And I'm told that sorcery digs through witchcraft, burrowing deep into places unseen to find the buried treasure—the power—below the surface. Sorcery consumes that power, creating a change then and there, not just influencing a future one."

It was how I'd explained it to him.

Eris said, "You know a lot for a wærewolf."

"I'm not just any wærewolf."

Todd thrust the paper at her and slapped three pens down in front of Eris. "Don't try anything," he growled at her. "The other witches here will know if your 'supplies' are accurate for your purpose."

Eris's look of surprise zeroed in on Nana. "I thought witches and wærewolves weren't meant to mingle? How the hell did *you* end up with these guys?"

"If you'd had the guts to stick around, I might respect you enough to answer that." Nana stood and shuffled away to the front room.

CHAPTER THIRTY-ONE

Eris finished her list, handed it to me, and lit another cigarette. The wærewolves had retreated to the corner and were whispering to themselves. Zhan leaned on the wall at the entrance to the hallway, arms crossed, and periodically glanced into the front area. Lance had given up on his ice pack, but seemed to be doing his best to be forgotten.

As I skimmed down the list, Eris said, "After you slammed the door . . . I thought I'd never have the chance to see you again."

For three heartbeats we stared at each other, then I laid down the paper. I grabbed the cigarette from her, stubbed it out, then tossed the pack into the garbage. "If Johnny didn't need you to do this—and what irony that it was *you*—then you wouldn't be seeing me." I sat and calmly resumed reading.

Or trying to read. My mind was still reeling from the knowledge that she, my deadbeat mother of all people, had been the one to magically dam up Johnny's power.

She recrossed her legs the other way, and the bouncing

resumed. "How does the vampire fit into this equation?"

"You're in no position to press me for information."

"But you're Erus Veneficus to a Regional Quarter Lord—I saw it on the news, Pittsburgh is part of his domain—*and* you're here with a wærewolf claiming to be the Domn Lup."

I ignored her and assessed the list. *Candles. Yellow, blue, red, silver, purple, green, black. Stones. Amber, moonstone, red jasper—*

"You've accomplished so much."

—*aventurine, amethyst, jade, hematite. Herbs. Cinnamon and rosemary. Eucalyptus and myrrh. Basil and allspice.* That wasn't even half the list. I wagged the sheet in the air. "Do you have all of this somewhere or are we supposed to hit your local witch supply store in a shopping spree? This stuff needs to be consecrated and empowered and we're in a waning moon phase."

"The moon is new tomorrow—" She stopped herself, stood. "Shit."

"What?"

"I told you: It took me a week to do this in the first place. If we're going to attempt to undo it, we have to get going and I mean now."

She had everyone's attention now, and she thrived in the spotlight. "The moon will be new at nine minutes after five, tomorrow evening. The sun will set at five-ten. In order to best break the bonds put on you, I have to banish those bonds, and that's best done under the sliver of a waning moon. There'll be no moon tomorrow."

"But that's magic," Johnny said. "This is sorcery."

"The influence of the energies is still relevant."

Johnny asked me for confirmation with a wordless glance. I nodded.

"So either we make this an all-nighter tonight," Eris said, imbuing her words with the sense of having the advantage in the situation, "or we get the gang together again in a few weeks and take a more subtle one-per-night schedule."

Johnny's dark look reminded her that she hadn't ever had the advantage here. "I don't intend to leave until it is done."

Eris tucked hair behind her ear, revealing three piercings in her earlobe and a tribal line tattoo behind and beneath her ear, along the hairline. "I have the supplies. Upstairs."

Zhan drew the gun from her shoulder holster. "Then let's go get them, shall we?"

Eris, Zhan, and I headed for the back door where Kirk still held his position. Zhan grabbed Eris's arm to hold her back. "You go first," she told me. To Eris, she said, "Don't try anything stupid. You *won't* outrun me or a bullet. I never miss."

I noticed Kirk's spine stiffen. "Never?" he asked.

"Never," Zhan affirmed.

Kirk gave her the once-over like he'd never seen her before. While wæres are notoriously horny, they would rather spit on a vampire's Offerling than look at one. But these two had a couple of things in common, for one, guns. Kirk was an ex-military sharpshooter. And they both were Asian.

"Keep your eyes in your head, fur-face," Zhan snapped.

Kirk sneered. "Blood whore."

In an instant, Zhan had released Eris and pressed the business end of her pistol against Kirk's temple. "Mind your mouth, dog, or I'll muzzle you permanently."

Kirk held his hands up as if he were surrendering. He said nothing, but his expression was a billboard proclaiming his approval.

I opened the door and discovered a metal staircase leading up to a small landing. An older blue Corvette was parked under it; the Tahoe the other wæres had driven was beside it.

Eris took a set of keys from a peg by the door and followed me up the stairs, then unlocked it and led us inside. "Welcome to my home, Persephone. If I'd known you were going to drop by and bring friends, I'd have picked up."

The dining area was right in front of us, the living room to the left. A pair of faux-distressed leather couches had an Aztec print area rug between them. One had a southwestern blanket crumpled at the far end, pillows with Aztec designs graced the other. A Pittsburgh Penguins jersey was draped on the back of one sofa. There was a TV on a table against the wall, DVD player underneath stacked with movies. I saw *The Fast and the Furious* and *Tokyo Drift.*

I took in the pizza boxes and empty two-liters perched on the corner of the glass-top dining table. A Steelers' hoodie was draped over the arm of one chair.

Beyond the table was an opening to a hall. The bathroom opened off it and, since the hall stretched in both directions, I assumed there were bedrooms, too. To my right was a doorway to the kitchen, where a cereal box sat out, a cabinet door hung open, and two granola bar wrappers lay on the counter beside a half-empty glass of milk. The uncovered garbage can was overflowing.

Seeing that she lived in a normal apartment with normal house items made her seem like a normal person, not the mean, cruel woman I had imagined her to be.

"It isn't grand, but it's paid for," she said proudly. "Magic stuff's this way." She led us through the kitchen to a black door in the back. Zhan inspected the bedrooms while I followed Eris. She took hold of the doorknob. "I call this the woogie room."

"Woogie? You got Chewbacca in there?" I asked.

"Woogie. Not wookiee." She frowned. "Nana doesn't like space movies, does she?"

"No."

"Don't give up on her, Persephone, she apparently doesn't hate wæres anymore. If that can change, anything can change."

"She's trying to quit smoking, too."

"No way!"

Eris was trying to be chummy, as if we were merely catching up after a few weeks of absence. It irritated me and I let her see the proof.

She opened the black door and hit the light switch. The inside was lined with shelves and the kind of do-it-yourself cabinetry that usually left folks wondering if the instructions lost something important in the translation. "Supposed to be a pantry," she said. "But we don't eat that much so everything stores in the kitchen."

"We?" I asked.

She spun around, cheeks flushing. "Don't worry, he's at work."

Of course she had a man living here. "When will *he* be back?"

Her fists shoved into her pockets. "He's a trucker. He'll be gone until midweek."

I held the list out to her. "Get your supplies."

As Eris moved about the room, opening the plywood cabinets, I took note of how organized she was. She collected the candles first, grouped them in a Baggie, then gathered the various stones.

Zhan drew my attention as she stepped up behind me and whispered, "All clear." I nodded and Zhan took a seat at the table facing the door.

When I turned back, my mother was holding a blade, unsheathed.

She wasn't threatening me with it, merely inspecting the naked blade. It was tarnished; real silver. She put it back and brought out another, checked it. Gleaming stainless steel with a black handle. Nodding to herself, she placed it with the other items.

In that moment I realized that if she'd meant me harm, she had weapons in this room to do so. If she'd meant Johnny harm she could have used the silver blade in the ritual.

I wondered what I would have done if deep desperation claimed me and left me with one chance to make a new life for myself . . . and all I had to do was ruin the life of one other person.

I'd staked Menessos in desperation. It didn't just ruin his life, it robbed him of it. The whole thing had been his idea. He had willingly submitted to it. Still, I'd felt plenty guilty over it.

And here was the one chance for my mother to absolve herself of her guilt. As an extra bonus, in doing so, she could prove her good intentions and try to gain a place in my life.

We were different enough that the places where we drew the line and declared our limits were miles apart . . . but we were alike in other ways. *In her place, wouldn't I do everything I could to fix this mess?*

I thought of Amenemhab. *Sometimes only forgiveness will do.*

I swallowed. *Maybe.*

Where to begin. Baby step. "Can I help?" I asked.

Her surprise was evident, but it changed into a warm smile meant for me, the one that as a child I'd tried so hard to earn. "I'd like that." She pointed to a box. "You can put this stuff in there."

I began filling the box.

She brought out the herbs. Some were already ground and some were in bulk form. She hefted a marble mortar and pestle to the table and ground the cinnamon and rosemary together. "Are you going to do this in one of the tattoo rooms?"

"I'd rather do it up here. I have an old massage therapist's table. We can move the furniture out of the way and have more room, and ensured privacy. Some of the artists have keys to the shop."

Once she was satisfied with the herb blend, she drew an equal-armed cross in the air over it, murmuring. Next, she dumped the mixture into a snack-size plastic bag and labeled it before passing it to me. She wiped out the mortar and combined the eucalyptus and myrrh next. I labeled the next Baggie while she worked.

"I often wondered if Nana taught you magic like she taught me," she said, her voice a little thick. "When I saw you on the news I knew she had. I am so proud of you." She seemed quite calm, immersed in the grinding of herbs.

"Most mothers wouldn't be."

"Well, we both know I'm not like most." Those syllables were laced with guilt. "But an Erus Veneficus . . . vampires don't want a lightweight. You have to be powerful to gain their consideration, and a Quarter Lord is even more demanding. It's no light honor."

"WEC considers it selling out."

"Of course they do." She repeated the gesture, murmuring over the mortar's contents, then emptied them into the plastic pouch I'd prepared, and took up the cloth to wipe it out for the next batch. "They have to stigmatize it. They're losing their best and brightest to a more glamorous world."

My heart was warming. What child doesn't want to hear that her parent thinks she's among the best and brightest?

After sealing and labeling the third Baggie, I said, "WEC is trying to update the image of the covens. Giving favor to the telegenic priestesses with marketing skills, appointing approved witches to the position of 'spokeswoman' in places of high media coverage."

"Doesn't surprise me at all." She was now pulverizing dried basil leaves and allspice.

"Do you belong to a coven?"

"No. Not in a long, long time. I prefer being a solitary."

Another thing in the "alike" column.

I thought back to the night the slate had given me the name Arcanum. It could have simply given me the name, but instead it gave me a reading, one that I now saw was an explanation. Nana had defined the problem: Someone wanted what was best for them and all my plans had to change. *True. She left me and my childhood was nothing like normal.* Factors: Poor judgment and chance encounters. *True again, according to her account of the events.* Advice: Think twice before taking action and masculine forces. *Okay. I'm trying.* Result: My take on it was "a spiritual, emotional, or material need." Nana's version was to "seek good advice." *I've talked to Amenemhab, but I don't know if I can forgive her. She still hasn't said she's sorry or asked me to forgive her. All I can do is give her the chance to absolve herself.*

By the time we had all the items gathered and moved into the living room, Zhan conveyed utter boredom.

"I'm going to get that table," Eris said, stepping out of sight.

Zhan gave me a single nod to indicate that was okay. "No way out back there."

I retrieved the satellite phone out of the inner pocket of my borrowed jacket, hit the speed dial I'd assigned Johnny, and asked him to double-check the front door lock, turn out the lights in the shop, and join us upstairs. In moments Eris returned as Lance and the wæres clamored up the metal stairs and came in. Johnny entered last, trailing Nana. I gave him a grateful nod; he knew she wasn't as steady on the stairs anymore.

After sharing the room-rearranging plan, the wæres moved everything in minutes. "You should go home," I said to the artist.

Lance shook his head. "I'm not leaving. Without her, AIE would fall apart."

"Then sit over there." Johnny pointed to the far corner of the couch. "Be silent and stay out of the way." The couches were now both tucked against the wall with the short side of the rustic coffee table separating them.

Eris moved the area rug to be centered in the open space, then placed her folded massage table and set it up. "The other wæres will have to leave soon," she said.

Johnny gave Todd and Kirk the go ahead. Kirk clasped Johnny's forearm. He said, "As agreed," then asked Zhan, "I didn't get a good view of your pistol. You packin' a ladies' .28, or was that a .38 you put to my head?"

"It's a .44."

"Oooo. That really kicks."

"Three hundred and ten foot-pounds of energy."

He regarded her appreciatively, then pointed at Johnny. "You know your stuff, China Girl. It'd be a shame to kill you, but if anything happens to him . . . you won't see me when I come for you."

"The Domn Lup's not my charge."

"Consider it a mandate. I carried your master to dark safety twice in one morning. You owe me this."

"Tell me, Wolfman Wang, are you saying you're a *team player*?"

Kirk glanced in my direction, then back to Zhan. "If my Domn Lup wishes, it is so. Can you say the same?"

"I can," she said with conviction.

Kirk gave Zhan a wink and exited.

Johnny and I shared a look that was multifaceted in its understanding. We'd both been shown the loyalty of our people. They'd confirmed that they could extend that allegiance to others; no light commitment considering how the various "nonsters" disliked and distrusted each other. Knowing their trust in us could bridge that rift felt good, if terribly heavy. Good, because there was unending hope in that. And terribly heavy because too many good people had already died.

Watching Zhan, I repeated a silent prayer to Hecate that such loyalty wasn't rewarded with death.

My somber moment was shattered as Eris said cheerfully, "All right. Let's get this party started."

CHAPTER THIRTY-TWO

Nana sat on the couch that Lance wasn't sitting on. I joined her. Zhan moved a dining room chair to the front door.

Eris patted the table top. "Off with your shirt and lie down."

Johnny pulled the black long-sleeved tee over his head and dropped it aside. My appreciation had to show. Johnny had ripples and bulges of muscle in all the places that screamed of strength and sex appeal. For all the beauty in the art that graced his skin—and I took a moment to acknowledge the artistic talent my mother possessed—these lines and curves and colors also condemned his flesh to the magic bound within.

We were here to liberate him from that sentence.

Eris whistled approval. "You sure grew into those," she said. "I hoped you wouldn't grow up to be a scrawny fella." She moved close to him, inspecting her work.

I bristled, but bit my tongue lest I say something stupid.

"Turn around."

Johnny revealed his back.

"Lord and Lady," Nana breathed. The red foo dog and black dragon tattoos were as intricate as any I'd ever seen.

Eris's finger traced the curved spine of the black dragon. "The colors have remained bright. Good. Good."

My jaw clenched. If I didn't grind my teeth together I would have shouted for her to keep her hands off my boyfriend. That would have been stupid. She had to touch him to undo this. It was just that she seemed to be appraising him with a regard that wasn't entirely professional.

"On the table," she said. "Head here." She indicated the end of the table closest to the TV as she twisted the blinds shut on all the windows in the long room.

"Why?" he asked.

"This is north." With the room dimmed, she cranked the thermostat, then grabbed a remote from beside the entertainment center and powered up the sound system around the big HD set. Mystical harmonies over drum circle rhythms flowed into our ears. She took the box of supplies and unpacked it all underneath the table, keeping the stones together, candles together, and so on. She returned to her "woogie room" and carried out a thatch broom on a birch staff.

Johnny didn't lie down on the table. He crossed his arms and said, "Earlier you claimed you couldn't do this."

"Impulsive magic isn't always the best."

"But you are going ahead with it."

"I lied. You called my bluff and said you weren't leaving until I fixed this." She shrugged. "We can do this another time if you're getting cold feet."

"No. I just want you to look me in the eye and tell me you can do this."

She didn't hesitate. "I *can* do this and I *want* to do this."

Johnny lay down on the table.

Eris placed the broom on the floor, and proceeded to cleanse the space with earth, air, fire, and water. "Ground and center yourself," she said to Johnny, with a light touch on his shoulder. "The rest of you observing should ground and center also."

We all took cleansing breaths and did as told.

Eris took longer to do this than the rest of us, but that was probably because we were watching her. *Stop being snide,* I chided myself. *Focus on positive things. She's probably taking extra time to be assured she is calm. This is a significant ritual, and calmness is essential.*

She had scattered salt across the floor as part of the earth cleansing, but now she made a wide circle of salt encompassing the table and all of the carpet.

> "I cast this circle round,
>   and conjure this sacred space.
> Between the worlds are we,
>   safe in this curved embrace.
> Here, magic is potent,
>   in a realm of day and night.
> Here, raised power's contained
>   where birth and death unite.
> Here, magic is possible.
> Here, magic is possible."

She lit a tea light candle and bent down to place it on the eastern edge of her salt circle.

"This circle must not be broken until I am done. And no one should interrupt a spell in progress." With that, Eris faced east and held her arms wide open in welcoming. "Watchtower guardians of the east! You are hereby summoned! Stir as I beckon to you. Come to me. Witness this rite. Protect this sacred space." She placed an incense burner, dragonfly charms, and feathers with a tea light candle at the inner edge of the circle.

She continued, calling on all the watchtowers in order. At each compass point she placed a candle and a representation of the correlating element. For fire she used a fist-size chunk of tiger iron, cinnamon sticks, and a round red candle. For water, she opened a glass bottle of water and placed a dolphin carved of aquamarine. For earth she sat out a bowl of salt, chestnuts, and colorful dried leaves and dried wheat tied together with a brown ribbon.

"Frigg, Queen of the Aesir, wife of Odin the shape-shifter, look down from Asgard, where you sit before your wheel in Fensalir spinning golden thread." Her arms slowly lifted as she spoke. "Don your lovely cloak of falcon feathers, transform and fly your inspiration to me. Though you will tell no fortunes, you peer into the universe, you know the fates of men. You know what I must do." She took a deep breath. "Come to me, attended by your creative maidens, and fill me. Guide me! Steer me truly, that the destiny your golden threads weave may be served by my actions."

I now understood why Great El's slate had given me her name in runes. She connected to the Norse pantheon. It indicated a severing of ties to the blood affinity her family had for the Greek pantheon, but a witch should answer the call of what pantheon calls to her, as that is the root of the spiritual connection.

Eris lowered her arms but kept her palms above Johnny's body, over his chest and bellybutton.

My attention flicked down to the items collected beneath the table, settling on the black-handled dagger I'd packed for her. *I should be in there with him. She could cut me a door and let me in. . . . No. I will give her my trust in this.*

"I now initiate the undoing of what was done before. What these hands once instated in magic upon this man, will now be rescinded. What captivity I cursed him with, I now release him from. What chains of confinement I placed upon him, I will now break."

Arms at her sides, her shoulders bunched just a little. Her fingers splayed, clawlike. It was very much the same pose the fairy Fax Torris had used to call and control her superheated beam of light.

"Answer my call . . . come to me . . . I draw you up, up from below. Power! Fill my circle. Seal my circle."

With the first gentle wave of energy, her hair lifted on the current. The second wave surged up before the first had ebbed, and as it tossed her hair around like thousands of snapping whips, sparks crackled from the tips.

This was ley line energy. This was sorcery.

Nana had taught me that sorcery was to be undertaken only as a "last resort," something to be used when immediacy demanded it. Right now, I could agree that Johnny's need was urgent.

But.

The power of the ley, the power of sorcery, was, as Nana would say, "like a bull in a china shop." It was eager, mobile, and brutish. It required strength of will to hold it, contain and control it.

I'd touched ley magic. I'd felt its sting at the first burning bite of contact. It was meant to protect, to keep the weak from tapping the line. I used a drop of that energy to power my house wards. That "drop" could numb my whole arm instantaneously. If more than a drop was being used—like it was here before us—the sensation faded too quickly into a euphoria that could render an unprepared or unlearned sorceress unconscious, either releasing that power unchecked, or leaving her helpless as it consumed her.

My mother's intoxication gave me great concern. I knew that the heated "almost-pain" was dulling into a nice buzz. She looked like a junkie who'd just taken a hit.

I checked Johnny for a sign that this was causing him any discomfort, but he lay still, calm and unaffected.

Eris clapped her hands over her head, fingers lacing together. She was breathing fast, but slowing with each inhalation. When she had control, she quit the pose and retrieved a long narrow tray and a yellow candle from under the table. She lit the candle, positioned the tray on the floor at the head of the table, and placed the candle.

"I invoke the will of the dazzling sun, with golden rays of warmth and light." She took up a Baggie and sprinkled the cinnamon and rosemary mixture on Johnny's arms. With a piece of amber dipped in Dragon's Blood oil, she traced the markings on his right arm, murmuring of Belenus, a Welsh sun god, and invoking the element of fire. When she switched to trace the marking on his right arm, her chant invoked Lugh, the god of the sun in Irish traditions.

Dragon's Blood, incidentally, was *not* a good thing to put directly on the skin, but I was confident that Johnny's wære healing ability would adjust for it.

I was feeling pretty good about this so far, at least until she climbed atop the table and straddled my boyfriend. Beside me Nana crossed her arms in a huff, drawing my attention to the belligerence she was expressing.

Eris grasped Johnny's wrists and lifted them until his arms were vertical.

> *"Guardians and loyal hounds*
> *Healers drawn and duty bound*
> *Rest now, you steadfast beasts*
> *Your vigilant watch now may cease."*

The flames of each candle sputtered and threw up smoke that swirled without dissipating. Taking the form of the lean hounds from the art, these smoke hounds loped happily around the circle three times before lying down and fading.

Eris climbed down from the table.

Johnny lifted his head to meet my gaze. I wasn't sure what he was trying to convey. If I'd been able to touch him, perhaps I could have heard him tell me in my mind.

Eris lit a blue candle, placed it beside the yellow one and moved the tray back enough to allow her to stand at the head of that table without jeopardizing the candles. She took up another Baggie. "Shut your eyes and keep them shut until I say you can open them," she said to Johnny. "I invoke the emotion of the shimmering moon, ruler of the tides, whose silver beams brighten the night."

She sprinkled ground eucalyptus and myrrh across his eyes, then lifted a piece of moonstone. Instead of dipping the stone in the oil this time—Dragon's Blood would be bad stuff to get in the eyes—she tapped the gemstone's edge against the oil-filled bottle three times. Murmuring invocations to the element of water, and calling on Thoth, the Egyptian god of the moon and knowledge and wisdom, and also on Amun, the king of the gods who was associated with hidden power, she traced the Wedjats.

Placing the moonstone between his brows she put her palms over him, chanting,

> "This man's desire is revealed.
>   Let him see it.
> This man's truth is revealed.
>   Let him be it.
> This man's power is revealed.
>   Let him free it.
> This man's destiny is revealed.
>   Let him believe it."

As she spoke, Johnny's exhaled breath became steam that flew like ibis and falcons, up and up, fading as they reached the ceiling.

She repeated the lines twice, lifted her hands, and shouted the chant a third time with upraised arms.

When she lowered her arms, however, she teetered to the left.

"Eris!" Nana called.

At the last, she caught herself with a grip on the table. "I'm okay," she said.

That may have been true, but simply being in a circle and saying the words wasn't enough to conduct magic, let alone sorcery. This was taxing her heavily and there were five tattoos remaining. She sat on the floor beside the table, dug a cloth from the box, and pushed it to Johnny's fingers. "Wipe the herbs from your face with this, then you can open your pretty blues."

He sat up to comply. When done, he blinked and peered around him, noticing where she was sitting. "Are you all right?"

"Yeah. Just need to ground and center again." She straightened her spine and imitated a yoga pose.

Johnny looked at me. I nodded. Silently questioning back, I tipped my head toward him and lifted my brows. He shook his head minutely and lay back down.

He doesn't feel any different. Since the ley power was crawling over my skin and I'd seen the hounds and birds in the circle, I knew it was working. Perhaps Johnny's immunity to magic was hampering his ability to detect the effects of it.

Eris broke her pose and stood with a dreamy sigh. She'd called the energy, it had answered again to refuel her. "The star on your navel is next." She glanced at me. "A fairy star, to be broken without fey magic."

She lit a silver candle, placed it with the rest. She gathered her supplies and, with her thumbs and forefingers, created a circle around the seven-pointed star on Johnny's abdomen. "I summon the speed of the planet Mercury, with quicksilver and light." She sprinkled lavender and mint on his stomach, then followed the lines of the star with a piece of aventurine, mumbling of Mercury, the Roman messenger of the gods and god of travelers, and invoking the element of earth.

> "Fate's path was once reborn
> With magic, ink, and art entwined,
> Sealed with seven points, seven thorns.
> But I command you now to unbind!"

Hands hovering inches above the star on his skin she chanted,

> "The way is clear.
> Barriers frayed.
> The way is clear.
> Obstructions fade.
> The way is clear.
> The path is remade.
> The way is clear.
> The way is clear.
> The way is clear."

My eyes detected a dark cloud. Analyzing what I was seeing, I realized that granules of the ground-up lavender and mint were sliding across his skin, floating into the air between his flesh and her palms, and forming the same lines as the fairy star.

The symbol floated there, first wobbling as each point dipped down in succession, tilting the whole.

"Clear the way," she said, and repeated it twice more.

On the third time, the spinning herbs massed together into a thick cloud, then exploded in a *poof!* that left a dusting of lavender and mint across Johnny's skin.

Eris leaned on the table, shoulders sagging.

"Stir," she murmured, twirling her finger clockwise in the air.

The air around them swirled hard enough to lift her hair and wipe the lavender and mint dust from Johnny. The sparks crackled around her again, but this time the sparks were red.

"You're going to need to remove your jeans for the next part."

Johnny rose from the table, on the far side, and removed his boots and socks, then dropped his jeans. With Nana sitting beside me I tried not to admire him too much and just be grateful that he'd worn underwear. *Bet he is, too.*

Eris grabbed his discarded things and shoved them into an empty space under the table. "And by the way," she told him, "this part is going to hurt."

She lit a red candle as he resumed his place on the table and placed it next to the yellow and blue candles on the tray. "I invoke the action of the planet Mars, of dynamic assertiveness and fearless heroics." From the third Baggie, she sprinkled basil and allspice onto his thighs. With an oblong piece of red jasper she'd dipped into the Dragon's Blood oil, she traced the image on his right thigh first, chanting odd Aztec names, and invoking the element of air.

These tattoos were the ones I had not studied much,

because when Johnny's pants were off, admiring the art on his legs was not my priority. However, I knew these images were blocky Aztec figures made with thick lines and curves, colored in with dark shades of red.

When she had completed the drawing on that side, she sat the stone on the top of his thigh and said,

> "Xolotl! Dog of the Underworld,
> Bringer of fire, at night the sun is in your keep.
> Cipatli! Dragon primordial,
> Your slain body became our earth, so deep.
> Dragon and dog together,
> Earth and fire forever!"

She moved around the table and drew the image on the left with a second jasper dipped in oil, then placed it atop his left thigh and said,

> "Quetzelcoatl! Feathered serpent,
> And ruler of the rains that cleanse,
> You are lightning and you are thunder
> Nahuatl! The lord of the Nine Winds.
> Serpent and human together,
> Air and water forever!"

She reached across the table to grip both thighs so the tattoos were under her palms, and her thumbs were on the stones.

> "Elements four,
> in Aztec gods once paired!

This seal is broken!
Separations are now repaired!"

She sucked down a trembling breath and enunciated the chant succinctly. "I take it back, I take it back, I take it back."

Johnny cried out sharply. He rose up and instinctively swung his fist at her, but halted the strike at the last second. To my far left, Lance was on his feet. Both Johnny and Eris were in pain. She ground her teeth, the scream in her throat building, building until she couldn't keep it down any longer. At once, both of them opened their mouths and anguish filled the room.

She jerked away, red jaspers tumbling to the floor as the room fell silent except for the mystical music on the stereo. Gasping, Eris clenched and unclenched her fists and shook them as if she couldn't feel them anymore. She took a step back and stared down into the palms of her now *badly* shaking hands.

Johnny was inspecting his thighs. "What the—" He struggled for the words, and blurted, "The color's gone!"

"No it's not." Eris showed us her palms. The palms of her hands were entirely red.

CHAPTER THIRTY-THREE

"How—?" Johnny demanded.

Her breath caught. "I took it back." She stumbled.

Johnny leaped from the table. He couldn't catch her before her knees buckled, but his grip on her arm kept her from tumbling out of the circle.

The rest of us rushed to that side of the table, careful not to cross the ring of salt.

Eris stared at her hands in dismay. "What I did to you was so wrong and I knew it." She showed him her hands again. "Air. Air was the final element. Air powers the mechanism that injected the ink into your skin. And now it's in mine, as if the universe has caught me red-handed." She laughed. The maniacal edge to it made the rest of us toss looks around like a hot potato.

"You have to stop this," Lance said.

"No!" Eris shouted. She twisted and struggled to get to her feet, obviously weak. Johnny helped her stand. "We can't stop!" When her knees threatened to give way again, he made her sit on the table.

Johnny retrieved his jeans from under the table and

stepped into them. As he tugged the zipper up he said, "I'm not convinced you're able to finish this."

"You can't leave the circle partially free."

"What? You took days to lock me up. You even said we could do this one at a time over the course of a week."

The guilt in her expression was heart-wrenching. "Locking it down piece by piece was like building a pyramid with blocks. It was systematic and each built on the other. I've just removed your foundation. If you did this over a series of days, we could keep you shielded from any other magic. But if you left now and randomly encountered any other magic, any surge of energy, it would be bad."

"But I'm—"

"Resistant. I know. This is different. You'd be walking around with magic in progress attached to you." Before he could protest, she added, "If you were trying to pick locks to get in a place without damaging the door or letting others know you had gained that access, you wouldn't pick *half* of the locks then let your impatience and temper get the best of you. If you ripped it off the hinges you'd defeat your own purpose and destroy the door."

He released a breath and put his hands on his hips. "I'm the door."

"Exactly." She reached up to his shoulder. "Right now, you're as fragile as an eggshell, tough guy."

He shied away from her touch. "What do you need to finish this?"

She examined her palms again. "I need . . . to accept what the deities intend for me to pay."

My thoughts ran to the Three-Fold Law. *What you*

do comes back to you, three-fold. It was a karma-in-this-life notion meant to keep witches' actions pure, good, and positive. Getting that goodness back in triplicate would be wonderful. Winning the trifecta of troubles, however, not so wonderful.

She flipped her hands over, hiding the reddened palms from her sight and pushed them out before her.

The hair on the nape of my neck prickled as she called to that ley energy and a pulse answered her. *And the junkie takes another hit.*

Eris eased from the table, onto now steady legs. "Unlocking that one hurt?" she asked Johnny.

"Hell yes. I nearly decked you before I realized what I was doing."

"This one will hurt more."

He rolled his shoulders as if preparing for it. "Why?"

"I told you before, each of the first four tattoos were locked to an element and set to a purpose. The fifth bound them all together. They weren't exactly happy about that." She showed him her palms again. "I need them free in order to unlock this one, which has your memories bound in it."

"Why did you take my memories?"

"These last three tattoos are all spiritual. They each required an offering."

"My memories were offered up?"

"Your past was relinquished. The man who paid me to do this requested that offering specifically. He said you had an unhappy childhood and wouldn't miss it anyway." Her tone had gone bitter and she was intently studying the floor. "That sounds stupidly weak now."

"Just undo it." Johnny sat on the table and stretched out.

This time a purple candle was added to the tray. "I call upon the expansion of the planet Jupiter, with golden rays of warmth and light." The mixture of nutmeg and clove was strewn across his chest. A heavy padlock was placed upon his sternum, right onto the pentacle, and a golden key was laid between the upraised wings on un-inked skin. Using an amethyst point, she traced the elaborate feathered details, then lifted the lock and drew the pentacle and circle beneath. She whispered, "Jupiter, planet named for the Great Roman god of thunder and lightning. Be generous. Hear me."

Slipping the amethyst through the loop of the lock and touching only the ends of the stone, she used it to hold the lock three inches above the pentacle tattooed upon Johnny's chest.

> *"Elements four, here combine.*
> *Elements meet, pentacle sign.*
> *Elements four, given wings.*
> *Elements meet, here a king.*
> *Earth: What was hidden now is found.*
> *Air: What was unknown is now explored.*
> *Fire: What was shackled is now unbound.*
> *Water: What was taken is now restored."*

The golden key began to twitch. Air lifted salt from the bowl and threw it around the circle while the water in the glass bottle bubbled and the flame of the round red candle stretched high and danced.

"Jupiter! Be generous, I beseech you!"

The key flipped into the air and glided into the lock.

"Open!"

The key did not turn.

"Open!" she commanded.

The key remained still.

Eris reached for the key, hesitated . . . and gently put thumb and forefinger to the golden surface.

As if the god Jupiter himself stood in the circle and had denied her, lightning exploded from the lock. It sent her backpedaling, stumbling and falling even as the lock thudded to the floor, breaking the head of the key as it struck.

Johnny yelled and clutched at his chest, rising up on his elbow.

That was when I heard gunfire outside.

It was followed by the clanging of feet on the metal stairs. Someone tried the doorknob. Zhan put a round through the door and the stairs thudded as if someone heavy had gone down hard. There were shouts from outside, a few screams, and the peel of cars burning rubber to flee the area.

Zhan dropped into a crouch, keeping her aim true. "Get down," she shouted to the rest of us. We obeyed; the shots continued outside.

Johnny's yell dwindled to a groan, then he collapsed against the table, his arms flopping over the edge. Though he was breathing, he didn't move.

I crawled forward.

Nana grabbed my arm firmly, holding me back. "Don't break the circle."

Amid the shots and shouts that were continuing out-side, one rattled the door and the knob flopped. Then the door burst open, ripping from its hinges and crashing into the chair Zhan had been sitting in. The chair flipped for-ward. One of the legs cracked on her forehead. Zhan went limp.

The Rege lurched through the entryway—it was his shoulder that had broken the door. He held a gun. His eyes locked on Johnny and he took aim.

"No!" I shouted, calling energy from the ley.

I heard movement to the side behind me.

The Rege got off two shots before the power of the ley enveloped him, but when he was wrapped in that dan-gerous energy, it required his full attention. The barrier around him, his own shields, blocked the magic. The bar-rel of his gun shifted toward me. My fists clenched, ris-ing up before me as if I dared fight him, but in truth, I was squeezing that ley power down, crushing him with its weight, until his shields were pulverized and every pore opened as if his skin was perforated with tiny funnels.

Weight pressed down on my shoulders as the Lustra-ta's mantle appeared on me, glowing soft white light.

I could never guess how many women he had ever raped, abused, and broken. But I was thinking of them, his faceless victims as I rammed ley power into him, vio-lating his body with it.

His eyes bulged. His hands shook like he had palsy. "No!"

Ley line power lifted him into the air and his body warped, sprouting hair and teeth.

I wasn't just stopping him. The Lustrata was

administering justice. I was doing what I never wanted to do to any wærewolf.

With a gasp, I loosed my fists, dropped the power, and stepped back. My mantle faded and disappeared. The creature dropped to the floor in a tangle of misshapen limbs, snarling and writhing. It flopped and groped, reaching toward my sentinel.

I pitched forward. "Zhan!"

At her name, she stirred. Seeing the inhuman thing so near her, she reacted swiftly. Before I could cross the room, she put four rounds into the thing's head. She pulled the trigger three more times before she realized she'd spent her bullets. I dropped to my knees at her side.

The sudden silence—inside and out—was deafening.

The Rege fired two shots at Johnny, who lay helpless.

I didn't want to look.

But I had to see. Slowly, my numb body responded. I saw a splash of red on Johnny's face. My heart sank into my stomach.

Then Lance surged forward, screaming, "Mom!"

Nana grabbed Lance before he could break the circle.

Eris moaned. "Fuck that hurts. Shit, shit, shit." Panic elevated her voice with each word. Behind me, Zhan got to her feet. I glanced at her. A trickle of blood ran down her face and her forehead was bruising. She checked the door even as she reloaded her gun.

Ignoring the mess that had been the Rege, I focused on the circle. My mother was bleeding, scraping her heels over the floor as she shouted another f-bomb.

And I found myself staring at Lance, who was trying

to remove Nana's grip from his arm. "Young man, get a hold of yourself," she was saying.

Mom. He'd shouted "mom." Shouted it at *my* mother.

The world swayed. My knees hit the floor.

Johnny may be dead. My mother's been shot. And I have a brother. A brother she kept. And raised. And didn't leave.

CHAPTER THIRTY-FOUR

The next minutes were a blur. I was completely numb until Nana's voice reached me. "Persephone, Johnny is not hurt."

My mind snapped back into working and I clamored to my feet.

"Eris blocked the shots," she added.

"We have to call an ambulance," Lance pleaded, cheeks wet with tears.

"Don't break the circle," Eris said, gritting her teeth.

"Mom, no . . ."

At that, Nana let go of him, finally catching on to what had torn through me like a hurricane.

Eris drew on the ley line—I felt the surge as she sucked power into herself. Even so, with great difficulty and much yelping, she twisted herself around and reached into the box with her left hand rifling around and coming up with the dagger. She clamped the sheath in her teeth and drew the blade. After spitting the sheath to the floor, she stabbed the black-handled dagger into the air. "Cut now the door, without breaking my circle." She dropped the dagger. "Persephone. You have to finish."

"You need medical attention!" Lance begged.

Zhan left the doorway, sliding her gun into her shoulder holster. "I have medic training. Let me in."

Nana jerked on Lance's arm. "Do you have an emergency kit?"

He blinked, seemingly as numb as I had been a moment ago. "Downstairs," he said. "In the shop."

"Go get it," she said.

He grabbed keys from a peg by the door, then stepped back as Kirk and Todd swarmed in with Gregor and two other Omori, all of whom had their wrists bound with zip-ties. Gregor dropped to his knees beside the grisly mess on the floor, saw a swollen hand with an identifying pair of rings. "The Rege! What have you done?"

Lance took to the stairs.

To shut Gregor up, Kirk whacked his head with the butt of a pistol.

"Is the Domn Lup—" Kirk's words stalled as he saw the same splash of blood that had distressed me.

I stepped through the door my mother had cut in her circle, feeling the static kiss of power as I entered. My hands roved all over Johnny, smearing blood but finding no wound. "He's unconscious but unhurt," I confirmed.

"Magic," one of the Omori cried, realizing what was happening on this side of the room.

"The energies are contained within the circle. For now." But we'd have to stir some more to finish this.

"The police are coming," Kirk said. "What do you want us to do?"

The wail of sirens was getting close. *Damn it, we have a spell going on, a dead half-formed wære, and—*

"This magic must not be stopped," I said. "Free the Omori and tell the—"

"What?" Kirk demanded.

I affixed the Omori wæres with as threatening a countenance as I could muster. "Your Rege is dead. All you have is your Domn Lup. Swear to me that you will go along with this, or I'll half-form you and have you shot where you are." *I hope they believe me. I don't know that I could harm anyone being submissive.*

Gregor's wide, despairing eyes shut. His mouth twisted in grief and fear. "And the witch strikes. . . ." he growled.

I moved as close to him as I could without breaking the circle. "If you prefer to die rather than see the new age your Domn Lup will usher in, so be it. I will give you that honor."

He looked up, eyes widening.

"But if you have any shred of hope inside of you, any desire to live in a better world, swear your allegiance now."

Gregor bowed his head. "I shall." He fixed his comrades with his stare. "And so shall you." They bowed their heads.

"Swear it," I demanded.

"On Ninurta's Hallowed Grave," Todd clarified.

Gregor lifted his chin. "On Ninurta's Hallowed Grave, I swear my compliance for now and my loyalty to the Domn Lup."

I breathed deep, sighed it out. "Tell the police this stranger attacked and broke in during the ritual, got too close, and it caused a transformation. He had to be put down. That's what the shooting was about."

Todd's head bobbed up and down. "If we're all guards of the Domn Lup, we have authority to protect him."

Lance rushed through the doorway with the emergency kit. A cell phone was pressed to his ear. "Come quick, she's been shot twice," he was saying. He'd called 911.

"Let me." Zhan took the kit from Lance and approached the circle. "May I come in?"

I indicated where Eris had cut the door in the magic circle. "Through here." Nana shoved a pillow and the crumpled blanket from the couch into Zhan's arms. She stepped over the salt circle and moved toward Eris. "Sealed again is the door." I visualized the circle whole once more.

The zip-ties were cut. "Let's get out there and figure out our positions and our story," Todd told the wæres. They headed out.

Zhan continued her examination of my moaning mother, murmuring to herself, "One shot to the arm. Passed through. That's how blood got on Johnny." She gently searched Eris's back. "No exit wound from this. Here." She ripped into a gauze pack from the kit and pushed the sterile fabric at me. "Hold this to the shoulder wound. Apply pressure."

When I did, Mom cried out.

"As much pressure as she can stand," Zhan corrected.

While I did that, Zhan wrapped an elastic bandage around Eris's upper arm. Eris's teeth chattered as she cried out again. Zhan grabbed up the athame to slice through the bandage. Black-handled ceremonial blades weren't to be used for actual cutting and were usually dull, but this one was sharp.

"I cannot leave the circle until this is done," Eris insisted.

Zhan dropped the blade and wrapped the remaining length of the bandage around Eris's ribs to keep her arm in place. "Then let's finish it," Zhan said, adjusting so she could hold Eris up while applying pressure to the shoulder. I covered my mother with the blanket, tucking it around her body.

Beyond the broken door, I heard the arrival of the police cruisers.

"What do I do?" I meant with the magic, not the police.

"You have to unlock the foo dog. He needs to be on his stomach."

Zhan had to abandon her patient temporarily to help me roll Johnny over without dumping him on the floor. The massage table had a cushion-edged hole in it so we could align him properly, and I checked underneath to make sure he was breathing normally.

"Light the green candle. Place it with the others."

I did so as Zhan returned to my mother.

"Take the lilac and vetivert, cover the red foo dog and only the foo dog, and repeat after me." She waited while I scattered the herbs. "I invoke the socialization of the planet Venus, whose duality in love and war finds harmony. Symbolized perfectly in this creature, that is not only a devoted dog, but a defender ready to make war to protect its own."

Though her words were harsh and fast, I repeated them slower. Then I took up a stone. "Jade?"

She nodded.

"Trace the edges and all details as smoothly as you can. Don't rush. Imagine the lines are strings, bindings that you're erasing."

As I did so, Eris murmured of Venus, of love and war and balance. Her brows furrowed in pain and concentration.

"I'm done."

"Is there any aspirin in the kit?" Eris asked Zhan, who was taking her pulse.

"Yes, but it would thin your blood. You can't have it." Zhan shifted slightly as if taking Eris's pulse at the wrist of her wounded arm.

"Fuck," Eris groaned. "Press the jade into the dog's mouth. Hold it there firmly. Pour your will into the foo dog, through the jade. You have to let the ley energy travel through you and that is going to hurt. It's sorcery and—"

"I'm no stranger to sorcery."

That statement cut through her anguish and she stared for a moment, then forced a weak, brief smile. "That's my girl." She swallowed. "Let it fill the foo dog and bring him to life. You have to feel his heart beating. You have to tell him to give Johnny back his wærewolf instincts. All of them. When the dog relents, you have to make it transfer that energy from within itself, back into Johnny."

"Got it."

"The dog won't give it up easily."

"Got it." I put the jade over the foo dog's mouth and positioned my hands.

"Repeat after me and mean it."

"I will."

When she spoke, I shut my eyes and repeated each line after her.

> *"Divine and auspicious,*
>   *Restraining motives vicious,*
> *Dignity once suppressed you*
>   *Power now arrests you.*
>   *Unleash his instinct*
>   *Unleash his nature*
>   *Unleash his instinct*
>   *Unleash his nature."*

As the chant continued, an alpha state filled me and a wave of ley energy rushed through me. I could feel the foo dog, feel it as if it were a real, three-dimensional, furry creature under my hands. *Live. Come alive.*

I squeezed, urgent to feel that heartbeat.

Live! Live!

With ley power I jolted the dog—and Johnny—as if my palms were the pads of a defibrillator. The next thing I knew, the foo dog was trying to bite me.

"It doesn't know you," my mother said. "Make him obey!"

Down boy! You have to give Johnny back his instincts!

The beast continued to snap at me. The edges of its teeth scraped at my palm. It couldn't get a bite of me because its nose was stuck against my palm and, apparently, it could not move its head.

Give him back his instincts!

Ley power dripped down my arms and into the dog in more moderate jolts, as if from a shock collar. Still, the animal snapped and growled at me. I imagined the flow stockpiling until there was a surplus in my shoulders. After holding it back as long as I could, I enveloped the foo dog's head with it like a muzzle and thought, *Give him back all his wærewolf instincts, now!*

The dog yelped as if struck. Though it had ceased snapping at me, it continued to whimper. I loosed my grip on the muzzle and put my fingers around its head and petted it gently.

Taking that it allowed me to do this as a sign the dog was ready to surrender the contained instincts, I thought: *Release what is Johnny's back into him. Return to him what you once held. Relinquish your duty and rest.*

For a full half-minute, it felt like kernels or pebbles dropping from the foo dog's mouth to bounce off my skin and tumble into Johnny. When that sensation ended, the dog licked my hand.

Instead of getting a wet palm, however, it knocked me back a step as if the dog had just shoved me back and jerked from me all the power that the ley had given me in one fell swoop.

I dropped down on one knee. My body was drained, my shoulders ached, and yet my soul felt electrified.

"Difficult?" Eris asked, gritting her teeth.

I realized there was a police officer in the doorway. He must've showed up while my eyes were shut.

He saw my surprise. "Just securing the scene, ma'am." He had placed markers around the Rege's body and around the weapon he'd used.

In answer to my mother, I said, "Yeah. Difficult."

She gave a quiet laugh. "The next one's going to be a *real* bitch."

CHAPTER THIRTY-FIVE

The paramedics arrived. Nana met them at the doorway. The sun would set soon; evening was rushing up on us.

"Are any of you wærewolves?" Nana demanded, placing her hands on either side of the doorframe.

"No, let us by!"

Nana snapped, "There's a spell going on in there and we've had one partial transformation already. I'm just protecting you."

"We received a 911 call. We were told there's an injured woman in there."

"That's right, but she's inside the circle."

To their credit, the medics pushed past the barricade that was my Nana and lined up just inside the doorway like mannequins in dark blue uniforms. Silent and still, the two men and one woman took in the scene, including what was left of the Rege on the floor. The woman moved closer to Zhan, but stayed back from the salt circle.

Zhan said, "She was shot twice by that man before his transformation set in. One broke her arm; the bullet passed through. I've bandaged it and bound it to her chest so it won't move. The other entered at the shoulder. I'm keeping pressure on it. The bleeding is minimal."

The woman had carrot red hair held back in a frizzy ponytail. "Did that bullet pass through?"

Zhan shook her head no.

"Then it may have bounced around causing internal injuries we can't see. We need to get her out of there."

"No!" Eris insisted.

"How's her pulse?" Frizz asked.

"Thready," Zhan answered.

Frizz nodded. "She may be going into shock. Is there a pulse in the right arm?"

Zhan shook her head again.

Lance came to the edge of the circle. "Mom. Let them take you now! Please."

Eris defiantly shook her head. "I have to finish the spell."

Frizz said, "Cut a door and let me take you out. The others can finish."

"You're a witch?" I asked, surprised.

"No. My aunt's a witch. I spent summers with her. Picked up a few things."

Eris held up her left hand, index finger vertical. "Just one more. One more spell and we're done."

"Your needs are more urgent, ma'am."

"Mom, please!" Lance begged.

"Lance, you know how much it means to me to earn Persephone's trust. I. Must. Do this."

I had been about to ask her to leave as well, but that shut me up. *I'm important to her?*

"I don't want to lose you," Lance said.

"I know. I love you, too, bitch boy, but if I fuck this up, I won't want to be here anyway."

"Ma'am. Your fingers look dark; that's not a good sign. You should get to the hospital immediately." Frizz's voice was more authoritative.

"If I leave, both that man and I are fucked."

"How so?" Nana cut in. She was pale, strained, her hands wringing. She was as worried as Lance. The prospect of watching her estranged child die wasn't a welcome one.

"I took something from him with the last tat. I have to give it back or all of this will be for nothing."

"What did you take?" I demanded.

"You're probably going into shock, ma'am," the medic announced firmly and loudly. It was a signal that she was about to forcibly take control of the patient. "This is irrational. Let us take you to the hospital."

"Everyone . . . just stop fucking talking." Even as she spoke, the hair at the nape of my neck prickled; she was calling the ley again. With her left hand and a scream of blinding pain, Eris snatched up the athame that had been discarded on the floor. She twisted and held it at Zhan's throat. To the medic she said, "Stop pushing me. Let us finish this. Then I'll go."

For a tense second, no one moved, not even to breathe.

Frizz nodded. "Everyone here is a witness that you refused."

"Back away." The medic didn't move fast enough and Eris shouted, "Get the fuck back!"

Nana crossed her arms and tapped her foot on the floor.

She looked as scared and frail as ever I had seen her, but her eyes were defiant. "I know you've been shot, Eris, but that's enough of that f-word."

I lit the black candle and placed it on the tray. I took the last Baggie from the box and sprinkled comfrey and patchouli on the black dragon, following its coiled body with a trail of the herbs. It smelled good. Earthy.

That was when I felt Menessos rise, far away in Cleveland. Wholeness surrounded me, and I took it as a good omen.

"I invoke the authority of Saturn," Eris said. I repeated it. "Where the crossroads meet, where the path is chosen."

I stilled. *Crossroads.*

Hecate.

"Where the crossroads meet, where the path is chosen," she repeated.

I said the words.

Taking up the shiny hematite, I dipped it in the Dragon's Blood oil and followed the lines of the dragon as Eris murmured, "Saturn, planet named for the Roman god of harvest, with a sickle in his mighty hands . . . hear me . . ."

Hecate also carried a sickle.

I gazed at the dragon tattoo.

And Hecate's chariot is drawn by dragons.

She continued, "You are also the god of the golden ages in history. A golden age is coming. A golden age is coming."

I knew that, astrologically, the planet we called Saturn was ruled by Capricorn, and together they symbolized the settling of accounts. What we were doing here, the un-locking of Johnny's tattoos and seeing the penance my mother was suffering . . . it definitely seemed more like karmic comeuppance than a golden age.

"Help me stand," Eris said to Zhan.

"That's not a good idea," my sentinel answered.

Eris dropped the athame. "Do it anyway."

Zhan knocked the dagger spinning onto my side of the circle. I helped her get my mother onto her feet. She was weak, moaning, and leaned heavily on the table with her left arm. Zhan stood behind her, steadying her.

"The hematite." Eris held her shaking left hand out to me. When I gave it to her, she placed it on the dragon's mouth, then grabbed at her right hand to maneuver it. She cried out and ended with "Help me."

"Ma'am, really—" the medic began.

Nana grabbed the EMT's elbow. "Zip it. And keep it zipped."

Zhan assisted in getting Eris's right hand to rest upon the stone and the dragon's gaping maw. My mother held her right hand in place with her left. Staring down at the now-covered dragon's head, I could guess how it would bite at her. Under her left hand, the fingers of her right were darkening.

Eris's knees buckled but Zhan held her firm.

"Mother . . ." I said.

"Help me," she said. "Hold my hands there no matter what."

I put my hands atop hers, fingers threaded across her knuckles and heels of my hands resting on Johnny.

She repeated, "No matter what."

"Got it."

> "Dragon! Master of elements,
>   here is divinity!
> Saturn! Power, luck, and
>   wisdom for infinity!
>   Restore to him what I stole!
>   Restore him, make him whole!"

She repeated the last two lines over and over.

Little by little, the room darkened, or at least it did inside the circle. It wasn't dimming because the sun had set. This darkness seemed to saturate everything with a damp chill. Even my clothes were weighted, heavy on my body. Wind swirled at the edge of the circle, faster and faster until it roared. Yet the barest of breezes caressed us. The candle flames were unhindered. The howling of dogs filled my ears as if a pack of wild hounds surrounded me, and the circle's edges darkened.

"And there be no time," Eris whispered. "Between the worlds are we." She shut her eyes tight.

> "Crown and brow, throat and heart
> Solar plexus, sacral, base.
> I free you from the art
> And end that magic embrace.
> That union is erased.
> That union is erased.
> That union is erased.

Unleash him from this cage!
Unleash his golden age!"

The whirlwind of the circle spat at us, rumbled and thundered at us.

The black dragon became real under our hands. Its body twisted around our arms, tangling and entwining us. The scales were rough and sharp, the cordlike muscles underneath bulged and squeezed.

Eris whimpered pitifully.

When the claws embedded in her left arm, a strangled scream percolated up her throat as if she were trying with all her might to keep it down. At the sound, the claws jerked, tearing the flesh until rivulets of her blood ran down her forearm.

Beneath us, Johnny stirred, moaned.

"Forgive me," she whispered.

I stared at her. Her eyes were clenched shut, a rictus of pain marring her features. She was asking this of Johnny. But I couldn't ignore the echo in my memory of Amenemhab saying, *Sometimes only forgiveness will do.*

Her words repeated, becoming a miserable, begging chant.

A dark figure stepped from the vortex swirling the circle's edge, and the aroma of raisin and currant cakes filled the circle. A cloaked figure with a sickle. That scent. I recognized Her wrinkled hands on the staff.

Hecate.

Her face was shrouded, hidden. She made no move but to bear witness.

"Forgive me, forgive me, forgive me," Eris continued.

I waited.

"Forgive me, forgive me."

And waited.

Forgive her, Red.

Johnny's voice!

Yes. Me. Forgive her already, he said.

Me? I thought back.

I already did. If we're still here . . .

But this isn't about me! I swallowed. Hard. I looked from Hecate to my mother and back again. *It can't be. I have no bearing on the breaking of this spell. I wasn't there when it was created.*

"Once, he sacrificed for her. Now she will sacrifice for him," the hooded figure said, walking the circle counterclockwise, crossing behind my mother and continuing around to stop behind me. "But you are here now, with me in the place of Time Eternal," Hecate spoke in her ancient but ageless voice, "in contact with the witch and the one who bears the spell. You have spoken the words. You have participated. And to achieve this purpose, you, too, must sacrifice something."

I understood.

In my hour of need, I'd asked Johnny to give a piece of his soul to me and another to Menessos. It was the last thing he wanted to do. But he had bravely given. For me. Now I was being asked to relinquish a piece of myself for him, a piece just as important because it had shaped and molded me. *It made me who I am.*

But now that you know that, do you still need to cling to it? Johnny asked.

It was more complicated than he knew. He was aware that she had rejected me, abandoning me with Nana. But he didn't know that she had gone on and, apparently, borne a child she then kept and cared for.

"How could you leave me and start your life over as if I'd never existed?"

My mother's visage of pain faded somewhat and her eyes opened. Mouth gaping, she stared at me, then beyond me to the goddess with the sickle at my back.

"Did you hate me? Were you running from *me?*"

Eris made no effort to answer. The dragon jerked its claws again, making the tears in her flesh a little longer. She screamed.

"How could you go on and *never* come back for me?" My tears dripped from my chin onto our hands.

"I made a terrible mistake, Persephone." Tears streaked her cheeks, too. "I wanted someone to make me feel important."

"Didn't *I* make you feel important? All I wanted to do was make you happy!"

"The responsibility was overwhelming. I wanted . . . I wanted to matter to an adult. Being an unwed mother meant I had baggage. Persephone," she sobbed, "that was so wrong, *I know that now,* but I didn't then. That's how I felt *then.* When Larry found out I was pregnant he threatened to leave. Until he found out it was a boy. His son. He stayed because it was a son."

"Why didn't you come for me if you had a perfect family going on?"

"Perfect? *Perfect?* We traveled like gypsies. You had stability with Nana. You had clothes and a bed and food.

We had a horse trailer. We slept in the hay. I wanted you to have better than that."

Looking at our hands, at the blood and tears and the darkening flesh of her right hand, I thought, *Excuses*.

"I left Lance, too."

At that, I focused on her sharply.

"When Larry got sent up, I had nothing—not even the hay to sleep in, and I had a child to feed. I left him with that woman I told you about, who had taught me to tattoo. I checked into that hotel with everything I owned in a backpack . . . and some downers. I intended to kill myself, Persephone. I got drunk, thinking I'd go back to the room, take the pills, pass out, and never wake up."

I was horrified.

"That was when he showed up. The man who offered me enough money to buy a new life for me and Lance. I'd never had a shot at independence before. I took it, and damn it, Persephone, I don't regret it. I grieve over what I did to the boy . . . this man. My only chance was in his loss. I've learned so much since then, about life, about myself. I'll give him back everything if I can. I owe him that and more. I'm doing this for him, because he deserves it, but I'm doing it for me, too. My conscience will finally be clear. And since *you* want me to do this, I'm doing it for you as well. I pray to the Lord and Lady that you will give me a chance to show you . . . to show you how sorry I am."

Sorry. She said she was sorry.

Hecate gripped my shoulder firmly, anchoring me.

Here it was again. A choice. *Do the right thing for the right reason.* But what was the *right* reason? Justice? Family? It was just like the situation with Beverley. Both were noble causes worth fighting for. Both hinged on me. What did I want? I could have justice for my past. Or I could have a family to lean on in the future. A family that might let me down. It was a risk.

Good fighters know when to stop *fighting,* Johnny said.

I took as deep a breath as my lungs would allow.

CHAPTER THIRTY-SIX

I forgive you, Mother."

Anger, resentment, pain, and anguish hardened on my skin like a thin film. I expelled the rest of my breath away, and all of that film cracked, flaked off, and fluttered away from me. I was free of all of it.

Sometimes only forgiveness will do.

The dragon released Eris, flipped and uncoiled its body, sinking back into Johnny's flesh as it had been. Hecate's touch faded away from me. She strolled back into the vortex, disappearing and taking the darkness of the circle, the wind, and howling dogs with Her.

Johnny stirred again. I lifted my hands; without pressure on Eris's hands, both dropped to her sides—the right hand completely dark. The hematite tumbled to the floor.

I took up the athame and gestured the tip at the circle edge. "I cut now a door." To my mother I said, "Go."

Zhan took my mother out through the space.

While I completed the ritual, thanking the deities, releasing the watchtowers, and taking up the circle, the paramedics put Eris on a gurney and strapped her down, then left.

Johnny sat up and seized me in an embrace. "I am so proud of you."

I squeezed him tight. "How do you feel?"

"Tingly. Weird." Then he stiffened, staring at the mangled carcass on the floor. "Who was it?"

I pointed to the rings.

Between the police taking statements and the arrival of Arcane Ink Emporium's other employees—one of whom showed up for the evening shift and called the rest when he learned what had happened—the next few hours weren't boring.

Nana made a call to Celia, who was delighted to have Beverley for another night.

I'd wanted to ask Johnny about the spell, about how he felt, but the wæres and Omori had commandeered him, citing that their world was about to be rocked in an unprecedented way. Johnny had simply said, "Yup. Rock is what I do."

The AIE employees set about getting a new door put on their boss's apartment. Once the police were done gathering statements, Zhan drove Lance, Nana, and me to the hospital following my brother's directions.

I can't believe I have a brother.

He sat up front. I observed him the entire way. He was worried about her, we all were, but I was judging him by other standards.

He'd responded to the initial threat by having his client hold the tattooing mechanism and keep it running so he could get the jump on Johnny. Had to respect the intelligence that had taken. And the courage.

"How old are you, Lance?"

"Eighteen. Why?"

"You look older," I said.

The awkward silence that followed was broken by Nana. "You'll graduate this year, then?"

"I took advanced courses and graduated last year. I go to the Art Institute now."

By the time we'd arrived at UPMC Mercy, parked, and found where we needed to be, we were told that Eris was in surgery. We waited for about an hour, then I sought out the vending machines. I bought sodas and goodies that I placed on the coffee table in our midst. No one touched them. There didn't seem to be anything to talk about. Interrogating Lance would be rude and insensitive and he wasn't in any shape to question us.

After another hour had passed, I had to take a walk around the hospital just for something to do. I ended up in another waiting area, one with big windows and a view across the parking lot and beyond the highway to the river.

"Ever since she saw you on TV, she's been talking about you a lot. She told me a long time ago I had an older half-sister who lived with her mother. Also made it clear she had no contact with you or her. Said it was for the best. Then she saw you with the vampire."

Over my shoulder I saw Lance, arms crossed and holding himself. He was so young. Overwhelmed. On TV, emergency surgeries are wrapped up by the end of the episode. Waiting like this was interminable.

I should have guessed he was Eris's son. The movies by the DVD player screamed "young man" more than "midlife crisis." I doubted now that there was a trucker boyfriend who'd be "home" later in the week. "I don't know what to say."

"She was nearly broken when she returned from Ohio a few days ago." He walked over and stood beside me. We stared out the window together. "Say you'll give her a chance. It's all she wants."

I faced him; he mirrored me. *My little brother.*

"My life is . . . complicated at best."

"She doesn't care. She just wants to make things right with you." He frowned. "The guilt is eating at her. And now . . . after this, if you don't . . ." He didn't finish.

I wrapped him in my arms.

His arms lifted in hesitant jerks, then surrounded me and, for a long minute, he gave up the tears he'd been fighting. He sniffled and eased away. "I hate crying."

"Must be a family trait."

He found a box of tissues beside a stack of magazines on a coffee table. After pulling a few he blew his nose. He rejoined me at the window.

"Why does she call you 'bitch boy'?"

He gave a half-laugh. "When I enrolled at the college I wanted to live in a dorm. She said that as long as she's paying for my classes and books, I had to live at home. I told her I didn't want people to think I was a bitch boy. She didn't know what it meant. I told her it was a rich kid, spoiled, who lives with his mom. She thought that was funny and . . . it kind of stuck after that." He drew a shaky breath. "Will you give her a chance?"

They hadn't seen or heard what was said while Hecate was present. So I told him, "I will."

When the surgery was concluded, a nurse ushered us into a private waiting room. "The doctor will be in shortly." He arrived minutes later, his grave expression cluing me in that this was going to be bad. "Ms. Alc-medi came through the surgery fine and has been taken to the recovery area. However, I have some unfortunate news."

The room was silent as we each held our breath.

"I was told that the emergency crew was forced to wait some fifteen or twenty minutes before Ms. Alcmedi agreed to be transported."

"That's correct," I said softly, thinking of how dark her hand had been.

"The bullet that entered her shoulder"—he touched the spot on his own shoulder to indicate—"transected the medial cord of the brachial plexus—"

"In English?" Nana demanded.

He reworded, unflustered. "The nerves were severed. The brachial artery was also severed. There was no blood flow in her arm for the time that it took for the medics to arrive, none while they waited, none while they trans-ported her here."

"What are you saying?" Lance was rigid, his voice tight.

"The arm was dead, son."

Hecate's words haunted my memory: *Now she will sacrifice for him.*

The doctor continued, "We couldn't save it . . . we removed it."

I was stunned. Zhan maneuvered Nana into a chair before her knees gave. Lance had paled again.

"She will be moved to her room in an hour—"

"Can we see her then?" Lance's voice cracked as he cut the doctor off. He was in tears again.

The doctor continued directly to Lance, conveying sincere pity, and I could tell he hated this part of his job. "For now we're going to keep her sedated. She's not going to be awake tonight." He paused, his own voice thickening. "Go home and get some rest."

Through gritted teeth Lance declared, "I'm not leaving."

The doctor left.

"I can't leave her," he said. "I'm all she's got. She wouldn't leave me and . . . she's all I've got."

I put my arm around Lance's shoulder. "No, she's not."

We stayed until Eris was moved from the recovery area to her room. Seeing her all bandaged up, with tubes and an IV, was terrible.

And yet, somehow, it was good. We all got to see her, see the new and strange shape of her without her watching us back, judging the pity and tears that inundated us. It would have been worse for us all if she had to endure our first reactions.

In time, weariness set in for everyone. I reasoned with

Lance and, though he resisted at first, he eventually relented and agreed to go home. Zhan went to get the car for us.

Lance kissed Eris's forehead and whispered something to her, then let Nana lead him slowly from the room.

I glanced from my mother to Nana walking down the hall, arm in arm with Lance.

This was the family I was born into.

Some families you join by way of vocation, location, or spiritual preference. And others are forced upon you when Fate decides to throw you into a niche societal group.

None of them are ever perfect.

I could see now that, for whatever reason, Eris had yearned to be valued by the opposite sex. She was the kind of woman whom men like the Rege chewed up and spit out. She sought her validation in the eyes of men when she should have looked inside—but she hadn't trusted her own judgment. She wouldn't back up and choose a different path, either. She kept stumbling forward, blindly. She chose a life that was awkward and thorny . . . a life fueled on nicotine, eyeliner, and alcohol . . . a life that made her travel the long road, the hard road, and it had quickly worn the soles right off her metaphorical shoes. But in the end—with nothing and closing in on self-destruction— she'd kept going. I had to respect that she did, if not the methods she'd used.

In spite of all that was wrong with the choices that led my mother to the brink of suicide, Fate gave her a fighting chance. And she fought.

I wondered what thoughts actually occurred to her when she had all that cash—payment for the terrible things she'd done to Johnny. I doubted reclaiming her life was the first thought, or even the second. But it had occurred to her at some point and she'd recognized it as the right thing to do.

Successful self-employment had taught her how to have self-worth, as opposed to believing her personal value was determined by the opinion of whatever man she was currently with. But that self-value had been bought with someone else's life. She'd carried the guilt, and because of it, doubt.

I had to believe that guilt over all the damage she'd done to me as a child was in there, too. And now she'd been absolved on both counts. It cost her, literally, an arm . . . the one that had made her alter ego, Arcanum, famous.

But I had seen in her eyes, as she gave back to him whatever it was that she had taken, that she'd finally proven to herself that she had her own value and deserved her own respect.

About damned time.

The drive back to their apartment was silent, and long enough that I began to wonder what Eris had given back to Johnny and whether I would detect a difference. *Will he be different with his powers free?*

When we arrived, we saw that a new door had been installed, the Rege's carcass had been removed, and his blood cleaned from the floor. The wæres and Omori were camped around the kitchen table playing poker. A bottle of whiskey sat open and everyone had a glass.

But my boyfriend wasn't with them. "Where's Johnny?"

"Kitchen," Kirk said, pointing. He had an impressive stack of quarters in front of him.

I stepped around the table and was surprised to find that Johnny *wasn't* cooking. He was leaning against the counter, staring into a glass of whiskey he held. I stopped in the doorway. Without looking up he asked, "She gonna be all right?"

I told him the news. I kept it brief. He nodded, but still didn't meet my eyes. It was beginning to worry me.

"The Rege put a tracer in your satellite phone."

I removed it from my purse.

"Inside the battery cover."

When I opened it, there was a little square of a feltlike material with wires running through it. I jerked it free, dropped it to the floor, and ground my heel on it. I picked it up and dropped it into the garbage can conveniently right next to me.

Johnny swirled his glass, making the ice cubes clink together, then finally his chin lifted. "Any chance my memories will kick in later?"

I remembered the golden key snapping in the lock. *Damn it.* "That tattoo was denied," I said. "It wouldn't unlock, but not because of us. The phoenix's claws must have damaged the magic."

He drained the glass. "That's what I was afraid of." He put the glass down and motioned me over to him. I approached, expecting a hug.

Instead he took me by the shoulders and turned me around. The wall I couldn't see because I had been standing in the doorway now filled my sight. My jaw dropped. My face stared back at me, made of, I think, ketchup and mustard.

"I dunno what came over me," he said. "But it's a good likeness, huh?"

EPILOGUE

Monday morning, we returned to the hospital. Since it was a new moon, I'd packed up a few of Eris's ritual things—a goddess statue and a few stones—and took them to her so she could commune with her deities that night. She wouldn't call spell energies—you never know who's in the hospital—but she could meditate. I figured it was always therapeutic for me.

My mother was groggy and kind of spacey from her medication, but all in all she wasn't surprised her arm was gone. The doctors said they'd never seen anyone simply accept such a life-altering trauma so easily. They cautioned the rest of us repeatedly to be wary of a rebound, and informed us of the signs to watch for concerning depression, post-traumatic stress syndrome, and other possibilities.

After talking privately with her, however, I was certain she'd be fine. Not that she was happy about losing a limb, but she said she'd "rather give her right arm than carry that guilt forever." She'd gotten what she wanted. As the justice-minded Lustrata, I could accept it. The only thing she cried over was not being able to drive her Corvette because it was a stick shift.

She told Lance the car was his now. That didn't make him nearly as happy as it would have under any other circumstance. Lance was taking this much worse than she was, though he put on a brave face for her. Nana and I had a private conference call with Celia and decided to stay for a week, to help Lance and Eris deal with this and make adjustments. That ten grand I'd packed wasn't used as bribe money, but it was useful.

The famous tattoo artist Arcanum had exceled—but on borrowed talent. Now I knew what she had taken from Johnny, and what she had given back. While the wæres have big plans for Johnny, he's going to be taking his guitar painting skills to another level. That, I'm sure of. And, since Nana, Zhan, and I were planning on staying here for a week, I was also certain that he wouldn't complain when we offered to let him take the Audi home.